HOURS TO KILL

HOURS TO KILL

SUSAN SLEEMAN

BETHANYHOUSE
a division of Baker Publishing Group
Minneapolis, Minnesota

Published by Bethany House Publishers
11400 Hampshire Avenue South
Bloomington, Minnesota 55438
www.bethanyhouse.com

Bethany House Publishers is a division of
Baker Publishing Group, Grand Rapids, Michigan

Printed in the United States of America

Library of Congress Cataloging-in-Publication Data
Names: Sleeman, Susan, author.
Title: Hours to kill / Susan Sleeman.
Description: Minneapolis, Minnesota : Bethany House, a division of Baker
    Publishing Group, [2021] | Series: Homeland heroes ; book 3
Identifiers: LCCN 2020046865 | ISBN 9780764233975 (trade paperback) | ISBN
    9780764238123 (casebound) | ISBN 9781493420261 (ebook)
Subjects: GSAFD: Mystery fiction. | Suspense fiction.
Classification: LCC PS3619.L44 H68 2021 | DDC 813/.6—dc23
LC record available at https://lccn.loc.gov/2020046865

Scripture quotations are from THE HOLY BIBLE, NEW INTERNATIONAL VERSION®, NIV® Copyright © 1973, 1978, 1984, 2011 by Biblica, Inc.® Used by permission. All rights reserved worldwide.

This is a work of fiction. Names, characters, incidents, and dialogues are products of the author's imagination and are not to be construed as real. Any resemblance to actual events or persons, living or dead, is entirely coincidental.

Cover design by Faceout Studio
Cover image of woman by Karina Vegas / Arcangel

Author is represented by The Steve Laube Agency.

21 22 23 24 25 26 27   7 6 5 4 3 2 1

For the Sleeman family—
Don, Mickey, Patti, and Barb

You all have been so supportive of my writing career,
and I am very blessed to have you on my side.

CHAPTER 1

THE BRUTAL KILLER put a knife to her mother's throat. Addison Leigh's mother blinked in terror, her eyes wide. The switchblade pressed against her crinkly neck. Right there in the small Portland home Addy shared with her mom.

Addy gasped.

"Back off, Agent Leigh, or else," the masked man snarled, his lips moving in the mouth opening.

Addy tried to breathe. To think.

The video playing on her computer screen in the U.S. Immigration and Customs Enforcement office was time-stamped five minutes ago.

Five minutes!

This man could still be in her house. With her mother.

Was it real? Staged? Was this armed man really at her house?

What should she do?

Think, Addy. Think.

She grabbed her phone and dialed her home number. One ring. Two. Three.

No answer.

"Warren, come here!" she yelled to her fellow ICE agent two cubicles down in the bullpen.

Ring four.

"C'mon, Mom, answer," Addy muttered as she jumped to her feet and tried not to lose it. "Please answer."

Voicemail. *No. No. No.*

She slammed her fist on the desktop.

Calm down. Panicking won't help.

A lack of answer didn't mean anything. Her mother could be napping, and her caregiver, Nancy, never answered the home phone.

"What's up?" Dressed in his usual khaki pants and white button-down, Warren sauntered her way.

"Watch this video." She clicked replay. "It's my mom. Or a Photoshopped version of her. I called the house. She's not answering."

Addy dialed Nancy's cellphone and watched again as the man pulled her mother's head back. He growled at the camera from behind a coward's ski mask, the brown skin of his hands telling her he might be connected to her current investigation. Something dark dotted his hand, but she couldn't tell what. A wound maybe.

His eyes focused on the camera, dark orbs in the mask's holes.

"Back off, Agent Leigh. Or else." His tone was high-pitched, obviously in an attempt to distort his voice, making it harder to do comparisons.

Back off. Back off what?

Was it Bruno Razo? A killer. A drug kingpin and gunrunner who was the focus of Operation Crossfire, her current investigation? A sorry excuse for a man.

Addy sucked in a gulping breath. Another and another, making sure to hold it together in front of her fellow agent as the call to Nancy rang in her ear, the sharp rings piercing Addy's brain.

Warren bent closer to the screen and let out a low whistle. "If it's Photoshopped, they would've had to film your mom at some point. And she would've needed a terrified expression like this when they did."

"Her dementia causes fear all the time, so they could possibly have caught her on a walk or at the park with me or Nancy."

The call to Nancy went to voicemail, and Addy's worry doubled as she shoved her phone into her pocket.

"In that case, it's a professional editing job." Warren frowned. "But I honestly think it's legit."

If Addy was on the verge of panicking before, the statement from an eighteen-year ICE veteran sent her over the top. "It's time-stamped five minutes ago. Mom's not answering the phone."

"They used a sheet for the background, so if they did indeed film it at your house, they disguised the room." Warren locked eyes with her. "Or it means it was Photoshopped."

"I need to go home. Check on her and see—" A sob grabbed Addy's voice, stealing it like a thief in the night, tearing away her last words.

Warren held her gaze, his normally calm powder-blue eyes darkened. "I'll come with you."

She nodded. She would be grateful for the backup, especially from an experienced ICE agent like Warren.

"I'll drive." He dug his keys from his pocket. "You're in no state of mind to get behind the wheel."

She thought to argue. Stand up for herself. A woman in law enforcement was often taken advantage of. Thought less of. But this wasn't that. He was right. Her hands were trembling, her heart thudding.

"Let's go," she said, but before she bolted for the door, she grabbed an extra ammo clip and shoved it in her pocket before pulling her jacket from the back of the chair.

Outside, a biting January wind whipped in her face, and she slipped into her jacket as she ran down the street behind Warren toward the parking lot.

She ignored him opening his car and charged over to the vintage Mustang she'd inherited from her father. She popped the trunk of the cherry-red vehicle and dug into a black nylon bag holding her Kevlar vest and emergency supplies. She slid into the vest and then joined Warren. He'd clicked open the locks on his nondescript sedan and was donning his vest too.

Seeing him dressed in tactical gear made the terror even more real. Her mother honestly was in danger, and they were heading to her house to rescue her.

Unbelievable. Totally unbelievable.

Addy breathed deep so she didn't lose it and climbed into the passenger seat. She buckled her seat belt. Took three tries with shaking hands to get the clasp into place. She had to calm down before they arrived at the house. If her mother was indeed being held captive, Addy had to be thinking clearly.

Warren slid into the driver's seat and started the car, the powerful engine roaring to life and vibrating the vehicle. He got his emergency light going and tore out of the lot, his hands steady on the wheel. Stalwart. A word she never used, except it somehow perfectly described him. He'd been like a father to her since she'd arrived back in Portland. At times smothering her with well-meaning advice, and other times leaving her alone. Right now she appreciated his help.

"Maybe I should call the local PD," Addy said. "Get them out there faster."

Warren gave a firm shake of his head. "First, you only live a few miles away and you don't know they'll arrive faster than us. And second, do you really want to risk some rookie rolling up on the scene and making a mistake that costs your mom her life?"

Her mother's life. In the balance. Her whole body trembled.

A car whipped in front of them and cut them off. Warren slammed on the brakes, saving their lives but wasting valuable time. She pounded a fist on the dash. She should have driven. At least she would feel in control of something. Anything.

She dug out her phone to call the house again.

Ringing. Ringing. Ringing.

Please, dear God, let Mom be okay. Please. Please. Please.

Warren turned his inquisitive eyes on her. "The warning on the video. It has to do with the investigation you're working on?"

"It's not like the guy came out and said so, but yeah, I have to figure it does. He's not Caucasian, and my chief suspect in this case is Hispanic."

Warren careened the car around the corner. "You've worked this investigation for months. Why the threat now?"

"There's something big. I mean like *huge* going down in six days. My suspect must have found out I got wind of his plans, and he wants me to back off."

She let the video replay in her mind, trying to find any lead or clue. "Bear. He wasn't barking."

"Your dog?"

She nodded. "Mom can't handle him so he's crated during the day. But as a retired police dog, he would sense the danger and be jonesing to get out. At a minimum barking."

"You think they hurt him?"

Dear God, no. Bear might live up to his name and be this big tough German shepherd, but he was her cuddly baby too, and she couldn't stomach the thought of anyone hurting him.

Warren turned onto her street. "Or maybe the guy on the video drugged Bear."

"We'll find out soon enough." She pointed out the window at the house three down from hers. "Pull up here."

She ran her gaze over the modest ranch that her parents had owned since the seventies—the house she'd grown up in. After Addison split with Mack, she'd moved in with her mom, and they'd just painted it a deep gray with white trim. The lawn was neat and tidy, thanks to a landscaping crew she paid to keep it that way. Nancy had parked her older model Honda in the driveway, but there was no sign of any other vehicle.

"Let me try calling again." Addy got out her phone and dialed.

The call connected and rang but went straight to voicemail. "No answer." She shoved the phone into her pocket. "Since we don't know which room they'll likely be in, we'll go in the front where we'll have the best view of the main living area."

He nodded. "I remember the layout from your party."

Party. Right. Remodel of the kitchen and family room celebration. Not something she could even imagine right now with her heart in her throat.

She eased out of the car and drew her gun. The wind, warning of coming rain, buffeted her body. She stayed low by the boxwood hedge that served as a fence and crept up to the front door painted a bright turquoise. Rain started spitting from the gray skies, dampening her hair and face. She swiped it away and dug out her key. As silently as possible, she unlocked the door, her hands trembling. The turn of the dead bolt sounded like a sonic boom in her ears.

If Razo is still here, please don't let him have heard that.

She turned the knob. Dreaded pushing on the door that stuck on the corner in humid weather like today. Why hadn't she gotten that fixed?

Because you didn't know keeping quiet could be a matter of life and death. How could you?

She put her shoulder to the door. Pressed. Wood rubbed against wood. The grating noise sounding like a piercing cry, giving them away for sure.

Addy couldn't hang back. She had to breach with confidence now.

Gun raised, she charged into the room that held the lingering smell of her mother's arthritis cream. Addy scanned the space. Saw her mom. Then Nancy. Both tied up. Both gagged. Otherwise unharmed and seated in wooden chairs in front of a sheet stapled to the wall.

"Are they gone?" she asked Nancy.

She frantically bobbed her head up and down.

"I'll clear the house while you stay with your mom," Warren offered and eased past her to the hallway leading to three bedrooms.

"Check on Bear," she called after him. "First room on the right."

As she stepped toward her mother, Addy's attention was drawn back to the sheet.

The perpetrator had painted a message in a fire-engine red color on the white fabric. The letters were big and bold, and paint dripped from them like blood.

Stop or next time they will pay, and so will you.

The message finally sank deep inside her, and Addy's heart nearly refused to beat. The video hadn't been faked. Razo, if it was indeed him, had come into her home. Taken her frail mother captive. Threatened her life with a knife and left her tied up like a trussed pig for Addy to find, then issued his warning.

Her legs threatened to buckle.

"Bear's in his crate!" Warren yelled. "Sound asleep. An empty meat wrapper by his snout."

Drugged. Razo had drugged Bear.

Drugging an animal. Taking her mother and Nancy at gunpoint. Calmly making a video.

The man was dangerous. A psycho.

Addy had to up her protection game. Just had to. Because despite Razo's aggressive, audacious actions—his issued threat—she was more motivated than ever to hunt him down and make him pay.

———

Mack Jordan shifted the strap of his assault rifle and was fairly salivating in the RED team's rental vehicle on the way to bust their suspect and find the missing girls. Mack and his fellow team members, Sean Nichols and Kiley Dawson, had waited countless months to bring the three Montgomery, Alabama teens home. And as the team member with a fugitive-apprehension background, Mack was in charge of the op to rescue the abducted teens.

Sean pulled the SUV over just down the road from their target, and Mack climbed out of the vehicle, his trusty cowboy boots thumping on the asphalt. Sun shining overhead belied their dark mission ahead. He grabbed the battering ram from the back of the vehicle, the girls' faces coming to mind.

Felicia. Becky. Izzie. All thirteen years old at the time of their abduction, disappearing without a trace. The RED team—his team often described as having superhuman skills—had been called in. But they'd failed and couldn't find the girls. The investigation went cold, and their supervisor closed the case. Didn't stop the team. They kept working in their free time until they tracked down the van that had driven off with the girls inside it.

The van was driven by Jim-Tom Williams, who was hunkered down in the dilapidated house just down the road. Their surveillance of this dump hadn't shown the girls living there, but they'd watched the place long enough. It was time for action. Time to lean on this guy and bring the teens home.

"Y'all ready for this?" Mack nearly cringed at how strong his Texas accent came across when under duress or with adrenaline flowing through his body. Didn't matter. Sean and Kiley were unfazed by it.

Kiley shifted her Kevlar vest and tossed her ponytail over her shoulder, the chocolate brown a similar color to young Becky's hair. Kiley's green eyes flashed from adrenaline. "Born ready for it."

"I'm all in. Way in." Sean, the most reserved member of the team, slid a hand into dark brown hair, his fingers getting caught in the slight curl.

"Then we're a go." Mack gave a final nod, cementing the mission in his mind, and set off, marching down the shoulder of the country road—steadily moving through the humid breeze toward the tiny clapboard-sided saltbox house. Rusty junker vehicles sat on blocks in the yard. Unmown grass billowed in the breeze. The invasive kudzu vine climbed up two vehicles and swallowed them whole.

The local SWAT team had cordoned off the street, and Mack had arranged backup from their department, their deputies manning the major thoroughfares in the area.

Mack crept up the weed-infested gravel drive.

His Spidey sense was tingling, and it never let him down.

Someone was in danger.

Was someone about to get hurt in the op? The girls? Sure, the team saw no sign of the teens on the premises, but the place had a root cellar, and Williams could be holding them captive down there.

Mack moved steadily forward, the others creeping behind him. Concern clawed at his soul. Growing stronger.

Should he abort? Continue?

Uncertain, he paused and flashed up his hand to tell his team to hold. He had to decide what to do. Quickly. If he didn't, someone could get hurt.

CHAPTER 2

"I'VE DIED ONCE BEFORE," Addy said in jest because this meeting was getting too tense, and she thought she might throw up right here on her supervisor's desk. "What's one more time?"

"Not funny, Leigh." Gala Harris, Special Agent in Charge of ICE's Portland office, closed her laptop after having watched the home-invasion video. She pushed the computer forward on a meticulous desk in an equally neat office, its shelves overloaded with reference books. The space smelled like a mix of vanilla and Harris's peach shampoo, but the sweet scent didn't put Addy at ease.

Harris tugged down the cuffs of her black turtleneck sweater while keeping her intense gaze pinned on Addy. "You need to take this threat seriously."

Addy knew that, but then saying out loud that a ruthless drug dealer turned gun smuggler was gunning for her and her mother wasn't an easy thing to admit. Verbalizing it for the first time made the threat very real. And scary. Even for a gun-toting agent. "I *am* taking it seriously. I promise."

"Your actions don't reflect that."

Addy wasn't about to admit her fear. And she wasn't about to let it control her either. "We've moved Mom and Nancy to a safe house with twenty-four seven protection. They'll be fine until Razo is behind bars. FYI, Nancy told me that my mom caused the injury to the man in the video. She stabbed him with a knitting needle."

Harris shook her head. "You're a chip off the old block, then."

Addy chuckled but it was forced. "Hopefully forensics found blood when they processed my house—should at least be on my mom's needle—and we'll get the attacker's ID from that."

"And if we don't?"

"I'm not going into hiding, if that's what you're getting at. I can't let this creep win. He won't run my life."

Harris brushed a hand over glossy black hair cut bluntly at her narrow chin. She didn't often speculate. She was a facts person and had often been accused of having ice flowing through her veins. Addy liked facts. Lived by them in her job. Most of the time. But she had also been told she let her emotions get to her on the job more often than she should, and she suspected right now was one of those times. After all, how could you not let a weapons smuggler abducting your mother shake you to the core?

"What exactly do you mean?" Harris asked.

Addy took a careful breath and let it out slowly, making sure Harris didn't pick up on her unease. "Like I said. I've taken a bullet before. Technically stopped breathing and died. And I promised myself back then that I wasn't going to live my life in fear."

Promised that to Mack—her estranged husband—too, but he wasn't in her life anymore so that really didn't matter now, did it?

Harris rested her hands on the glass desktop, her manicured nails clear-coated. "I'm not saying to live in fear, but I am telling you to be cautious. You're on to something big in your investigation, and Razo means business. If in fact he's the person behind the threat."

"I don't see how it could be anyone else. You reassigned all my pending investigations to Warren, and no one else has a reason to tell me to stop."

Harris locked gazes with her. "Exactly. The guy is dangerous, and that's why you need to be extra careful."

Addy knew that too. Razo was primarily a drug importer, getting his drugs from the Mexican cartels. He used the I-5 corridor running through Portland to move the drugs. The Interstate was a main artery from Mexico to Canada and was a very common route for smuggling drugs. Not just for Razo but for countless other dealers.

But lately he got involved with gun sales too. Not just any gun, but miniguns. The diminutive name *minigun* didn't do the weapon justice. It was a six-barreled rotary cannon that could fire up to a hundred bullets per second. The cartels in Mexico were slaughtering people with them. She'd seen the photographic proof.

Word on the street was that he'd bought five guns from the cartels and was going to smuggle them into the U.S. in six days, yet she didn't know how. She also didn't have a clear indication of his plans for the weapons. There was great money to be made in the sale of these special guns, but if he kept them, he could use the guns to quickly eliminate his competition and greatly expand his drug-distribution territory. Either way, she'd been charged with stopping him before innocent people lost their lives.

"I can call in a favor from Seattle and try to get a protection detail on you too," Harris offered.

Addy shook her head. "Not necessary. I'll be more cautious. And I have Bear. No one is going to get past him."

"Bear?"

"He's a retired police dog Mack and I adopted. Big German shepherd. He lives with me. Razo drugged him when he broke into the house. After I dropped Mom and Nancy at the safe house, I took him to the vet. She says he'll recover, and right now he's home snoozing off the drugs."

Harris arched an eyebrow. "Clearly someone can get past him, then."

"Yeah, I guess. But I wasn't home, and my mom ignores him. I wouldn't. I can also stay at a hotel tonight until he recovers as my watchdog, and I'll be fine." Plus, she wouldn't have to deal with the fingerprint powder scattered around her house tonight.

"The hotel is a good idea. Not just for tonight either. Until we have Razo in custody. Let's book the room under a bogus name like we'd do for someone we were protecting. And to the extent that's possible, try not to be out and about alone."

Addy nodded but wondered who would run necessary errands for her. Like get her mom's meds that were waiting at the pharmacy for pickup. Addy didn't have a man in her life. Not even one on the horizon.

She'd been separated from Mack for a year and a half, and she was still in love with him so she hadn't even contemplated dating someone else. She'd left D.C. to move to Portland to care for her mother. Addy sure wasn't going to ask her seventy-eight-year-old mother to come out of hiding and accompany her into danger. So who then?

"I'll also have IT try to track down the email with the video and enhance it," Harris continued. "Maybe then we can see distinguishing marks on the masked assailant. At least on the little bit of skin that's showing."

"He had something on his hand, but I couldn't tell what it was, other than the knitting-needle injury." With Addy's past experience in network security, and as a former RED team member, she knew tracking the email back to an actionable location bordered on impossible, but they could get lucky.

"And I want an update on the investigation. Maybe I'll find something that can pinpoint this threat even more."

"I don't want us to lose focus on the investigation to concentrate on my safety, though. That's just what Razo wants. Especially now. Something big is going down in six days. Word on the street says he's stepping up his game in a big way and bringing in five miniguns."

"Okay." Harris looked at her watch. "Give me two hours, and we'll meet in the conference room."

"Can we push it to later in the day?" Addy asked, as she'd been on the verge of a breakthrough when the video popped up in her email.

Harris turned to her laptop. "I can do four o'clock, but that's the latest. Bring all your files. I want details, not just a cursory update." She flicked her fingers in dismissal, then grabbed the handset of her ringing phone.

Addy headed out to the small bullpen area, where the smell of stale popcorn lingered in the air. Warren sat behind his desk and looked up at her, his eyes inquisitive. A veteran agent, he was still sharp and didn't miss a thing. "I take it you showed Harris the video."

Addy rested her arm on the padded wall of his cubicle. "I did. She's fired up about it."

"I told you she'd take it personally." He leaned back in his chair and clasped his hands behind his head. "You don't mess with her agents."

"I appreciate that, but she also wants an update. I need to get my files organized and prepare a report for her."

"I should've warned you she'd ask for that." He scratched his reddish-blond hair, messing up the neat haircut.

Addy pushed off the cubicle. "How'd you know that?"

"She's always one step ahead of us. Sure, she wants more info to see if the threat is credible. But this investigation has the potential to be a press-worthy bust, meaning she also wants to gather enough details so if something does happen to you, she can carry on your work."

"When you say it that way, it sounds pretty heartless."

He snapped his chair forward and planted his feet on the worn tile floor. "She isn't called Cruella for nothing."

Addy wanted to argue. To defend a fellow woman in the workplace. To point out that Harris had a softer side, but if that side existed, Addy hadn't seen it since the woman had taken over their small office six months ago. She was a little heartless at times, exactly what Warren was alluding to. Yet she was also very good at her job, and Addy respected that, so she would never call Harris *Cruella* or any name. And she shouldn't stand here gossiping either.

Her still-crisp white blouse was suddenly feeling restrictive, and she tugged on the collar. "Only Harris knows her own intentions, and I need to get to work."

Warren raised an eyebrow, deep grooves on his forehead melding together in a single line. "You are the most diplomatic agent I have ever met. You should go into politics."

"Now, that would be the worst thing I could think of doing for a living." Addy faked a shudder and continued down the aisle toward her cubicle.

She dropped into the black mesh chair and glanced around her desktop, which held little more than a wide computer monitor and a keyboard. The only personal item she'd brought to her work was an Echo speaker. Nothing else. Not even a plant or a solitary knickknack. After what happened with Mack, she didn't believe in mixing work with her home life anymore. It just got too complicated. If she hadn't met and fallen in love with him while part of the RED team in D.C., she would still be on the super team, working important cutting-edge investigations instead of her usual immigration cases here in Portland.

She opened the Operation Crossfire folder stored on the network server. A subfolder labeled Research contained all the articles she'd downloaded and saved for their records. She needed to go through them one by one and determine which ones to print for the update meeting.

She clicked on the first PDF about the implementation of X-ray security systems in the front lines of some border towns. Customs and Border Patrol had recently moved the nonintrusive scanning technology to the front lines. Much like an E-Z pass system, the scanners allowed traffic to keep moving as they generated a detailed image of the inside of every vehicle before it reached the official checkpoint, giving the officers a head start on suspicious cargo.

The document had been downloaded into a PDF file along with other articles for that date listed on the side. She tried her best not to get distracted by the extras and quickly back-tracked through the PDFs until she had three of them open. Each screenshot had similar related headlines posted on the side.

On the last PDF, her investigator's sixth sense started tingling, and she could hardly sit still to finish reading it. "Yes! Yes! This is it. This will break the investigation wide open. Give me what I need to arrest the creep."

"You say something?" Warren called out.

"Never mind." She closed the file, stood, and grabbed her jacket from the back of her chair. She needed more information, and she knew just the person who could give it to her. She pressed her hand on her sidearm for comfort. Despite playing down the threat with her boss, Addy was very concerned for her own safety. She bolted for the door.

"In a hurry much?" Warren asked when she reached his cubicle.

She slowed for a moment. "Got a new lead."

His eyes narrowed. "What about your update with Harris?"

"I'll be back in plenty of time."

"Are you sure?" He gave her a father-knows-best look. "Are you ready for the meeting?"

She waved a hand at him. "I have time. Don't worry."

She raced for the door.

"It's your funeral," he called after her.

Maybe he was right, but finally figuring out how Razo was

getting this weapon into the U.S. could be a game changer in apprehending him. The threat would no longer be an issue once she slapped cuffs on the creep and put him behind bars.

———

Mack burst through the door, Kiley and then Sean behind him in their normal stacking order. The room was as trashy as the exterior of the house, and even the bright sunshine beaming through the front door didn't make it seem any less so. A strong odor of stale fish mixed with the musky smell of marijuana permeated the space.

"Police!" Mack called out instead of shouting the acronym ICE. Every suspect understood the word *police* and knew how to react to it. "Hands. Hands. Hands. Where I can see them."

The skinny guy in a recliner flung his arms in the air. A woman on the couch lifted hers.

Mack fixed his rifle on the guy. "I've got Williams."

"I'm on the woman," Kiley said.

"Moving on." Sean passed Mack, heading into a hallway to clear the rest of the house.

Mack glared at Williams. "On the floor. Slowly. Hands where I can see them at all times."

"Hey, man," he said. "What'd I do?"

"On the floor" was all Mack said. He wasn't going to get into any discussions until he had cuffs on this guy and had searched the root cellar.

"I need my hand to work the lever," Williams whined.

Mack moved into position so he could see the side of the recliner. "Slowly."

Williams lowered his arm, his hand dropping straight to the lever. He hitched his string-bean body out of the chair and knelt on the floor littered with empty takeout bags. "Can't we talk about this?"

Mack gave him a shove until he was flat on his face, his

greasy blond hair hanging limp around his head. Mack nodded at Kiley.

"Your turn," she said to the plump woman with equally dirty hair and a white T-shirt that was stained yellow at the armpits—a match for Williams's undershirt.

Eyes wide and terrified, she slid to the floor and flopped onto her face near a pizza box.

"Hands behind your back," Kiley said.

She moved her scabbed arms, likely injured from drug abuse, and Kiley glanced at Mack.

He nodded, indicating he had both suspects covered and Kiley was free to search and cuff this woman. She shouldered her rifle and knelt, grabbing cuffs from her belt on the way down. She secured the woman's hands, then made a thorough search.

Sean came back into the room. "We're clear. No sign of the girls."

"Girls?" Williams asked. "What girls?"

So he was going to play dumb. Not surprising.

Mack looked at Sean. "Cover this creep."

Sean took a wide-legged stance as Mack searched Williams, nearly reeling from the ripe body odor emanating from the man. Mack cuffed him before calling the lieutenant in charge of the county support team. "Subject secured. Get your team in here for transport. We still have the cellar to clear."

Williams scoffed, "Ain't nothing down there. Wasting your time."

He might as well have said, *Don't go down there. I have something to hide.*

Mack glanced at Sean and then Kiley. "One of you good to stay here with these two?"

"I got it," Kiley answered.

Mack nodded his thanks. Sean was lead on the initial investigation, and he more than any of them was desperate to find the girls.

Mack and Sean moved through the kitchen, dirty dishes piled high and roaches scurrying over the walls. They exited the back of the house to a yard covered in knee-high grass and weeds. Mack let Sean go first, and he stopped by two ancient-looking cellar doors built into the ground, white paint flaking in the breeze.

"No dirt or dust on the right door," Sean said.

"So it's been opened recently." Mack's hope for finding the girls skyrocketed, but he quickly tamped down the excitement.

"Cover me," Sean said. "I'm going in."

CHAPTER 3

ADDY STEPPED OUT of the sleek office building and into the chilly wind whipping in from the Gorge. She was pumped. Ecstatic. Her impromptu meeting had gone well, and she'd gotten the information she needed. Most of it anyway. Still, she couldn't lose sight of her safety.

She took a good long look around the parking lot for any danger. The shrubbery and wooded area near the two-story glass and steel building held a dusting of snow from a minor overnight snowfall, but nothing else appeared out of the ordinary.

She hurried to her Mustang, double-checked the locks, and got the heat going. She grabbed her travel mug and took a sip of the coffee she'd bought on the way over to her meeting. Thankfully she'd poured it into her mug and the brew was still warm.

Her phone rang. She jumped and nearly tipped over the mug. She grabbed her cell and accepted the call from Warren.

"Where are you?" he asked by way of greeting.

She didn't care for his tense tone. "In my car."

"You better be on your way back here." He sounded like her dad when he'd caught her out after curfew.

She resisted sighing. "Why?"

"Harris had a question about your investigation, so she came looking for you. She was less than pleased that you weren't here prepping for the meeting."

"Did you tell her I had a new lead?"

"Yeah, and she still wasn't pleased."

Addy tightened her grip on the mug. "She'll be fine once I tell her what I learned."

"Your lead panned out?"

"Did it ever." She smiled, but as she thought about her next step, it vanished, and her stomach knotted. "I just have to make a phone call to get the final details and I'll be on my way back."

"Make it quick. You only have an hour until the meeting."

"Don't worry. I have this." She hung up and wished she believed what she'd just told him. In order to get the final details, she had to call Mack for the RED team's help. She could call Cam, the team analyst, directly. After all, he would be the one to do the work, but somehow she thought Mack should know that she was communicating with the team and asking for a favor.

She tapped his name on her phone. She hadn't talked to him in months, and she had no idea how he would feel about her calling. She took a sip of the warm coffee while the phone rang and watched the wind whip through brown ornamental grasses with tall seed heads flowing in the breeze. She remembered so many walks in the park with Mack while they'd admired a similar landscape near the RED team's office. At first getting to know each other, then just enjoying each other's company.

He kept things bottled up and was a hard guy to get to open up. Turns out he didn't open up. Not fully. And they'd been married before she learned of his issues with PTSD, which stemmed from his deployments as an Army Night Stalker, an elite aviation regiment known for their proficiency in nighttime operations. He frequently piloted missile drones that took out high-value targets, but sometimes innocent people died too, and he carried a lot of guilt over that. Addy wanted to help him, but she couldn't. He had to handle this on his own. But he wouldn't stay with her. He refused to subject her to his dangerous flashbacks after he'd once tried to strangle her in the night.

She touched her throat. Remembered the strength in those hands. Her air cut off. She'd punched him in the face. Brought him back to reality just in the nick of time. And he'd been shattered. Remorseful. Broken. She couldn't stand to see him that way. It hurt to her core.

His recorded voice came over the phone. "This is Mack. You know the drill."

Voicemail. Sigh. The deep tenor of his voice and his smooth Southern accent wrapped around her, easing out her disappointment at getting the message. The beep sounded. She hesitated. For only a second.

"Mack, it's Addy." She tried to keep her emotions out of her tone. "I need a favor from the RED team—Cam especially—for an investigation I'm working. It's a big one. One that means saving countless lives. Can you call me back ASAP to discuss? Thanks."

She put her phone in the dash holder, not surprised her heart was beating hard. Her heart always thrilled at the mere sound of his voice. She loved this man. How she loved him, and if it had been up to her, they would still be together while he worked through his issues.

A car door slammed shut, jerking her back to the present. She couldn't sit there daydreaming over the past. She had a gunrunner to catch, and an irritated boss to pacify.

She started the car, headed out of the lot and onto the winding road. Miles rolled under the wheels until she started to feel drowsy. Beyond drowsy. Confused.

The road blurred ahead. She held on to the wheel, but her fingers couldn't grasp it, and she crossed into the wrong lane. A truck came at her. Big. A semi. Lights cutting into her eyes.

Oh, well. No problem. Life was good. She relaxed.

The driver laid on the horn. She blinked hard. Tried to focus.

She jerked the wheel. Her muscles responded as if they were made of elastic, but she got back into the correct lane.

What was going on?

Seeing a sharp curve ahead, she tried to lift her foot from the gas. Her leg was a wet noodle. It wouldn't move. She tugged hard, lifted it, and thumped on the brakes. Failed to activate them.

The car plunged off the road. Down the embankment. Hit a tree. Metal rent. Groaned and complained. Her rag-doll-limp body fell forward. Her head crashed into the steering wheel.

Blinding pain radiated through her skull. She fell back against the seat.

She opened her eyes but couldn't see. Blackness surrounded her brain. The darkness calling. Rest. Sleep.

No. No. She had to get help.

She reached for her phone, still clasped in the holder. She tried to pry it free. Her hands were clumsy. Her fingers lifeless. She couldn't move it.

Her car door groaned open.

Oh, good. Help.

She swung her head in slow motion. Saw a man. His face fuzzy. His body fuzzy. Was he wearing a ski mask? No. It was just her blurred vision. What was wrong with her?

"I'm hurt. Need help." She tried to say more but the words wouldn't form.

"You don't want that phone," he said, reaching over her and pushing her hand out of the way. "This is your wake-up call. Pay attention. Keep yourself and your mother safe. Now relax. Let the drug take hold."

He was right. No help needed. Relax.

The drug. He said drug. What drug?

Her thoughts jumbled, tangling like the yarn her mother used for her knitting. Addy couldn't form a coherent thought. The effort just too much for her. She let her arm drop and fell back into her seat. The blackness descended. She didn't care and let the dark haze envelop her like a soupy fog of death.

———

Mack held his breath.

Sean pulled up the cellar door. "Police!"

He turned on his rifle's light and slowly descended. Mack followed, watching behind as he moved. A strong musty odor wafted out. Thankfully not the smell of death, but also not the smell of three girls confined in this space for a long time.

Sean ran his light over the four-by-four-foot room. Jar after jar of marijuana filled the shelves lining the cellar walls.

Mack's hope vanished. "Williams did have something to hide. Just not the girls."

Sean muttered something under his breath and lowered his rifle. "We didn't expect to find the girls here, but still."

"Yeah, but we hoped for a lead at least." Mack met Sean's gaze and shared a moment of commiseration. "Let's get Williams processed so we can interview him and maybe find something to go on."

Mack headed back into the house, passing the deputies who were hauling the couple off. The prisoners glared at Mack, but he ignored them and climbed the steps. Kiley gave him an expectant look, and he shook his head.

She grimaced.

"I'll update Eisenhower while you two search this place," Mack said. "Let's find anything that says the girls were here."

She dug latex gloves from her pocket. "If it exists, we'll find it."

It was the *If it exists* that had been the bane of this investigation. Never finding a solid enough lead to move forward until the only eyewitness underwent hypnosis and remembered the van.

Now what did they have? Looked like nothing.

"Let's get to it," Mack said, trying to sound hopeful but failing miserably. He normally tended toward being grumpy, and in this case his anger was threatening to join in.

Sean and Kiley started going through the room littered with takeout containers and ashtrays overflowing with marijuana-cigarette butts. He stepped onto the ramshackle porch and took a long breath of the warm country air. He got out his phone that had been on silent for hours. A missed call and a voicemail from Addy popped up on his screen. His gut clenched. She never called unless it was important.

His Spidey sense had been tingling and yet nothing had gone wrong on the op. Was she the reason for his unease? Was she in trouble? They might be separated, but he still felt responsible for protecting her, even if she lived an entire country away from him.

He wanted to return her call. Desperately. But couldn't. Not just yet. Not until he saw this op through. He started to dial their supervisor when an unknown call came in with a Portland, Oregon area code.

He should ignore it. Should. But he wouldn't. Not with the call from Addy and the worry that had his gut in a knot.

"Mack Jordan," he answered.

"Oh, good, Mr. Jordan. Glad I caught you. This is Beth Ann Rogers. I'm an ER nurse at St. Vincent Hospital. Your wife was in a car accident and sustained a serious head injury."

Mack's gut cramped harder, and his leg muscles turned to jelly. He spotted a rickety wooden stool and dropped onto it. "Will she be okay?"

"It's too early to tell," she replied. "We're still assessing the extent of her injuries, but you should get here. Soon."

Soon? As in she was going to die? "I'm in Alabama."

"Then do your very best to get here," she said, and the call ended.

Shocked, he pocketed his phone and stared over the lawn, if you could call it that. He could hardly focus. Not on anything but the thought of losing Addy. He couldn't lose her. And he had to be with her. But he was needed here. Tough. She needed him more.

"You have to see this," Kiley said from the doorway, taking a long look at him. "What's wrong? Is it the girls?"

He managed to think clearly enough to shake his head. "Addy. Car accident."

"Sean, get out here!" Kiley shouted as she rushed over to Mack and squatted by his knees. "Will she be okay?"

"They don't know yet."

Sean joined them. "What is it?"

"Addy's been in a car accident."

"The nurse told me to come as soon as I can."

"Then why are you just sitting here?" Kiley made shooing motions with her hands. "Go."

"I need to—"

"Do nothing. Get in the car and head to the airport. Now." Kiley got up and tugged him to his feet. "We've got things here."

"But the girls—"

"We got them," Sean said. "Go."

"I didn't get ahold of Eisenhower."

"I'll call him," Sean said.

Mack nodded, the reason he was stalling becoming clear. The minute he got in their rental SUV to drive to the airport was the minute he had to admit he'd failed the person he loved most on this earth. Failed her big-time, and she was clinging to life in an emergency room.

CHAPTER 4

THE SMELL OF ANTISEPTIC and vomit comingled in the emergency room waiting area, but Mack didn't care. All he cared about was finding Addy. Ten long hours had passed since the phone call and it was nearing midnight. He was tired. Cranky. And hungry. Not a good combination, and it didn't bode well for anyone who crossed his path.

Hoping to at least freshen his breath, he popped one of his favorite mints into his mouth. He marched up to the desk and took a second to compose himself so he didn't snap at the young woman behind the desk. "I'm Mack Jordan. My wife, Addison Leigh, was brought in this afternoon. Car accident. I need to see her. Now!"

"Let me check." She offered a kind smile and let her fingers race across her keyboard. Her eyes narrowed, and Mack braced himself for bad news. She looked up. "She's been moved to a room."

"What's the number?"

"Um, I'm afraid I can't give that out without Addison's permission."

"But I'm her emergency contact."

"Sorry. That's not in her file."

He was so close to losing it. "The nurse—her name's Beth Ann—called me from here. Told me to come. Can't you check with her?"

"Um. Well. Okay. Hold on a second." She tapped a button on

her phone and her index finger on the desktop. She explained the situation to someone on the other end of the line. Her finger stilled, and suddenly she looked up and gave him a tight smile. "It'll be just a second while they check it out."

For some reason, the *Jeopardy* theme song started playing in Mack's head, and he could hardly stand in one spot. He was so antsy after sitting on the long flight. And he wanted to get to Addy. Desperately.

"Okay, yeah, sure." She nodded as she spoke. "Yeah, I can do that."

She hung up. "Beth Ann is coming out to talk to you."

"Thanks." He moved to the side.

A woman wearing bright orange scrubs stepped through the locked door, running a hand over her black hair slicked back into a ponytail. "You must be Mack. I found your name in an address book in Addy's purse, so I'm okay with sharing. She's in ICU. Room three. But I'm not sure they're going to be as flexible and let you in to see her. They're real sticklers on letting only family or emergency contacts in. Since you aren't listed as her emergency contact in our system, I'm guessing she didn't want you added when they entered her data."

He would ignore that part for now and focus on learning about her condition. "So she's awake then?"

"Yes. We're uncertain how long she was unconscious. She's confused about the accident. Doesn't remember it. Not at all."

Memory loss. He didn't like the sound of that. "Is that concerning?"

"Could be, but it can happen after a traumatic incident and brain injury."

"How serious is the injury?"

"Like I said, we don't know how long she was out, and time is a huge factor when assessing an injury of this nature. A minor or mild brain injury is defined as loss of consciousness for thirty minutes or less. Then thirty minutes to an hour and you have a moderate injury. More than an hour, severe. She was conscious by the time she arrived here, though she wasn't completely lucid, and we had trouble keeping her awake."

"So which one is it?" He was starting to get frustrated. "Mild? Severe? What?"

"The doctor is uncertain," she replied. "Imaging wasn't remarkable for hematomas, but she has brain swelling and many other symptoms consistent with a traumatic brain injury. The type of swelling she's experiencing generally doesn't peak until forty-eight to seventy-two hours from the time of injury and then diminishes from there. So her status could change."

"What happens now?"

"They'll watch her intracranial pressure in the ICU and act fast if it rises to unsafe levels."

"And if it does?"

She clamped down on her lips and then shook her head. "That's a bridge they'll cross if needed, and we really don't need to talk about it yet. I prefer to think optimistically that the swelling will stabilize or go down."

He'd like to think that way too, but his worry wouldn't let him. "Will she make a full recovery?"

"It's uncertain. If the swelling doesn't progress to those unsafe levels and the other deficits she's experiencing resolve, she'll be discharged soon. As to a full recovery, it's not unusual for someone who suffered a TBI to have lingering effects." Her phone rang, and she grabbed it from her pocket. "I have to take this. Sorry. ICU's on the first floor."

"Thank you," Mack said, though he didn't know if he was thankful or not. He just didn't know what to think. Other than when he reached Addy's room and saw her, he would likely lose it unless he took a few moments to process this news and gather his composure.

He got directions to the ICU, but once he reached the locked unit, as much he wanted to see her, he couldn't pick up the phone to call the nurse to let him in. Not yet. He wasn't ready to deal with hearing any bad news. It was almost better not knowing.

He leaned against the wall. Closed his eyes. Breathed. Just the way his counselor taught him when he started into one of his flashbacks. Find his center. Breathe. Breathe. Breathe.

Problem was, Addy was his center. She was where his mind went when he had to clear out the horrors of war. To find a place where he could keep breathing and moving.

Father, help me to be the man Addy needs right now. And heal her. Please. Heal her. Not for me. For her. For the amazing woman she is. For all she has to do in this world still. All the people her crusading personality will help.

The ICU door opened. He let his foot fall to the floor and opened his eyes.

"Oh, hi," a female nurse with a bright smile and wavy blond hair said. "Can I help you?"

"I'm Addy—Addison Leigh's husband, Mack," he said. "Mack Jordan."

"Husband?" She appraised him, and her smile fell, her eyes narrowed. "I don't understand. Addy didn't say she was married, and she isn't wearing a ring."

"We're separated," Mack explained but didn't like the way the nurse's eyes tightened even more when he did. "But I'm still her emergency contact so the ER called me."

"Oh, right. Right." She nibbled on her lip. "Did she go back to using her maiden name?"

He shook his head. "She never changed her name when we got married. For professional reasons."

The nurse nodded. "This is going to sound insensitive, but if it wasn't an amiable split, she doesn't need to see you right now. With the brain injury, she needs to maintain a calm environment and avoid agitation. I can't have you cause her distress."

"We're cool," he said, though they really weren't. They were an emotional tangle of a mess, yet they still loved each other.

The nurse tilted her head. "Let me just check with her, okay? See if she wants to see you?"

"Sure," he said, because he was positive she would say yes.

"Wait here." She turned back into the ICU pod, and he had to fight not to barrel in after her.

He couldn't stand still so he started pacing, counting the floor tiles while moving back and forth. He'd reached 253 when the door swung open. He shot a look at the nurse. Her mega frown said it all. Addy had turned him down.

"I'm sorry. They're doing some additional testing right now, and I couldn't disturb them." She gave a tight smile. "It's well past visiting hours anyway. Maybe come back in the morning."

No way. He wasn't leaving. Not by a long shot. And especially not without getting more information on her status. "They brought me up to date on her condition in the ER. Has anything changed? The swelling increased?"

She scratched her neck. "I checked her patient record while I was back there. You're not listed as her emergency contact or family. Means I'm not at liberty to share anything with you."

"Please." He sounded pitiful even to his own ears. "Can't you just tell me if she's stable or has gotten worse?"

She eyed him for a long time. "She's stable."

"That's good, right? Means the swelling hasn't reached that unsafe level."

"Yes. Now head home." She widened her stance and made a shooing motion with her hands. "Come back at nine when visiting hours start. I'll still be on duty, and if she agrees to see you, I'll let you go on back."

"I'm not going anywhere." He firmed his stance. "I'll be hanging in the lobby for the night."

She tsked and shook her head. "You won't sleep well, and it's in Addison's best interest for you to be well rested."

"No matter where I lay my head tonight, I won't sleep." He shoved his hands into his pockets. "Not with Addy in the ICU. And besides, I live in D.C. Flew in just an hour ago."

"Oh, I see. But the lobby isn't meant for overnight guests."

"I get that, but I'm going to stay anyway." He forced a smile. "I need to be close by. If you'd take pity on me and let me know every few hours how she's doing, I'd appreciate it."

"I can't—"

"Tell me anything. I know. Just say stable or worse. That's all I need to hear." He gave her another smile. "And between updates, I'll be praying to hear only the word *stable*."

———

In the ICU, Addy shifted in her bed, careful not to disturb the wires and tubes running from her body or make her head hurt any more than it already did. She looked around the room but couldn't remember a single detail of her day before arriving at the ER and going in and out of consciousness. Not one thing. The nurse had told her that she was involved in a car accident, but Addy had no idea where it happened, where she was going, or why. Her mind just blanked it out. The doctor told her this was normal, but it was anything but normal to her.

The door opened, and Gala Harris stepped in. "Thank goodness you're alive. I was concerned when you blew off our meeting, and then a Detective Palmere called to tell me you were in a car crash."

"Meeting? What meeting?" Addy asked.

Harris rested her hands on the back of a nearby chair. "You were going to update me on your investigation this afternoon."

Addy quickly explained as much as she'd been told about the crash.

Harris narrowed her eyes. "At first I thought this was just an accident, but when Palmere informed me you just drove off the road without braking, I questioned it. Especially with what's going on with Razo."

"Razo?" Addy blinked, searching her memory for the name. "Who's Razo?"

Harris's eyebrow went up. "Why would you even ask that?"

"My memory. It's more than the accident I can't remember. I don't know what I was last working on. Or that I had a meeting with you."

"That's not good." Harris tightened her grip on the chair. "What are the doctors saying about that? Will your memory come back?"

The question of the hour. Maybe day. Addy hoped it wouldn't be more than a few days until she started remembering things. "They're uncertain because they aren't sure of the cause. They don't know if it's the trauma or the brain injury."

"Which direction are they leaning?"

"They don't think my injury is severe enough to warrant memory loss, so they think it's trauma. The good news is, the swelling's going down so things should be getting back to normal on that front." She didn't add that the doctor also told her she might never return to normal again. That was the last thing she wanted to tell her supervisor right now.

"Palmere says he has your weapon and your car. He'll return the gun to you when you're discharged, and he's processing the car."

"How is my car? It was my dad's and has special meaning to me."

"He didn't say. But crashing into a tree can often total a vehicle."

Addy nodded but refused to believe the car was a lost cause until she saw it herself.

"The crash happened in northeast Portland." Harris rattled off an address. "Any idea why you might have been over there?"

She gave it some thought, her brain burning with the strain, but nothing came to mind. "None."

"Warren said you bolted from the office," Harris stated. "Said you had a new lead. Do you remember that?"

"No. Sorry."

"Well, I tasked Fitz with reviewing the last files you accessed on the network to see if we can figure out what you were looking at that made you take off. Might give us a reason for your visit."

Thankfully, Addy remembered their IT tech guy. "I appreciate your getting started on it right away. I only wish I was in better shape and could do my own digging."

"Maybe tomorrow. Until then we've got you. Fitz's also tracking down CCTV footage for the accident location, if there are any cameras in the area. Maybe seeing that footage will jog your memory too."

Addy hoped for the same thing. "I also don't have my phone. They said it wasn't in my car. Not sure what could have happened to it."

"Things can get misplaced at accident scenes." Harris pushed off the chair and rolled her shoulders. "I'll have Fitz run the app to find it. Worst case, if he doesn't locate it, he can disable the device."

"I'm sorry for making more work for Fitz and putting the agency at risk."

Harris shook her head. "You have nothing to be sorry for. You were incapacitated. You couldn't keep track of your phone or gun."

"Still, I feel responsible. If this guy cracks my password, he could get to the network."

Harris tilted her head. "Tell me you had a secure password. Not something like 12345."

"Very secure, and random. No way he could connect it to me." She was happy to report that at least.

Harris watched her for a long moment. "Is there anything you can do to speed up the process of getting your memory back?"

"The doctor mentioned several therapies, but he thought the best one might be hypnosis. He said by using relaxation coupled with a method called age regression, that it's possible to retrieve lost memories."

"Are you planning to do that?"

Was she? Not knowing people and what had been happening in her life was horrible. "I think I will once I'm discharged."

"I don't know anything about memory loss, but if it were me, I'd be doing everything I could to get it back."

"Yeah," Addy said and decided to change the subject. "So why was I supposed to meet with you?"

The nurse poked her head in the doorway. "Visiting time is up. Addy needs to rest."

Harris gave a sharp nod. "I'll just say good-bye."

The nurse smiled and closed the door.

Harris met Addy's gaze. "I'll get with Palmere and make sure he includes me in your accident investigation. Then I'll clear my schedule for tomorrow morning and come back with your new phone and laptop in case you feel up to reviewing the case files. Later, we can review the details of the threat."

"That would be great if you have the time," Addy said, as she was too out of it to even contemplate reviewing case files tonight.

"Razo is a killer, and we need to bring him in. I'll make the time."

CHAPTER 5

THE NEXT MORNING, just before visiting hours were to begin, Mack stood outside the regular hospital room Addy had been transferred to about an hour ago. He held a bouquet of white roses, her favorite, the fragrant scent perfuming the air around him.

He ran into Addy's new nurse, who was coming out of the room. She eyed him and blocked the door. Talk about bad timing. She was just like the ICU nurse last night. Protective and willing to confront him despite the gun on his hip. She insisted on making sure Addy wanted to see him before letting him in the room.

He should be thankful all these nurses wanted to defend Addy, but he was starting to get irritated. He was her husband, for Pete's sake. He had every right to see her. Okay, fine. They were separated, and he had no rights. He just didn't want to acknowledge that now. He wanted to see her.

Forget this waiting business.

He pushed through the door and came to a stop. Addy lay on the bed looking pale and washed-out, her long lashes resting on her high cheekbones. Shoulder-length red hair that he'd tangled his fingers in so many times spread around her ashen face. Even her freckles were pale. A large bruise darkened her forehead, and she wore a white-and-blue hospital gown. Cords and wires traveled from her body to beeping machines, and Mack thought he might hurl.

He'd never seen Addy sick. Not a single day. She was so very fit and healthy, and he didn't know how to act. Other than to swallow down the anxiety crawling up his throat and threatening to strangle him. Maybe it was a good thing he never got to see her in the ICU where he bet there'd been even more tubes and wires.

"Addy." The nurse named Patsy approached the bed. "Your husband, Mack, is here to see you."

Her eyes opened. She blinked a few times. "Mack?" she whispered.

"Yes, he's in the hallway."

"Actually, I'm right here," Mack said, stepping forward and earning a frown from the nurse. He held the roses out to Addy. "Your favorite."

She flashed her gaze to the roses and then up to his face. She stared for a long moment, then blinked a few times. Closed her eyes and held them closed.

Maybe she wasn't glad to see him after all. Or didn't want the flowers.

She slowly opened her eyes and ran her gaze over him from head to toe, lingering on his face for the longest time at the end.

"I'm sorry," she said.

Was she going to tell him to go? That she wanted to recover alone?

That would be nearly the worst thing she could say to him. His heart clenched, and he laid the flowers on the nearby table.

"I'm not married. Never have been." She scooted up and away from him like a cornered animal. "I don't know who you are or what you're playing at, but I've never seen you before. Never. Not once. And it's pretty low to try to pretend to be my husband when I'm in no position to defend myself."

Oh, man. He was wrong. Way wrong. This was the worst thing she could say to him. The very worst.

———

Addy couldn't breathe. This man. This very handsome—big eyes in an unusual grayish-green color, a hint of red in slightly curly hair, and close-cut beard—but big and frightening man who stood there looking at her as if he'd been punched in the gut. As if she'd physically punched him in the gut.

He was lying, right? She wasn't married. She might not remember the accident, but she would remember a husband, for goodness' sake.

She looked at her hand. No ring. But he knew she loved white roses. How could he know that if she didn't at least know him?

"It has to be the brain injury," he said, sounding like he struggled to get the words out over a closing throat.

"Be that as it may." The nurse named Patsy stepped between them as if she thought this Mack guy might hurt them. "I'm going to have to ask you to leave until we can sort this out."

"But I . . ." He moved to the side, and his pleading gaze landed on Addy.

In her line of work, she was truly into personal protection, and yet she had the oddest desire to tell him to stay. They'd figure things out. But that was just because she found him attractive—his broad shoulders under a leather jacket. She had a thing for guys in leather jackets. And the cowboy boots and Southern accent? Those were a bonus, as one of her favorite pastimes was to watch professional bull riding.

He adjusted his jacket on his shoulders, and she suspected he wore it for warmth, but there was a gun at his hip too, and he didn't want to draw attention to it. Law enforcement? Seemed like a good bet to her.

"You a cop?" she asked.

"Deputy U.S. Marshal," he said proudly, his smooth accent blanketing her in Southern charm.

Right. She pegged him. Meant he might be safer to have around, but also could mean he wasn't. What if they *had* been married? He was abusive and they split? A guy in law enforcement would be the very worst in that situation. So no. She couldn't let him hang around. Couldn't be alone with him.

"We worked on the RED team together in D.C., remember?" he asked, sounding a bit desperate, and his eyes reflected the need. "Before you kick me out, think about it. Please."

"RED team?" She ran the name through her brain, but it didn't ring a bell.

"Kiley. Sean. Cam. Our teammates."

He was either a good liar or he'd made up this story in advance. But he was wrong. She lived here in Portland with her ailing mom. Took care of her. Not D.C. "Sorry, no. I'm an ICE agent here in Portland."

"I know. When we separated, you couldn't work on the team anymore and your mom was getting frail too. So you moved back here to take care of her."

She gaped at him.

How did he know about her mom too? How could he possibly know that?

A bolt of fear burrowed into her. "I need you to leave now. I need to rest."

"Yes, come on." Patsy pointed at the door. "You and I can sort this out."

He continued to stare at her, and she felt an anguish so deep that she started to believe they were married. Still, that was impossible. She would remember. Wouldn't she?

She couldn't look at the pain on his face any longer, so she closed her eyes again. She listened carefully as the sweet nurse led him out of the room. The moment Addy heard the door close, she opened her eyes and stared at the door. Had she forgotten this man? He seemed unforgettable. A larger-than-life person physically, and though she only got a hint of his personality, she could see he felt things deeply. Lived life large.

She would call her mom to ask, but she had dementia and couldn't be relied upon to remember a wayward husband. Because if he was telling the truth, they might be married and separated. Why? What had happened?

She thought. Hard. Searched her brain. Nothing. Just nothing. It was all a void. A black, uncomfortable void. She wanted to pound on her head, but it ached so badly she couldn't do that.

Panic threatened. She closed her eyes and breathed. In. Out. In. Out.

The doctor had said to rest. Not to worry about not remembering the day. Wasn't unusual. No biggie. It would come back when she was ready to remember it.

But would this guy come back to her memory? Would she remember him or was he lying? And if so, why? Did it have anything to do with an investigation? With the killer, Razo?

She would ask Harris when she came by. Or call Warren. One of them would know—they had to know. Because she couldn't be married and not remember it. That was completely unacceptable.

———

An hour passed before nurse Patsy came to the lounge door, her expression serious and not boding well for Mack.

"I'm sorry," she said. "Unless you can prove you're married to Addy, she doesn't want to see you."

Panic crept up Mack's back and nearly capsized him until an idea came to mind. "Addy called me yesterday. Left a message. Wanted the RED team's help. I could play it for her. Then she'd at least see that we know each other and that the RED team exists."

Patsy frowned and didn't respond.

"Can you just ask her if she's willing to listen to the message? I can even give you my phone and let you play it. That way she won't be intimidated by me being in the room."

"I don't know."

"Please. Don't say no." How could he convince her to help him? Because it was clear he needed her help if he was going to see Addy again.

Make it personal. "Think about it from both of our points of view. It's like a gut-wrenching thing to have your wife not recognize you. It's tearing me up inside."

Patsy arched a flawlessly plucked eyebrow. "Wife you're separated from."

Rats. "Yeah, well . . . yeah." He firmed his stance. Switched tactics. "We might be separated, but I still love her and want her to get well. Maybe I can help with her recovery. She doesn't have anyone else. I mean her mom . . . yeah . . . sure. But she has dementia and there's no way she could look after Addy. She needs a full-time caregiver as it is."

Patsy's expression softened.

"Speaking of her mom." He stepped closer. "Do you know if anyone has called her? Or what about Bear? Our dog. Has he been fed?"

"I don't know."

"You should ask. She needs to know. And ask about the message too." His mouth went dry and he grabbed his mint tin, opening the lid and offering one to Patsy first. She shook her head, her expression relaxing.

He popped a mint into his mouth, the strong peppermint exploding on his tongue. He felt like he'd succeeded in gaining her empathy. He just needed to go in for the close.

"I'll wait here. I promise." He shoved the mints back into his pocket and dropped onto a chair to emphasize his point. "See. Right here."

"Fine." She clenched her hands and released them. "I'll talk to her, but if you show up in the room, I *will* call security and have you thrown out." She glared at him. "You might be this big tough guy, but you don't scare me."

She planted her feet, looking like a tiny Chihuahua attempting to be a Great Dane, and he had to fight hard to keep his mouth from quirking into a smile.

"I'm grateful for your help, and I won't move a muscle." He leaned back on the cold vinyl chair and propped his leg on his knee, trying to appear casual when his gut was screaming at him to go racing down the hall to see Addy. At the very least stand outside her door to defend her. Keep her safe from any other harm.

Patsy gave him one last lingering look, a warning mixed with disapproval, before she spun. Her shoe squeaked on the tile, and she marched away with solid footfalls.

Alone now, he had nothing and no one to keep his mind busy, and worry curled into place like a snake taking up residence in his brain. He couldn't lose Addy. He just couldn't. Sure, he was the one who broke things off. He'd woken up from a flashback to his Middle East deployment, and he had his hands around her neck. Choking her. Her eyes wide and bugged out. Red-faced. Gasping for air.

Then he'd had to look at purple-and-green bruises circling her delicate neck for weeks. Bruises he'd put there. She didn't blame him. Even so, it was his fault. He'd refused to acknowledge his PTSD and then let it get out of control instead of seeking help. He'd been going to counseling since that day. He'd gotten things under control. Pretty much anyway. His focus was now on God and how He empowered people. Mack had been focusing on the Bible verse in 2 Timothy—"For the Spirit God gave us does not make us timid, but gives us power, love and self-discipline." His mantra now whenever things went south. Over and over he would repeat it.

But honestly, he still didn't trust himself. Maybe that meant he really didn't trust God. Because if he really believed this verse, he wouldn't lose his cool, would he? When he was overworked and tired, he was still very vulnerable to the effects of PTSD.

And what if he hurt her again?

No. He could never do that. Never take the risk. They just couldn't be together until he figured all this out. That was final.

CHAPTER 6

ADDY LAY BACK and closed her eyes. She tuned out the beeping of the monitors, and the IV needle pinching in the crook of her elbow. The blood-pressure cuff on her bicep and the oxygen monitor on her finger. All of it. Forgot it all. So she could concentrate. Figure out what was going on.

The doctor said Addy needed to rest her brain, but how could she rest when a strange man had shown up to say he was her husband, and she had no recollection of him? None. Not one tiny hint of a memory.

But she *had* called him, or at least he claimed she had. He would soon join her to play the message. So she *did* know him, but did she know him that well? As in his wife?

She sighed a long breath, and her lungs felt like they were collapsing and she couldn't pull in enough oxygen to keep going. The medical trauma mixed with this emotional trauma was just too much, wasn't it?

She was getting a glimpse into her mother's world. She lived in a fog like this all the time. Not remembering. Getting upset when someone presented themselves and she didn't know them. Addy being one of those someones.

A knock sounded on the door. Addy's eyes flashed open. She tugged up her sheet and blanket to her chin, protecting herself from this man. "Come in."

The door creaked open. As if in slow motion, he entered. He stopped just inside the door. "Thank you for seeing me."

She started to nod, but pain lanced through her head so she stopped. "Just for a few minutes."

He gave a sharp nod and crossed the room. He had a confident swagger—powerful, as if he didn't let anything get in his way. She looked at his face. His eyes. There the confidence evaporated. Instead, uncertainty mixed with a deep, abiding pain. He'd been hurt. Badly. By something. And it drew her to him as if being pulled by an invisible magnetic field.

He moved a chair close to her bed and straddled it. His muscular arms came to a rest on the padded back. He dug out a tin of mints from his pocket and offered her one.

She found it odd, and yet something niggled at her brain that mints were a hint to his personality. What kind of hint she had no idea, and it likely didn't matter, so she refused one and left it alone.

He tossed one in his mouth and got out his phone. "May I play the message for you?"

"Go ahead."

He tapped the screen, then held out his phone.

"Mack, it's Addy." Her voice sounded from the speaker, but there was an underlying hesitancy in her tone. "I need a favor from the RED team—Cam especially—for an investigation I'm working. It's a big one. One that means savings countless lives. Can you call me back ASAP to discuss? Thanks."

She stared at the phone and swallowed hard. What in the world had she been working on? "Yeah, that's my voice all right. But I don't remember leaving the message. When did you say I called?"

He tapped the screen and leaned forward to hold it out, his peppermint breath drifting over her. The message was left at three o'clock yesterday.

She massaged her temples, making sure to avoid the big goose egg on her forehead. "Tell me more about this RED team. You said I was once on it?"

He nodded and shoved his phone into his pocket. "We work out of HSI's Cyber Crimes Center in D.C. There are four of us on the team now. FBI agents Sean Nichols and Kiley Dawson and analyst Cameron—Cam—Linn. We work high-level and top-priority investigations for criminal activity conducted on or facilitated by the internet."

"So big cases," she said, taking it all in. "Like?"

"Like . . ." He paused and held her gaze. "You have the clearance to be read-in on these, but I know Eisenhower wouldn't approve. Still . . ." He shrugged. "A couple of biggies we worked in the last few years are the WITSEC database being hacked and terrorists smuggled into the country who were planning to kill millions of people on the 9/11 anniversary."

"Wow." She was impressed. "And I willingly left the team?"

He cringed, and that sadness he'd kept at bay so far took over his expressive eyes. "I don't know if *willingly* is the word for it. But yeah. You decided it would be too hard to work together after we broke up. So, since your mom isn't doing so well, you came out here to take care of her. After you left, our supervisor, Barry Eisenhower—he's the ICE Special Agent in Charge of the Cyber Crimes Center—decided not to replace you. I think he was hoping we'd get back together and you'd rejoin the team."

"Okay, so I'll go along with the premise that we're married for now," she admitted reluctantly. "How long have we been separated?"

"Going on a year and a half."

"And we didn't divorce?"

He shook his head.

"Why'd we split up?"

He grimaced. "My fault, totally. I served as an Army Night Stalker for many years. Had some issues linger. PTSD. Thought I had everything under control. I thought I was trusting God. Turns out I didn't, but I'm working on it."

She didn't like seeing his pain, but she was glad to hear he believed in God.

"I started having flashbacks and nightmares again." He clasped his hands together so tightly his fingers turned white. "One night was particularly bad. I woke up with my hands around your throat. I thought you were an enemy combatant. The guy with a knife who took out two of my team."

He met and held her gaze. "You were so amazing. You punched me in the face. Brought me out of it. Otherwise . . ." He shook his head and looked down. "I couldn't let that happen again. We couldn't be together. So I moved out."

Wow! Just wow! How did she handle something like that? Had she really punched him? Did she want to get away from him?

She scooted back. He caught her move and scowled.

"I understand your reasoning," she said, "but couldn't we have just slept in separate beds until you got it under control?"

"Yeah, that's what you said back then too." He relaxed his hands. "I've had a few daytime flashbacks—not enough to make me leave the job—but my counseling is working in that area, and they've pretty much stopped. The dreams too, but I still occasionally have them."

His upset troubled her, and she wanted to get up and give him a hug. He felt terrible for hurting her, and she knew beyond a shadow of a doubt that he was telling the truth. She was married to him—this man who clearly still cared about her. Cared enough to walk out on her. She had to admire that, even though it frustrated her because she thought it was something a couple would work through. Together. After having lived through the horrifying experience, how had she actually felt about it? She sure would like to know.

Mentally and physically exhausted, she lay back and closed her eyes.

"I'm sorry," he said. "That was too much for now. I'll go."

He was probably right. Resting her brain was a good idea. But she didn't want him to leave. Not yet.

She heard him push off the chair and stand. "Has anyone called your mom?"

She looked up at him. "I called Nancy. Mom's caregiver. No point in worrying Mom when she might forget it anyway."

He rested a hand on the back of the chair, and she admired his long fingers. "Do you remember the accident?"

"I—not really. They said I just ran right off the road and didn't brake to try to stop. Plowed into a tree."

His eyebrows shot up. "Seriously?"

"Yeah."

He tightened his fingers. "You never were a drinker and didn't do drugs. But did they do a tox screen to check that?"

"Not that I know of." She sighed and thought about what the accident scene must have looked like. She'd been alone. Coming from or going to where? She had no idea. She hadn't gotten the details from anyone yet.

He stood, looking at her, his eyes narrowed. "Have the police interviewed you?"

"No. I remember them being in the ER. They wanted to ask questions, but the doctor told them to come back later. Surprisingly, they complied."

"Do you remember any of the accident details at all?"

"I have hazy vague memories." She closed her eyes, hoping her thoughts would sharpen. "I remember feeling like I was outside of my body when it happened. Like I was watching from above and seeing myself but not feeling like myself."

He frowned. "Is there any way you could've been drugged?"

"Doubtful. And by who? No one is trying to kill me." She opened her eyes and forced a smile, though in her line of work threats did occur, so it was possible she supposed.

"What about the investigation you needed Cam's help with? Could someone connected to that case want to hurt you?"

"I—" she started to say, but she couldn't come up with any details or reason for why she'd called him. "I don't know. I can't remember why I left you a message. Maybe my supervisor knows. Or Warren even."

"Warren?"

"He's a longtime agent in my office. I think of him as my work dad. I bounce ideas off him sometimes." She took a deep breath. "My supervisor is coming by this morning to update me on the investigation and bring me a new phone."

He arched a brow. "It wasn't in your car?"

"No. I don't know what . . ." A fragment of the accident flashed into her mind, and she paused to let the memories flood in like a river rushing over a cliff. "Oh my gosh! That's it. I remember being in the car after the accident. Before I blacked out. A man. Masked face. Fuzzy memory."

She pinched her eyes closed and let the memory play. It was vivid. Bright. Real. "He had a deep voice. I had my phone in my hand. He said I didn't want it, and he took it from me. Told me to relax. I remember being fine with that. Not afraid at all." She flashed her eyes open. "He also said this was a wake-up call. To keep Mom and me safe. Then he said to relax and let the drug take hold."

"He drugged me. But who *is* he?" She frantically searched her memory for a face. Didn't see one. "Why did he want my phone? And the warning. My mom. Is she in danger? Am I in danger?"

———

Stunned, Mack dropped back onto the chair and swallowed, trying to wet a dry throat. He didn't like hearing what happened to Addy. Didn't like it at all. A strange man taking her phone. Drugging her. Warning her off. Why?

The accident clearly wasn't an accident. Addy could've died. Right there in the car.

Mack's heart nearly refused to beat. He couldn't think. Couldn't focus. But she needed him to. And that meant he had to remember God was in control and gave him strength.

"The Spirit God gave us does not make us timid, but gives us power, love and self-discipline." Mack repeated his mantra once. Twice. Focused on the problem.

He looked at Addy.

"Maybe he took my phone to stop me from calling 911," she said. "From getting help. He wanted me to die." Her eyes darkened in anguish. Raw. Terrible. Living, horrible anguish, and she wrapped her arms around her slender waist as if she could protect herself.

It took everything Mack was made of not to come off his chair and take her in his arms. He missed holding her. Missed everything about her. And yet his touch wouldn't comfort her right now. It would add to her pain. The thought was like a sucker punch to the gut.

"I'm assuming you use your phone to log on to your network using a VPN," he said and didn't explain the abbreviation. She would know he meant a Virtual Private Network that masked the physical location of a person's internet access.

She nodded. "You're thinking he took the phone to gain access to our network."

"It's possible, but I would think if he just wanted the phone, he could've found an easier way to steal it."

"You're right. This still seems to be about killing me," she said matter-of-factly as if talking about her grocery list, not her potential murder.

"I'd like to talk to your supervisor. What's his name?"

"Her. Gala Harris. Special Agent in Charge of the Portland office. But I don't want you to contact her." Addy shook her head, then winced and stopped. "How can I remember her just fine and not you? Or the investigation?"

He suspected both their marriage and the investigation included a boatload of stress, and this Harris person didn't bring along the same baggage. But he wouldn't say that and further upset Addy. "I guess that's just the way the brain works."

"Yeah, I suppose." She nibbled on her full lower lip.

Memories of kissing that lip were vivid and real, and he was powerless to look away.

She released her lip and frowned at him. Right. She didn't want him drooling over her. Shoot, she probably didn't what him here at all. "I'll let you get some rest, but I want to check on you a little later. Also to see if you've regained any of your memory. Maybe help figure out who this guy might be who stole your phone. Would that be okay?"

"I don't know. I mean I would like to think I *should* want to see you, but I . . ." She shrugged and continued to stare at him. "It's just so confusing."

He hated that his presence made her life worse, yet he had to be nearby. And to that end, he wasn't leaving the hospital. He would be hanging out, sleeping in the lounge, and checking in with the nurses at regular intervals. "I don't want to make things worse for you. I honestly don't. But I need to be sure you're on the mend."

"Fine," she said finally and sighed. "Stop in. It's okay."

He reluctantly got up and put the chair back where he found it. He faced her bed. "Thank you for talking to me. I'm sorry I'm adding stress to your already tough day. I hope you get some rest."

She gave a brief nod, and he started for the door.

"Mack," she called out.

He turned.

"Were we happy once?" She searched his gaze. "I mean really happy?"

The question shocked him but he made sure to hide his surprise. "Yeah. Until the PTSD ended it. Yeah. Was the best time of my life, and you said yours too."

She tilted her head. "Seems like I should be able to remember such a special time."

He would never forget the joyful days they'd spent together. Thought about it—about her all the time. And he wanted the relationship back. He just didn't know how to go about it. Now with her memory loss, no matter how well he did in his PTSD therapy, that might not happen for him. Ever.

CHAPTER 7

THE MOMENT MACK LEFT the room, doubt settled into Addy's brain. Married? Was it true? Was she married to Mack? He'd looked so worried for her. Terrified, if she was right. He seemed genuine. Kind. Caring. Maybe still in love with her. But despite studying that handsome face ad nauseam, not even a spark of recognition registered in her brain. A thick five o'clock shadow darkened his jaw, and she tried to remember touching that rough beard. That scruffy hair. Kissing him. Being held by him.

Nothing. Nada. No memory.

She might have believed him when he was in the room with her, but now that he was gone, what did she feel?

She couldn't think about that anymore. Not when she had an accident to sort out. She tapped her nurse call button and asked to have Patsy come to her room. Not more than five minutes later, the kind nurse stepped through the door.

She ran her gaze over Addy, her green eyes narrowed. "Everything okay?"

"Fine." Addy smiled to ease her worry. "I was wondering if the doctors ran a tox screen when I was brought into the ER."

"Not that I know of, but let me check." Patsy stepped over to the computer in the corner and brought up Addy's records. She ran her finger down the screen. "No. No tox screen." She peered at Addy. "Is there something we need to know about?"

Addy suddenly felt foolish because she had no proof of being drugged, but she had to see this through. "I'm not sure. I remembered a bit of the accident scene, and I was woozy. Way too woozy to be driving. If someone drugged me, that would explain why I ran off the road and didn't stop."

"It would." Patsy frowned. "Would you like me to call your doctor and request the tests?"

"Yes. I think it's a good idea."

"If you were drugged, hopefully there's still enough in your bloodstream to register it. I'll call the doc and get the orders going." Patsy squeezed Addy's arm and hurried from the room.

Addy leaned back on her pillow. If any drugs were still in her system, they weren't actively affecting her, thank goodness. Or at least she wasn't feeling any odd effects that weren't from the head injury. She was feeling plenty of those, but she wasn't one to dwell on the negative.

She pushed the table away from her bed and closed her eyes. If she was married to Mack, she had so many questions. Tons of them. And her brain was spinning. Just what the doctor had told her to avoid. He'd prescribed cognitive rest for a few days. He said they'd once recommended it for much longer, but they'd since learned that the so-called cocoon therapy that limited the brain from even the most basic tasks of checking email, social media, et cetera, had detrimental effects. She was thankful her neurologist was up to date on treatments. The sooner she could get back to work, the better.

She grabbed a notepad and started jotting questions for Mack. She filled a page. Then a second one. But her head started hurting worse, the very sign the doctor told her to watch for. If any symptom became more exacerbated, she should stop. She wanted to be able to review her files when Harris brought them over, so she set down her pen and relaxed her muscles until she fell asleep.

She dreamt of a faceless man standing over her. His tone oddly comforting as he gently pried the phone from her hands.

She trusted him. At least that was the feeling she was getting. She would do what he said and not question him.

A knock sounded on the door, and she bolted upright. Taking a deep breath, she raised the head of her bed even more from the already high position that the doctors insisted she maintain and pressed her hand over her hair to settle wayward strands into place.

"Come in," she called out and expected Harris to walk through the door.

Mack poked his head inside. "Is this an okay time to check in?"

"Okay?" she asked, not sure how to answer. "I guess."

He strode into the room, his booted feet pounding on the floor. He'd shaved and changed clothes since he'd left, and he looked refreshed, if still tired. He smelled fresh too—mint and musk combined in a scent that tugged at her memory but failed to produce one.

He came to a stop next to her bed, looking down at her, his presence seeming to fill the room. He held out that same tin of mints. She shook her head, and he popped one in his mouth before pocketing them. "Harris been here yet?"

Addy shook her head and straightened her covers.

Another knock pounded on the door.

"Maybe that's her now." She called out for her to enter, keeping her gaze pinned to the door.

A burly man with shocking white hair and wearing a black suit with a green shirt stepped inside.

"Agent Leigh?" he asked. "I'm Detective Oliver Palmere with the Portland Police Bureau. I was hoping you were up to answering some questions now."

"Sure," she said, thankful to have someone else in the room before the conversation with Mack turned personal.

Palmere looked at Mack. "And you are?"

"Addy's husband, Mack Jordan." He glanced at Addy, likely trying to see her reaction to him sharing their relationship that she had yet to confirm. He swung that intense gaze back to Palmere. "I'm a Deputy U.S. Marshal out of D.C. Mind if I sit in with the two of you?"

"Two Feds to interview. What could be the problem with that?" Palmere's sarcasm was liberally applied to his tone, but he didn't tell Mack to leave.

Addy pulled her blanket up to her chin, bracing for Palmere's questions, but first she had one of her own. "Could you be sure I get my service weapon back before discharge?"

"I'll have someone bring it by." He got out a small notepad and pen. "Tell me about the accident."

"I don't remember much, but I do remember feeling off as I was driving. Woozy. Unable to focus. Blurred vision." She swallowed before the memories actually played before her eyes. "But the tox screen will tell us what happened for sure."

"How could someone have drugged you?" He pursed his lips.

"I don't know." She fidgeted with the edge of the blanket to calm her nerves. "I mean, I just don't remember where I was going or anything before getting behind the wheel."

"You're a huge coffee drinker," Mack said. "Did you stop for a cup?"

Did she? She shrugged. "Maybe there's a cup or mug or something in my car that can be tested for drugs."

"I'm way ahead of you there." Palmere puffed out his chest. "When I heard that an ICE agent had wrapped her car around a tree without attempting to stop, I thought it was worth looking into."

Likely to find fault with a Fed. Addy had half a mind to mention it, but what good would it do to accuse him of wanting to call out a Fed? None. In fact, it might make things worse, so she clamped down on her lips.

"So I had your car hauled into the state crime lab," Palmere continued. "They're processing it as we speak. And in answer to the coffee question, you had an empty paper coffee cup and a warm travel mug in the car. Enough coffee was left in the spill-proof travel mug to take into evidence."

She nodded. "So I was probably drinking it around the time of the accident, and it could contain a drug."

He kept his focus pinned to her. "Tests are being run. Should know something soon."

She closed her eyes and searched her brain, trying to remember where she'd been before the accident and how someone would have access to the cup. "What if I got the coffee—left it in the car while I went inside somewhere—then this man broke into my car and put the drug in there?"

"Sounds possible, but where did this occur? Why were you in that neighborhood at that time of day? And who would want to drug you?"

She clutched her hands together, wishing she could come up with something. "I don't know. I just don't know."

"What about an investigation you're working on? Maybe you made someone mad and they were getting back at you."

"It seems to be the best explanation," she said, "but I don't remember anything about my current investigation."

He arched an eyebrow, his posture rigid.

Fine. He didn't believe her. She couldn't change that. "Trust me, I want to remember everything about the accident. It's awful not knowing what you should know."

"I assume you'll get up to speed on the investigation soon, and I'll need to be read-in on it too."

"My supervisor is coming by later to update me, and that won't be a problem if you have the proper clearance."

He grimaced. "Right. The Feds' security clearance side step."

"It's not a side step. It's a necessary part of our work."

The door opened, and Patsy entered. Her footsteps faltered, and her gaze traveled between the men and Addy. "I'm sorry. I didn't know you had company."

"It's okay," Addy assured her. "Feel free to do what you need to do. Blood pressure. Whatever."

"It's well . . . I . . ." She took a few hesitant steps forward. "I don't need to *do* anything. But we got the results back from the test you asked for."

"The tox screen?" Addy's heartbeat picked up. "Already?"

Patsy nodded.

"And?" Addy held her breath, and she saw Mack do the same thing.

"The test was positive for Rohypnol."

"Roofies," she cried out, her mind spinning as she tried to process the fact that someone had used the popular date-rape drug on her. "Someone roofied me?"

"Yes," Pasty said between clenched teeth.

"So your accident was as far from an accident as possible." Mack's nostrils flared, and he clenched his hands. "Someone roofied you knowing full well that you were going to get behind that wheel. That's as clear-cut a case of attempted murder as can be."

———

Detective Palmere and Patsy had barely departed when a petite woman charged into the room, a laptop case swinging on a strap slung over her shoulder. Mack took in her black power suit and crisp white blouse. Her inky hair was straight to the chin and shiny, her eyes narrowed and intense. She might only stand a few inches above five feet, but she presented herself with confidence, and he assumed she was Addy's supervisor. He was glad she'd finally arrived. Maybe now they would get some answers.

The woman looked up at Mack, then at Addy and back at Mack. "You must be the wayward husband."

Mack didn't like her tone but gave her a tight smile and held out his hand. "Mack Jordan."

Harris grabbed his hand and pumped it hard as she rattled off her name and title. "Addy didn't tell me you were in town."

"I was still listed as her emergency contact," he said, as if that explained everything going on between them.

Addy paled and looked at Harris. "You know about Mack? That we're married?"

"You didn't make a secret of it, so yeah. I knew."

"So it's true? He's my husband?" Addy gaped at her supervisor.

"You don't remember?"

Addy shook her head, and an awkward silence fell over the room.

Harris hustled into action and set the laptop on a green vinyl recliner.

"Addy says you're here to bring her up to speed on her current investigation," Mack said.

Harris cocked her head. "That's right. Operation Crossfire."

Hearing the op's name raised Mack's interest even more. "Did she mention that she called me before the accident to request help from our team?"

"No." Harris shifted her focus to Addy.

"That's because I have no idea why I called them. The message Mack played for me said I wanted Cam's help. He's the team analyst. So I must have wanted data that wouldn't be easy to come by."

"I've been doing some digging," Mack said. "Comparing the time of the voicemail and the time you were brought into the ER. Seems like you left the message shortly before the accident."

"Likely," she said, her expression downcast. "By the way, I remembered something." Addy shared about her phone being taken from her. "Could've been Razo. Do you know if we have his prints on file?"

"Who's Razo?" Mack asked.

"He's a suspect in Leigh's latest investigation, and we do

have his prints," Harris replied quickly. "He's been in and out of prison over the years and has a long sheet."

"Then maybe we'll have recovered his prints at my house or in my car."

"Maybe." Harris's doubt lingered on her face.

"I really don't want to think of someone like Razo in possession of your phone." Harris frowned. "Fitz was unable to locate it using the app. Seems like whoever took it removed the battery. But he'll keep monitoring it in case is comes back online."

Addy rubbed her head. "I'm hoping once I dig into my files, I can figure out who took it."

"Fitz is still working on getting the CCTV footage for the area of the accident, but I brought your computer so you can access your files."

Mack wanted to say that last night he'd gotten Cam started on locating video files, and that Mack suspected Cam would have better results, but he didn't want to antagonize Harris or Addy, so he kept his mouth closed.

"Let's get the technical things out of the way first." Harris picked up the laptop. "Your new phone's in the outside pocket of the case, and it's all set for our VPN so you can log on to the network and download your files."

Mack met Addy's gaze. "Seems to me your taking a rest after all of these visitors is a better idea."

"All?" Harris asked.

Mack told her about the detective.

"Right. I'm already coordinating with him on the car and other evidence." Harris's focus flashed to Addy as she handed her the laptop. "Especially the coffee cup. I could see Razo drugging you after his threat."

"Threat?" Mack asked, his pulse kicking up. "What threat?"

Harris grimaced and curled her hands into fists. "A man went to Leigh's house, drugged her dog, tied up her mother and caregiver, and put a knife to her mother's throat. Then he sent Leigh a video of him holding her mother hostage."

"My mother!" Addy shot up in her bed and wobbled before she clutched the side rail. "Is she okay? And Bear?"

Harris held up a calming hand. "Fine. You moved your mom and her nurse into protective custody. You arranged that before you tore out of the office on the new lead. Your dog is sleeping off the drugs at your place."

Addy sighed, her breath going on and on, sounding like a leaking tire.

"No one's taking care of Bear, then?" Mack asked.

Addy shot him an odd look. "You know Bear?"

Right. She wouldn't know that. "We adopted him together."

She gave a long, frustrated sigh. "Then please say you'll go feed him and let him out."

"Of course. Glad to." He smiled in earnest at the thought of seeing Bear after the time they'd spent apart.

Harris glanced at Mack. "We believe the person behind the video is Bruno Razo or is connected to him. Razo is a major local drug dealer turned gunrunner, and he's the target of Operation Crossfire. He's in bed with the drug cartels, and rumor has it he's moving five miniguns from Mexico to the U.S. in five days. We don't have details on the shipment, but we need to find it and stop it before Americans are slaughtered with this weapon. Are you familiar with the minigun?"

Was he familiar? Boy howdy. "I was an Army Night Stalker, so I'm well aware of the weapon's destructive power. It's a descendant of the Gatling gun and is legally classified as a machine gun."

"That's right." Harris sounded impressed.

"And he's working out of Oregon to import guns from Mexico? Seems odd to me."

"First, you should know Razo is a U.S. citizen born and raised in Hillsboro, one of Portland's western suburbs. He took over the local drug trade and is the top dog now. So it's a no-brainer for him to operate in an area where he has contacts. And even more important, the I-5 corridor runs through Portland and is a main artery from Mexico to Canada. Huge numbers of drugs are moved on this route every day, and Razo takes full advantage of the high traffic volumes. He uses nondescript vehicles to hide the drugs. Cars like a soccer mom might drive, and they make sure to stay under the speed limit and blend in. He could be doing the same thing for the guns."

Mack let out a low whistle. "The way I see it, we have two issues here. Not only the sale of the weapons, but civilians can't legally own these guns in our country. Means he's on the wrong side of the law in several ways."

Harris frowned. "That's almost right. Unlike assault rifles—which are perfectly legal, by the way—machine guns are banned for civilian ownership without an FFL."

"Federal Firearms License," Mack muttered. "You just have to have a license to own something this deadly."

"That's right," Harris said. "Razo doesn't have a license, but someone with an FFL working with him might, and the guns couldn't be confiscated from them."

Addy cringed. "So we could be looking for someone with an FFL who could be holding these guns for him when they arrive."

Harris shifted her focus to Addy. "You were looking into that but hadn't run down all the possibilities yet."

Mack's pulse started thundering in his ears over news that was far worse than he could imagine. A weapon like this one trained on Addy would instantly end her life, and Mack could do nothing about it. He needed to find Razo and find him ASAP. He would have Cam search for FFL holders who fit the bill, but first . . . "I need to see that video of the abduction. Now!"

Harris looked at Addy. "It was emailed to you. You should have it on your computer."

SUSAN SLEEMAN | 69

"Let me pull it up." She dug the phone from the case and started tapping the screen.

"FYI, I'm having Fitz try to track the email and enhance the video." Harris looked at Mack. "He's our tech person."

Mack nodded, though he knew his team would do a much better job of both tracking and enhancing the video than this local tech might do, and he wanted to ask to take over. But he'd just met Harris and didn't want to come on too strong and ruin any chance of being involved in the investigation. Instead, he'd wait until the right time to broach the subject.

Addy fired up her laptop and used her phone as a network hotspot for security. The computer hummed through the expectant silence. The lights flashed on the screen, highlighting the planes of her face. Her forehead was still swollen and all kinds of eggplant purple. The lighter red highlights in her hair shone in the light, and he wanted to brush it away from her wound and gently kiss away the pain that still had to be plaguing her.

She frowned at the screen and turned the computer so that Mack could see it too. Still, he stepped closer. He would relish a reason to be near her, but he'd never use her mother in danger for an excuse.

The video played, her mother's eyes wide and terrified. The man stepped behind her and lifted the knife to her throat. Addy gasped and grabbed Mack's arm. He'd been hands off until now, yet he wasn't going to let her watch this terrible video without support. He pressed his hand over hers. She didn't move it, so he settled on the bed next to her and took a solid hold of her hand.

While touching her felt so right, the horrific video usurped any joy of the connection. The man warned Addy to back off or else, and his adamant tone declared he would follow through. Mack wanted to find this guy and make him pay before the creep could inflict more harm.

Mack looked at Addy. "He means business."

"Maybe when I took off from the office yesterday, I'd actually figured out what was he was up to, was tracking it down, and Razo tailed me. When he saw where I went, he got spooked."

"Could be," Harris said, her eyes fixed on their hands.

Addy must have noticed, as she pulled her hand free. Mack got the not-so-subtle hint and stood again but continued to look at Addy. "If you were on your computer before you took off, your tech should be able to figure out which files you had open at the time. That could tell us where you might have gone."

"Good idea," Harris said, sounding impressed. "I'll have our guy check it out."

"I don't like the sound of this Razo guy and the threat. That's not something we can take lightly." He kept his tone calm, but his gut was swimming with acid. This Razo dude was clearly bad news, and the thought of him in Addy's house—of holding a knife to her mother's throat—sent Mack's head spinning.

"Agreed." Harris widened her stance. "And there's no way I'll let a local detective run an investigation into an attempted murder of one of my agents. Especially when it's looking like it's tied to one of our top investigations."

Harris had Addy's back in the investigation. That was clear. Addy also needed someone to look out for her health, to make sure she rested and didn't exacerbate the head injury.

He faced Harris. "I want in on the investigation."

Her eyebrow shot up. "Excuse me?"

"I want to bring the RED team in on this. We have resources beyond your wildest dreams. And it's clear Addy thought she needed Cam's help. So, let me get the team here, and once we're up to speed on the investigation, we can partner with you to figure out who wants Addy dead."

Addy sat up in her bed. "I don't—"

"Your team has a reputation of hijacking investigations."

Harris planted her hands on her hips. "I won't allow that. I *will* remain in charge. If I agree to your help, that is."

"No worries. You call the shots. We'd just be here to support you in any way we can." Mack hoped he'd be able to follow through on that, but truth be told, if he thought something needed doing to keep Addy safe and find the man who wanted to kill her, then Mack would do that something whether Harris wanted him to or not.

"Give me some time to think about it."

Mack frowned. "We don't have time to waste. Not with this guy planning something big. Time is of the essence."

"Hey." Addy met his gaze. "I have a say in this too. And I'm not sure it's a good idea for us to work together."

"I have to do this, Addy. I just have to. Please understand. I can't let anything bad happen to you." He sounded desperate, and he was. His chest was tight with pain, his stomach convulsing. He loved this woman. More than life itself, and if she wouldn't let him stay at her side until the man wanting to end her life was caught, he'd have to covertly watch her, which had all kinds of creeper vibes. No matter, though. He would do it.

Addy gnawed on her lip. "I don't know."

"No need to decide just yet," Harris said. "I'm not sure I'll allow it anyway."

Mack wanted to snap out a snarky reply. To say something, anything, to make this woman do the right thing here. Instead, he shoved his hands into his pockets and clamped down on his lips before he made things worse.

"Go ahead and make sure you can log in." Harris shifted to face Addy. "And then I'll get out of here so you can rest."

Addy ran her finger over her trackpad and frowned. "My files. They're not here. They're gone."

"What do you mean *gone*?" Harris asked.

"Everything in my account." Addy stared at her supervisor. "There are no files. No folders. Nothing."

Harris blinked, long lashes fluttering. "Did you delete them?"

"No . . . I mean, I don't think so." Addy bit her lip. "Why would I?"

"That's the question of the hour," Mack said, letting the latest development settle in. "Do you think the people you're investigating could've hacked the system and deleted them?"

"Impossible." Harris glared at him. "We have strong security in place."

"Actually," Mack said, trying to sound calm and in control when he was anything but, "some of the smaller federal offices aren't as protected as they could be. And you do manage one of the smaller offices. Plus if he cracked Addy's phone password . . ." Mack shrugged as the rest was obvious.

"Yes, but . . ." Harris shook her head. "I'll head straight back to the office and have Fitz look into it."

Mack didn't like that they might've been hacked, but he could use it to his advantage. "If your server has been compromised, our team is just the group you need to assess the risk and put measures into place to stop it from happening again. We have years of both private and agency experience as well as advanced IT degrees. You won't find anyone more qualified to work this IT piece."

She looked up at him and suddenly gave a sharp nod. "I don't want to let any more time pass, leaving us vulnerable. Call them in, and let's see if the rumors are true and your team really does respond in record time."

CHAPTER 8

MACK WASTED NO TIME but headed straight to the lounge to call Eisenhower. Thankfully, Harris had invited them to partner in the investigation, saving the team from any jurisdiction or authority issues.

He lifted his phone and explained the situation to his supervisor. "I hate to ask for the team to join me when we're finally getting somewhere on the Montgomery Three Investigation, but—"

"Don't even think about it," Eisenhower said. "Addy has to come first right now, and we have to stop this gunrunner in his tracks. We can't let such dangerous guns get into the wrong hands."

"But the girls . . ."

"Are important too. Which is why I'm planning to head to Montgomery to take over for the team."

"You'd do that?"

"Of course," Eisenhower answered quickly. "Addy is one of us, and we always have each other's backs. Always."

Mack had come to respect his supervisor over the years, but never more than at this moment. Heading up such an important ICE division took every minute of very long days, and yet, for the good of a former employee on his team, he was agreeing to work even longer hours.

"I'll get a small team together and be in Montgomery before the day's end. Since Cam is in the office, I'll send him your way and get the others on the next flight to Portland. I'll check in with Sean for an update once I'm set to leave."

It had taken Mack ten hours to get to Portland, but it was early in the day yet so Sean and Kiley shouldn't have any issues finding flights and would arrive in less time.

"And even though Addy doesn't remember us right now," Eisenhower continued, "give her my best. Tell her I've got her back. Anything she needs that she's not getting from the team or anyone else in the department, have her call me. Same for you on the investigation into the gunrunner. You need something, you call."

"Understood." He looked out the window and thought ahead to when Addy would be leaving this place. Would she allow him to provide protection for her?

"And Jordan." Eisenhower's tone held a note of caution.

"Yeah," Mack replied, trying his best not to sound worried.

"I know this has thrown you for a loop, but don't let it interfere with your judgment. Take things one step at a time, focus on procedure to keep her safe, and then nail this guy."

Mack nodded. Why, he didn't know, as Eisenhower couldn't see him. Maybe Mack just needed to do something physical to cement the thought into his brain. If another attempt was made on Addy's life, he could easily see himself doing just what Eisenhower warned against. Acting based on emotion rather than instinct and training could be deadly to the one person he loved most in this world.

He ended the call and quickly forwarded Addy's video threat to Cam. Thankfully, she'd agreed to email it to Mack, though his gut clenched just knowing it was on his phone. He headed out of the hospital, his mind a mass of worry. Worry for what Addy was going through and for leaving her in the care of Warren, her fellow agent, so Mack could go feed Bear. Sure the dog needed him too, and Warren was capable. Didn't mean Mack wasn't worried. And that could trigger his PTSD.

He couldn't let that happen.

"For the Spirit God gave us does not make us timid, but gives us power, love and self-discipline," he mentally recited as he jogged to his rental vehicle. He repeated it time after time until he believed it again. Believed he could control his emotions that caused the flashbacks brought on by stress and rendered him helpless.

Once on the road, he used the vehicle's infotainment system to get their analyst, Cam, on the phone before he left the office. Mack wanted to get him moving on Addy's investigation during his flight.

"Yo," Cam said. "I'm packing up now. Catching an Air Force hop out of Langley. Wheels up in an hour so I've gotta hustle."

"Then I won't keep you. Just wanted to tell you I emailed a video to you." Mack brought him up to speed on the situation. "The local ICE supervisor is having their tech track the email and try to enhance the video but figured you might have more luck. Addy saw something on the guy's hand, so start there."

"How's she doing?"

"Better," Mack said, but didn't want to bog down the conversation with details. "I also want you to get started on doing a deep dive on a man named Bruno Razo. Guy's a shady drug dealer turned gunrunner. We believe he's the one who tried to take Addy out."

"I'll access the internet on the plane and get going on it right away."

"I also want a list of his known associates."

"Can do."

"Did you have any luck getting the CCTV footage for the area of the accident?"

"I've got warrant requests out and hope to have it by the time I land."

"Great. So the minute you hit town I want you to head to the ICE office. Someone might've hacked their network and deleted

Addy's investigation files." Mack shared about the theft of her phone too. "We need to find where this hack and the email sent to Addy originated."

"You gotta know by now that tracking hackers rarely leads to their physical location."

Mack had indeed learned that lesson from his years on the team. Still, he had to remain hopeful. "Sometimes it does, and this is our best lead right now."

"Then you don't have much." Cam blew a breath over the line. "And if they used the office VPN and her phone as a hotspot, that makes it nearly impossible to track. That's one of the reasons VPNs are used."

Mack hated to think this guy used the ICE office's own technology against them, and he didn't want to acknowledge Cam's statement, but it was true. VPNs masked a user's IP address, so the transmissions were virtually untraceable. "I need you to try anyway."

"Sure thing. Just want you to have legit expectations."

Mack did, but he didn't like it. "The office tech is looking for her files in their backups, and I gotta hope he finds them so we won't have to start her investigation over at the beginning."

"She must have some paper notes, right? I mean even I do, and I'm a die-hard electronic-only kind of guy. And what about files on her laptop?"

"I haven't asked, but I assume yes on the paper. The tech is also trying to see what she was doing on her computer right before the accident. I hope it'll tell us where she was headed."

Mack heard talking in the background of the phone.

"Hey," Cam said, "my ride's ready. I gotta go."

"Let me know if you find anything and shoot me a text when you arrive at the office."

"Will do."

Mack ended the call and focused on the road until he reached Addy's house. He grabbed his phone and placed a video call to Kiley and asked her to get Sean too. She moved the phone, and he glanced at the screen showing Sean behind the wheel of an SUV.

"Hey, man, we're on the way to the airport," Sean said before Mack could say a word.

"So I guess you've talked to Eisenhower and he brought you up to speed on the situation here," Mack said.

Kiley moved the camera back to her side of the car. "He did. Loaded the SUV the minute he told us we were being reassigned to you. Just parking at the airport now."

Mack took a long breath before continuing. "I know you won't want to leave the Montgomery investigation behind, and I'm sorry about that."

Kiley shook her head, her pencil bun holder falling out and her ponytail swinging free. "Of course we're coming to Portland. You and Addy need us."

He heard brakes being applied, and Sean leaned into the video. "I won't pretend that I don't want to keep at Williams, but if anyone can get anything more from the guy, it'll be Eisenhower. And besides, Addy needs us more."

"Now what do you want us to get started on?" Kiley asked.

He brought them up to date on Razo and the hack. "Kiley, I need you to come to the hospital and image the drive on Addy's computer. Then start trying to figure out what she might have been doing before she took off from the office. The local tech is working that, but it's always good to have a second set of eyes on it."

She nodded. "Will do."

"I'm heading back to see Addy tonight and get her buy-in on setting up a safe house and protection detail for her," Mack said. "Sean, can you arrange the safe house? I thought maybe we could stay at one of the places we used when we had to protect the twins."

Sean eyed him. Mack knew it wasn't because he didn't know

who Mack was talking about. The team provided protection for witnesses Dianne and Dustee Carr when their lives were threatened by a hacker, and Sean led that investigation. Which was when he'd met his fiancée, Taylor Mills, so he could hardly forget it.

"You think Addy's going to agree to ride this out in seclusion?" Sean asked.

The question of the hour in Mack's mind. "Her supervisor has already agreed. I hope Addy will too."

Sean arched an eyebrow. "She really doesn't remember you? Or us?"

"Not at all."

"That's a bummer, but it might work in your favor with no bad blood between you to muck things up right now."

"Yeah," Mack said and decided to move on. He'd never told the team why he'd split up with Addy, and she hadn't said a word either. The team knew about his PTSD, however. Not the full extent of the problem, but they'd seen him in flashback mode a few times. He'd told them he was going to counseling, and they accepted it as a part of who he was and kept his issue confidential. He did know that if he'd had any problems on the job that put anyone in danger, they would be forced to report it, but so far that hadn't happened, and now that he was seeing a counselor, that was very unlikely. "So you good with finding a location, Sean?"

Sean nodded. "I'll coordinate with the local FBI office, and if the place we stayed at before isn't available, I'll find another location by the end of the day."

"Thanks," Mack said. "I'm hoping Addy will agree to let us stay with her. If not, I'll need you to find a house nearby."

"Where are you staying now?" Kiley asked.

"Hospital lounge, but if I can't get a shower here today, I'll check into a hotel to get cleaned up."

"We will all appreciate that." Kiley chuckled.

Mack wanted to share her lighthearted spirit, but with Addy in danger, he just couldn't. "Okay, that's it. Other than use any spare time to read up on a Bruno Razo. Cam's doing a deep dive on the guy. He'll have a preliminary report for us by the time you get here, but it wouldn't hurt to do some extra reading. He's the guy we suspect is behind her accident."

"On it," Kiley said.

"Oh, and FYI, Bear will be joining Addy at the safe house."

"Ooh, good." Kiley smiled. "I love that dog."

"And he loves you too, so be prepared for slobbery wet kisses." Bear was extremely affectionate for a former police dog. He didn't know his own size and thought he was a lapdog.

Mack got out of the SUV and headed up the walkway. His eagerness to see Bear grew with each step, but the excitement vanished the minute he entered the house and spotted black fingerprint powder clinging to Addy's home and possessions.

He glanced into the family room on the way to the office where he heard Bear howling and was glad to see that someone had removed the white sheet from the video. His gut tightened at the mere thought of it.

Bear's cries grew more frantic, and Mack hurried to the room. The dog was whining and clawing at the door of his crate.

"It's okay, boy." Mack raced to the crate and pulled the door open. Bear pounced on him, taking him down. He licked Mack's face and danced on his chest. Mack ruffled his neck. "I'm glad to see you too, but let's take this outside before you have an accident in here." Mack squirmed out from under the dog and got up. "Sit."

Bear immediately complied.

Mack tapped his leg. "Come."

Bear walked alongside Mack to the back door. Mack pushed it open, and Bear bolted into the grassy backyard to do his business. Mack watched the dog sniff around for the perfect spot. He really was a majestic-looking dog—tan with a black saddle, long square-cut muzzle, and black nose.

The dog's next need would be water and food, so Mack looked around the kitchen until he found Bear's food and filled his dish along with his water bowl. Bear came racing inside and started lapping up the water. Poor guy was thirsty. Mack wished he'd asked about Bear sooner instead of assuming he was being taken care of.

Addy said he'd been sleeping off the drugs for most of the night at least, but he'd had a long thirsty day. He shifted to the right and buried his snout in the food, gobbling it as if he didn't think he'd be fed again. Mack wanted to hug him and ruffle his fur again, but he would never try to touch Bear while he was eating. He would defend his food, and Mack didn't need to be nipped with those sharp teeth.

Mack slid down on the floor to wait and just enjoyed watching the dog.

Memories of living with Addy and Bear came flooding back. Mack had lost so much. Addy. Bear. A life outside of work other than counseling. He didn't want things to continue that way, but what choice did he have? None that he could see.

Bear finished his meal and came to sit on Mack, then gave him slobbery kisses, his rough tongue cold and wet.

"What do you think, boy?" Mack said as he rested his forehead on the dog's head. "I know you'd like it if we were all together again. So would I. But how do I fix things? Just how?"

———

Addy closed her internet research on Razo, dragged in a gulp of oxygen, and tried not to hyperventilate. The guy was a killer. A ruthless killer who'd never been convicted of any of the murders. Arrested many times, but there was never enough evidence to prosecute. And she'd been investigating this guy. Would continue to investigate him. With Mack of all people.

He was staying in Portland. Was working the investigation. Would be at her side. And yet, she didn't know him.

Was that what was making her so uncomfortable? That she didn't know him, or that she was afraid she might fall in love with him all over again?

She couldn't stop thinking about him. Maybe it was best if she didn't ever remember. Her life without him would be so much easier. She wouldn't have to deal with their baggage. Wouldn't have to think about how she'd failed at being married. She would be free to fall in love with someone else. Just not Mack. Not again. Not when it had ended so badly.

But after spending the rest of the day researching Razo so she could hit the ground running the moment she was released from the hospital, she was glad for the help of the RED team in locating the dangerous weapons Razo was smuggling into the U.S. Though it might be awkward with her not knowing them, she would welcome their assistance all the same.

Her phone dinged. Thankful for the interruption, she glanced at the text from Harris: *Network was indeed hacked. Taking it down for protection. Your files were deleted.*

Addy's heart sank, and she thumbed in her response: *Could they be in a network backup?*

Will check and get back to you.

Addy thanked her and set down her phone. So Razo was either skilled in computers or had someone on his payroll who was. Her gut said she really had discovered something that would help her locate him. Otherwise, why would her files have been deleted? She had to come up with what she'd found. If not, he was going to move the weapons across the border, and countless lives were at stake. All because she couldn't remember.

Father, please . . . please help me stop this guy. Help me remember.

Mack poked his head in the doorway and held out a large

to-go coffee cup. "I thought you might want a mocha. I got decaf since it's so late."

Yeah, he knew her all right. "Thank you. I would very much like that."

He beamed a smile at her, and she almost gasped at the sharp jolt of awareness that plunged through her. He was a fine-looking man—she'd figured that out already—but when he smiled? Oh, man. Wow. Just wow. She was putty in his hands.

He held out the cup. She tapped her table. No way she was going to risk touching him. If a smile left her breathless, what would physical contact do?

His head tipped in question. She wouldn't explain.

He set down the coffee, the pungent scent filling the sterile air.

He straddled a chair and watched her carefully. "So how has the rest of your day been? Is your head still pounding?"

"Yeah, but it's manageable." She clutched the stiff sheet in her fingers and thought about what she should share, how she should act with him. Especially with the way his focus was so intently pinned on her.

"Any word on when you might get out of here?" he asked, solving the problem for her.

"Doctor said if things don't change for the worse, he'll discharge me in the morning."

"That soon? Great." He frowned.

"Why the frown? Doesn't look like you think that's good news."

"No, it is." He quirked a tight smile. "We just have to figure out a protection plan for you is all."

Protection plan? No way. She lifted her shoulders. "I won't be coddled and locked up in a safe house like my mom. I'm going to work the investigation right alongside you."

"Yeah, I knew you'd say that. But you can't go home either."

"That's true."

"You know as a Marshal, I'm well-versed in protecting people. So would you let me come up with a plan and find a safe place for you to stay?"

She could already tell that he was the kind of guy who was used to giving directives, and yet he'd asked her. That meant a lot to her and warmed her heart. "I'm okay with that, if Harris is."

"I called to update her on the team's arrival. She's good with it."

Addy picked up the coffee cup, the warmth feeling good in her cold hand. "She doesn't usually give in so easily."

"Who said it was easy?" He grinned, and the tiniest of dimples formed in his left cheek, giving him an adorable vibe so at odds with his tough-guy exterior.

She was quickly starting to see that he had many sides to his personality, and she shouldn't even be thinking about his personality at all. But honestly, even if she wasn't attracted to him, she would want to know what kind of man she'd fallen for and said the big "I do" with.

"But I'm glad Harris agreed because you need protection." Mack's smile fell. "I've been doing some research on Razo to try to formulate the best plan. He's one bad dude and has a lot of Mini-Me types following in his footsteps."

"Yeah, I checked him out today too." She had to work hard not to shudder over the photos she'd seen of people Razo had allegedly brutally murdered. She wouldn't focus on that, though, or she would live in fear and lose her effectiveness as an investigator. "But honestly, Razo's profile doesn't scream computer savvy, and I really can't see him deleting my files."

"He might not be tech savvy, but I'll bet he has someone on his team who is."

"You mean because a lot of the illegal drug-and-gun sales are conducted on the dark web nowadays?" She didn't bother to explain. His job on the RED team made him well versed concerning the hidden layer of the internet, accessible only via a special browser where criminals conducted illegal transactions of all kinds.

"Which is why it's even more important that the RED team is tagging in on your investigation," he said. "You might not remember us, but we truly are the best."

"I Googled you and the team too," she admitted. "Not that I expected to find much. Not with you all being law-enforcement officers. And I didn't learn anything other than the formal HSI press releases about the team."

"We do our best to make sure we don't share anything. I know you do too."

"I do."

"Could you look up your phone records online too?" he asked. "You could've made a call that will help us figure out your movements."

"Already done. No calls from before the accident. So, either I didn't need to call who I was going to see, or I used the office landline. Which is something I usually do when I'm in the office. Harris is requesting the call log. I also checked my credit cards. I did purchase a cup of coffee at a cart near the office, but nothing else to give us a lead."

He nodded, his expression pensive. "What about your email?"

"I reviewed it. Nothing there to help. I didn't send any messages that day at all. And earlier that week, they were are all business emails unrelated to this investigation."

"I assume you were driving the Mustang."

She nodded, and the thought brought an ache to her heart.

"No navigational system to check, then." He pursed his lips and looked like he wanted to spit tacks at the lack of leads.

She wanted to help move things along, but she couldn't very well pull leads out of thin air. "What time does the team arrive?"

"Cam's already at your office." Mack glanced at his watch.

"The others should be touching down anytime. They'll be staying at the safe house if that's okay with you. I figured having three Feds on duty would improve the odds of keeping you safe."

"Sounds like a good plan," she said, feeling a bit nervous about interacting with the team when she didn't know them.

"Kiley will come by to image your computer just in case there's any information we can use. But knowing you, you don't keep important files on your computer."

"You *do* know me," she said and tried not to frown at the thought. "I'm a security freak when it comes to electronic files. I figure laptops can be stolen, so I don't keep anything important on my computer. And our office is basically paperless, so I have very little there either. But I do sometimes print items I want to follow up on. I take notes on them so that anything I printed could point us in the right direction."

He leaned closer. "Do I have your permission to have Cam make copies of the files so we can review them?"

She knew they would be involved in the investigation, but at the moment his request felt like he was taking over. She didn't want that to happen. "That's fine, but I want to see anything he copies before you all review it."

"Of course." He smiled, and her heart flip-flopped. "I'll just text him to make sure he knows."

She watched him take out his phone and type the texts. When he looked up, she was still studying him, and he quirked an eyebrow. If they were going to be working together, she would have to get better at covering her feelings. "FYI, Harris confirmed that the network was hacked and my files were deleted."

Mack frowned, and he looked so tired, her heart went out to him. "Have you gotten any sleep at all since you got here?"

"Some. But I'm good. You're the one who should concentrate on getting enough rest. You're not known for sitting still, and I don't want to see you hurt your health even more."

Oh, man, he really did know her.

He searched her eyes. "Did I say something wrong?"

"I keep forgetting how well you know me, so when you say something that pegs me like that, it hits me odd."

"Oh, right. That makes sense."

"You know I appreciate you and the team offering to help, right?"

His eyes narrowed. "Yes, but . . ."

"It's going to be awkward for all of us, but most definitely for you and me."

"I know, and I'm sorry about that. But it's the right thing to do. Don't you agree?"

"I wish I didn't, but yes, I want to stop Razo from selling such dangerous weapons, and to accomplish that I'll do just about anything."

"Even if it means working with me?" He sounded so sad and disillusioned.

She wanted to assure him that she didn't mean that, but it was better to let him think she could barely tolerate being with him. If he knew how attracted she was to him, she'd be sunk before they even started.

CHAPTER 9

MACK HAD WANTED TO STAY with Addy, but Sean texted saying they'd arrived and were at the safe house. Mack needed to check in on any progress they might've made as they had only five days to figure out Razo's plans. Plus Mack needed a shower in the worst way, and he wanted to bring Bear to the safe house since no one was going to be around to take care of him. With another ICE agent standing watch at Addy's hospital door, Mack felt like he could take off for a little bit.

Sean had arranged to use the same safe house they'd stayed at in the past, and Mack found the team settled in as if they were at home in the finished family room in the basement. The lingering smell of spicy pizza filled the air, making Mack's stomach rumble.

Bear sniffed with his big snout as he strained on his leash, leading Mack into the large carpeted room that held comfy leather chairs and a sofa grouped by a wood-burning fireplace. A round game table, large pool table, and a foosball table took up the far side of the room, and an old upright piano sat in the other corner. Not that anyone was taking advantage of any of these items. All three of his teammates were in the seating area, laptops on legs, concentration so focused they didn't seem to notice him come down.

But Bear noticed them. He jerked on the leash, and Mack released him. He bolted for Kiley, pushing his nose at her computer screen.

"Hey, fella." She closed her laptop and set it aside.

Bear leapt onto her lap and pressed his head under her hand. His large body barely fit on her legs, and he shoved his snout into her neck.

"Sorry about that," Mack said.

"Are you kidding?" She ruffled the dog's neck. "I love this guy."

Mack looked at Bear, who was watching him with careful eyes. Man, Mack loved this guy too. Loved him a lot.

Kiley smiled at him. "Looks like you two missed each other. Too bad you're separated."

"Yeah," Mack said and left it at that, even though Kiley was clearly fishing for information on Addy. "Bring me up to speed on what we have so far."

"Sorry, I wasn't able to track the email sent to Addy with her mother's video." Cam lifted his head. "And I've got a lot of digging still to do on Razo, but I just emailed his initial background info to everyone. Dude's suspected of involvement in twenty-five murders."

Mack's gut clenched.

Kiley shot Cam a surprised look. "Seriously?"

Cam nodded. "Many different incidents. All in Mexico, but he used one of the miniguns to take out a supplier who'd done him wrong and his gang in one mass killing."

Sean let out a low whistle. "So, if he's the guy who took Addy's phone, and he really wanted her dead, she would be."

Mack's gut tightened more, forming a hard ball as he grabbed a marker sitting in the tray of a portable whiteboard. Bear came to stand at Mack's side, looking up at him with pleading eyes.

Mack had to work hard to ignore the dog for now. "Okay, so we have two investigations going on here." He uncapped the marker and released the caustic scent into the air. He noted *Addy Attempted Murder* on one side of the board, and *Razo Gunrunning* on the other side. "We think they're related, but as of now, we have no proof."

He looked at Cam. "Unless you were able to enhance that video and find something damning on Razo."

"I've done my best with the footage and don't see anything new," Cam said. "I also sent it on to D.C. to have one of our video guys work his magic. I did find a voice recording of Razo online. They'll isolate the background, then do a voice comparison, but with the way this guy disguised his voice in the video, it might not be possible."

Kiley cocked her head. "You found a voice recording for Razo?"

"Yeah, can you believe it?" Cam rolled his eyes. "The guy was dumb enough to do an interview with a Texas reporter five years ago or so. When will people realize that what shows up on the internet stays on the internet?"

"We might benefit from his ignorance." Mack jotted the information on the board and turned back. "Let me know as soon as they finish the voice comparison and video evaluation."

Kiley shifted her computer. "Even if it's not Razo himself in the video, it's likely one of his men."

"Yeah, likely," Mack said. "Can you get me a list of his key players?"

"I'll do my best," Kiley replied.

Mack held up the marker. "What else have we learned?"

"I need to image Addy's laptop. I can come with you when you go back to the hospital or work on your other requests first."

Mack hadn't said he was returning, but his team knew him well and would know he wouldn't be this far away from Addy overnight. Not even if a guard had been posted at her door. In fact, now that he heard about Razo's kill count, Mack would work hard to convince her to let him sleep in the recliner in her room all night.

"Go ahead and start on the other items, and I'll text you when it's a good time for Addy." Mack turned his attention to Cam. "Did you have any luck in locating backup files?"

He shook his head. "Fitz is still working on it. Some sort of glitch in the most recent backup."

Sean swiveled to look at Cam. "If he doesn't have something for us by the morning, I'll take over so you can focus on tracking that video."

Cam frowned. "Hey, thanks, man, but I hope to have that in hand by morning."

Kiley and Sean both rolled their eyes, and Mack took it to mean that Cam was overly optimistic about finishing the tracking by then.

"That video was horrible." Kiley shuddered.

Mack nodded. "I never thought it would be good to have dementia, but I hope in this case, Addy's mom has forgotten all about it."

Kiley's forehead furrowed. "Her nurse won't have, though."

"No," Mack said. "And being put in a safe house is likely giving her a lot of free time to think about it. Which is another good reason to make this guy pay."

Mack jotted down *Forensics* on the board. "I doubt our forensic team will be allowed access to Addy's car or house, but Harris is coordinating with the detective on the car and running down results from their forensic team. I'll take point in communicating on this."

Mack tapped the gunrunning heading before bending down to give the still-staring dog a scratch behind the ears. "Until then, I think we should also search the dark web for any sign of Razo's gun sales or chatter on whatever he has planned."

"Glad to do that," Kiley said.

"I'm still waiting on the CCTV for the accident area," Cam said.

Mack added that to the board, his marker squeaking. "Get after them. Time is ticking down to figure this out."

"I'm nagging my sources, but short of flying back to D.C. or doing some illegal hacking, I'm at their mercy."

"Still, keep after them." Mack had to work hard not to snap at Cam and looked at his teammates. "I know this isn't much to go on. Any other thoughts that I haven't covered?"

Kiley looked at Mack. "Well, yeah. The obvious."

Mack met her gaze. "Enlighten me, oh wise one, because nothing else is obvious to me."

She snickered. "That drugging Addy has nothing to do with Razo at all. Someone else is gunning for her."

"We did make a huge assumption here," Mack admitted. "But it fits Occam's razor—the simplest answer is almost always the best."

"Not sure I agree with that," Cam said. "Someone else could be just as simple."

"Then why didn't Addy mention anyone else?"

"Um, hello." Cam tapped his head. "Brain injury."

"Fine. I'll ask her about that. Anything else?"

He received a shake of heads in response. "I'll take a quick shower and go back to the hospital, then. Want me to crate Bear or are you guys good with watching him?"

"Are you kidding?" Kiley smiled. "I'm glad to take care of him until bedtime. Then I'll crate him."

Mack nodded his thanks. Having a retired working dog could pose problems. They weren't always the easiest to handle and didn't warm up to others, but Bear loved women more than men, and Kiley had made fast friends with him.

"I'll take him out for a walk before I go, and that should help him settle down when I leave." Mack grabbed Bear's leash, and the dog's expression perked up, but he was so well trained that he waited patiently until Mack directed him to move.

Outside, Bear strained a bit on the leash, wanting to go faster. Mack had a flash of brilliance. PTSD was like this leash. Holding him back in life when he wanted to soar. He was straining on the leash, trying to gain control of his issues. Straining hard, hoping he could find that place where he might feel comfortable in asking Addy to reunite with him, but the healing process wasn't in his hands. At least not completely. God had control, and if Mack's progress was slower than he hoped for, maybe God wanted it that way. Or maybe Mack was getting in God's way.

Some days he felt like David facing Goliath. A problem too big to overcome. But David didn't gear up. Didn't try to become a warrior. He simply grabbed the stones. Something he knew how to use. And slayed his dragon.

Did Mack need to simplify? Go back to the basics, starting with trusting God?

Yeah. Yeah. He needed to work on that, and maybe it would make all the difference.

Bear tugged him forward, and Mack decided to run. To let Bear get out his energy. Maybe to let him get his own stress out too. To find that place of submission instead of control. To release himself to it.

Father, please, he prayed as his feet pounded over the pavement. *Please help me. I want to be with Addy more than anything. I can't make that happen. I know that now. Only you can. Will you bring us back together? Please?*

Mack ran harder. Faster. Charging down the street and then circling back to the house, sweat beading up on his forehead. When he got Bear back into the basement, Mack was sweaty, his throat dry.

Kiley looked up at them. "Looks like you took quite the walk."

Mack nodded, his thoughts mixed. Had he just been running to God or from Him?

————

Addy sat up in her bed, eager to hear about Mack's delivery of Bear to the safe house. "How is he?"

Mack straddled the same chair he'd sat in earlier, and a

broad smile brightened his expression. "Good. I took him for a run and then left him with the team. He's in love with Kiley, so he'll be a good boy."

Addy's heart lifted at the good news. "I'll bet he was happy to see you."

"It went both ways. I miss him too."

She studied his strained expression that had plagued him much of the time since they'd reconnected. Was he always this troubled, or was it the PTSD or even the danger to her? Or it could be her injuries and her loss of memories fueling more anxiety than usual. Seemed like he could use Bear in his life to help him cope.

"Why did we decide for Bear to live with me?" she asked. "Other than I'm sure I was more than happy to have him."

Mack rested his arms on the back of the chair, the corded muscles playing beneath the surface of his skin. "It was my fault we split up, so the least I could do was to let you have him. And I felt better knowing he was with you for protection when I couldn't be there for you."

"You really are a sweet man, Mack Jordan," she said without thinking it through. "I can see why I fell in love with you."

His mouth dropped open, a big gaping hole, before he recovered and grinned. "You're the only person who has called me sweet and gotten away with it. Kiley tries, but I shut her down."

At the fondness in his voice for another very attractive woman, Addy frowned. "Sounds like you and Kiley are close."

He nodded. "She's the kid sister I never had."

"Do you have siblings?" she asked, suddenly wanting to know everything about him.

"Two brothers. Older."

"So you're the baby." She mulled that over. "Explains a few things about you."

"Such as?"

"You're charming. Confident. Seem to be creative. Independent. Adventurous."

"Yeah. That's all true. My brothers, of course, would say I was spoiled and got away with everything." He grinned. "And they'd be right."

She enjoyed this mischievous side of him. "Where did you grow up? I mean, I know with your accent and cowboy boots it wasn't D.C."

"Born-and-bred Texan and proud of it, ma'am." He mocked tipping a cowboy hat and smiled at her.

She could easily see him on a ranch. A horse. Maybe riding a bull. In the rodeo, breaking all the young girls' hearts. A bolt of jealousy stabbed through her chest. Shocked, she drew back.

He lifted an eyebrow. "You got something against Texas or the rodeo?"

"No. Not at all. I love watching bull riding. Did I get that from being with you?"

He nodded. "Surprising, the things you're remembering."

She had to agree. "I could totally see you riding a bull. Did you?"

He frowned. "Yeah. For years."

"You don't look happy about it."

He didn't say anything, as if he was considering if he really wanted to tell her more about his past. He blew out a breath. "I liked it all right, but my dad was a big-time champion. He put a lot of pressure on me. It was all about winning for him. I just liked the thrill. When he got too involved, I quit and found the same thrill as a Night Stalker and then in fugitive apprehension."

"And now?"

"Now." He furrowed his forehead. "Now, the PTSD keeps me pretty grounded. Sure, the arrests we make can be thrilling, but I find that can be a trigger if I don't remain calm. This job means too much to me to mess up, so I make sure to stay calm. It's the dreams I can't control, yet."

He pressed his lips together and rested his chin on his hands.

"What is it?" She leaned forward, desperate now to hear what he had to say.

He looked up, and that pain she'd seen all along was deeper and penetrating. "I don't suppose you remember the Montgomery Three Investigation."

"Yeah, it was all over the news." She kept her gaze trained on him. "Was that a RED team investigation?"

He nodded, but it was in sad resignation.

"But the girls were never found and the case closed, right?"

He sat up and stiffened his back as if needing to protect himself. "Officially closed, but we never let it go. Kept after it until we had a solid lead. That's where I was when I got the call about your accident. We were raiding the house of the guy who stole the van the girls were abducted in. He's admitted to stealing the van but won't say what he used it for."

"I'm so sorry. It's got to be hard not to be able to resolve something as important as finding missing girls." She wanted to reach out to him, but instead clasped her hands on her blanket. "I'm starting to feel frustrated about this Razo guy. I assume I was very passionate about bringing him in."

Mack placed his hands on the chair back and looked at them. "If you called me for help, you had to be desperate."

She leaned down to get him to look at her again. "Were we on bad terms?"

"Bad? No. We just didn't communicate at all. Hurt too much when we did."

She tried to remember the pain, but nothing came other than sympathy for the anguish in Mack's expression.

"And speaking of the investigation," he said, "I met with the team to hand out assignments."

She listened carefully as he reviewed them in detail, impressed with how thorough the team had been. "Sounds like you have things covered. So does Harris, and this investigation is well under way even if I'm trapped here."

He beamed under her praise. "We were wondering if you can think of anyone other than Razo who might want to hurt you."

She shook her head, the pain receding some. "I spent some time thinking about that but couldn't up with anyone. I suppose I could be forgetting someone else, yet my gut really says it's Razo or one of his guys."

Mack took a long breath and let it out slowly, his frustration nearly palpable. "Are there any places near the accident scene that you're familiar with?"

She'd given this very question hours of thought today, even consulted a map. "I know the area, but as to a place I would normally visit? Nothing comes to mind."

"Did you follow the road in both directions on a map to see if anything became clearer?"

She nodded. "I have a college buddy who works at an IT start-up about ten miles out, but otherwise nothing."

"Would you have gone to see him or her during a workday?"

"Him. Rob, but I don't see why. He's helped me with IT info in the past, but gunrunning isn't likely something an IT guy could help me with."

"Still wouldn't hurt to give him a call tomorrow."

"I was already planning on it."

He gave a firm nod. "About tomorrow. I've already met with the hospital administrator to arrange your transport."

She appreciated his concern and help. He might be her husband, but they were separated and she didn't want him to decide things for her. "What if I want to go to the office instead?"

"If there's something you need from there, we could get it for you."

"There's nothing. I just don't want anyone deciding what I do or don't do because of this threat."

He chewed on the inside of his mouth as if he was fighting saying something. He cleared his expression. "Sorry. I should've asked."

She sighed and shifted in her bed, the clean smell of bleach emanating from her sheets. "No, I'm sorry. I'm just being touchy. Not remembering things is awful. I have a tendency to control things, and this is out of my control. And I don't much like this headache either. It's all making me cranky so I want something I can control. Where I go from here is something I can decide on."

"Hey, I get it. Trust me. Put me in your shoes and I'd be far more cranky." He smiled.

She ignored the smile before she let it draw her further under his spell and thought about the transport instead. Deputy U.S. Marshals managed the witness-protection program, so they were experts at transporting vulnerable people.

She would be safe under Mack's direction. "I suppose you're going to run one of those crazy car drills where you have several of them leaving every which way at once so Razo doesn't know which vehicle I'm in. You were always a master at that and loved, loved, loved running them."

His mouth fell open, but she had no idea why.

She eyed him. "What's so shocking?"

"You remembered something."

"I did? I . . ." She rehashed what she'd just said and tried to recall a transport situation that he'd shared with her, but she came up blank. "It sounds like I did, except I can't think of any particular incident. Still, I knew that about you, didn't I? Maybe my memory's starting to come back. I'll have to ask the doctor about it tomorrow."

"Sounds promising." He looked so hopeful.

She hadn't really thought about how difficult her inability

to remember him had to be on him. She was too busy protecting her own emotions. That selfishness stopped now. She needed to be more sensitive to him. Not in a way that led her to fall in love with him, but in the way a fellow Christian might behave out of Christian love. She offered a quick prayer for him. For her memory. For their past and God's will in their future.

Mack cleared his throat, maybe trying to gain her attention. She wasn't going to share her thoughts, but she could tell him more about her doctor's visit.

"Speaking of promising," she said, putting them on a more neutral footing. "The doctor also suggested I try hypnosis. He said using relaxation coupled with a method called age regression might bring back those memories. He gave me the card for a doctor here for after I'm discharged, and I want to try it as soon as possible. I'm hoping the doctor will come to the safe house."

"We'd have to be very careful about that."

"I know, but if he won't do a house call, I'll have to find a way to return to the hospital."

Mack nodded, but his grimace said he didn't like it. "FYI, I'm not planning to use a car drill. Too many pedestrians around here. We'll first do a drone flyover of the immediate area, looking for anything out of the ordinary. Sean and Kiley will also run a detailed surveillance. Then we'll bring in a linen delivery truck. I'll ride with you in the back. Sean will drive. Kiley will ride shotgun."

"Sounds like an adventure." She smiled to reassure Mack that she was on board with his plan.

"The administrator has also agreed not to officially discharge you and leave the room under your name, so if anyone checks to see if you're still here, they'll be told you are."

"What about the nurses? They'll know I've left."

"The administrator will inform them of the situation. And

we'll leave an agent at the door who will turn everyone else away."

Addy gave the plan some thought. "It could work."

"I'm confident it will." Mack's tone sounded convincing. "Our team will be paying for the room at full price, so the administrator has motivation to keep the sham going. She'll make more money per day, and her staff won't have to lift a finger. It's a win-win situation."

"Then she'll likely do her best." Addy considered the logistics. "And I'm good with it as long as it doesn't screw up my insurance paperwork. I can't even imagine how much my bill is going to be."

"I'll personally make sure it doesn't." His vehemence took her aback.

He planted his boots firmly on the floor again. "You'll have to wear a delivery uniform in case you're spotted on the loading dock. A wig too. Your hair color isn't exactly subtle."

"I can handle that."

He looked down and stabbed his toe into the floor. "I was wondering if I could spend the night in your recliner."

"Here?" She eyed him. "But why?"

"Cam's report on Razo." Mack clamped his mouth closed as if he didn't want to say more, then gave his head a slight shake. "Guy's implicated in the murder of twenty-five people."

She gasped. "I read that he was suspected of murdering people, but not twenty-five."

Mack responded with a solemn nod. "He's implicated in quite a few different killings and also turned a minigun on a rival gang. If your intel is right—and I have no reason to doubt it—he has something big planned. *What* is the big question. And he could be gunning for you. I can hardly breathe when I think someone this vicious has you in his sights."

She'd just seen pictures of the horrific results from the use of these guns, and she didn't know what to say. How to respond.

Should she let Mack stay here? Even if he did, he was no match for such a weapon. None of them were.

Not that she could see Razo hauling a minigun into the hospital, but he could be lying in wait outside. So yeah, she needed Mack. Needed him to securely move her to the safe house tomorrow. And if he felt better about staying with her tonight, then so be it.

Staying alive trumped any of her uneasy feelings.

CHAPTER 10

MACK TOOK A SWIG of his energy drink and watched Addy where she sat on the edge of her hospital bed the next morning, waiting for the all-clear to leave. A bright beam of sunlight caught her body as she wrung her hands together where they rested on the dark blue uniform pants she'd paired with a matching jacket over a Kevlar vest. A blond wig covered her glossy red hair. If they were in any other situation, he might comment on how amazing she looked as a blonde, but now wasn't the time for flirting. With their history, there might never be.

She'd been jumpy and jittery since she'd woken up. Maybe he was to blame. He hadn't meant to scare her last night with his talk of Razo. He just wanted to make her more cautious. Or maybe his presence or the danger of leaving the hospital had darkened her mood. Either way, the area surveillance and drone flyover had been completed, and they would soon step out of the hospital, praying that Razo wasn't waiting somewhere with a minigun.

Anxiety clawed at Mack, and he felt his control slipping. He closed his eyes and focused on the sunlight warming his back.

"For the Spirit God gave us does not make us timid, but gives us power, love and self-discipline."

God gave Mack and the team the skills they needed to safely transport Addy. And God gave Mack the ability to hold off any flashbacks. He could do this. He really could.

He opened his eyes. Addy looked over her shoulder at him

and bit her lip. She pressed her hands on her knees and scrubbed them over the fabric.

"It's going to be fine," he said, thinking it a good thing to acknowledge the stress in the room. "With my teammates' help, I'll get you to the safe house without any problems."

"I know." The corner of her mouth lifted a fraction, then dropped. "At least I know it in my brain. I sure don't want to let this guy get to me. I want to be independent and strong and live my life, but I'd be lying if I said I wasn't apprehensive about walking out that door."

"It's only natural to feel that way."

"Do you?"

"I shouldn't admit it, but yeah. I know our plan is sound, and we've done everything within our power to be sure you'll be fine, but . . ." He shrugged.

"Yeah, it's the *but* that's getting to me."

Mack's phone chimed, and he glanced at the text from Sean saying they were good to go. He responded with an affirmative, then texted the administrator to clear the loading dock area.

He waited for her confirmation before stowing his phone. "We're a go."

Addy slowly took a seat in the wheelchair. She placed her computer and a bright green bag with her belongings on her lap. Mack wanted his hands free for the trip down to the loading dock, but he had no choice. The administrator insisted that with Addy's head injury, the patient should be wheeled out, and Mack didn't want anyone else in on the move, so he would be pushing her chair.

She put on large sunglasses. No one would recognize her. Not even Razo.

Mack propped open the door and grabbed the wheelchair's rubber-gripped handles. In the hallway, he nodded at the agent on duty.

Addy looked up at him. "Thanks for your help."

He gave a tight smile back. "Glad to do it."

Mack rolled the chair down the hallway, catching the smell of orange-scented cleaner, until he reached a service elevator that he'd been given a keycard to access. Inside, he let out a breath at making it through their first hurdle and watched the numbers count down above the door. The tension in the small space was so thick, it felt like fingers choking off his air, and he opened his mouth to take deeper breaths.

Dressed in a uniform that matched Addy's, her hair up under a cap, Kiley met them at the door for the loading dock and held out a box. "Drop your things in here to disguise them, and I'll load them in the truck for you."

"Thanks." Addy placed her belongings in the box.

"No worries." Kiley closed the cardboard flaps and took off for the loading dock, her booted footfalls thudding in the silence.

Mack locked the wheels on the chair. "You'll be hoofing it from here."

Addy pushed out of the chair and rested her hand on her sidearm worn under the jacket. He understood her actions. Knowing she was packing gave her more confidence in facing her foe. At least it did for him. Even if this foe packed a weapon that could take them all out in one fell swoop.

They moved to the end of the hallway, where Mack pulled open the door for the loading dock. Vehicle exhaust along with the biting cold hit him. He could easily imagine the place bustling with workers, but the only person he saw was the dock supervisor, who gave him a nod of acknowledgment.

Kiley bounded out of the back of a large delivery truck and stepped to the side to surveil the area. She turned and waved them on.

Mack took Addy's arm and hurried her into the back of the truck. "The floor is going to have to do."

"No problem." She sat and drew up her legs.

Mack didn't want to sit, putting himself in a vulnerable position, but he would be visible through the windshield if he stood. No way he would give Razo any hint that this wasn't a normal delivery truck.

Mack squatted next to Addy and looked up at Kiley. "Let's get this thing moving."

"On it." She marched out the back, and the lock clicked into place. She climbed into the passenger seat. "Let's roll."

Sean shifted into gear, and the big truck rumbled forward. Mack wished he could see outside. Instead, he just had to trust that his teammates had things under control. Not something Mack was very good at doing when Addy's life was on the line.

"Update," he demanded.

Kiley was sharing her attention between the windshield and side mirror. "We're clear."

"Sean?"

"She's right," he said. "We're clear."

Fine. Things were going well. Still, Mack wouldn't relax. Not until they had Addy in the safe house. Then he was going to have to figure out a way to try to convince her to stay there. No way his heart could handle another round of racing at the speed it now pounded in his chest.

He waited until he could wait no more, then asked for another update.

"I promise to tell you if someone shows up on our tail," Kiley said.

Sean looked in the rearview mirror. "Me too, so you can quit asking."

Mack clamped his mouth closed and rode in silence, the tension nearly his undoing, but before long they were on their way out of town.

"I'm going to make a few turns just to be sure we're alone," Sean announced.

"Good plan." Mack shifted as the truck took a sharp left.

Addy rested a hand on his knee. "My turn to tell you to re-lax."

At her touch, he nearly jumped out of his skin. The shock even trumped his adrenaline, but he worked hard to give her a smile in return. "Adrenaline."

"Oh, I get it, but we're in the clear now."

They rolled around two additional corners.

"She's right," Kiley said. "We're good."

"Don't let your guard down," Mack warned.

"Not planning on it." In the side mirror, he saw her roll her eyes.

If Mack were in their shoes, he wouldn't appreciate all this backseat driving. He needed to back off. And he did, but the moment Sean stopped at the safe house, Mack leapt to his feet.

"Check it out, Kiley," he demanded.

As she slid out of the truck, Mack stood to face the back door and rested his hand on his weapon. Thoughts of what would happen if they'd been followed pinged through his head like a tennis ball volley. He shook his head to stop them.

The door opened, filling the cargo area with sunshine and nippy cold that Addy had told him usually accompanied the sun in January when the constant drizzly rain wasn't falling.

"We're clear," Kiley said.

"Bring in Addy's things, please." He looked at Addy. "I want us both to have free hands."

She frowned but stood.

He jumped out and looked around. The house had been selected by the FBI for its location on a high hill, allowing them to see the countryside in all directions and determine if a threat was imminent. Feeling certain they were in the clear, he held out his hand to help her down. She didn't argue and stepped out. Mack kept his head on a swivel as he hurried her up the stairs and inside the large daylight ranch.

Kiley carried the box with Addy's belongings inside. "We'll drop off the truck and be back soon."

She reversed course outside.

Mack locked the door behind her, double-checking it for safety.

"Let's meet up with Cam. He's likely downstairs in the family room." He led the way, and they did indeed find Cam sitting on the sofa, his laptop on his legs. Bear was curled up next to him.

"Hi, boy," Addy said.

Bear cried out in a piercing bark and leapt from the sofa to run to her.

"Sit," she said with authority.

He did, but his feet danced with urgency, and he whined. She dropped down and hugged him. He lunged and knocked her over. Mack was about to command Bear to come so she could get up, but she laughed and tussled with him on the floor. When her head hit the carpet, she winced.

"He's happy to see you," Mack said.

Bear suddenly looked up and bolted to Mack, shoving his bony head under Mack's hand. Mack petted the dog as Addy got back up.

"Hey, Addy." Cam smiled. "Long time no see."

She frowned. "You must be Cam."

"Oh, right. The memory thing. You must've really taken a blow because I'm a pretty memorable guy." He laughed.

She laughed with him, but it was awkward on her part. Mack didn't want to see her in another situation that she found uncomfortable, but he was glad to see that the way she'd been acting with him wasn't all that different from her response to Cam.

Wait. Was that a good thing? Mack wanted her to react to him with gusto. With passion. Even if it was negative, he wanted to evoke something inside her that made her remember their past together. Their love. The sparks. The longing.

Cam eyed them. "You guys look like old-fashioned milk delivery men in those uniforms."

"Feel like one too." She shrugged out of her jacket, the uniform seeming totally out of place now.

"We could go change if you want," Mack suggested. He wouldn't mind getting out of the tight uniform.

"I'd rather get a plan going so everyone can be working while we change."

He pointed at the furniture. "Then go ahead and have a seat. The drop site for the truck isn't far, so Sean and Kiley should be back soon and we can begin."

She nodded and chose one of the club chairs near the sofa. Bear climbed up on her lap and shifted a few times to settle in. He dwarfed her, but she looked content. Even now, in the safety of the basement, Mack wanted to be nearby and ready to protect her if the need arose, so he sat in the chair closest to her.

Cam lowered the screen on his laptop and looked at Addy. "I tracked your vehicle as best I could. From what I could gather, you went straight to an office building. Spent about an hour there and then took the same route back."

"Do you have the address?" she asked.

He nodded and was about to say something when her phone rang, and she glanced at the screen. "It's my friend, Rob."

"The guy who works near the accident scene?" Mack asked.

"That's right."

Eager to hear from this guy, Mack sat forward. "Answer and put him on speaker so we can listen in."

She tapped her screen and held out her phone, resting her arm on Bear's side. "Thanks for calling me back, Rob. I've got you on speaker so my associates can hear."

"Let me guess," he said, his tone deep and sounding amused, "you want more info on the ocean cables."

She cast a surprised look at Mack. "Ocean cables?"

"What?" He snorted. "You forget about coming to see me about them, or are you just messing with me?"

"Actually, I was in a car accident, and there are holes in my memory from the last few days." She ran a hand over her hair. "When did I come by?"

"Tuesday around two."

Mack tried to make eye contact with Addy, yet she was staring ahead as if trying her best to remember.

"What's your office address?" She gave Cam a pointed look.

Rob rattled off the address, and Mack shot a look at Cam to see if this was the same office he'd located. He nodded.

Addy shifted in the chair, waking Bear. The dog's head came up and he peered around. "And I wanted to know about ocean cables?"

"Yeah, internet cables run along the ocean floor. You said some bad dude—a gunrunner—might be cutting them to take out the new border X-ray imaging systems so he could smuggle his guns."

Her mouth dropped open. Bear whined as if he were sensing her discomfort. She stared at the others. "Are you familiar with these recently added frontline systems?"

"Machines placed just before the border to X-ray every vehicle for contraband," Mack said. "So when they reach the actual border, the customs officers can search the questionable vehicles."

Addy nodded.

"I take it you don't remember that visit," Rob said.

She petted Bear's head, soothing him. "Not exactly."

Rob let out a breath that hissed through the phone. "You said you had someone who could help you figure out if the border agencies own any of the cables or were leasing them."

"Cam," she whispered.

"Hurt my feelings, girl," Rob said. "Like anyone is better than me."

Cam opened his mouth to say something, but Mack assumed it would be a smart-aleck response so he slashed a hand across his neck to tell Cam to keep quiet.

Addy blinked a few times. "Anything else happen at our meeting?"

"I showed you the map that lists all the cable locations in the world and explained a few things. Other than that, not really." He let out another long breath. "Glad to review it with you again if you want. Or find that additional data you need."

"Thanks, Rob," she said, sounding sincere. "Could you text me with the link to the map, and I'll let you know if I need additional help?"

"So you're going to two-time me with the other geek, huh?" He chuckled.

She stared at her phone. "It's a clearance thing."

"Yeah, you said that when we met. Wouldn't give me any details at all, other than you were dealing with guns being smuggled into the U.S."

"I didn't give you a specific location, then?"

"Nah. You were tight-lipped." He sighed. "I'll send the link the minute we hang up."

"Thanks again." She tapped her screen and looked up, her eyes awash with a mixture of concern and excitement. "There you have it. Confirmation of where I went that afternoon and why."

Mack turned to Cam. "We need to get on this right away."

"Already on it." Cam looked up from his computer. "Found the cable map."

"One quick question about the CCTV first," she said. "What about cars that were behind mine on the way back? Did you catch any plates?"

Cam shook his head. "There *was* a black Honda Accord a few miles back from you on the drive over, but it didn't turn into Rob's parking lot. A black Accord tailed you on the way back too. Not sure if it was the same vehicle or not. And I couldn't get a clear look at the driver, but it was a guy. I sent the video off to our lab to see if they can clear up the image."

"Let me know what you find out," she said, looking even more uncomfortable than she had earlier. "And I'll follow up with Rob to see if his company has parking-lot cameras."

Cam nodded. "Also, you should know you were swerving on the road for most of the drive."

Mack tried not to respond, but he grimaced over the thought of her driving under the influence.

"I was roofied," she said.

"Ah," Cam said. "That explains it."

"What do we do next on the cable issue?" she asked, looking happy to change the subject.

"Put the map up on the TV, Cam," Mack directed, and when Cam did, Mack studied the world map with red, green, blue, and orange lines running from continent to continent, and in some cases just hugging a country's coastline.

Mack frowned. "Way more cables than I imagined."

"Looks like there're nearly four hundred submarine cables in service around the world." Cam looked at Addy. "You know much about oceanic cables?"

"Some. I know that most people think internet connections are all wireless. Not so. Huge fiber-optic cables run across the ocean floor, essentially hardwiring continents and firing data over these connections."

"Well, duh." He leaned back. "I didn't think you'd get that basic."

She rolled her eyes. "I also know the cables fail all the time and are even accidentally cut or taken out by natural disasters. And there's been some sabotage too, but very little. Mostly because there's no point in it."

"Exactly." His expression brightened as if he was starting to get into the subject. "Companies that seriously depend on undersea cables distribute their data across multiple routes, all of which they own. That way, if one fails, customers aren't cut off and don't suffer any downtime."

"But that's not true of all companies who use the cables, right?" she asked.

"Right." Cam crossed one leg over the other and shifted his computer. "Mostly we're talking about the big data users like Google, Amazon, Facebook, Microsoft. Usually companies with heavy cloud storage use. But when the bubble burst in the early 2000s, operators unloaded cables for pennies on the dollar, so there are some smaller companies who own them."

"We need to figure out if any of our border agencies bought up these cables or are leasing them," she said.

Mack had to play the devil's advocate here. "Razo cutting cables sounds like a long shot to me."

"Yeah." Cam crossed his arms. "But possible."

"Sure . . . yeah, possible," Mack said. "But think about it. After it was sliced a few times, I would think security would get suspicious."

Addy faced Cam. "Could he do it in a way to make it look like he didn't just slice through the cable? Like it was an accident?"

Cam tilted his head. "Run a boat motor over the cable and let the propeller cut it. Or use a ship anchor. Something along those lines. Maybe change up the method and location so it varied." Cam tapped his chin. "But still, even after he takes out the X-ray machines, he still needs to get past border patrol."

"He's been concealing drugs for so long," Addy said. "I have no doubt he knows how to do that. Is there a way to track cable outages?"

Cam rested his hands on his keyboard. "I'll get started on locating recent cable failures that have been made public, but I'm going to need a location to narrow it down."

She shook her head. "I don't even know if I had that information when I talked to Rob, and now? I don't know a thing."

Cam kept his focus on her. "Okay, how about dates?"

Addy's hand paused midair from petting Bear. "I'm guessing all that data was stored in the files that were deleted."

Cam frowned. "Then we'd best hope your tech has come up with a backup of your data. Otherwise it'll take some time to track down every cable failure I find. And with each passing hour, it could mean those guns could be delivered to a man who clearly has no respect for life, and people will die."

CHAPTER 11

ADDY WAS GLAD they'd figured out her destination on the ill-fated afternoon, but what good did it do them if she couldn't come up with additional information? None. That's what. And she wanted to pound on her throbbing head to make her brain work right.

How were they going to locate Razo if she never remembered? They had to stop him before he unleashed his big plan, whatever that might be. Right now it was looking like cutting cables so he could move the miniguns, but she couldn't even be sure of that. Or of what he planned to do with the guns. She needed more information, and she needed it now.

"I'm going to call Harris to see if Fitz has fixed the backup issue." Phone still in hand, she made the call to her supervisor. Tension clawed at her stomach, although having her big love buddy on her lap was helping to keep her calm. Even if he did weigh eighty pounds and was crushing her legs.

"You still at the hospital?" Harris asked by way of greeting.

Addy pressed the phone against her ear as the connection was glitchy. "Discharged and at the safe house."

Kiley and Sean entered the room and settled in the seating area. They locked their focus on her as if questioning if she remembered them. She hadn't recognized Kiley last night when she came to image Addy's computer, or Sean at the loading dock. Seeing them again hadn't jogged her memory. She didn't enjoy being the subject of their study and tried to ignore it as she updated Harris on her visit to Rob.

When she finished, she took a long breath before continuing. "We desperately need information. I'm hoping Fitz has located a backup of my files."

"He's still working a technical glitch."

Of course. Nothing was easy in an investigation. "With your permission, I'll have one of the RED team come by to help him resolve the issue." She looked at Mack for his approval.

He nodded, but Harris didn't reply. Addy could easily imagine her expression. A mixture of dislike for bringing in outsiders, and resignation that it had to be done to expedite their investigation and save lives.

"Time is of the essence," Addy reminded Harris, not caring if she might be stepping on her supervisor's toes. "We only have four days to find out how he's shipping the guns."

Harris let out a rush of air. "I'll tell Fitz to expect someone."

"Thank you. I know it's hard to give an outsider access to our files."

"If you only knew. But it's the right thing to do." Addy could hear a frown in her supervisor's tone. "Did you get doctor's clearance to be working?"

"Not exactly. He wants to see me back in a week before releasing me for active duty. His main concern is my using a weapon while I have some dizziness and headaches. But I can still work the investigation from the safe house where no weapons will be required."

"So he cleared you for light duty?" Harris's tone had sharpened.

Her voice grated on Addy. Usually, she appreciated that Harris was detailed and by the book, but right now she wished the woman would cut her some slack. Still, Addy had to give an answer. "No."

"Then consider yourself on official leave until I receive something in writing from the doctor telling me you can return to duty."

"But the investigation," Addy cried out, bringing Bear's ears perking up. "It's okay, buddy," she cooed in a low tone so her boss wouldn't pick up on it.

"The RED team and I can handle it." Harris took a long breath. "I can't be put in a position to violate wage-and-hour regulations."

Addy appreciated that, yet she had to find the person who'd tried to kill her and put Razo behind bars before he unleashed more terror. "And if hypothetically I continued to work the investigation on my own time, and I needed something from you?"

"I'm forming an official task force to facilitate communication. Small group. Just me, Warren, and the RED team. They'll try to take over the investigation anyway, so why not let them do their thing? I'll designate Deputy Jordan as lead." She paused for a moment. "To that end, I want to talk to him if he's there."

"Can we do it on speaker?"

"I'd rather not."

"But—"

"You're on leave," Harris stated firmly. "Please put him on the phone."

Addy stifled a grumble and looked at Mack. "Harris wants to talk to you. She put me on leave, so I can't be included in the conversation."

He arched a brow and held his hand out for the phone. "Good morning, Special Agent Harris."

Addy buried her fingers in Bear's fur and leaned closer to Mack to try to make out Harris's words, but she couldn't. Mack tipped his head, his gaze intense, and he nodded occasionally as if Harris could see him.

He glanced at Addy. "And you told her about that?"

What had Harris asked him? Addy really wanted to know.

He listened to the information that she wasn't privy to, and she wanted to stomp her foot on the floor and demand to be included. But acting like a big baby wouldn't help anyone.

"Don't worry. I've got it. We'll be in touch." He held the phone out to Addy.

She grabbed it from his hand, but Harris had ended the call. "What did she tell you?"

"She mentioned the task force and gave us carte blanche to run the investigation."

"And what else?"

"Um . . . well." He clasped his hands together. "Sorry. I'm not at liberty to say."

"Seriously?" Addy clenched her teeth, finally understanding how Rob must have felt when she went to him for help but withheld information from him. "The two of you are really going to keep secrets from me?"

"Not secrets, really." He scratched his head. "Just something I can't share."

"Not sure I see the difference." She tried not to be annoyed, but she was. "With the stubborn set of your jaw, I can tell there's no point in trying to get you to talk."

Hoping for support, Addy shifted her focus to the others. She looked at Kiley, her hair held up by a pencil, her eyes as determined as they'd been when she stopped by to image Addy's computer. Her socially awkward personality keeping her quiet. Quiet or not, Addy knew she'd liked Kiley. Just an innate sense that she'd connected with this woman.

Addy then turned to Sean, who'd taken a seat on the couch on the far side of Cam. She hadn't talked to him since he'd been in town, so she dredged up a smile and hoped he didn't notice it was forced. "I'm Addy, but then you already know that."

"Sean." He cocked his head, his deep brown eyes remaining locked on her. "Must be tough not to remember."

"It is," she admitted. She never wanted to show weakness at

work. "But I remembered something yesterday, and the doctor said that's a good sign. I hope the rest comes back soon."

"It'd be nice if you could remember how well we used to work together. You were once an integral part of the team."

While she appreciated his kind comments, he was just another stranger who shouldn't know these things about her but did. "I need someone to work with our tech guy to figure out his issues with the backup."

Sean looked at Mack. "I can do that."

Mack nodded. "I was about to suggest you go so that Cam can focus on this internet cable aspect. Go ahead and take off. If you gain access to the electronic files, forward them to us the minute you have them."

Sean stood. "You got it."

"I appreciate your sense of urgency," Addy said and knew they would be using the RED team's secure network to send the files to prevent hijacking.

"Good to see you again, Addy, even if you can't remember us." Sean grabbed his laptop and departed, taking the stairs two at a time.

"So let me get all of this straight." Kiley grabbed a pillow and fluffed the teal fabric. Something about the action niggled at the back of Addy's memory, though she had no idea why.

"From what I've read online," Kiley continued, "we have a suspect who has smuggled drugs from Mexico to the U.S. undetected for years, but most recently he turned to gun sales?"

"Correct," Addy said.

"Then you come on the scene, and he has to find a new way to move the drugs and guns, right?"

Addy nodded. "Although I have no recollection of how he got away with it for years. Or if I even knew."

"Do you remember how your investigation got started?" Kiley asked.

"No," Addy said. "But Harris said a detective came across

Razo in another investigation. When the detective called our office to loop us in, I was the agent who took the call. I have no idea how Razo learned about the investigation, but if we assume the threat to my mother was directed by him, then it's clear he knows I'm investigating him."

Addy took a breath and shook her head. "What I don't get is if he *is* the guy who took my phone, why didn't he just go ahead and kill me to get me out of his way? He obviously isn't against killing. And he had to have followed me when I went to talk to Rob, so he might even have figured out that I knew about the cable. Or maybe he tapped my phone."

"Maybe we have this all wrong and he doesn't want to kill you." Mack frowned. "Sure, he might gain some satisfaction from revenge for a perceived wrong he thinks you've done. But taking you out would make things worse for him."

"How so?" Addy asked.

Mack leaned closer. "You don't murder a federal agent and get away with it. Harris would bring in every resource to hunt him down. And even if you were taken off Razo's investigation, it wouldn't go away. Someone would replace you."

"I guess that makes sense," she said, thinking it over. "So, he really might just be warning me to back off."

"Not that we can let our guard down. Not for a second." Mack wrote Razo's name on the board and underlined it with a vicious slash of his red marker. The discussion about Razo was obviously bothering him, and she didn't like seeing the worry in his eyes. He cared deeply for her. His feelings had become clear in the time they'd spent together, and she was being drawn to him in a way she couldn't explain.

"Okay," Mack said. "We have this guy who once had carte blanche to move drugs across the border from Mexico. And at the same time, we're deploying X-ray machines at the front lines. Now he needs to work harder to keep up the business. So he does what?"

"Rob may have given us that answer," Addy said. "Seems like I believed Razo discovered the X-ray imaging systems were operating on one of the cable feeds. So he finds the location—maybe from the map Cam put up on the TV—and he cuts the cable to take the systems offline."

"It's not quite that easy, though," Cam said. "The map isn't exact. It's stylized and only shares the general location, but he could do additional research."

Cam clicked on one of the blue cables. "See here? It lists the company who owns the cable and their contact information. And if he's behind the hack of your office, he either has hacking skills or he's had to hire someone. I suspect he hired someone."

Addy held Cam's gaze. "Can you try to find out who that might be?"

"I can put out feelers." Cam's eyes narrowed. "But don't hold your breath. Unless the guy's bragging about cutting the cables, I doubt we'll find his worker bee."

"If I worked for Razo," Kiley said, "I wouldn't be bragging about anything. I'd be too afraid he'd take me out for talking."

"Exactly." Mack pointed at the screen. "Walk us through what we're looking at, Cam."

"The different colored lines seem to distinguish between multiple cables in a particular area. So if you look closely at the U.S. here—" he paused and used the mouse to zoom into the West Coast—"you can see the routes that originate on the Oregon coast. Clicking on one of them brings up the cable owner's information." He clicked on one of the lines, and the sidebar displayed company information.

"If the Feds or a state owned any of these cables, it would show up here," Mack clarified.

Cam narrowed his eyes. "I'm not familiar with this map, but that's my take."

"I have to say, it's impressive that Razo figured it out and went this route," Mack said.

Addy didn't want to be impressed with Razo. Not at all. "If he did, I have no proof of it, and not remembering why I thought it was a possibility, I can't even defend my position."

"So if we knew where Razo was taking guns across the border, we could check the cable owners at those locations."

Cam nodded. "And if not, we can look at every border crossing area, but I just checked and there are fifty crossing locations."

"If we have to, we review and clear each one," Mack said.

Kiley arched an eyebrow. "That's a large number of crossings to research."

"It'll take time, but it's doable." Mack looked at Cam. "Most of the crossings don't have the X-ray systems on the front lines yet. Or at least they didn't back when I lived in Texas. Shoot, one of the locations is nothing more than a hand-pulled ferry crossing the Rio Grande. Can you knock locations like this one off the list right away?"

Cam shook his head. "I doubt it's public knowledge which ones have the X-ray imaging systems, and I'd have to go one by one. It would take some time to do alone."

"I'll call Eisenhower and put analysts back in D.C. on it," Mack said. "Hopefully we'll soon have actionable information and can move this investigation forward."

CHAPTER 12

SILENCE FELL OVER THE GROUP, and the mood turned dark and ominous. They had to keep the dire consequences foremost in their minds to remember innocent lives depended on them and finding the guns had to be their top priority.

"You get to work on this map, Cam," Mack said. "Addy, Kiley, and I will go change and be right back."

The three of them hurried up the steps and went to their respective rooms, Bear trailing Mack. Bear jumped onto the bed and watched warily as Mack made quick work of changing, forcing his mind to think about Razo's operation and not on how Razo was targeting Addy. If Mack focused on the danger that seemed to be growing with each minute, he could trigger a PTSD episode, and as lead on the investigation, he couldn't afford to lose his cool.

His phone rang, and seeing Eisenhower's name on the screen, Mack sat on the bed to answer it. Bear settled his head on Mack's knee, melting Mack's heart into a big old puddle of love. He stroked his short, dense fur and answered.

"Glad I caught you," Eisenhower said. "How's Addy?"

"Doing as well as can be expected. She's been discharged, and we have her at the safe house."

"Is her memory returning?"

"Not really. She has some vague feelings of overall things but nothing specific, except a man taking her phone at the accident." Mack brought Eisenhower up to speed on the investigation, trying his best to be succinct and unemotional. He succeeded on the first, failed on the second.

When Mack finished, silence stretched out on the phone. Mack wasn't sure if he should say something else or wait it out.

"You good to lead this investigation?" Eisenhower finally asked.

"Of course."

"I have half a mind to pull you, what with your personal connection and all, but if you keep a level head, you should be able to handle it."

"I'm fine," Mack said and hoped he wasn't lying.

"If I get word to the contrary, you're out of there. Got me?"

"Yes, sir." And he knew that word would come from Harris. Eisenhower would've already talked to her and told her to inform him of any issues Mack might have.

"We're making some progress here." Optimism raised Eisenhower's tone. "Williams is starting to cooperate, and my gut says he knows something that can help propel things forward. It's just going to take a little more finesse to get it out of him, but I'm confident I can do so."

The weight on Mack's shoulders lifted a fraction. "Has he shared anything of value yet?"

"Only that he didn't actually sell the van. Gifted it to a friend who he won't name." Eisenhower blew out a sharp breath. "I've got agents running down the friends, but so far we struck out."

"And the woman?"

"Pretty much ruled her out as a one-night stand. I'm still keeping her in custody and questioning her. She could've heard Williams say something that will help. If she did, I'm going to get it out of her."

Mack felt sorry for the woman. One, because she was the type of person who engaged in casual sex, and two, she was caught in a situation she wouldn't get out of easily and the problem wasn't of her making.

"I wish I could be there," Mack said. "I know the others do too."

"I'll keep you updated," Eisenhower said. "I'll check in with you tomorrow or sooner if I learn anything."

The call went dead, and Mack sat for a moment, staring at his phone and digging his fingers into Bear's wiry undercoat. Mack's mind swam with everything on his plate. The Montgomery girls needed him. Addy needed him. A callous gunrunner was selling terrifying weapons, and Mack needed to stop him.

Mack repeated his mantra over and over so by the time he got back downstairs, he felt stronger and in charge again. Good thing, because Addy and Kiley had returned to sit next to Cam on the sofa and all three looked at him. He relayed Eisenhower's update.

Kiley rested her fingers over the keyboard of her open laptop. "I sure wish we were there."

Mack nodded. "I told Eisenhower the same thing. He says he'll let us know the minute anything goes down."

Mack shifted his focus to Cam. "How are you doing on gathering that list of Razo's known associates?"

He kept his eyes glued to his computer. "I've got an analyst in D.C. who's working on it. Should have something soon."

"Can they also get details on his associates' vehicles?"

Cam looked up. "Sure, but it's going to take longer."

Mack nodded his understanding. "I know Razo isn't personally moving guns over the border. Too big a risk. So I'm hoping we can figure out who is actually transporting them."

"Makes sense." Cam started typing on his keyboard.

Kiley's head popped up, and she looked at Addy. "Hold everything. I'm done looking at your laptop files. Immediately before leaving your office, you were viewing PDFs stored on the network."

"The files that are missing, I assume," Addy said.

"I assume so too," Kiley said. "But I'll print a list of the file names for you to review. Maybe they'll jog a memory." She kicked off the printer.

Addy hopped up and grabbed the pages. Mack opened his mouth to tell her to stop, then closed it. Harris might have banned Addy from the investigation, but she was the right person to review these files. He knew if he talked to Harris, he could probably get her to agree, but he wouldn't put her in that position.

Addy grabbed her laptop and sat at the nearby dining table. Cam remained working on the sofa, while Kiley joined them and placed her laptop on the table.

Addy spread out the pages, and Mack leaned over her shoulder, catching the familiar peach scent of her conditioner. He'd always loved the fragrance and remembered her coming out of a steamy shower, the room holding the same smell as the warm peach cobbler his mother often made for Sunday dinners. He let the memory play, a desperate urge to have Addy regain her memory and come back into his life making him lean closer.

"Look!" Her head snapped up, nearly hitting him as she tapped the corner of several pages. "These links refer to stories about the cables."

"Okay." Mack blinked a few times to focus. "So these stories appeared on the pages you viewed. Other stories appear on web pages all the time, but why did you connect them with your investigation?"

She looked over her shoulder at him. "I don't know. It's not obvious from this article. Let's look up the links. I'll take the first one and you two do these." She handed one to Kiley and one to Mack.

Mack dropped into the chair next to her and entered one of the URLs in a browser on his computer. The article opened on the screen, reporting a cable malfunction three weeks earlier in California. "Cable sliced. Possibly on purpose. Confirms what you were on to when you took off before the accident."

Addy nodded but kept her focus on the article she was reading.

He crossed the room and dragged a clean whiteboard on an easel next to the table. He jotted down location and date details from his article. "Tell me where and when the outage occurred in your story, if in fact that's what it's about."

"Mine took place four months ago in California." Kiley grabbed another article and entered the link in her laptop.

"Last month, an outage occurred in Tijuana, Mexico." Addy's eyes narrowed. "That's definitely a border town."

"So is this. It happened in Redondo Beach, California." Kiley rattled off the date. "Let me bring up the last one."

He and Addy both watched as Kiley's fingers flew over the keyboard, and she scanned the article. "Nada."

Mack stood back and studied the board. "We have three locations where a cable was cut, and the links appeared on internet pages that you previously downloaded. That can't be a coincidence."

"Agreed," Kiley said. "Something in these stories or the key words attached to them made the search engine think the articles on oceanic cables might be of interest to you."

"Let's carefully read the stories to see if we can find a common thread." Mack picked up the page he'd looked up and read the story about gunrunning in California. He underlined any reference to the internet or dark web, but he found no mention of cables. When he was done, he sat back to wait for the others to finish and focused on Addy.

She was so absorbed in the article that she didn't have a clue that he was watching her. Her tongue poked out the corner of her mouth, a habit he'd come to associate with her when she was concentrating. It darted back in as she circled something on the page, then soon poked out again.

How many of her actions had Mack stored in his memory that he had forgotten about? Their years together had given him a huge data bank of memories. He couldn't possibly recall them all, but each one told him a lot about the woman he knew and loved. He would give anything to find a way to be with her again.

He was seeing a Christian counselor for his PTSD, and the counselor kept reminding him that he was a child of God, who was watching over him at all times. God knew what was happening and exactly where Mack was in His plan and purpose for Mack's life. So God knew that Mack wanted to be with Addy, and it was Mack's job to figure out if that was what God wanted and then how to make it happen. After all, he wasn't one to easily give up. He always embraced the Night Stalkers' motto, *Night Stalkers Don't Quit*. This would be no different.

Addy's head lifted, and she gave him a quizzical look. He certainly wasn't going to share his thoughts in front of the team, so he pointed at the page. "What did you find?"

"My story's about Michigan State University researchers," she said. "They infiltrated the dark web to find out how firearms are anonymously bought and sold. They knew guns were being sold online similar to illicit pharmaceuticals and narcotics, but not to the extent drugs were being sold. They found that the majority of guns sold were handguns, and because the dark web allows for total anonymity, the buyers are people who couldn't purchase a firearm legally."

Mack digested the information. "Surprises me that it's mostly handguns."

"Yeah, me too. I would've thought rifles. Especially assault rifles." Addy looked back at the page. "It goes on to say the sellers shipped the product in pieces and hid them in books, shoes, cocoa, computer parts, and other harmless things. Many of them were international shippers."

"Razo could be one of them," Mack said. "Not for the min-
guns, but other weapons."

"He totally could be," Addy said. "So, what's your story
about?"

"A guy with an FFL who was caught making parts for a
gunrunner," Mack said. "Not miniguns, but Barrett sniper
rifles."

Mack shook his head. "Which is totally wrong, as the sniper
is in the person, not the rifle."

"What do you mean?" Kiley asked.

"Absolutely any rifle can be used by a sniper. In fact—not so
much these days, but in the past—military snipers would use a
standard-issue weapon they would prepare and sight in because
many of these guns needed to be ditched, and they didn't want
to lose pricey rifles."

He paused and took a long breath. "Anyway, the story
says this .50 caliber rifle is one of the most popular weapons
among Mexican cartel fighters. Only guns that best it are
the AR-15 and AK-47. The Barrett has a range of more than
a mile and can shoot through a wall of concrete block with
no problem."

Kiley shuddered. "Not the kind of gun you want in the hands
of a drug dealer."

Mack nodded. "Surprisingly, it's not restricted for civilian
ownership in our country. If you can pass a background check,
you pay cash for one—no paperwork whatsoever—and you
aren't breaking any laws."

"Which makes them easy to resell," Addy said.

"Yeah," Kiley said. "And someone can go in and buy as
many as they want, take them home, and sell them at their
leisure. Even if ATF knows about the purchases, they'd have
to sit on these guys twenty-four seven to wait for a sale. That's
just not practical, so these buyers get away with it most of
the time."

Mack shook his head, letting his disgust flow through it. "The guy in this story with the FFL was making replacement parts to be smuggled to a big cartel."

"Speaking of FFLs," Cam said, "I struck out on finding anyone holding one who would be a strong suspect in our investigation."

"Thanks for digging into it." Disappointed in another failed lead, Mack turned his attention to Kiley. "And your story?"

She lowered the screen on her laptop to look at him. "It's an article that dispels the myth that criminals get guns by stealing them."

"Then how do they get them?" Mack asked.

"Number one method is through straw purchases, like the .50s we just talked about. Someone who can legally buy a gun does so for someone who can't and sells it to them. And the next biggest source are sales made by legally licensed but corrupt at-home and commercial gun dealers."

"Do we think Razo is dealing in other guns?" Mack asked.

"I wish I knew." Addy frowned. "We should watch for it as we go through my files. But I would have to think if he is, I didn't catch him in the act or he wouldn't still be on the street."

"Does he have priors for illegal gun sales?" Kiley asked.

"He does," Cam called out. "He did time back in the nineties, which is when he first came onto the Feds' radar. I just got this info, and I'll email it to everyone in a few minutes."

"Thanks, Cam," Addy said but looked at Mack and Kiley. "What's the connection to the internet cables in the stories? Why did a search engine connect these links to my stories?"

"My article mentions how they believe some of these dealers use the dark web to expand their business," Kiley said. "Maybe the internet connection created a link to cables."

"Okay," Mack said, trying to process. "But with such a loose connection with Razo to the internet, I still don't see why these links would connect to our stories."

"It's gotta be metadata-driven," Cam said, talking about the key words that search engines indexed and attached to internet stories. "I can look into that for you, but you should know, it probably won't help the investigation. It's more likely a search engine dynamic than anything else."

"We need a stronger connection." Addy studied the whiteboard. "What about dates? Or towns? Or maybe both—maybe that's what caught my attention. I really think I need to look at the actual case files."

"Then we better hope Sean's as good as he claims to be," Mack said. "If he can't locate them on your office server, no one can."

———

As dinnertime approached, Mack could feel the clock ticking down while they continued to research the cable lead, and they weren't getting anywhere. They really needed Addy's files, but Sean hadn't called yet so there was no news on that front.

Mack looked at Addy's face, hoping to find clues to tell him if she was still doing okay or if her medical condition was worsening. She looked tired, and she massaged her head.

"Do you need to rest?" Mack asked.

"No."

"Are you sure? Because you won't be any good to anyone if you burn yourself out."

"I'm good for now." She smiled, but it was strained.

He didn't want to let this go. Not when he felt responsible for her. Not only because Harris told him to keep an eye on her to make sure she rested, but also because he loved her and wanted the best for her. "Will you agree to take a nap soon?"

She wrinkled her nose at him. "Yes, Mom."

His mind went back to their married life when she'd often

said the same thing to him after he'd suggested she take a break. She was never mad about it, but she did question why he never told the others on the team to step back for a while. He had a simple answer. He wasn't in love with the others. And that usually ended the discussion with her circling her arms around his neck, telling him how she loved him, and a passionate kiss, leading to anything but rest.

"So what's it like, Addy?" Kiley asked. "Having these blank spots in your life?"

Mack glanced at Kiley. "Leave it to you to be so blunt."

"Oh, oops." A sheepish look crossed her face. "Addy, you wouldn't know that about me. Sorry. I'm like a big nerd, and my social skills aren't the best."

Addy waved a hand. "I have the feeling we were friends, and I wouldn't mind the question."

"Good friends, actually." Kiley sounded so sad that it put a hitch in Mack's heart. She'd never really expressed her sadness over losing Addy from the team. It was obvious that all of them missed her, but Kiley had a hard time making friends, so losing a close friend had to hurt even more.

He thought to tell them to move on. To get back to work. To remember how little time they had, but maybe it would do them all some good if they took a few minutes to think about something else.

Addy frowned. "It's odd. I mean I look at you or Mack—any of you—and I know I should have this recognition, but it's blank, and I only know what I've learned since being with you all again." She paused and chewed on her lip. "Here's something weird, though. Earlier, when you were fluffing that pillow, I got this sense that it was something I'd either seen you do before or it was important somehow."

Kiley clapped her hands, and her eyes lit up. "I love to decorate and do home improvement. I decorate when I get stressed. You're probably remembering that."

Addy's expression perked up. "Yeah, hey, good. Something else. It's like with Mack earlier. I had a feeling about him. Not a specific memory, just a feeling."

"Maybe that's how things are going to come back."

"Yeah, maybe."

Kiley held out her hand and wiggled her ring finger, boasting a large solitaire diamond. "I should tell you that I got engaged since we last talked."

Addy squealed and admired the ring. "That's wonderful. Tell me about him."

Kiley grabbed her phone and woke it up. "His name is Evan Bowers. We go way back. I blamed him for the death of my friend, but we ended up partnering on an investigation together and worked that out." She held out her phone.

Addy looked at the picture on the screen. "He's very good-looking."

Kiley smiled. "I know, right?"

"Have you set a date?" Addy asked.

"We're waiting on Sean and Taylor to finalize their plans." She looked at Mack, then back at Addy. "Sean and Taylor Mills got together while working an investigation too. Now you and Mack are working together. I wonder if—"

"Leave it alone, Kiley," Mack warned.

She held up her hands. "I'm just saying. Something to think about."

"Yeah," Cam said. "Everyone's dropping like flies, so why not you two?"

Kiley cast Cam a mischievous look. "Then that means you're next."

He rolled his eyes, but his grin remained.

Mack's phone rang, the sharp peal startling him and the others. He pulled it from his pocket. "It's Sean."

Mack tapped the screen. "You're on speaker. Tell me you have good news."

"I do." Sean's deep voice boomed from the phone. "I fixed the glitch. Addy's files are on the way to your inbox."

A smile erupted on Addy's face, and she sat up higher. "That's great news."

"You're the man, Sean," Mack said.

"I'll be back soon, and you can tell me in person how great I am." Sean laughed and hung up.

"I'll download the files and get them printing." Mack moved to his computer and opened the first file but felt Addy's gaze on him. "I'll start with your timeline. We can review that while the other files are printing."

Mack sent three copies of all the files to the printer, then jumped up to grab the timelines. Kiley and Addy continued to talk about Evan—a great guy as far as Mack was concerned— yet Mack wasn't going to let Kiley try to play matchmaker with him. Addy didn't need any pressure in her quest to remember Mack. If indeed she was even trying to do so.

He handed out the timeline. Thankfully the women turned their attention to the pages.

Kiley tapped the top page. "This is fantastic."

Mack looked at Addy. "You always were good at paperwork."

"While you, on the other hand?" She clapped a hand to her mouth. "Another feeling. Am I right?"

"So right." Kiley grinned. "He stinks at doing reports and often avoids it."

Mack rolled his eyes. "Why don't you really say how you feel."

Addy glanced between them, a smile on her face. "You two sparred this way a lot, am I right? Like a brother and sister."

"Yep." Kiley looked proud of the fact. "And we still do. Mack's the big brother I never had."

Mack smiled and prayed that Addy would remember Kiley soon to know what an amazing person she was.

"So your dates," he said, taking them back to the task at

hand. "Looks like you thought Razo was moving guns on the dates we have on the board."

Her eyes narrowed. "Look at the last entry. It's bolded and footnoted. Maybe means it's the big event coming up."

"And would confirm your thoughts of something going down in four days."

"If so," Addy said, her gaze bouncing between them, "we don't have long before Razo uses the minigun in a mass shooting."

CHAPTER 13

AT THE BASEMENT TABLE the next morning, Addy watched Mack connect the TV to a video feed with Harris. She'd wanted to come to the safe house and meet with the team in person, but Mack had forbidden it. He didn't want any chance that she could be tracked to this house. Nor did he want her to see that Addy was frantically reviewing her files.

An easy solution. The team gathered in front of the TV with a camera mounted above, and Addy remained off to the side at the table with her files. Obviously, Harris had to suspect that Addy wouldn't step aside in the investigation, but Harris couldn't have any proof that Addy continued to work the case. That would make Harris complicit in violating those wage-and-hour laws, and Addy didn't want to put her boss in that position.

Harris leaned toward the camera. "Got our office call logs for the day of Leigh's accident. She didn't call anyone. Not even Rob Alberg. Anything new on her visit to him?"

"We hoped parking lot video from his office would ID the person who drugged her," Mack said. "But the camera range doesn't reach the area where she parked."

Addy wished she'd parked closer in instead of trying to protect the Mustang. But she was thankful that Mack shared the information she'd gotten from Rob, so she didn't need to talk to Harris.

"FYI, I got a call from Palmere," Harris said. "The coffee in

Leigh's travel mug tested positive for the Rohypnol, confirming that's how she ingested the drug. With her car being so old, it would've been easy for someone to use a slim jim to break in."

Addy curled her hands into fists. She might've prevented this, if she'd only been thinking about potential ways Razo could harm her, instead of protecting her car and satisfying her need for caffeine.

"What are the plans to check out these internet cables?" Harris asked, thankfully moving them on before Addy said something.

Cam looked up from his computer, which Addy was learning he had open most every moment. "We've got analysts back in D.C. reviewing all border crossings that might have X-ray imaging systems plus have an oceanic cable in the area and experienced an outage. We hope this will narrow things down considerably."

"Sounds like a solid plan."

"Only problem is, it's going to take time that we don't have," Mack said. "Addy's timeline confirms the big event happens in three days."

Harris muttered something under her breath and shook her head. Addy itched to weigh in on the discussion and not hold back, letting the team interact with her boss, but it couldn't be helped.

"Did Addy ever stake out Razo?" Sean asked.

"We did several times but to no avail. Even got a wiretap for his phone, but he's too cagey. Either he was speaking in code or he has burner phones we don't know about." Harris frowned. "All of this should be in Leigh's files. Have you reviewed them yet?"

"Spent most of the night doing so," Mack said. "But we've been focusing on data revolving around the internet connection. I'd like to get some boots on the ground and put Razo under surveillance again."

Harris scowled. "Could be a waste of time."

"Why's that?" Mack asked.

Harris took another breath, and Addy knew her supervisor didn't have good news. "The prints on Leigh's steering wheel came back to Razo's lieutenant. A Dante Zamora."

Addy gaped at the screen and had to clamp her mouth shut not to say anything.

"So it wasn't Razo himself, but his errand boy who tried to take her out," Mack said, his voice tight, his fingers clenched on his knees.

Harris gave a grim nod. "I don't know a lot about Zamora, but I'm guessing Leigh was all over him, and you'll find plenty of information in her files. I'm working on getting an arrest warrant right now. We'll have to find him first, of course. If he's not at the residence listed in DMV records, hopefully her files will hold a secondary address."

Mack glanced at Addy, and she recovered enough from the news to give a shrug. She had no idea what the files contained on this guy or where he lived. His name didn't ring a bell any more than anything else had in the last few days.

Mack faced the television again. "The guy's not real careful if he left prints on the wheel."

"Probably grabbed it when he leaned into the car to take her phone and didn't even know he was doing it." Harris pressed her lips together, a look Addy was very familiar with.

"Could mean he won't be careful when we question him, and we'll be able to get him to crack under interrogation." Mack lifted his shoulders into a hard line. "I want to be there for the questioning."

Harris gave a firm nod, and Addy was thankful she was including Mack, as Addy suspected he had great interviewing skills. He could be tough and yet caring. Two things combined together that might get a suspect to talk.

"I'll call you once we have him in custody," Harris said.

"What about forensics from the house?" Kiley asked. "Did you receive anything on that?"

"Sort of," Harris said. "Techs found a bloodstain on the sheet the attackers used for a backdrop and on the knitting needle Leigh's mother used to stab him. They're running the samples for DNA, and we should have results anytime now."

Addy was tempted to clap at the news. She wanted the person who'd threatened her sweet mother and Nancy found so he could pay for terrorizing two defenseless women.

"FYI, we don't think Razo was at the house," Harris continued. "One of the techs at the Oregon State Lab has been following a new development in bloodstain analysis. This test can determine the age of the person from the recovered blood sample."

"Never knew they could do that," Sean said, echoing Addy's thoughts.

"It's experimental and isn't a readily accepted science in a court of law yet, so no one is officially using it. Still, the tech ran it through Raman spectroscopy and has narrowed down the age range. It doesn't fit Razo's age."

Mack leaned forward, his attention fixed tightly on Harris. "Does it fit Zamora's?"

"Yes."

"Not surprising that Razo doesn't want to get his hands dirty." Kiley crossed her arms. "Send in his lieutenant, so if anyone gets busted, he can run his business as usual."

"Exactly." Harris's mouth turned down. "You should also know that a guy fitting Zamora's description was seen in the hallway outside Leigh's hospital room a few hours ago. When he caught sight of the agent on duty, he did an about-face and took off down a stairwell."

"Actually, that's kind of good news, right?" Sean asked. "Means Razo and Zamora don't know she's been discharged."

"Hadn't thought of it that way." Harris laid her hands on

her desktop. "That's all I have. Please tell me the Wonder Team has something to report?"

"I've got a couple of things," Cam said. "First, CCTV footage from Addy's drive to Rob's office couldn't be improved enough to get a look at the driver who tailed her. But it sounds like you might know who it is anyway. Good news is that we were able to improve the video from Addy's house. The guy on the video not only has the cut on his hand from the knitting needle, but he has a unique birthmark just above it on his wrist. I'll send out enhanced footage to everyone."

Mack shot Addy a look. "Do we have any pictures of Razo's or Zamora's wrists?"

Addy and Harris both shrugged, but Addy would look through her files for pictures and information on Zamora the minute this call ended.

"The audio recording didn't pan out either," Cam added. "Due to the way the guy at the house distorted his voice, they were unable to match it to Razo. The experts did use his fill words and speech patterns, and they don't believe it's Razo. This is just based on their years of experience and won't hold up in court."

Harris pressed her hands flat and leaned forward. "Hopefully, the blood from the sheet or needles will return our attacker's ID, then."

Cam nodded. "I'm still working on tracking the hack of your office. But you should know." Cam paused dramatically, and Addy leaned forward in anticipation of what was coming next. "There's nothing in your network logs to suggest there was an outside hack."

Harris gaped at him. "But there has to be, right? The files didn't just delete themselves."

"The only option other than an outside hack would be if someone inside your office deleted them."

"Not possible." Harris crossed her arms. "None of my staff would do that."

"If Cam thinks it's possible," Mack said, "we need to look at your security system logs to see if anyone was in the office that night."

"The files were deleted at 2:18 a.m.," Cam said.

"I'll get with Fitz and let you know what I find." Harris's shoulders drooped.

Addy didn't know if Harris was disappointed in Cam or if she was beginning to suspect someone they worked with had deleted the files. Addy couldn't see anyone in their small office doing so. They didn't have traitors on their staff. No one who would do Razo's dirty work.

"Anything else?" Harris asked.

"I'm still scouring the dark web for Razo's gun sales." Kiley smoothed a hand over her hair. "So far I've discovered that he's set up shop and is selling handguns via shipment. No sign of selling miniguns, but then I would think those would be custom orders."

"Any way to track him to a physical address?" Harris asked.

"Not really," Kiley said. "But I created a bogus identity and contacted him to try to set up a local buy for a gun. Since I don't know his location, I just had to approach it as a shot in the dark—like hey, if you're near me, can we meet to buy the gun because I need it ASAP. That sort of thing. We'll see if he goes for it. And I'll continue to look for other sites he might be running."

"Good work, Agent Dawson," Harris said.

Kiley sat up straighter, preening under the compliment.

It was still hard for women in law enforcement, and any encouragement from Harris was welcome.

Harris gave a sharp nod. "We'll do a video meeting again in the morning unless there's urgent information to share before then."

"You mean like you've arrested Zamora," Mack said. "Because right now that's the most urgent thing we have going and getting him to talk could break this investigation wide open."

———

Addy started going through her files for any information and pictures on Zamora, and Mack began researching the guy because he thought Zamora was now the key to their investigation. Find him and they'd find Razo. Problem was, after hours of searching, Mack didn't come up with much.

Addy sighed and got up to pace the family room floor like a caged animal. Bear followed her, his tail down. The poor guy was as anxious as Addy. She'd asked to take a walk earlier to clear her head so she could be more efficient, and Mack wanted to let her go but wasn't willing to risk exposure. He didn't even want her to set foot out on the back deck, but that was the best solution to her need for a change.

He waited for her to pass nearby and stepped in front of her. "How about we go out on the deck? Stick close to the house in the pergola, and I think it should be fine."

Her face brightened. "Yes, please. The fresh air will clear my head of all those images of Zamora and Razo and the people they murdered."

He looked at his teammates. "Heading out to the deck for a few minutes. Text me if anything happens."

They nodded, their focus never leaving their computers.

Addy hooked Bear up to his leash, and they bolted up the stairs.

Mack followed, but at the top he rushed ahead to reach the patio door first. "Stay here. Let me have a look around."

"Sit," she said to Bear, a frown on her face.

Mack grabbed the binoculars by the door, slid the door open, and stepped onto the wood structure on tall stilts. He slowly glassed the area, looking for a person hunkered down in the woods. For a glint of a rifle scope or a set of binos pointed their way.

He didn't see anything, which was what he expected, but he

could never be too careful. He dragged a chair back to the door. With the height of the deck and the ground far below, even the best of snipers wouldn't have a shot at Addy there. Still, no way Mack would sit down and relax when on guard duty.

He turned to Addy. "You're cleared to come out as far as this chair. Not another step. Okay?"

She nodded but didn't seem as if she liked it. Tough. He wasn't going to risk her life.

She sat in the chair, and Bear lay over her feet as if he knew she was in danger. She lifted her face to the sun and took long, cleansing breaths.

Her phone rang, and concern marred the peaceful expression. She quickly dug it from her jeans pocket—jeans that fit her like a glove, emphasizing her curves, something he couldn't help but notice when he'd trailed her up the steps. And he knew those curves well.

He shook off the thought and looked back at the ravine below while she talked. From what she was saying, he gathered it was the hypnosis-therapy doctor for her memory loss. She was trying to get him to come to the house, but he didn't seem willing.

"Then we'll go with today," she said firmly. "Four o'clock, your office. And thank you for squeezing me in. I sure hope this works."

Mack tightened his hands on the coarse wood railing. He didn't appreciate her agreeing to an appointment without first checking logistics with him. He wanted to spin around and tell her as much, but he needed to cool it. He was the one with the problem, not her. Her life hung in the balance, and she could make an appointment if she wanted to.

He took a few deep breaths, then turned and leaned against the railing, crossing his ankles to make it seem as if he was relaxed. He studied her face. Her expression held a mix of hope and apprehension.

"That was the doctor who'll do my hypnosis," she said, confirming Mack's thoughts. "He has an opening at four today at his office, and I took it. It's in the medical center attached to the hospital."

Mack swallowed to be sure his tone didn't sound defensive or angry. "He wouldn't come here?"

"It's not that he wouldn't, but he couldn't come today and make his other appointments due to travel time." She paused and looked deeply into Mack's eyes. "I know this isn't ideal, but if I start remembering things, we could really get this investigation moving. Can we make it work?"

At her vulnerable tone and question, Mack's heart softened and he nodded. "Of course."

"Thank you. I know that means we only have a couple of hours to figure out transport, but after hearing someone matching Zamora's description was outside my hospital room, I can't imagine that he or Razo are expecting me outside of the hospital."

"I would agree with that." Mack started running ideas through his head, rejecting some and moving on. "Off the top of my head, I'd suggest we use the doctors' parking area for our arrival. It's undercover and away from the public parking lot. And we can use their private entrance too."

"Sounds good to me." She smiled. "If you can arrange it."

"No worries there. One thing, though. We'll have to take hospital corridors to get to the medical building, and you're going to be out in the open. There's nothing we can do about that."

She frowned. "But I'll be heading to the medical center, and again, they won't expect me to be there."

"It's still dangerous. I'll need you to wear another disguise and keep your guard up." He met her gaze and held it. "Will you promise to do that? For me?"

"I'd do that even if you didn't ask, but yes, for you I will be extra careful." A soft smile played on her face and wrapped warmth around his heart.

Her comment made it seem as if they'd anchored something between them, and yet, in less than three hours she might remember him, and their relationship—or whatever they were developing between them now—might end. They could be back to the same impasse.

"What are you thinking about?" she asked, her chin lifting ever so slightly, as if she felt a need to defend herself.

He thought to blow off her question, to make light of his thoughts, but he wouldn't want her to do that to him. He crossed over to her and squatted down so he was at eye level with her while continuing to keep watch on the deck. Bear popped up to stare at him, and Mack patted the dog's head to reassure him everything was okay.

Mack looked at Addy. "I was wondering what will happen if at this appointment you start to remember me—if you remember my issue and how you feel about me and our past together. Will you let me keep working with you? Protecting you?"

"I hadn't even thought of that." She tangled her fingers together. "I mean, I hope to remember, but I didn't really consider what would happen then."

"And now that I brought it up?"

"I . . . I don't know—I won't know until the memories come back." She reached out and touched his cheek. Gently. Softly. Like a butterfly landing. "Our time together has told me you're an amazing man. Someone I could see myself falling for all over again, so I assume everything will remain the same."

"Addy, I—" He reached up to capture her hand and hold it tightly in his and was suddenly very thankful they'd stepped out on the deck and away from his teammates. "I want you to know how much I still love you and want to fix my issues. To get back together as husband and wife. But I—"

"But licking the PTSD is still going to be a challenge." She sounded so sad it broke his heart.

He was disappointing her again, and he hated that, but he needed to explain. "It's like your memory loss. You can't change it. You can try today with the hypnosis and do other things I imagine in the future, but you can't just will it to come back. Just like I can't will the PTSD to go away."

He took a long breath to clear his head. "It's so much better than when we were together, but I still have flashbacks and bad dreams. And although they're rare, it would take only one horrific episode for me to hurt you again." He lifted her hand to his mouth and kissed it, then looked her in the eye. "I'd rather die than hurt you. I just can't take the risk right now."

She frowned. "And if I remember, and I'm okay with the risk? Then what?"

"Then we're right where we were when we split up," he said, his heart cracking.

His phone rang, and he had to force himself to drag his gaze free to look at the screen. "It's Harris." He answered and listened as she updated him on the blood found on the sheet at Addy's house. "You're sure?" he asked.

"Positive," Harris said and ended the call.

Mack shoved the phone back into his pocket.

"News?" Addy asked.

He nodded. "DNA taken from the blood on the sheet and knitting needle—the results are back from the lab. It's official. The blood belongs to Zamora. He's the jerk who took Nancy and your mother hostage."

CHAPTER 14

SITTING IN THE MINIVAN, Addy tugged on an itchy blond wig. She didn't like the wig, but she had to admit being blond was fun. Especially with the way Mack had looked at her before they'd left the safe house. She'd warmed to her soul under his intoxicating study. Had she worn a blond wig in the past and it was bringing back memories, or did he just enjoy the hair color change? Maybe in an hour or so she would remember their past and know the answer to that question.

She glanced at him, sitting next to her in the back of the van as they whisked down the treelined road. His intense focus said he couldn't care less about her hair right now. He had his head on a swivel, watching every inch of their progress. Riding shotgun, Kiley was doing the same thing. Even Sean was hyperalert while driving.

They'd left Cam back at the house. As an analyst, he didn't carry and couldn't provide protection. He'd cast a longing look at them when they exited. If Addy was right, he wanted to be in the thick of things. Maybe he wanted to be an agent. She might soon know the answer to that and remember all these wonderful people too.

She looked around the van. What secrets or insights had they revealed about their personalities to her in the past? Since seeing them again, Kiley had shown herself to be sweet, if awkward. Sean, a straight shooter who seemed intense and by the book.

And Mack? He was proving to be the guy she'd always imagined being with. The kind of man she could see herself marrying.

He caught her eye and smiled. A tight, nearly forced number, but still devastating to her heart. She was falling for him for sure. She shouldn't be surprised. Not when she'd married him once before.

He looked away, and her mind went to Zamora. Maybe she would remember him in the hypnosis and know how to find him. Mack was sure the guy would lead them to Razo, so she would tell the doctor that it was a priority to focus on. Not that she thought you could list out things you wanted to remember, but still, she hoped they could emphasize that because time was disappearing faster than she could imagine, and they had to make some progress soon. Just had to.

They approached the medical facility, and she became alert, her hand resting on her sidearm. Warren had done a thorough threat assessment of the building for Mack, taking pictures and drawing a rough layout so that Mack could plan their arrival. She was so thankful for how her fellow agents were cooperating with the RED team, even taking a backseat when needed.

Sean pulled into the center's secured parking area and punched a number provided by the administrator into a silver keypad. The gate lifted, emitting a high-pitched squeal that grated on Addy's already tight nerves. Sean wound up the ramp to a private elevator. Kiley hopped out and called the elevator car to their floor.

"Okay. We're a go." Mack looked at Addy. "Straight inside the car. Kiley and I'll be with you all the way. Once you're settled in the office, I'll stay with you, and Kiley will join Sean out front for your return trip. We good?"

She nodded, though her heart was thundering in her chest and warning her not to get out and expose herself to a potential gunshot. Still, she opened the door and slid out. She had to for the investigation. For the people who might die if she didn't try to remember. Mack came to her side of the car, pulled her close, and hurried her into the elevator. Kiley took one last look outside and closed the SUV door. Addy saw Sean drive off before the elevator doors whisked closed.

Mack let out a long breath. He obviously felt the same stomach-clenching tension she was experiencing. The doors opened on the third floor, and Mack took her arm again. She didn't protest but stayed by his side, her hand ready to go for her gun if needed. They moved through the hallways at top speed, Mack knowing exactly where they were going.

They arrived at the doctor's office, where he stopped outside the door.

"I'll check it out," Kiley said and stepped into the office.

"Can I take this wig off now?" Addy asked. "I'll put it back on when we leave, but I want to be my real self for this."

"Sure," Mack said.

She jerked the irritating wig free and stuffed it into her hand-bag. She shook out her hair and finger-combed it. Mack reached out to move a strand crossing her face, and their eyes met. Interest and longing deepened the blue of his eyes. She couldn't gauge the intensity of his feelings, as she was only getting to know him, but his obvious interest touched her deeply, an unseen force drawing her to him.

She took a step closer. He sucked in a sharp breath and held her gaze. She wanted to touch him. To kiss him. To find out what they had together. She inched closer, slowly, savoring his gaze as she moved. He reached out and circled her waist with his powerful arms, and it felt as if he was calling her home. Calling her to where she belonged but hadn't yet known it.

The door opened, and Kiley stepped out.

Mack's hands fell to his side, and Addy moved quickly back. A hot flush crept up her neck and over her face. How had she allowed herself to be caught in a compromising position?

Kiley's eyes traveled between them, a wide smile spreading across her face. "Sorry to interrupt, but all's clear."

Mack nodded and gulped in air as he gestured for Addy to go in.

"I say you two should go for it." Kiley patted him on the arm.

Addy all but fled into the office, and Mack didn't respond either. She heard his footsteps trail her into the small waiting area, but she put him and their recent encounter out of mind. She was here for one reason and one reason only. To remember everything she possibly could. She needed to focus on that.

The doctor stood at his inner door. Tall, maybe six-foot-three, his white dress shirt hanging on his slight frame, the collar with a navy-striped tie loose on his pencil-thin neck.

He gave her a genuine big-toothed smile and extended his bony hand. "Dr. Galt."

"Addison Leigh." Addy was surprised by his firm grasp as she shook his hand.

"Come in." He stood back.

"I'll be right out here," Mack said.

She smiled at him and entered the small and tidy office with modern décor. She didn't know what to expect, but the furnishings really didn't matter. It was the doctor she had to evaluate and become comfortable with before she could relax enough to be hypnotized.

"Go ahead and have a seat." He gestured at a smooth leather recliner. "Get comfortable."

She sat in the plump chair, and her nerves jangled with unsettling emotions much the same as she'd experienced on her first date. Or the first time she spoke in public. Or the day she took her oath as a federal law-enforcement officer.

The doctor sat in a nearby low-slung chair. "There's nothing to be nervous about. In fact, you'll need to relax if this is going to work."

"I'm trying," she said. "I just keep wondering what made me lose my memory, and if I want to know what that thing is."

"I understand your concerns, but you should know you will be in total control during our session. If the memory comes back and it's too painful for you, you'll likely let it go and move on." He smiled at her, but it did nothing to ease her mind. "You should also know that you'll be fully awake during the process. All we're doing via hypnosis is slowing down time, freezing the memory so it can be explored in detail."

"I'm not sure I follow," she said.

He tapped his index finger on his desk for a moment. "You're an agent. Imagine you're interviewing a witness to a crime you're investigating, and you can slow down the crime so the witness can view every detail as it unfolds. They would be far more able to give you details of what occurred than just having the flashing memory we often recall."

She was glad he put the information in a way she could understand. "That makes sense."

"You'll be in an altered state and have that time distortion too. And the other big difference is that you're thinking with feelings rather than thoughts. If you enjoy the feeling, you'll likely continue the thought. If you feel uncomfortable, the hypnosis might cease." He paused and met her gaze. "Because you will be recalling traumatic experiences, we might not succeed."

She nodded, but deep down she hoped he was wrong. That she was an exception and would recall her life in D.C., Mack, the accident, and the investigation.

He settled back in his chair. "Now, tell me a bit about what you're struggling to remember."

She took a long breath and launched into her story, pointing out how important it was above all else to remember Zamora. "I can't help but think these things are all linked together, and if I figure out this link, it'll all come back."

"Maybe," he said but didn't look convinced. "The best thing

for us to do right now is to begin the hypnosis. I will guide you back in time and into your memories. Are you ready?"

She nodded.

"You're comfortable?"

She nodded and swallowed hard.

"Okay then. Let's begin our session."

———

Mack sucked on a mint as he paced the small waiting area. He'd been doing this for nearly an hour, and the receptionist with cat-eye glasses and purple hair eyed him. He didn't want to make the woman uncomfortable, but how could he sit still when what was going on behind the adjoining door could dramatically change his life?

He wanted to be in the office with Addy. To hear the doctor take her back through the last few years of her life. Hear what she had to say about him, if she said anything at all. Would she remember him? Remember how very much he loved her and wanted to be with her, but couldn't?

He didn't know if he could bear it if she came out and looked at him with that hint of suspicion still in her eyes. That doubt. He'd rather have her anger or even hurt over their breakup. He just wanted her to know him so he could hope for a future together, even though that future seemed impossible.

Mack paused. His feet planted, he closed his eyes. Bowed his head, right there in the middle of the room. His mantra came to mind. *"For the Spirit God gave us does not make us timid, but gives us power, love and self-discipline."* Everything Mack needed to mentally succeed at a time like this. Everything! So why couldn't he embrace it?

The hallway door opened behind him, and he spun, his hand whipping his jacket out of the way and landing on his sidearm. The silver-haired woman who entered startled and gasped. *Great.* Now he'd scared a little old lady. He released his jacket and cast her an apologetic look, but her hand remained clutched at her chest as she hurried over to the receptionist, who glared at him from behind her glasses.

He couldn't keep making these women uncomfortable. He stepped into the hallway and took several long breaths. He faced the open end of the hallway where any threat might originate and planted his feet. No way he was letting Razo or Zamora get to Addy.

His phone rang. Harris. A lump in his throat, he answered it.

"Thought you might want an update on Zamora," she said. "He's in the wind. I've got Warren watching the guy's house, but if word gets out that we're looking for him, he's not about to come home."

Mack's spirits fell even lower. "Addy's undergoing hypnosis right now at the medical center. After I escort her back to the safe house, I'll meet with the team, and we'll come up with a plan to fish Zamora out."

"I have other agents beating the bushes," she said. "Don't do anything without consulting me first."

Mack didn't want to hold off on anything. And he wouldn't. Not with their deadline fast approaching, but in the spirit of cooperation he could at least let her know what was going on.

"Keep me updated, and I'll do the same," he said and ended the call.

He shoved his phone into his pocket and thought ahead to the transport. Most people would think he would reverse their arrival procedure, but when transporting a high-value target, you could never know if you'd been made known on arrival, and it wasn't prudent to take the same route back. He'd arranged to borrow a medical-transport van, which was this very moment idling at the curb out front with Sean behind the wheel and Kiley riding shotgun. Addy would be exposed in the twenty feet or so between the hospital and van, but then she would be exposed in any transport arrangement.

The office door opened, and he breathed deeply to prepare himself for whatever Addy had remembered.

"Thank you," he heard her say. "I'll see you then."

Then? She was coming back. Did that mean she didn't remember?

Mack shoved his hands into his pockets. *Not safe.* He jerked them out to keep them free for her protection. Still jittery, he kept his eyes on the hallway. Not only to assess the risk, but he didn't want to see the disappointment in her expression.

Even so, in his peripheral vision, he saw her step out.

"Ready to go?" she asked.

Right. She didn't even want to talk about her session.

"There's a restroom at the end of the hall where you can put your wig on." He tapped the mic on his comms unit. "We're ready to leave. Both in position?"

"Roger that," Sean said, and Kiley echoed his reply.

Mack also needed to make sure the officers he'd arranged via local law enforcement were in place. "And the officers at the door?"

"In position," Kiley said.

"Have them clear the area. I don't want any vulnerable patients in the loading zone. We're stopping in the bathroom so Addy can put on her wig. Let me know when the area is clear and you've made your final assessment."

"Roger that." Sean sounded confident, and Mack trusted him one hundred percent.

Mack set off, making sure Addy was right behind him. At the end of the hallway he held up his hand and stepped out to assess. The elevator area was empty.

He signaled for her to follow, and he moved on to the bathrooms. "Stay here. I need to check it out."

"Okay," she said.

He pounded on the women's restroom door. "Officer coming in." He pushed it open and squatted to confirm the small bathroom was empty. He stood back and let Addy go in. He didn't make eye contact. What was the point? If she'd remembered him, she would've said so by now, and he couldn't take seeing the confirmation that he was still a stranger to her in every way that counted.

He let the door close and waited, his brain firing on all circuits and blurring his thoughts. Not good. He shook his head. Blinked his eyes. Swallowed hard. All to pin his concentration to where it needed to be—on protecting Addy. He eyed everyone who stepped into the area and sighed in relief when they departed on the elevators.

She opened the door.

He held up his hand. "This is a good place to wait for the all-clear." He kept his back to her and tapped his foot.

"You're good to go," Sean reported.

"Roger that. On our way." He released his mic. "Stay by my side. We move straight through the lobby and into the van. No stopping for any reason. Got it?"

"Mack?" she asked. "Why won't you look at me?"

His stomach clenched. "The hypnosis didn't help, did it?"

"It did actually. I can remember the investigation and even the accident now. And I—"

"But me?" He shot her a desperate look.

She took a step closer to him, then stopped and met his gaze. "No. Not you or the team. We ran out of time for that."

Time. He'd assumed she would've made him top priority during her first session. Obviously not. He'd known it would hurt to hear she didn't remember him, but it was worse than he imagined. Like a serrated knife plunged into his gut and jerked upward. Still, he should know that she would do the right thing and try to recall the investigation so she could find the miniguns before time ran out.

He needed to support that. "I'm glad you remembered things."

She laid a hand on his arm. "I have another session scheduled, and Dr. Galt is hopeful from today's success that I will remember more. He warned me, though, it could take several sessions. I need to tell you about what I did remember. It's important."

Mack gave a nod, but it felt stiff and falsely reflected his feelings. He had no hope or positive emotions to emit. "That will have to wait until we get back. We need to get going and keep our attention on our surroundings."

He gestured for her to move to his side. She did, wreaking havoc on his senses. He swallowed away every emotion and put on his professional demeanor. He had one job right now. Get her to the vehicle without incident and back to the safe house.

She stepped closer to him, and they made their way to the elevator where he jabbed the button with a force that wasn't necessary.

"You're upset," she stated plainly.

Once more, he kept his head on a swivel, watching areas where hallways intersected. "I can't talk about this now. I need to concentrate on your safety."

"All right. But when we get back to the safe house, let's take a few minutes to have a private conversation."

"Sure thing," he said, but would rather go to the dentist and have a tooth pulled than hear her remind him that the investigation came before him.

CHAPTER 15

ADDY DIDN'T WANT TO BREAK MACK'S HEART and hoped to talk more, but with the exit doors right in front of her, she had to think about her safety and not leave it all up to Mack. The automatic doors split wide, the cold, damp air washing over her face helping her to remain alert.

Mack took her arm. She was glad for his touch. It gave her more confidence and a sense of well-being. Kiley stood by the van's sliding side door. She nodded at Mack. He urged Addy forward. She was aware of his head turning. Turning and watching. She followed suit, the misty rain coating her body as she stepped quickly toward the vehicle.

Mack suddenly stiffened. "Sniper!"

Addy gasped, drew her sidearm, and searched the area. Time seemed to slow. Like in the hypnosis. Each sight. Each sound. Intensified. Her feet still moving but barely.

Kiley, weapon out, spun.

Mack shoved Addy forward, pushing her into the vehicle, then hurling his body on top of her. She heard the crack of the gun. A loud boom. Rifle. Mack jerked and sucked in a quick breath.

"Go!" he yelled as Kiley slid into the vehicle.

Sean floored the gas, and the van jerked forward. The side door hadn't closed, and she knew Mack hadn't made it all the way inside. She felt his leg move, and he shoved his body farther in, remaining on top of her like a large burlap bag of potatoes, heavy and solid. The vehicle raced around a corner, and he held fast, his body rigid and braced.

Sean suddenly slammed on the brakes. "Pedestrian! Move. Move. Move."

The van soon roared forward, and they were off again.

Another shot rang out, the bullet hitting the door above her head with a sharp ting, piercing the van and exiting through the other side. Had to be a powerful caliber to rip holes in steel like that.

"He's got to be using .50s," Mack said. "Get this vehicle out of here!"

"Doing my best." Sean sounded calm amidst the chaos.

"Reporting the shooter's location to locals at the hospital door," Kiley announced.

Addy had no idea how Kiley knew the shooter's location, but Addy wouldn't ask now and disturb Kiley's focus.

"It's gonna take time to get to him," Mack said, his breath warm on her neck. "God willing, we'll be out of range before then. Hopefully they'll still be on time to bring this guy in."

All conversation stopped, the van silent and bursting with heavy tension. Addy listened to the wheels spinning over the wet pavement. Mack's heart thundered against her back. She heard and felt the rapid beating—was aware of every touchpoint of his body, but she didn't ask him to move. She was afraid if he did, he would fall out of the vehicle.

Time slipped by. Miles with it. She didn't know what to say, so she didn't say anything.

Mack cleared his throat. "You okay?"

"Fine."

He shifted. "I know I'm heavy, and I'll get off as soon as we're out of range."

"We're a few miles out and no tail," Sean called out.

"Which means we can pull over to regroup," Kiley said.

The vehicle slowed and stopped. Mack pushed off Addy, and

she heard him grunt. Not the sound of exertion, but a grunt of pain.

"Are you hit?" She came to a sitting position to make room for him and searched his body.

"Maybe," he said.

"Your pants are soaked in blood!" she cried.

"Yeah." He scrambled into a sitting position. "Let's get this door closed and get moving."

Her heart racing, she eyed him. "We have to go to the ER. You need to have that looked at."

He waved a hand. "It's just a scratch."

"How do you know? You haven't even looked at it."

"Trust me. I know."

"Because you've been shot before, right? I mean, I don't remember it, but you have."

"Enough times to know this will be fine." He slid the door closed. "Get us moving, Sean."

Sean didn't question but started the van forward again.

Addy glanced into the back of the vehicle. "There's a first-aid kit back here. At least let me look at it and stop any bleeding."

"Sure." His reluctant expression belied his agreement.

She didn't care what he thought. She was going to tend to his wound. Thankful they were in a medical transport vehicle that was equipped with a kit, she climbed over the seat and grabbed it. Once settled back in her seat, she put on her seat belt and looked at Mack. His face was flushed, and he was sweating. He was in more pain than he was letting on.

She would be as gentle as she could be. "Put your foot on my lap."

"Yes, ma'am," he said, drawing out his accent and ending with a cute smile.

Here he was bleeding and in pain, and he was trying to make her feel better with his Southern charm. She loved his kindness, but she wasn't going to let it interfere with her concentration. She got out the scissors to cut his pant leg.

"Oh no, you don't. Not my favorite jeans." He tugged the pant leg up to his knee.

Just above his boot, blood oozed and ran down. She felt queasy and had to work hard to dredge up a smile of her own as she shifted his leg for a better look. He sucked in a sharp breath.

"Sorry," she said. "I'm doing my best not to hurt you."

"No worries." A broad smile crossed his face, but he was still perspiring.

"You thinking it was Razo?" Sean asked.

Addy didn't want to talk about Razo, yet she knew it would help keep Mack's mind off the injury.

Mack nodded. "One of the stories in Addy's files was about Barrett sniper rifles. They're .50 cal weapons, so yeah. I figure he or one of his minions took the shot."

"Razo was selling them too," Addy said as she remembered intel she'd received. "My source says he bought broken and discarded guns for a song and had a gunsmith fix them up for him."

Kiley looked over the seat. "Sounds like you remember the investigation."

Addy nodded and started to remove Mack's boot.

"Be careful with that," he warned. "Don't want my boot damaged."

"You and your precious boots." Addy rolled her eyes but knew deep inside how much he loved his boots.

"You remember more than the investigation?" Kiley asked.

Addy shook her head. "It's just another one of those feelings."

"Not hard to remember that," Sean said sarcastically. "The man would rather die than lose those boots."

"Hey." Mack grinned. "You should know to never get between a cowboy and his boots."

Despite the blood. Despite the danger. The adrenaline. The near loss of her life. Addy had to chuckle. Probably Mack and Sean's intent.

She studied Mack's wound. A three-inch gash ran across the outside of his leg, the skin splayed open, revealing the muscle below. She gasped.

"Hey," Mack said. "It's just a flesh wound. Not even bleeding anymore."

She stared at him. "I can see the muscle. A doctor needs to make sure there's no muscle damage, and it's going to need stitches."

"Yeah," he said. "I'll get it looked at after you're back at the safe house. But FYI, docs don't stitch up minor gunshot wounds. Bullets leave a lot of debris in the wound, so too big of a risk for infection."

She couldn't imagine leaving the gaping wound open, but at least it would be bandaged. While she wanted him to head to an ER right now, she knew no matter what she said he wouldn't budge.

Kiley looked over the seat. "You got lucky, man."

Addy shot Kiley a look. "You call this lucky?"

"If the shooter really was pumping off .50s, a fraction of an inch closer and Mack wouldn't have a leg at all."

Addy knew .50 caliber bullets did serious damage, but she'd never witnessed the destruction, and she shuddered at the thought. Not only at Mack losing his leg, but one of them could have lost their lives. She swallowed away the horrific thought and got out gauze pads. She gently laid them over the wound. He winced and gritted his teeth.

"Sorry," she said.

"No worries." He smiled again, but now it was tight, and his eyes narrowed. "It's got to be done, so go for it."

She wrapped gauze around his leg to secure the pads and finished it all off with tape.

"Done," she said. "I wish I could do more."

"You could kiss his boo-boo and make the pain go away," Sean joked.

Mack laughed, a deep belly chuckle, and that lightened her heart.

"Or just kiss him," Kiley added, a spark of mischief in her eyes.

Mack's laughter fell off, and he looked at Addy, his expression telling her he wouldn't mind that at all. They sat there, locked in each other's gaze as the miles passed under them.

At some point Kiley turned back in her seat, but when they pulled into the safe house driveway, she shook her head. "You two need to get over whatever's keeping you apart, because it's clear you need to be together."

"It's not at all clear to me." Addy closed the first-aid kit with a snap.

Mack pulled his leg down. He jerked on his boot and took a gulp of air. He panted and looked up at the ceiling, pressing his hand on his knee as if he was trying to stop the pain from racing up his leg. She reopened the kit and grabbed some Tylenol.

He reached for her hand to help her out of the vehicle, but she held out the tablets. "Take these. It'll help with the pain."

He tossed them in his mouth. She watched his bronzed neck as he swallowed, and the need to touch him again was almost overwhelming. She'd become so acutely aware of his physical presence since the hypnosis. Could the memories she recounted to the doctor have opened the pathway to remembering Mack and all they'd once had together?

He offered his hand again, but she couldn't touch him and keep her focus, so she scooted out on her own. He gave her a pointed look.

"I don't want to risk hurting you." She made a beeline for the front door before he asked if that was her real reason. She didn't want to hurt him. Never. She was telling the truth, but . . .

Inside the house, she went straight to the basement and hoped Mack was able to navigate the steps. She soon saw his boots clomp down the open stairwell.

"Everything go okay?" Cam asked.

"No." Addy sat by Cam and Bear and shared the incident with him, ending with Mack taking a bullet.

"Whoa." Cam's eyes widened.

Mack waved a hand, dismissing the shocked response.

"Hey," Cam said, a grin forming. "It's no biggie, right? Your boot's still intact."

Mack laughed with Cam as Sean and Kiley joined them.

Kiley started moving furniture around. She was stressed. What was she so worried about? Sure, the shooting had everyone off-kilter, but Kiley seemed to be focused on something in particular.

Addy thought back to the shooting. The memories playing like a video in her mind. The terror coming back, inching up her back. Addy had focused on Mack's injury and hadn't really thought about the fact that she could've been shot too. She was standing very close to the first bullet's landing spot.

"I'm going to call our local contact to see if they arrested the shooter." Mack stepped to the side of the room holding the piano and gingerly lowered himself onto the bench. Bear trotted across the room and looked up at Mack. The poor dog knew something was up, and he whined under his breath until Mack gave him a reassuring pat.

"One question, Kiley." Addy looked at Kiley, who'd paused, chair in hand. "How did you know where the shooter was located?"

"Oh that." She set the chair down, dropped onto it, and used the tips of her toes to push a glass bowl in a kaleidoscope of colors to the center of the coffee table. "We're testing a military program—Tactical Communication and Protective Systems. TCAPS has microphones on our comms unit that record two acoustic waves from bullets fired at supersonic speeds. It does a lot of things I won't go into, but basically it gives the direction of arrival of those waves, and that provides the location of the shooter's hideout."

Addy was confused. "But how do you get the info?"

"It's sent via Bluetooth or USB to our smartphones, which use a data-fusion algorithm to calculate the shooter's position. Takes only about half a second to receive the information. The military hopes to be deploying it any day now."

"It's some sweet program," Cam said. "Wish I'd thought of it."

Mack got up and limped over to them, his eyes darkening. "Locals are still looking for Zamora, but we can't rely on them anymore. We need to come up with a plan to track him down."

"I can help with that," Addy said.

Mack flashed her a look. "How?"

"I told you, I remember the investigation and the accident."

"Yeah, so?"

"The day of the crash, I was coming back from seeing Rob just like we thought. But I had one more stop to make."

"Where?" Mack jumped up and limped across the room.

"In my research, I found a local guy, a Vadim Yahontov, who did time for, get this—" she paused and looked Mack square in the eyes—"tampering with internet cables on the ocean floor."

———

Addy couldn't believe Mack actually let her join the team in questioning Yahontov. She'd had to plead, but after she pointed out that this guy's rap sheet was all about internet crimes and with no hint of violence, plus pointing out that she knew the investigation best, Mack agreed.

She'd also made sure he gave in to her demands to stop at the ER, where his wound was examined—no muscle damage, thank goodness—cleaned and bandaged, and he was sent on his way with a prescription for painkillers. Which he refused, saying he would never take them while responsible for her protection, and he would manage the pain. She planned to keep an eye on him. If she saw him suffering, she would talk to him about it.

They rolled up on the apartment complex in Milwaukie, a suburb of Portland. The two-story building was old but in good condition with fresh blue paint. Sean parked the SUV, and they all got out. They'd taken the precaution of dressing in body armor but wouldn't carry assault rifles for a knock-and-talk.

Addy was starting up the sidewalk when Mack held out a hand, stopping her and allowing Sean to take the lead, Kiley behind him.

"We stack in this order so if there's a problem, we'll be ready," Mack said.

She glanced up at him. "And you have me safely at the back of the group."

"That too, but honestly I'm more concerned with maintaining our routines."

"Where did I used to fall in the stacking order?"

"You had Kiley's slot, and she took up the rear."

Was there was any real significance to this order? She would ask, but they reached Yahontov's door before she could get the question out.

Sean used the side of his hand to pound on the door. "Police! We need to talk to you, Yahontov."

"Movement inside," Sean said, his focus pinned to the door, his hand on his sidearm.

Addy clasped the butt of her gun, ready to draw if necessary.

"I need to see some ID." Yahontov's voice came from the other side of the door.

"I got it." Kiley stepped forward and held her credentials up to the peephole. "FBI Special Agent Kiley Dawson."

The dead bolt clicked, and the door opened.

"You Vadim Yahontov?" Sean asked.

"I am." He lifted a bushy black eyebrow. "What's this about?"

Sean eyed the guy. "We'd like to come in and talk about that."

Yahontov shifted his focus to the group. "And it takes four people to talk?"

"We can have a conversation here or we can escort you to our office." Sean's tone left no room for the guy to argue.

Yahontov stepped back, his eyes narrowed. They marched past him, and Addy took in his sloppy jeans and baggy T-shirt with an anti-government slogan. He had a slight body, scraggly hair, and his face was unshaven, the dark whiskers making him look dangerous.

His apartment held very little other than a giant leather couch, big-screen TV, and a wall of computer equipment. Much like Addy would expect in the apartment of a computer geek who lived alone. Yahontov dropped onto the sofa next to a pricey laptop, the team remaining on their feet. Wouldn't do to let their guard down, not when they knew so little about this guy.

Kiley stepped over to the computer wall and took a long look at the equipment. "Sweet setup. What do you do for a living?"

Yahontov hesitated for a moment. "IT consulting."

"Specifically what kind of consulting?" she asked.

He waved a hand. "You wouldn't understand."

Addy watched Kiley intently, waiting for her to respond with a smart-aleck comment. She locked gazes with him. "Trust me, with a master's in IT, I would."

He swallowed, his Adam's apple bobbing in his scrawny neck. "You know. A little bit of everything, but mostly PHP and SQL stuff."

Kiley shared a skeptical look with Sean. They clearly recognized that the guy was being evasive, as he was making it pretty obvious.

"Do you know a man named Bruno Razo?" Mack asked.

Addy knew he was hoping the name would spark a response. And it did. The guy paled, which told them far more than words ever would.

Yahontov recovered and lifted his chin. "Nah. Should I?"

"We think you're *consulting* for him," Sean said.

Yahontov shook his head, then clasped his hands in his lap and chewed on his lip.

Kiley tapped his computer. "If we were to look at your hard drives, we wouldn't find any information on Razo, would we? Nothing about cutting internet cables in the ocean?"

Yahontov gulped. "No."

Mack, his expression tight and deadly, moved closer to Yahontov. "If you lie to us, and we find out, we'll not only charge you with anything illegal you're doing for Razo but add a charge for obstructing our investigation."

"Fine," he said, running his palms over his legs. "So I helped him find a few cables. If they were cut, it was all him."

"And which cables might those be?" Addy held her breath for the answer, as it could lead them straight to Razo.

Yahontov blinked a few times. Ran his gaze over the group. Shook his head. "I can't say. He'll kill me if I do."

"Might as well speak." Mack moved even closer to Yahontov. "We'll be taking you in and getting a warrant to search this place and review your computers. Means we're bound to find the information anyway. Why not make it easier for yourself?"

"I . . ." He sighed. "I can't talk. Just can't. So I guess that's what you'll have to do."

Sean took out his cuffs. "Stand up."

Instead of standing, Yahontov shoved his hand into his pocket and rolled off the sofa.

Addy drew her gun, as did the others. But he shot forward, reaching out to the computers, a large red key, not a gun, in his hand. He shoved the key into the USB port on the main computer.

"He's trying to erase data." Kiley jerked him away, put a knee in his back, and yanked out the key.

"Let me take a look." Sean rushed over to the computer and woke it up. "You caught it in time."

Mack cuffed Yahontov and hauled him to his feet. "Thanks for letting us know which machine to look at first. I personally would've started with the laptop."

Yahontov glared at Mack. "You have no idea who you're dealing with here. He's going to kill me just for talking to you. Putting me in jail guarantees that."

"A risk we're willing to take." Mack dragged Yahontov toward the door. "And if you're going to die anyway, you might consider telling us exactly what Razo is up to."

CHAPTER 16

ADDY WAS DISAPPOINTED that they came away from Yahontov's interview with so little information, and that Cam had imaged Yahontov's hard drives but the data was encrypted and would take time to crack. She flipped through the remaining surveillance photos, looking for anything to help find Zamora, her head pounding and begging her to take a break, but she wouldn't. Couldn't. Not yet. Three days to find the guns before they were deployed in the U.S. Not even three whole days anymore, as the hours were racing by and they'd passed the end of a normal workday. Not that they would quit working. They couldn't.

She closed her eyes to search her memories, to comb and sift through any fragments. Just like Dr. Galt told her to do. She didn't know if she'd remembered everything or if there were key elements she was forgetting. And if so, why? Dr. Galt had said since the hypnosis had worked so well that if there were any details missing, they might be connected to further trauma her brain simply didn't want to remember. There could be some trauma surrounding Zamora, she supposed. But what?

Bear trotted across the family room to join her, his eyes pleading with her. He wanted to sit on her lap again. If time wasn't of the essence, she would move to the sofa or a comfy chair and let him climb up. But time was their most valuable commodity right now, and she had to use every second wisely. She ruffled his neck and gave him a kiss.

"Bed." She pointed across the room.

Head hanging, he trudged back to his bed and curled up, his eyes remaining fixed on her.

Mack came down the stairs with a tray filled with spaghetti, green beans, and garlic bread, the pungent smell making her mouth water. He loved to cook and often did so to clear his head and make a plan. Kiley followed with another tray, this one holding dishes and utensils.

They set them on the far side of the table.

Cam stepped over to them, grabbed a plate, and started filling it with food. "I'm starved."

Mack raised an eyebrow. "You might want to leave a little for others."

"I did. I did." He took his plate over to the couch and somehow managed to balance it with his opened laptop.

"Do you sleep with that machine?" Addy asked.

"Sometimes." He grinned and then shoved the end of the crispy bread into his mouth.

Bear whined from his bed. He wasn't usually a whiner. Sure, he begged for food at times, but only with his eyes.

"Poor baby. He's out of sorts." She looked at the dog's pitiful face. "I wish I could comfort him, but we have no time."

"You have to make time to eat, though." Mack moved her folder aside and set a plate and silverware in front of her.

"I can eat while I review the photos."

"But you won't taste my magnificent meal."

"I promise I will." She loaded her plate and, after giving thanks for the food, dove into the spaghetti, twirling it up and taking a big bite. "Mmm, good. Thank you."

Mack just shook his head, and after Kiley got her food and sat at the table, he made a plate for himself and took the chair between them.

She chomped on the melt-in-your-mouth bread and took up a magnifying glass to study the next picture of Zamora. She ran it over every bit of the photo but paused at his wrist and racked her brain for recognition. Nothing came.

She slid the photo over to Mack. "Does that look like a birthmark on his wrist?"

Mack peered at the photo with the magnifying glass. "There's something there, but it could just be dirt or a bruise. Or even a tattoo."

"Yeah, and no amount of enhancing is going to make it clear enough." She sighed. "I'll keep looking."

She started flipping again, getting a good feel for the many hours she must've spent watching these men, only to come up short every time. She noted the locations of the photos. Outside Razo's big, expensive house. By Zamora's cheap apartment. Near the storefront of a Mexican grocery store. And in front of a massage parlor. She knew Razo wasn't connected to the businesses. Zamora either. Or any of the other thugs she'd identified in Razo's gang.

It appeared to be one of the coincidental places she found them talking. Like near the post office. A gym. A nail salon. That one made her laugh.

Mack lifted his head, a forkful of spaghetti in his hand. "What's so funny?"

She held out the picture. "Think they got manis and pedis?"

Mack rolled his eyes. "More likely waiting on girlfriends or wives. Are they married?"

"Razo is. Zamora not."

"Maybe we can get to them through these women," Sean suggested.

"I don't see how. I don't see anything in my surveillance that would indicate that they're involved in Razo's business. I remember Razo has two kids—grade school—and seems like his wife is just being a dutiful wife and mother. Active in her kids' school. Volunteers at their church."

"Church?" Mack's mouth dropped open. "Razo goes to church?"

"Nearly every Sunday from what I remember."

Mack shook his head. "That makes me want to haul him in even more. What about Zamora?"

"He's more of a party guy. Likes the ladies, and they seem to like him."

Sean took a drink of his water. "So we have one guy who's pretending to be upstanding, and the other who's embracing who he is."

"You could be right, and I don't see how those things will help us nab either one of them." She resisted sighing, as it would do her no good.

"Except that I sent the list of Zamora's known night-spot hangouts to Harris," Mack said, referencing a list they'd found earlier in Addy's files. "If she doesn't locate him before then, she's going to stake out these locations."

Kiley arched a dark eyebrow. "Does he party during the week?"

Addy swallowed her bite of beans. "Guess that's the thing with being an illegal gunrunner. You don't have to keep regular work hours and can go out every night."

Kiley set down her fork. "We're in the wrong line of work."

"Did we like to party?" Addy asked Mack, wanting to know more about their past.

He shook his head. "We were homebodies."

Addy had suspected they weren't big into socializing, as she didn't do much of it now either. She continued eating and flipping through the photos, pausing at one of the later ones.

"Zamora might not frequent nail salons, but he's starting to dress better." She showed Mack a picture of Zamora wearing a pricey Nike tracksuit, and something about the picture tugged at the back of her mind. "Before this, it was worn jeans and muscle shirts."

Mack took a long drink of his water. "You think Razo is suddenly cutting Zamora in on the profits?"

Addy dug deep in her memory bank for more information on the pair. There was something there. Just beyond her reach. But what?

Kiley picked up her bread. "Can you see anyone as brutal as Razo deciding to pay his flunkies more money?"

"Not really." Mack sat back. "So maybe Zamora is moon-lighting."

Kiley swallowed her bite. "You think Razo would allow that?"

"No, and if Zamora is up to something, Razo wouldn't approve of Zamora flashing his new wealth in front of him," Addy replied, still trying to think of what she might know about him that her brain didn't want her to call up. "So maybe he saved the money."

"That doesn't seem likely either." Mack tapped his finger on the pictures. "Maybe Razo wanted Zamora to dress better and gave Zamora hand-me-downs."

Kiley cleaned her fingers on her napkin. "Any other signs of money?"

"Let's see." Addy put down her fork and flipped through additional photos. She found one of Zamora wearing a big chunky gold necklace. She laid the photo in front of Mack and Kiley. "You mean like this?"

Mack let out a low whistle. "That had to cost a pretty penny."

Addy nodded, the necklace sparking even more attention in her brain. "Razo isn't in this set of pics, so maybe Zamora *is* moonlighting and he felt free to wear the gold without Razo around."

Mack stabbed his green beans with force. "The guy's a fool if he's doing anything to make Razo question him."

"I have to agree." She held Mack's gaze. "From what we're learning about Razo, he would sooner kill Zamora than let him explain."

———

Mack hauled all the dishes upstairs and brought down gooey chocolate-chip-and-hazelnut cookies that he'd warmed in the oven. The local office had supplied them with groceries and given them a basket of Oregon goodies that included the cookies. He watched Addy carefully as she took one and chewed as if not even realizing she was eating. Between bites, her expression was tight as she went through the photos. She moved forward but kept going back to the pictures with the necklace, pausing and chewing over it each time until the cookie was gone. She closed her eyes, placed her hands flat on the table, and began to take deep breaths and slowly exhale. She'd said Dr. Galt had told her if a memory was pressing in, to relax and let it flow. Maybe that was what she was doing.

Mack bit into the oozing chocolate and thought about the doctor. Mack believed the guy was capable. After all, one session and she'd remembered some very important details. But time was slipping away, faster than Mack would hope. Another day was almost gone and they hadn't gotten very far. If they were going to stop Razo from killing a large number of people, they needed more help.

Mack closed his eyes too. *If there's something she's trying to remember, please let her recall it. Please. We are bordering on desperate here and need your help.*

He should've asked for help long before this. Why did he wait until he felt out of control? If God was the center of Mack's life, he would've thought to call out before now. But the PTSD thing had put a wedge between them. A wedge Mack needed to eliminate.

I'm sorry. So sorry. Please forgive me. I should trust. All the time. In everything. Help me to do that too.

"This is it!" Addy shouted, bringing Mack's eyes open. "How could I not remember this?"

"Tell me." He scooted closer, his heart thumping with adrenaline.

She pushed the photo where Zamora wore the cross toward Mack.

He scanned the picture. "I don't see it. Is it the cross?"

She shook her head. "And that's where I was going wrong. I was focusing on the cross, not the person in the background."

Mack studied the photo. A woman with gleaming black hair and wearing a bright green knit top, jeans, and tall boots stood behind Zamora, a patronizing expression on her face as she looked at him. "Who is she?"

"Camila Baca. She's my informant. In fact, she texted me on the day of my accident asking to meet, but I never got back to her."

"Informant?" He looked up. "There's nothing in the files about her."

"I wanted to protect her identity. I didn't even have her information in my phone."

"How did you contact her?"

"By a prepaid phone. It's at my house. I kept it there so she couldn't be compromised."

Her desire to protect this woman was admirable but broke protocol. He locked gazes with her. "You didn't file a report and tell Harris about her?"

"Don't look at me like that." She narrowed her eyes.

"Like what?"

She crossed her arms. "Like you're judging me. Like I'm a bad agent. Don't tell me you've never kept your informants from your supervisor. Or if not that, then something else."

After Eisenhower closed the Montgomery Three case, Mack and the team had kept months of continued investigating from him. So yeah, Mack was guilty. "You're right. I have. So why did you hide Camila?"

Addy frowned. "She was so terrified of Razo that I promised not to tell anyone. It was the only way she would talk."

"How does she know Razo?"

"Actually, she knows Zamora. She's his jilted girlfriend."

Odd. "And she's still hanging around with him?"

Addy nodded. "She took up with another guy in Razo's gang. At first she wanted to get back at Zamora, but then when she heard about the miniguns, she couldn't live with knowing about them and doing nothing."

Mack leaned back and pondered the information. Something seemed off to him. "Unusual to have a gang member, or in this case a gang girlfriend, with a conscience."

Addy nodded and fell silent.

Mack was stunned. Not over the secret but over the memory loss—forgetting an informant was a big deal. Something he thought she would have recalled when she remembered so many other details in hypnosis. "Any idea why you didn't remember her at first?"

Addy pursed her lips. "Dr. Galt said my brain might be refusing to remember things if there was any trauma around the situation. The last time I talked to Camila, Razo almost caught us talking. I got away in time, but it scared me nearly to death. Please, let's not tell Harris."

He never wanted to disappoint Addy, yet he had no choice. It was protocol. "I have to, Addy. You know that."

Addy sighed. "Then let me talk to Camila first. Make sure she's all right."

No way he was going to let Addy venture out to an area where Razo frequented. "I can't let you do that."

"I appreciate your concern, but I can make my own decisions." She lifted her chin.

She'd always been headstrong, and he loved that about her. But in this case, it went against everything he needed to do to keep her safe. "I can't agree to it. It's just too dangerous."

She clasped her hands together on the table. "I have to do it. Camila could know where Zamora might be hanging out. And if she does, it could blow this investigation wide open, and we could confiscate the guns. Save lives."

Her this-is-not-negotiable look tightened her face. There would be no stopping her from going. Could he let her meet Camila? Maybe. With proper planning.

"If I agree to this . . ." He paused and held up his hands. "And I'm saying *if*, then I'm coming with you."

She narrowed her eyes, determination beaming at him. "Only if Camila agrees to it."

"No." He shook his head. "I *will* be with you, so make sure you get her to agree."

"I have to get the phone before we can do anything."

Another nonstarter with him. "I'll do that. Just tell me where to find it."

"It's in my dresser. The top drawer on the right."

Her dresser. Where she also kept her personal things. Maybe she didn't want him to look through it. "I can have Kiley get the phone."

"Kiley?"

"Figured you wouldn't want me going through your things."

She tilted her head. "Actually, since we're married, I think I'd prefer you going through my things rather than a stranger."

"Kiley's not a—"

"Stranger? Not to you, but at the moment she is to me. And at least I know I shared a life with you."

"Right. Okay. Also, if you'd make a list of items you want from there—like clothes and stuff—I can get that too."

"Thanks. I'd love to have clean clothes and not wash out my things every night." She grabbed a paper and pen and jotted down a list. He watched, and she was very detailed on where he would find each item.

She slid it over to him. "Thanks for offering. But please be careful. Razo or one of his goons could be watching the house."

She got out her phone and dreaded the call to Harris, but Addy tapped her supervisor's icon and took a cleansing breath.

"Leigh," she answered. "You better not be calling about the investigation."

Addy's dread intensified. "Sort of. I went to hypnosis, and I remembered the investigation and my accident."

"Great. Wonderful even. So why do you sound like you lost your best friend?"

"There's something else I need to tell you." She explained about Camila, sticking to the facts and making it short.

Harris drew in a sharp noisy breath. "That's not good, Leigh."

"I know. I shouldn't have done it, and I'm prepared to accept the consequences. Camila won't talk to anyone else, so please, if you're going to suspend me, don't do it now. Not yet anyway. And don't say I can't meet with her because I'm on leave."

"I'll hold off on weighing in until I can process the information." Harris let the call go silent. "I'm not even going to pretend you're not working anymore. You need to talk to this girl, and if I get any flak, I'll deal with it."

CHAPTER 17

TENSION SURROUNDED MACK as he drove the SUV, Addy sitting rigidly beside him in the passenger seat. Sean and Kiley had gone ahead in their own vehicle to set up surveillance for the meeting with Camila on the east side of Portland, and Addy was wired for sound and video. Camila had agreed to let Mack join the meeting, and nothing would stop him from being right by Addy's side.

He glanced at her. She sat rigidly and peered out the window. His nerves might be taut, but he didn't like seeing her so anxious.

"Tell me about Camila," he said to cut the tension.

She looked at him. "She started dating Zamora at sixteen and reluctantly became part of Razo's gang. He brought her in at a slow pace. Regular dates. Compliments. Gifts. It was six months before he asked for a favor."

Mack nodded. "The guys in gangs are paranoid. They think their girlfriends will set them up."

"Exactly. He was building trust. And when he thought he could trust her, he asked her to take messages for him. Then to help cut drugs. She was in love with him by this point, so she agreed."

"A pretty typical process." Mack shook his head. "Maybe not the age difference, though."

"Yeah, twelve years is a lot. I was surprised when she told me that."

Mist started falling, coating the windshield. Mack turned on the wipers. "Let me guess. She started carrying more packages for him. Drugs and weapons."

"Right," Addy said, the single word laced with revulsion. "Until she got pregnant. He didn't want a kid so he told her to get rid of it. She said no. He punched her in the abdomen, and she miscarried. He dropped her. That's when she started to hate him, but she couldn't get out because she knew too much. So she hooked up with another guy in the gang."

"And plotted to take Zamora down." Mack glanced at Addy. "The hookup with another gang member is par for the course, but planning to take down the ex? Haven't seen that before."

"I have to give her credit for finally standing up for herself. Especially when it's so dangerous."

"How did she find you?"

"She went to the sheriff's office and asked to speak to a female deputy. She'd only talk to a female. Figured they would better understand her plight. This was at the same time they'd contacted our office on Razo. So they passed her name on to me."

"And now here we are, going to meet her."

"The good thing is she hates Zamora so much that she'll tell us where to find him. We could have him in custody within the hour."

"Yeah, that's the good news." He thought ahead to the meeting and then to taking Zamora into custody and of everything that could go wrong. "You know the protocol for our meet-up. I want you to keep that in mind, and you know the code if you need help."

"Bear with me," she said, repeating a phrase they chose for agents needing help. Using Bear's name made it easier to remember the phrase in a time of stress.

"You know Camila. I don't." At a red light, he looked at Addy and held her gaze. "You might pick up on something in her behavior, speech, whatever, that I don't see. So don't be afraid to use it, even if I'm right beside you."

"I got it, Mack." She pressed her hand over his on the gearshift. "Don't worry so much."

"I can't help it. I love you and don't want to see anything bad happen to you."

She removed her hand.

"Sorry. I know that's not something you want to hear."

She let out a slow breath. "Think of it from my point of a view. A virtual stranger tells you he loves you. It's a little unsettling."

"I imagine it is," he said and let the conversation drop for two reasons. One, he didn't need another reminder that she didn't know or love him. He'd had enough of those in the last few days. And two, he didn't want to distract them from the upcoming op.

He focused on the road as he got them going again, driving over the wet city streets. As they approached their rendezvous spot, he checked in with Sean. "Everything quiet on your end?"

"Affirmative." His deep confident voice coming over the comms unit should bring Mack comfort, only he was too jazzed to settle down. "Contact hasn't shown yet."

"Let me know if she does before we get there." He ended the conversation.

Addy shifted in her seat, adjusting her Kevlar vest under her jacket. "I hope Camila doesn't notice this and get freaked out."

He cast her a shocked look. "You didn't wear a vest on your other meet-ups with her?"

She shook her head. "We met at a coffee shop that she thought Razo never frequented."

"Guns can come out at a coffee shop too. No matter how well-lit and crowded. Especially when you're talking about gang members."

"You're right." She averted her eyes. "I should've taken precautions, and would have after the last meeting when he almost caught us."

Mack had made her feel bad when that was the last thing he wanted to do right now. "Sorry. You don't need me quarterbacking one of your ops."

"I appreciate your saying that." She gathered her jacket around her and crossed her arms over it.

He cringed. They sounded like strangers. Total strangers. How could that be when he knew so much about this woman? What was it going to take to get beyond this?

He made the last turn onto a dark street with rows of older two-story apartment buildings. They were meeting behind the three hundred building. Mack had scoped it out online, and Sean and Kiley had done recon before Mack even agreed to the meeting. It was an open space, which was both good and bad. Good in that he could see anyone coming. Bad in that it allowed easy access to them. Still, it also allowed Sean and Kiley to have clear eyes on the meeting.

Mack parked in a visitor lot and contacted Sean. "We're here. Getting ready to move to the location."

"No sign of contact," Sean said.

"She could be inside one of the buildings watching for us."

"True that."

"We'll do sound checks now." Mack muted his mic and looked at Addy. "Go ahead."

"Testing," she said. "Testing."

"Got you loud and clear," Kiley replied.

"Then we're a go." Mack kept his focus on Addy. "Anything happens out of the ordinary, just the slightest little thing, we bail. No questions asked."

"Got it," she said, but didn't sound like her heart was in it.

He understood. He desperately wanted to bring in Zamora too, but not at the expense of their lives.

———

A sharp, biting wind mixed with cold drizzle hit Addy when she stepped out of the vehicle. She lifted her hood but resisted bending her head from the rain as they moved through dark shadows to the back of the building. She had to stay alert and watch for danger.

She glanced around the end of the building into an open area with a small playground, a rusty swing squeaking in the wind. A faraway streetlight cast a weak glow over the area, leaving most of it shadowed. The darkness allowed Sean and Kiley to take cover, but it also allowed other people to do the same thing, raising Addy's concern.

"Keep your eyes peeled," Mack said as they swung around the end of the building. But he didn't need to issue any warnings as Addy was scanning the area before he got the words out.

A person crept out from one of the apartments down the way. Addy instinctually went for her gun until the person's identity became clear. Then she let out a breath and waited for Camila to join them. "You live here?"

She shook her head, her eyes locked on Mack. "My friend does. One that Razo and Zamora don't know."

Mack stepped forward, and Camila backed up. She'd developed real trust issues with older men.

Addy smiled at her to help ease her nerves. "Thanks for meeting me and letting Mack come with me."

She gave Mack a wary look. "Only agreed because you're married and you vouched for him." She turned back to Addy. "Almost didn't come 'cause you didn't respond to my earlier text."

"I would have if I wasn't in that accident and lost my memory."

"So you said on the phone."

"Don't you believe me?"

"Yeah, sure." Camila narrowed her eyes. "So, what do you want?"

That was Camila. Direct and to the point. "I need to talk to Zamora, but he's gone into hiding."

"What's he done?"

Addy debated telling her, but if Camila heard he'd threatened Addy's mother and nurse and drugged Addy, she thought

Camila would be more forthcoming. She decided to share the story in detail.

Camila's eyes tightened in rage. "He's gone too far this time. Your poor mom."

"Can you tell me where he is, then?" Addy asked, hoping she wasn't being too pushy and sent Camila running.

"Yeah, sure." She rattled off an address in Hillsboro. "It's his new girlfriend's place. He's holed up there and doesn't leave for anything. Sends the girl to do all his dirty work. Too big of a baby. Afraid he's gonna get collared."

"Odd that the police didn't check her place out," Mack said.

"They probably don't know about Mariana. When I say new, I mean *new*. As in a few days. At least it's only been that long since he's been bringing her around. She's just a kid like I was. Parents are dead. She lives with her older sister now, who doesn't care about what Mariana does."

"Thanks for the information." Addy smiled at Camila again.

Camila looked around and stepped closer. "There's something else. The reason I asked to meet you before."

"What is it?" Addy held her breath, awaiting the information.

"The guns. Razo is keeping two for himself and selling the other three to a sovereign-citizen group."

"Sovereign citizen?" Addy's heart fell, and she tried to run everything she knew about these groups through her brain. Basically the members believed anything U.S. government-related was illegitimate, and they rejected all federal laws. Not something Razo ever championed. "How did he hook up with them?"

"Dark web. He's keeping it on the down-low, but I overheard his latest girlfriend talking about it to a friend."

"Girlfriend?" Addy stared at Camila. "But he's married."

"Doesn't stop him from messing around." Camila pulled her collar up, acting as if she wanted to disappear behind it. "He often goes by BloodyFox as a screen name."

"Appropriate name," Mack said.

Camila grimaced. "Look, that's all I got. I gotta go."

"Before you do, is there anything I can do for you?" Addy asked.

"For me?" She gave Addy an incredulous stare. "Yeah. Arrest the creep. Make sure he doesn't know I ratted on him and put him away for a long time. And while you're at it, do the same for Zamora."

She turned and walked away, disappearing into the shadows. Addy watched her go, wishing she could do more for the young woman. To help her get out of the gang. Addy had offered to help before, but the only way that was possible was if Camila left the area, and she didn't want to move away from her family.

Mack took Addy's arm. "Let's move."

He led her back to the car. The moment she sat, she got out her phone, opened a maps app, and entered the address Camila provided. Mack climbed in and peered at her. "You had no idea about the sovereign-citizen connection?"

She shook her head. "But it raises our investigation to a whole new level. We have to assume, with their hatred of all things federal government, that the miniguns will be used on a federal target. The guns could be staying in Oregon or going anywhere in the country. The targets are endless. With three of the guns in the hands of the sovereign citizens, so many lives could be lost."

Mack grimaced. "Makes me think of the Oklahoma City bombing of the federal building. Not the method, but that what happened in Oklahoma was in retaliation for the ATF and FBI's handling of Ruby Ridge and the Waco siege."

Her mind raced over the details. "Maybe the guns are staying in Oregon and this is retaliation for the way the occupation of the Malheur National Wildlife Refuge was handled here."

"Could be. I'll have Cam make a list of all federal targets in the state."

Her stomach knotted. "Our office could be one of them. Razo could be looking to pay me back for investigating him and make it seem like a sovereign citizen did it."

"I could see him thinking that way."

"Other than our office, I think the most likely target is the Edith Green–Wendell Wyatt Federal Building in Portland. It's like eighteen stories, and I think its offices include around twelve hundred federal employees in over sixteen agencies. A shooter could take out a lot of people at this location."

"I'll have Cam research the security there."

"And I need to let Harris know. Plus we have to get the word out in case we don't stop the guns from coming across the border."

"We aren't going to fail," Mack stated. "And I'll let Eisenhower decide who should be notified. Agreed?"

She nodded, and he got his phone out.

Addy's phone rang, and Harris's name displayed on the screen. Addy answered it.

"Got a call from Palmere," Harris said in her no-nonsense tone. "They recovered casings from the hospital parking garage and lifted Zamora's prints from them and also the garage railing."

Addy sat up straight. "He was the hospital shooter?"

"Looks like it," Harris said. "Tell me you got info on his whereabouts."

"Just did. He's holed up with a new girlfriend. We're headed there now."

"You'll need the arrest warrant to serve him. I can get that from Palmere, but if Zamora's at a girlfriend's place, she'll likely come to the door and refuse entry. I suggest you get a search warrant too."

Addy agreed. The law required if they needed to enter the residence of a third party where the resident refused entry and where the suspect didn't live, they also had to obtain a search warrant. To do that they had to establish probable cause that Zamora was at the specified location and that it was necessary to seize him in the interest of justice. They could easily produce that information, and it would be good to get it in case they needed it so they didn't have to walk away from the house without Zamora in handcuffs.

Addy cupped her hand over the phone. "Harris wants to know about a search warrant."

Mack held up his phone. "Was just about to run it through Eisenhower. He'll have a better chance of turning one around fast."

Addy relayed the information to Harris.

"Let me know if it falls through," Harris said. "I have a judge on speed dial who'll come through for us."

"Will do." Addy took a long breath. "You should also know that Camila told us Razo is keeping two of the guns and selling the others to a sovereign-citizen group."

"Seriously?" Harris went silent. "That's a whole other ball game. Our office could be a target for all I know."

Addy didn't think she could respond to that without getting emotional. Since Harris always reminded Addy to remain impartial in her job, Addy moved on. "Mack is informing Eisenhower now. I assumed you'd want to coordinate with him on how we should proceed."

"Will do as soon as we get off the phone."

"Let me know what you decide." Addy was ready to end the call, breathing easy because Harris didn't ask about Camila.

"You can be sure we'll talk about the informant once Zamora's in custody." Harris disconnected.

Mack was still talking as panic started to form in Addy's gut. Her friends and co-workers could be targets of this very deadly gun. She could be a target. Her heart started pounding, her breath shallow.

No. Stop. Keep busy.

She tapped the map program again and continued to look at the various views of their target house as Mack relayed the pertinent details for the search warrant to Eisenhower.

When he finished his call, he looked at her. "You okay?"

"Not really."

"Worried about the new threat?"

"Terrified actually."

"Yeah, this really brings home the danger of a minigun."

"How are we going to stop him? Just how? We only have a couple of days to find him and the guns. What if we fail?"

"The RED team doesn't fail." Mack took her hand and held it tight. The warmth seeped into her, and only a tiny bit of her anxiety vanished. For despite his comment, the team *had* failed in the Montgomery Three Investigation, so they weren't as infallible as Mack liked to think.

"We just have to keep our focus," he added.

She swallowed hard and nodded, taking another beat to re-member she was an agent. A professional. She'd faced danger-ous situations before and could keep calm. She had to remain in control. Lives depended on her.

She squeezed Mack's hand and freed hers. "What did Eisen-hower say?"

"He's hoping Zamora will roll on Razo, and we'll have the information we need to locate the guns, ending the federal threat. I'll call him back after it all goes down."

"Sounds like a good plan." She showed Mack the map on her phone. "Where Zamora is holed up. It's an area known for drugs, and deals frequently go down in a nearby park."

She switched to street view to show him a small square box of a house surrounded by tall weeds, on a large lot at the edge of the city.

"We need to get together with Sean and Kiley to make a plan. But first I'll have Cam get better images of the property and the area." He made the call to Cam. "I need you to drop whatever you're doing and get me surveillance images for the house where we'll be making an arrest."

He explained about Zamora and about the latest news on the sovereign citizens. "Then make a list of federal targets in Oregon. It's not like Razo or the sovereign citizens can go into a federal building carrying a minigun. They'd need to plan to get something like that inside the building. Find the target with the lowest security threshold where they could inflict the most damage. And I want a list of sovereign-citizen members in Oregon who've been active and might have the kind of cash to buy these guns. If you don't find anyone here, then branch out to surrounding states."

Cam must have agreed, as Mack ended the call.

"I was thinking," she said. "How is Razo going to keep using the gun and not get arrested? It's not like anyone else has one, so if he uses it, he's implicating himself."

"He must have some plan to keep it quiet or have one of his gang members do the work for him. Still, he'd need a secure location to store the gun so it doesn't tie back to him."

She thought about the situation as Mack called Kiley and Sean to ask them to meet up at the parking lot of a nearby grocery store. Her mind was still on the gun while they reviewed the images Cam sent and formed a solid plan. They'd received both warrants and printed the documents on a portable printer kept in the RED team's supplies. She was coming to see that they were prepared for most everything, and she was wishing she was still on the team.

Mack pushed off the front of the SUV where he'd been leaning. "Once we reach the property and conclude our surveillance, I'll call the locals so they know we're going in."

Neighbors often called the police when an op was going down, so it was typical procedure to let them know about a bust. But the federal team didn't want to make the call too soon or the locals would ask to be in on the arrest, and that could produce unnecessary friction.

Mack ran his gaze over them. "We good to go?"

"Couldn't be better," Addy said. She was pumped about being able to personally slap handcuffs on the man who'd drugged her and could've killed her. Not to mention terrifying her mother and Nancy.

They climbed into their respective SUVs. Kiley and Sean would cover the alley in back, and Addy would accompany Mack to the front. There was no way Zamora could skate on them.

Mack slowly drove down the treelined street and pulled over to the curb three houses down. She grabbed his binoculars and lifted them to take a careful look at the house. Light spilled out of the front window and a window near the back.

"Wish we had a layout of this place," she said. "He could be in the front or back."

"Doesn't really matter." Mack killed the engine. "Once we announce ourselves, he'll most likely try to squirt out the back."

She glanced at him. "Which is why you want me at the front. You want the guy running away from me, not toward me."

"Exactly."

She handed him the binoculars. "And you're giving up the chance to take him down because you want to be by my side."

"See. You *do* know me." He chuckled and raised the binoculars.

She looked at his strong profile and wished she did actually know him. She liked what she'd come to know, and she was starting to believe he deserved to be loved by a woman as intensely as he seemed to love her. She hoped she'd been that woman for him once, but could she be again?

He lowered his binoculars and pressed his mic. "Report."

"All quiet in the back. A woman is moving around in the back bedroom. Not sure if it's the sister or girlfriend."

"Then be cautious if someone comes running out the back," Mack said. "Could be her."

"Roger that," Kiley replied, her voice jazzed. "We're good to go."

"Then let's move." Mack dropped his binoculars and opened his door.

Addy had discarded her jacket for better access to her weapon, and the cold sent a deep shiver over her body. She ignored it and marched behind Mack up to the door with black chipping paint.

Mack pounded hard. "Police. Mariana Morales. We need to speak to you."

They'd agreed to call her out instead of Zamora, so he didn't come to the door, guns blazing.

Addy heard footsteps and saw movement through the front blinds. Two shadows. One large and burly. One small.

"Just a minute," a female voice responded. "I need to put some clothes on."

Footfalls headed away from the door.

Addy pressed her mic. "Be alert. Looks like suspect's fleeing toward the back."

"Roger that," Sean replied.

Addy heard a commotion on the other side of the door, followed by silence. She wished they could just break down the door and go in, but their warrant didn't allow it.

Finally, footsteps approached again. Addy and Mack both went for their weapons.

The door opened. A pretty young girl with ebony hair that fell in waves below her shoulders stood in jeans and a T-shirt. Her hair was perfectly combed, so she likely was already dressed when they knocked and was giving Zamora a chance to escape.

"You Mariana Morales?" Addy asked.

She nodded.

"We know Dante Zamora is in the house. We have a warrant for his arrest. Please step aside so we can arrest him."

"This is my place and you're not coming in." She took a defensive stance.

Mack handed her the search warrant. "We have a warrant to search the premises. I need you to stand aside."

"Male fitting Zamora's description is exiting the back," Sean said over the comms unit. "Moving in to take him down."

Addy made sure not to show her excitement over the possible arrest and waited for Mariana to move out of the way. When she did, Addy bolted past her to go after Zamora.

"Addy, wait," Mack called out.

She felt bad. She'd left him in a precarious position. He needed to remain with Mariana to arrest her for refusing to let them in and watch the front door when Addy knew he wanted her to be out of danger. But she had to go. Had to take this creep down if she could. Make him pay. Her mother deserved that. *She* deserved that.

"Coming out after him," she said into her mic as she reached the back door.

To her surprise, Zamora stopped, then turned and raced in her direction. He wasn't armed. He was barely dressed. Just sweatpants. No shoes. No shirt.

"Police! Stop!" she shouted.

He lowered his head like a charging bull and came straight for her. At the last moment, she dodged him, and he went barreling into the house, slamming headfirst into a wall.

She pivoted and got her gun on him. When he rolled, he looked like he was going to try to get up and run.

She stood over him with her gun and glared at him. "Don't add resisting arrest to your charges."

"Behind you," Kiley said, and Addy heard two sets of footsteps enter the house.

"Good collar," Sean said. "Mack will want to be in on this. I'll go spell him."

Sean brushed past her.

"Cover me, Kiley." Addy holstered her weapon and returned Zamora's glare. "On your belly. Now."

Zamora tightened his eyes and lay lifeless.

"Really?" she asked. "You really want to argue when there are four federal agents here?"

Mack charged into the room and gave Zamora a look that would make Addy quake in her shoes.

Zamora groaned and rolled over.

She grabbed his hands and slapped on the cuffs.

"I didn't do nothing wrong," he muttered.

"That will be up to a DA and jury to decide." Addy stood and looked down at him, satisfaction curling through her body. She couldn't wait for the day when this guy stood before a judge and she got justice for the terror inflicted on her mother and Nancy.

CHAPTER 18

MACK TOOK A SEAT IN THE CHAIR across from Zamora in the Mult-nomah County Detention Center. The man glared at Mack and crossed beefy arms over a powerful chest. He was a big guy with bushy black eyebrows that drew together when he frowned. Wavy hair cascaded down to his shoulders, and his dark eyes looked combative.

Mack wanted to say, *Bring it on, I got this*, but the guy had an air of contempt that gave Mack a moment's pause. Mack was surprised Zamora hadn't called the attorney who represented Razo's gang members. Seemed like Zamora would do that right off the bat, but he didn't even hint at it. Not that Mack was complaining. Not at all.

He shifted on the hard chair, and a stabbing pain raced up his injured leg. He had to work hard not to suck in a breath and reveal the pain that had worsened during the arrest. He changed his position again, hoping to find a more comfortable spot, moving as subtly as possible.

Addy was watching through the one-way glass, and he didn't want her to feel bad about his injury or worry about him. He wished she wasn't even watching. After the shooting, he hadn't wanted to bring her to the detention center, but Harris agreed that Addy could observe the interview, and there was no stopping her. He recognized that from the moment Addy fixed her determined gaze on him.

Plus with Zamora in custody, Mack didn't have a reason to

keep her away. Sure, Razo was still free, but it would take him time to get another one of his henchmen in position to cause Addy any harm. And as she'd said, if she wasn't safe from Razo and his men inside the interview area of a secured jail with deputies all around, where was she safe?

He couldn't argue. Even as much as he wanted to.

The door opened, and Harris entered. They'd decided Mack would be the tough guy, and she would go easier on Zamora. Between the two of them, they hoped to get him to roll over on Razo.

Harris sat next to Mack, laid a pen and notepad on the table, then tapped the play button on the video recorder. "I'm Gala Harris, Special Agent in Charge of ICE's Portland office. And I'm joined by Deputy Mack Jordan with the Marshals Service, questioning Dante Zamora."

She added the date and leaned forward. "You are under arrest for attempted murder, two counts, and kidnapping, Mr. Zamora." She read Zamora his Miranda rights. "Do you understand the charges and your rights?"

Mack didn't know how she could call this creep "Mr." In Mack's Southern upbringing, the word was a sign of respect, and there was no way he respected Zamora.

The guy crossed his arms and gave Harris a snarky smile. Mack noted the birthmark on his wrist, cementing in Mack's mind that the guy had been the knife wielder in the video.

"I understand," he said. "But I didn't try to kill or kidnap no one."

"See, here's the thing." Mack planted his hands on the stainless-steel table. "We have the casings from the hospital shooting with your prints all over them. Plus the slugs. Our top-notch forensic staff is processing it all right now, and we'll have your DNA and prints from every touchpoint. And they've lifted your prints from the railing where you took your stand. It's all enough to put you away for a very long time."

Mack paused and waited for Zamora to speak. He slumped back in his chair and clamped his mouth shut.

"And we have your DNA from Agent Leigh's house, and prints from there and her car," Mack added, this time taking the guy by surprise. "So you're looking at multiple counts of attempted murder and two counts of kidnapping. Without your cooperation, you have no hope of getting out of prison until you're an old man."

"I . . ." He closed his mouth and stared at them. "I want to see my lawyer."

Having this creep lawyer up frustrated Mack beyond words, and he wanted to lay into the guy. How he wanted to. Desperately. He fisted his hands on his knees instead.

"We'll make that call, Mr. Zamora, but just know, telling the truth about everything will go a long way in reducing your sentence." Harris's tone was softer, kinder. "We know you committed these crimes for someone else. If you cooperate, I can tell the DA about your assistance and recommend a lighter sentence."

Zamora crossed his arms again, the tattoos vivid and gaudy. "I ain't no snitch."

"Don't think of this as snitching as much as you saving your own neck," Mack suggested.

Zamora shook his head. "Just the opposite will happen. This guy runs with the big dogs, and he'll have me killed."

"You mean Razo," Harris stated.

"Nah. He don't know nothing about this," Zamora said with a vehemence that Mack believed. "And I aim to keep it that way or he'll want to take me out as well."

———

Addy's mouth fell open, and she suspected Mack and Harris felt the same way. If Zamora was telling the truth, this was a shocker. A big, honking, crazy shocker. If Razo wasn't the force behind Zamora, who was? And why did this person want her dead?

Mack shoved his chair back from the table. "Think about it, man. We'll only go to bat for you if you come clean, and soon."

Mack spun and limped out of the room. The door opened, and Mack walked in, favoring his injured leg. "Do you believe Zamora?"

"You should get off that leg." Addy tapped the chair.

He complied, his lack of protest telling her he was in more pain than she first suspected. She wouldn't comment, though, or he might go back to being the strong, invincible guy, working hard to hide his pain. No point in putting him through that.

She took the chair next to him. "Seems like he's telling the truth."

"My gut says the same thing. He's working for someone in addition to Razo, and that someone is the person who wants you dead." Mack moved his leg again, and she wished she'd been allowed to bring her purse in so she could give him some Tylenol. "Probably the reason he didn't lawyer up right away too. If he's two-timing Razo, he couldn't call Razo for the gang's attorney, and Zamora wouldn't implicate this other guy who scares him so much. But who is he?"

"I have no idea." She searched her brain and came up blank. Did she know this boss's identity but couldn't remember? She couldn't be the reason that these guns came into the country and countless people were murdered. They had to figure this out, and there was little time left to do it.

A tinge of panic raced through her, her heart starting to beat faster. She swallowed it down and forced herself to clear her mind. "The only reason I can see Zamora two-timing Razo is if he's profiting big-time."

"The pricey clothes Zamora was wearing in your photos sure suggest he has money." Mack lifted his injured leg over the other one, acting casual. Not his expression. That told

196 | HOURS TO KILL

another story. He was feeling the same pressure she was. "You think someone is trying to take over Razo's business, and they convinced Zamora to help?"

She shrugged and wished she knew. How she wished she knew. Or could remember if she *did* know.

Harris entered the room, her hand sliding through her blunt-cut hair. "I thought I was going to get him to flip. Then he goes and lawyers up, even before we can ask about the miniguns."

Addy nodded and faced Mack. "I don't remember thinking there was another person in the picture, but we need to get to the safe house pronto. I can go back through my files. Maybe I have a lead on this guy Zamora's protecting."

Harris lowered her hand. "I'll let Zamora stew for a while. Once his lawyer arrives, I'll take another crack at him on this mystery person. I'll also impress on him that he can go away for life as an accessory to the deaths of countless federal workers if he keeps quiet about the miniguns."

"If that doesn't get him to talk, I don't know what will," Addy said.

Harris nodded, but she looked more worried than Addy had ever seen her. "Keep me informed of your progress."

She exited the room, her steps crisp and quick.

"She's worried big-time," Addy said.

"Yeah, I guess we all are." Mack stood, grimacing as he walked to the door. He held his hand out. "After you."

They made their way down the hall to the security area, where the guard released their phones and weapons. Sean and Kiley were waiting in the lobby and got to their feet. Addy studied them for a moment, willing herself to remember anything about them, yet she only got a sense of goodness and friendship. Maybe that was enough for now. At least it seemed like that was all God wanted her to know.

She expected them to ask questions, but instead they remained silent. A uniformed deputy escorted them to a side entrance, where Sean and Kiley exited first. Mack held Addy back at the door until Sean gave the all-clear. She hustled to yet a different vehicle, this one a white ten-passenger van. The transport was becoming familiar to Addy. Sean driving. Kiley shotgun. Mack in the next seat. Her beside him.

He looked at her. "I'd like you to get down until we're sure we're not followed."

With Zamora in custody, Addy thought it was overkill, but no point in arguing and stressing Mack out more. She dropped to the floor.

"We're good," Mack said. "Let's get moving."

Sean got the vehicle going, and Mack recapped the interview for him and Kiley.

Mack shifted his attention to Addy. "Something's been nagging at me."

"What's that?" she asked, uneasy now.

"Zamora being at the hospital entrance we chose. How did he know we'd use that entrance? I can't believe it was one of those 'in the right place at the right time' kind of things. Especially since logistically that would be the least likely place for you to leave."

"You're right. It couldn't be a coincidence, could it?" She met Mack's gaze. "How did he know?"

Mack's eyes narrowed. "I would suggest maybe a bug on your phone, but your phone is new."

"What about a GPS tracker of some sort," Sean suggested. "But where? It's not like we're using your car. Or even the same vehicle twice."

Kiley swiveled to look over the seat. "So where could he have planted a tracker? And if he did plant one, why wait until today to take the shot?"

Addy took a moment to think. "The only item that's been with me all this time is my purse."

"Yeah, yeah." Excitement burned through Kiley's voice. "He could've put something in it when you crashed."

"Only one way to find out." Addy lifted the strap of her cross-body bag off her shoulder and started unloading items one at a time onto the seat by Mack. He was getting a firsthand look at the things she considered important enough to carry every day, but if he had an opinion on the items, he didn't comment. She pulled out the last thing, a can of pepper spray.

"Nothing so far." She ran her fingers over the bag's lining, then went through each compartment again and came up empty-handed. She was both glad not to find anything and disappointed as they needed to figure out how Zamora had discovered her location. She started putting the items back into the bag. "Nothing."

"Okay, so not your purse." Mack tapped his finger on his knee. "Who in your office knew about the hospital transport plan?"

She paused with compact in hand and eyed him. "You're thinking one of my fellow agents ratted me out?"

"Not on purpose," he said. "But somehow the person let it slip."

"But to who and where? It's not like the people in my office have contact with Zamora or his associates."

Mack locked gazes with her. "Since we don't know who Zamora is protecting, it's possible they had contact with this person."

"I suppose," she admitted, but wished she didn't have to. "As far as I know, only Warren and Harris had any information."

Mack worked the muscles in his jaw, his finger tapping faster on his knee. "And you trust this Warren guy?"

She firmed her shoulders and made sure she sounded resolute. "Absolutely. Fully."

Apparently, her tone left the others in contemplation as they fell silent and no one spoke for the remainder of the drive. At the safe house, she went straight to the basement, the others trailing after her.

Cam looked up from the same position on the sofa, his lap-top still on his knees. Bear was curled up in his bed. He shot to his feet and bounded over to the steps. Addy scratched under his chin, and he rewarded her with a contented look. She knew he'd been picking up on all the tension, and she felt bad for him. His days as a police dog left him ultrasensitive, and her goal had always been to give him a happy and contented life in his senior years.

She went straight to her files—she had no time to waste—and when Bear followed her, she let him rest his head in her lap.

Cam looked at them, his expression bright and cheerful. "Glad you guys are back."

"You find something on the federal targets?" Mack went to the small refrigerator and grabbed a can of Red Bull.

"Not yet." Cam closed his laptop and rested his hands on it. "But Fitz just called me. He finished reviewing the office security video, and the cleaning people were at the ICE office on the night of the hack."

Sean dropped down next to Cam. "You think one of the cleaning crew deleted Addy's files?"

Cam scratched his neck. "I think it's worth looking into."

"But they all would have been thoroughly vetted before being allowed to work in our office," Addy said, still stroking Bear. "I mean thoroughly."

"People change." Mack popped open his Red Bull. "Any-one can suddenly have financial issues and be susceptible to a bribe."

"Or maybe one of the crew used a bogus ID," Kiley sug-gested.

Addy looked at Kiley. "You mean like the guy Zamora is protecting hired someone just to hack our network?"

"Exactly," Kiley said.

Addy liked this thought a whole lot better than thinking one of her fellow agents had performed the hack. "Then we need to delve into backgrounds on the crew members on duty that night. Also take a look at the owners of the company and their connections."

"Already ahead of you on that." Cam grinned, his cocky little smirk so familiar to Addy, though she had no concrete memories of it. "Fitz gave me the workers' and owners' names, and I'm writing an algorithm to search for their backgrounds. He also said Harris will request personnel files from the cleaning company and will forward them the moment she receives them."

"Espionage at our office." Addy shook her head, and Bear's head popped up, his eyes seeking the cause for the new anxiety in the room. "This is all just too unbelievable."

Cam's expression sobered, his look very severe for the happy-go-lucky guy. "You might have to believe it. It's looking very much like someone infiltrated your office. And prepare yourself. We may have only found the tip of the iceberg on the damage they've done."

CHAPTER 19

ADDY HAD REVIEWED her files again while Mack planned transport to her office so she could determine if her desk had been compromised. Even with the time pressure mounting, she didn't find any hint of another boss. Now as she sat in the worn chair that had seen years of use, she was hoping a search of her desk would give them another lead.

The small office was low on the priority list for new equipment and supplies, which also meant they didn't have advanced security measures. Not that they could've stopped anyone on a cleaning crew by enhancing their security system, but they might've had interior cameras to record their actions. They didn't, and she had no time to waste on thinking about what could've been.

She opened a file drawer, and her gloved fingers were clumsy as they thumbed through the folders. She didn't note anything odd or missing so she moved on to other drawers and then her desktop files. Everything looked exactly as she'd left it. Although her desk was free from dust and any crumbs she might've left from eating here, which she often did, fingerprint powder from the forensic staff covered the desktop and her keyboard.

Just the sight of the powder brought back visions of her house after forensics processed the place. She had to brace herself to keep from shuddering and drawing attention from Mack, who was talking with a white-suited forensics tech named Lyle. Mack caught her attention and split away from the tech.

Cam followed him and stopped next to her. "Did you find anything odd?"

"No." She peered up at him. "What did Lyle have to say?"

Cam planted both hands on his narrow hips. "They lifted prints from your keyboard that didn't match your prints on file. Says someone used it for sure. They processed every key and will map out the ones holding the unknown prints. Might tell us something."

She hated that someone had sat here. In her chair. Using her computer. Stealing information. Her indignation rose. "If this crew member was hacking the network, or even looking at my files, why wouldn't they wear gloves?"

"Ever try to type with them on?" Cam asked. "It can be done, but not fast. And this person likely had to be quick."

Mack leaned against her cubicle wall, looking right at home. "Still, they could at least wipe down the keyboard when they finished."

"The guy might not have been savvy enough," Cam said. "Think about it. Hackers usually work at home in the dark, in hiding. They don't come out into the open and visit the place they're hacking."

"Yeah, I suppose." Mack narrowed his eyes. "But still."

"Don't try to analyze it," Cam said. "Just take it as the gift that it is. Someone's prints served up on a platter."

"You're right. It could be a real lead." Addy turned to stare at her desk, looking for anything else out of the ordinary. Her eye caught on her Amazon Echo. When she worked late alone in the office, she played music on the device. The bottom looked odd. She reached for the Echo with her gloved hands.

"What is it?" Mack moved closer.

She held it up. "Looks like someone tampered with this."

Cam leaned over her shoulder, and she could almost feel

him jonesing to grab the speaker. She glanced up at him. "You want to have a look?"

"Do I!" He jerked it from her hands and turned it over. "The bottom's been removed." He shoved his hand in his pocket and came out holding a multipurpose tool. "Mind if I have a seat?"

She got up and let him take her chair. He all but collapsed on the seat and soon had the rubber base removed. He quickly pulled the plug and shook his head. "It's been hacked. Turned into a listening device."

"Listening device?" She stared at him, her mind racing. "If Harris told Warren about the transport plan within earshot of this thing, whoever was listening in could've heard the details of our transport plan."

Cam grimaced. "That's rough. Using your own device to listen in. IoTs are great, but unscrupulous people are getting better and better at hacking them. Not in person like this but via the internet."

Addy knew IoT meant Internet of Things, which described any device connected to the internet.

"Smart TVs, security cameras, thermostats, even refrigerators can be hacked these days, leaving people more vulnerable than ever." Cam snorted. "We don't need all this stuff to be smart-based. I mean, who needs to see what's inside their refrigerator from clear across town?"

Addy had to agree but was surprised to hear a tech lover like Cam hold such an opinion. "Is there any way to tell who did this?"

"I'll get a tech to print the device." Mack stepped over to Lyle, who they'd been speaking to earlier.

She watched Mack as he talked with Lyle, his mannerisms sharp, the tech bobbing his head in agreement, then quickly grabbing his kit and following Mack back to her desk.

"Get up, Cam," Mack ordered, "and give Lyle room to work."

Cam traded places with Lyle and looked at Addy. "With your permission, I'll take the Echo back to the house when Lyle's finished with it and see if I can figure anything out."

"Of course," she said, watching Lyle as he was taking out a small device she'd never seen before.

"And might I suggest you don't use an IoT device at work in the future? Not that you'll be able to." Cam smirked. "I'm going to warn Fitz not to allow them."

She tried to smile with him but couldn't find any humor when she had obvious evidence of someone having invaded her personal space. Evidence that she might have compromised her agency, which was an even worse feeling.

"Yes!" Lyle shouted. "We have DNA."

She looked at Lyle's hands. "What is that thing?"

He glanced up. "A new technological breakthrough that the RED team is testing."

"But what does it do?"

"Saves me a lot of work is what it does." Lyle continued to look at her. "Nearly half of all DNA samples we take at crime scenes don't result in useable DNA profiles. This device clearly indicates whether a trace is worth further examination. It works kind of like a pregnancy test with a yes and no. You load a potential DNA sample, and a *no* response means move on and look elsewhere. *Yes* means that human DNA is present and that the trace is good for DNA profiling in the lab."

Lyle looked at Mack as if he were a superhero in a cape. "You guys have all the cool tools. I never even knew this prototype had been developed, but man. It's great. Really great. It proved that I lifted good DNA samples from this keyboard and worked here too. It's awesome."

Mack gave a firm nod. "We are blessed with the latest and greatest toys."

Lyle shook his head in amazement and went back to work.

Mack jabbed a finger at her monitor. "I'll have Fitz image

all hard drives in the office for our review, but I'd like Cam to personally do your desktop machine. See if it's been compromised."

She nodded. "Let me know what I can do to help."

"Other than review your desk for any other evidence of tampering," Mack said, "there's nothing."

"I've finished that. I should head back to the safe house to keep looking for Zamora's mystery boss."

Mack looked at Cam. "Can you handle wrapping things up here?"

"Absolutely."

"Then we'll go, and I'll send Sean back to pick you up when you're ready to leave."

"Sounds like a plan."

"Thanks, Cam." Addy grabbed her jacket from the back of her chair and slipped it on. Mack went into his protective mode and arranged with Kiley and Sean to get the vehicle and prepare for their departure.

Addy had to admit that leaving the ICE office could be more dangerous than departing from her doctor's office. She was known to frequent this location, and Razo could have his guys staking the place out. Yet with Zamora behind bars now, she figured it was safe enough to leave. Especially since they were using the back entrance, located in a more controlled environment.

And she'd been right. The transport went smoothly, and they arrived at the safe house without incident. She was soon standing in the small basement kitchenette where she set an individual cup of coffee to brew to keep her alert for the long hours ahead. Her skull felt like someone was trying to pry it into two pieces with a crowbar. She really should take a nap, but she wouldn't give in to the pain and fatigue. Not when there was something she could do to move the investigation forward. Because right next to the sharp agony in her head was the time counting down. A reminder that they had to figure out Razo's game plan before he delivered the miniguns into the hands of brutal killers or used the guns himself . . . all in less than forty-eight hours.

Mack came back from taking Bear outside, opened the refrigerator, and grabbed an energy drink.

She leaned against the counter, listening to the coffee drip into her cup. "You know they're saying those are bad for you. That they increase the risk of stroke due to rapid heartbeats."

"Yeah," he said and popped the top. "I really should give them up."

He didn't sound all that convincing.

She met his gaze. "Would you do it if I asked you to?"

"Yes." He set the can down. "I'd do anything for you."

"Anything?"

"Pretty much."

"Even break the law?" she asked, pressing the issue and hoping to learn more about him.

"Depends on the situation. If your life was in danger and I had to break the law to save you, I would." He planted his hands on the edge of the counter. "No questions asked."

She continued to watch him, and he didn't flinch or back off at all.

"I wasn't sure if I wanted to remember what we had together." She looked him directly in the eye. "But now I want to know in the worst way."

As the coffee gurgled its final breath, he moved closer to her. "Maybe there's a way for you to know."

"How?" The word barely came out through her dry throat.

"What if we didn't just talk about what we had? What if I kissed you?" He gently tucked a strand of hair behind her ear. "Maybe the emotions would come back then."

"I'm not sure . . ." She started to refuse when his fingers slid into her hair. He drew her close, and she knew she was going to let him kiss her. Not just let him. She wanted him to. With all her heart.

She suddenly couldn't wait and circled her arms around his neck, one hand traveling to the back of his head and drawing it down. His hair was soft and sharp at the same time. His body warm.

He bent closer, eliminating the final space between them. Their lips touched. His were warm and gentle but quickly turned urgent and insistent. She gave herself to the kiss. To the emotions. Waiting. Waiting. Hoping for memories to flash into her head. But all she had was now. His lips. The warmth. His touch. And a tremendous urge to explore it all.

His free hand circled her back and drew her tightly against his muscled body. She might not have an actual memory of being in his arms before, but she knew she was where she belonged. Knew that kissing this man was only the tip of what she felt for him. Knew that they were good together. And also knew she might never remember, but hoped—no, prayed—that she was wrong.

———

Footsteps sounded on the stairway, breaking through Mack's brain fog. He might be fine with kissing Addy, and she seemed to be equally fine with it, and yet there was no way he'd expose their personal life to the team.

He ended the kiss and pushed back, gulping in air to calm his emotions. Her eyes opened, and she looked confused. Maybe disappointed. Or maybe he was wishing she was disappointed and wanted to continue kissing him—continue getting closer to him again.

Kiley settled onto a club chair and opened her computer, but her focus continued to move between him and Addy.

Mack didn't want Kiley to get into a personal discussion, so he nodded at her laptop. "Are you going to keep searching for Razo on the dark web?"

"If that's what you want me to do."

"I do."

She gave him a knowing look, and he returned it with a little shake of his head, warning her off the direction he knew she was heading.

"Okay," she said, but sounded as if it was taking a herculean effort to move on. "I get it."

"Get what?" Sean took a seat on the couch.

"Nothing," Mack and Kiley both said.

Sean held up his hands. "No need to let me have it."

"Sorry." Mack scrubbed a hand over his face. "Tired. Need some caffeine."

Sean pointed at the counter. "You have your energy drink right there, so power it down and you'll be good to go."

Mack looked longingly at the drink. "I've decided to give them up."

"Seriously?" Kiley flashed her eyes at him. "We are *so* in for a horrible time."

"Maybe I'll make a cup of coffee." He turned to the machine, and after handing Addy her cup, he started one brewing for himself. He liked coffee just fine but usually only drank it in the mornings. Or when he needed caffeine and there wasn't an energy drink in sight. As of this moment, that was going to change, because he meant what he'd said. He'd do anything for Addy. He would. And if she wanted him to give up his favorite drink? For what he'd put her through, it was the least he could do.

Mug in hand, he stopped at the whiteboard to update outstanding leads by adding the fingerprints and DNA from the ICE office. He noted Harris's name beside it since she would coordinate with the forensic staff.

He took a sip of the strong brew and looked at Sean. "I need you to take charge of vetting the cleaning crew once Cam gets their files from Harris."

"Sure thing," he answered readily.

Mack gave his teammate a tight smile. Not long ago he and Sean hadn't gotten along, and Mack was thankful that the uneasiness had been ironed out and replaced with mutual respect.

Mack's phone chimed, and he read the text. "It's the data on the border crossings. Analysts have narrowed it down to two likely locations in California—San Ysidro and Calexico. Both have X-ray technology installed."

Kiley looked up. "I read up on both crossings. These locations are crazy crossings to try to move guns through. San Ysidro is not only the busiest land border crossing in the U.S., but in the Western Hemisphere. Seventy thousand passengers travel from Mexico to the U.S. every day on that route."

Addy sat in a chair at the table, Bear coming to rest at her feet. "Makes sense to use those crossings. The busier the crossing, the less time border patrol agents have to search the vehicles. My research said they take like twenty seconds per vehicle to make a decision. At slower, more remote crossings the agents can take their time."

"I didn't know that." Kiley looked at Addy with respect.

"We need to trust the analysts' findings," Sean said. "The good news is that we have far less than fifty crossings and an actionable list."

Mack turned to Cam. "What do you have on federal targets and sovereign-citizen members in Oregon?"

Cam frowned. "Not as much info as I would hope for. With banking federally regulated, these guys don't have accounts, and I couldn't locate any financial information that way. I did find info on members suspected in a fraud case who were never charged. They got away with a nearly half a million dollars, so they would have the coin to bankroll a minigun."

"And if they're scammers, they likely have the nerve to plan an attack," Mack said. "What are their names?"

"Joshua Ross, Randy Turner, and Eric Woods."

"Get going on researching them, and I'll ask Eisenhower

to put a tail on each of them. Then Sean and I'll research the border crossings." Mack looked at Sean. "You take San Ysidro, and I'll take Calexico."

"On it." Sean opened his laptop.

Mack sat next to Addy and wished he could talk to her about the kiss. But getting agents on the tail of the three men and researching Calexico was far more important. His personal happiness had to take a backseat to a violent man selling monster guns.

Mack got out his phone and called Eisenhower. After hearing about the latest development, he promised to have someone surveilling these men by the end of the day. Mack could always count on Eisenhower. He possessed more of a sense of urgency than any boss Mack had worked for.

Confident the task was taken care of, Mack opened his computer and got started on his research. He read article after article about the Calexico crossing, learning statistics and issues, but found nothing that helped move their investigation forward. He raised his fist in frustration, planning to slam it against the table.

"Mateo Pena!" Sean called out, stopping Mack's hand mid-air. Sean focused on Addy. "Name ring a bell?"

She looked up from her files and shook her head.

"Should it?" Mack asked.

"Maybe." Sean dipped his head to focus on his computer. "Not long ago, he tried to cross the border with four barely concealed semiautomatic pistols, fifteen AK-47s, thousands of rounds of 7.62 ammunition, and over thirty high-capacity magazines. Serial numbers were obliterated on all the weapons. This was enough to shock the guards, but then they found a big military-style battery with a heavy-duty electric cable. Took some time to figure out what it was, but it's the power supply for a minigun."

Mack let out a long whistle, and his radar went up. "This guy wasn't messing around. Where did he try to cross?"

"San Ysidro. He's in custody there."

Mack jumped to his feet. "I need a plane ASAP. I'm going to talk to Pena before the day is out."

"You'd rather follow this lead than the guys I found?" Cam asked.

"Absolutely." Mack met and held Cam's gaze. "If we stop the guns before they enter the country, these men can hardly use them, can they?"

CHAPTER 20

ADDY STOOD WAITING in the jail hallway, thinking about the military flight she and Mack had just taken to San Ysidro. She'd likely ridden in a military aircraft as a member of the RED team, but she sure didn't remember it, and the sounds and smells were memorable. She'd sat next to Mack but couldn't talk to him about their trip or Mateo Pena. Privileged conversations were out of the question in a plane carrying airmen who didn't have clearance to overhear such a discussion.

She'd had to settle for reading Pena's file. An American citizen, he had a long sheet of minor charges from his teen years. Burglary. Assault. Disorderly conduct. But no weapons charges of any kind, making this arrest unexpected. Even more so, as it had been six years since he'd had any interaction with law enforcement at all.

A tall uniformed deputy who looked harried and overworked joined them. He rested his hand on the interview room doorknob and looked back at them with interest. He probably didn't have many Feds visit the prison, especially those from out of state. Yet possessing this illegal machine gun was a federal crime, which gave Addy and the team jurisdiction wherever their investigation led in the country.

"This guy has been very cooperative," the deputy began. "Seems scared to death. But you never know with these gunrunners. Keep alert, and I'll be right outside the door."

She gave a sharp nod and stepped into the room, Mack following. Pena was dressed in blue prison garb. His shoulder-length hair was deep brown, and he had sparse facial hair that looked like he'd been trying to grow a beard but failed.

She held out her ID, then they introduced themselves.

"Yeah, yeah," he said, sitting forward. "They told me you was coming. I'm Mateo. I think I really screwed up."

"How's that?" Addy asked as she took a seat.

He laid his cuffed hands on the tabletop. "I mean, I've been in trouble before, but nothin' like this. I didn't know, you know? What was hidden in the car. I just agreed to go to Mexico, pick up the car, and drive it over the border for a grand."

"Come on, Pena." Mack gave the guy an incredulous look. "Your rap sheet says you've clearly been around the block. You had to know there was something illegal in the car."

"Yeah," he said, staring at his hands. "I mean . . . sure, but I figured it was smack or something. Not guns. And not that battery thing." He shook his head, his hair brushing his shoulders. "They seem more upset about that than the AK-47s."

"Do you know what the battery is for?" Addy asked.

He looked up at her. "Nah. They didn't say—just that it was big."

"The battery powers a minigun," Addy went on, "which is like a Gatling gun, if you know what that is."

"Um, yeah." He bit his lip. "It's like a really big machine gun."

She nodded. "It's a mass-casualty weapon that drug lords are using in Mexico to kill people at an alarming rate."

"Oh, man." He lowered his head and swiped a hand over his face, the chains holding him down jingling. "I didn't know. I swear. You gotta believe me."

"Who paid you to drive the car?" Mack asked.

Pena lifted his head, his eyes dark with sorrow. "Some guy I met outside a bodega. I never seen him before, and he only gave me his first name. Dante. I remember because I thought he kinda looked like the devil. I mean his expression." He shook his head. "I never shoulda hooked up with him, but my wife, she's pregnant. I've been out of work, and we need the cash so we don't get evicted. If I don't pay the rent by tomorrow, we'll be thrown out on the street." Tears formed in his eyes. "She's flipping out over my arrest. What am I gonna do? The baby . . ."

Addy felt sorry for him, yet there was nothing she could do to reduce the prison time he was facing. "Can you describe Dante for us?"

He gave a physical description that matched Dante Zamora, just as Addy expected.

She shifted on the hard metal chair and laid a photo of Zamora on the table. "Is this the guy?"

"Yeah. That's him all right."

Mack eyed Pena. "Where were you supposed to find the car and deliver your cargo?"

"They gave me a car to take into Mexico. It had the coordinates programmed in for leaving the car and picking up the other one. There was a man there with coordinates on a piece of paper for the drop-off location. He told me to memorize them, then took the paper back." Pena shared the GPS coordinates.

Addy wrote them down. "Do you know where that is?"

He nodded. "Just north of the border, out in the middle of nowhere."

Addy was shocked that a man who seemed to have gotten his life on the right track would take such a risk. "I know you're upset over being caught, but you do realize that meeting gunrunners in some secluded spot would not have gone well for you."

"Yeah, I know that now." He clapped a hand on his forehead. "Stupid. Stupid. Stupid. I knew it was too good to be true. My *abuelita* always warned me about that."

His grandma was right—the guy should've listened. "Do

the names Joshua Ross, Randy Turner, and Eric Woods mean anything to you?"

"No. Should they?"

Addy shrugged.

"What about the bodega where you met Dante?" Mack asked. "Where's it located?"

Pena mentioned cross streets in San Ysidro, which Addy also recorded in her notebook.

"We live just down the street. I went to get ice cream for my wife. Cravings." The tears glistened in his deep brown eyes.

"Do you have any family she and the baby could maybe live with?" Addy gave in to her emotions like Harris always accused her of doing.

He nodded. "But I . . . my son. He will be how old when I finally get to truly be his father?"

Addy's heart was breaking for this man, and she wished she could do something for him. "We'll make sure the judge knows you cooperated. That should help the judge be more lenient with the charges. Still, you have to know this is very serious."

"I do. I really do. How else can I help?"

"What about Dante?" Mack said. "Is there anything else you can tell us about him?"

"He seemed respectable. Except for the way he watched me. And his clothes . . . man, they looked expensive. You could tell he'd dropped a lot of money on them and on a gold necklace he was wearing."

Pena described Zamora's clothing in greater detail, as well as the same necklace she'd seen in her photos, further confirming they were on the right track.

"What about his car?" Addy asked. "Can you describe what he was driving or give us a plate number?"

He shook his head, hard. "I didn't see it. He just walked off."

Mack shifted on his chair and grimaced, likely from the toll the long plane ride had taken on his painful leg. "And did he warn you about what would happen if you didn't drive the car to the right location?"

"Yeah. Said there was a GPS tracker on the car, and he would be following my every move. He said I couldn't even go home to tell my wife that I was leaving." He shook his head again. "I wish I had. She would've talked me out of doing this. She's the reason I stopped wasting my life. Turned me right around."

Addy resisted shaking her head over the man's lack of street smarts. For a guy who had a juvie sheet, he had to know Dante couldn't be trusted. But Pena was desperate, and desperate people did desperate things. Addy had seen that often enough. And she'd seen men like Zamora take advantage of people in these positions. It never ended well for the pawn, but the knight got richer and richer and lived in a big castle on the hill.

———

Addy couldn't sleep and padded to the kitchenette in the hotel suite she shared with Mack. The only light in the room came from a nightlight casting deep shadows around the space, and she didn't turn on another one for fear of waking Mack.

Four a.m. and he and the town were silent, but she was wide awake. She needed to pass a few hours until they could go to the bodega. By the time they'd left the jail, the shop was closed, so they'd gotten a hotel suite for the night. On the way to check in, they'd stopped at a grocery store to buy a few essentials.

She dug through the paper bag until she located a single-serve pack of Cheerios. She pulled out the files on the three men with sovereign-citizen connections, sat at the hotel room's small table, and opened the pack to start nibbling on the cereal while she looked through the folder again.

Her thoughts drifted to Pena and his wife. He'd made one stupid mistake and now his entire life was destroyed. The same thing had happened to her and Mack, she guessed. Mack hurt her one time only, couldn't live with it so he walked out, altering their lives forever.

The difference was that they could still change their consequences. Pena couldn't.

She sighed and scooped out some Cheerios. She munched on them, her mind clouded, her emotions raw. She so desperately wanted to remember Mack. Even just a tiny bit so she knew her emerging feelings were real and that she did actually love the man. It was easy to see why she might. He'd proven himself to be honorable and dependable. Kind and yet strong at the same time. Loyal and trustworthy. Everything she could hope for in a husband.

And she was also physically attracted to him. What woman wouldn't be? She hadn't asked him if he'd dated since they'd broken up. If her memory was right, she hadn't gone on any dates. At least she didn't remember a guy in her life. Which told her she either hadn't had the time, what with work and caring for her mother, or she was still in love with Mack and didn't care to date another man.

Another sigh whispered out in the silence, and she shook her head. She had to get control of these emotions so she could focus on the investigation. She had to be clearheaded and ready to go in the morning. Especially now that they knew the names of three men who might be buying the guns and would likely be targeting federal employees.

None of the three showed any means of employment, and all of them lived on compounds in rural Oregon. Joshua Ross had a wife and ten children. So how was he feeding all those kids? The scam? Likely. Randy Turner was married too but had no children. And Eric Woods, the youngest of the three, was single.

Cam had located an online connection to all three men on an imageboard called *8run*, which was composed of user-created message boards. The board had been linked to many right-wing movements, racism and anti-Semitism, plus hate crimes, mass shootings, and child pornography. Though shut down many times, it continued to resurface elsewhere, most recently as a Russian-hosted site on the dark web. Cam didn't find any information about the guns or Razo, but he was looking into the users for possible screen names and monitoring the site for any new posts.

A sound came from Mack's room. Groaning, she thought. She went to his door and listened. Sounded like he was having a bad dream. Maybe a nightmare.

Should she knock on the door? See if he was all right?

It really wasn't her place to do something like that anymore. She continued to listen and heard footsteps, then water running. Okay, he was in the bathroom and didn't need her intervention.

She went back to the table and her Cheerios. His door soon opened, and he stepped out, dressed in athletic shorts and a T-shirt. He limped toward her, but the moment he caught sight of her, his limp disappeared. He still didn't want her to know how badly his leg hurt. She looked at the bandage on his calf, then ran her gaze up his torso. He really was a fine-looking and fit man. Handsome, even with his tousled hair. But it was the man she was coming to know that she was really attracted to.

She caught herself staring and blinked a few times. "Couldn't sleep?"

He shook his head. "You either, I see."

"Yeah. Kept thinking about Pena and how he ruined his life with one choice."

Mack went to the kitchenette. "You were always the softie in the group."

"You mean the RED team?"

He nodded and started a cup of coffee brewing.

"I wish I could remember everyone," she said. "They seem like great people."

He turned and leaned against the counter. "They are, and you got along very well with everyone. Even Eisenhower."

"Is he a good boss?"

"The best." Mack's expression brightened. "He might be controlling at times, but he also gives us free rein in many ways. Allows us to do our jobs our way."

"With our personal connection, I'm surprised he let you take lead on this investigation."

Mack frowned. "He had to know I wasn't walking away from you at a time like this and would ramrod the others anyway. So why not let me lead?"

"Yeah, I suppose."

"Besides, he told me if I let it get in the way, he'd replace me."

"Then you must be doing a good job of keeping your emotions in check."

He raised an eyebrow. In the shadowy light, he looked darkly dangerous. "I'm doing my best, but let me tell you, it's a constant battle. I want to . . ." He shook his head and turned back to the coffeemaker.

"I was thinking," she said. "We're a lot like Pena. One thing happened and our married life was over."

He spun to look at her. "You remember?"

She shook her head. "But that's what you told me, right?"

"Right." He faced the coffeepot again.

She inhaled the tantalizing scent filling the air and waited for his cup to finish and for him to join her. If, in fact, he planned to sit with her instead of going back to his room.

She polished off her Cheerios, and he came to the table. His eyes were dark with anguish.

"Bad dream?" she asked.

He nodded and looked down at his mug. "I think it's the deadline fast approaching and creating so much tension. This event is supposed to go down tomorrow, and we're no closer to finding the guns than when we started. I'm in charge and failing to bring everything to a close. Failing big-time."

"And you think that triggered the dream? Want to talk about it?"

"There's really nothing to say. I was reliving a particularly bad day in the Middle East. Lots of gunfire and civilians in the way." He took a long sip of the coffee. "If you'd been next to me . . ." He shrugged.

"I would've woken you before horror played in your brain for very long."

He set down his mug and rested his hands on the table. Beautiful, strong hands that could also be so tender. "And how might I have responded?"

She leaned forward and took his hand. "I don't know, but God knows. We have to stop thinking what if and let Him take charge."

"Easy for you to say." He slipped his hand free. "First, you can't remember how badly I hurt you. Second, you aren't the one doing the hurting."

"But I'm still half of the equation, and my opinion should count for something."

He crossed his arms and leaned back, physically withdrawing from her. And, she suspected, mentally going to that place in his mind where she was off-limits.

He met her gaze and held it. "There's really no point in discussing this. Not until your memory returns. And after the nightmare I just had, maybe not even then."

CHAPTER 21

MACK MADE SURE they were at the bodega the moment the doors opened. They had no time to waste today. The gun transport went down tomorrow, and they had to stop it. He scanned the strip mall in an impoverished area of the city and immediately spotted the bright colors of the place. The morning sun reverberated from the red-and-orange paint chipping from the walls. A small green fence ran along the front but was falling down in places. Several of the stores in the mall were vacant. The others held sketchy tenants such as hydroponic growing supplies, a marijuana shop, and a tattoo parlor.

Mack parked in front of the bodega and took off his sunglasses. "Not the best part of town."

Addy leaned forward. "It's what I expected, though."

He pulled the key from the ignition. "You think Zamora chose this location at random or he has an affiliation with the place?"

She reached for her door handle. "Let's go find out."

He clasped her free arm. "Be careful, okay? I doubt Razo is here, but you never know."

"Got it." She slipped out of the vehicle.

He hurried to catch up with her, taking in the parking lot and surrounding area as he moved. He spotted a homeless camp on the corner and obvious drug deals going down in broad daylight. It was hard, but he ignored it all to open the bodega door for Addy.

They stepped inside, and a spicy aroma made Mack's mouth water. He saw tamales and burritos in a glass case with a warmer. His stomach grumbled. He should've eaten breakfast, but after the nightmare, he wasn't able to stomach even a bite of food. It wasn't the dream itself, but the proof that he was still capable of hurting Addy.

He looked around the store at shelves holding groceries and tall glass candles. Brightly colored piñatas hung from the ceiling, and a fan hummed in the background. A stooped older woman stood behind the counter. She was dressed in a multicolored top and long skirt, her hair pulled back in a bun. Wrinkles lined her weathered face, but she had a ready smile for them as they approached.

Mack wasn't about to flash his creds in a border town. That was a sure way to silence anyone they talked to. He'd even worn a jacket to hide his sidearm, and so had Addy, though the temperature outside was balmy.

He smiled at the woman. "I'm looking for Dante. Heard he was here today."

"No. No Dante." She shook her head, a suspicious look on her face. "Not today."

"But he does come here, right?" Addy asked. "His friend Mateo Pena sent us to talk to him."

Mack wanted to tell Addy good job for bringing up Pena's name to give them credibility with this woman, yet this wasn't the time or place to compliment her.

The woman's smile widened. "Ah, Mateo. Baby yet?"

"Not yet," Addy said. "Does Dante have a regular schedule?"

She shook her head. "He come whenever."

Mack wanted to start asking questions, but since Addy had connected with this woman, he held his tongue and let her take charge.

"What does he do when he comes here?" Addy asked.

"Hires workers. They are glad." She mimicked handing

someone money. "Too many out of work. Not good. Dante help."

Mack wanted to say, *I'll just bet he does*, but he nodded instead.

"When was the last time you saw him?" Addy asked.

"He was here a couple days ago. Gave Mateo job. Good for bambino to have his papi working."

"Does Dante come into the store?"

"Yes. Yes. For burritos. Says they are the best." Her grin widened enough for Mack to see she was missing several upper teeth.

"Does Dante do anything else but buy your burritos?"

"He likes Mexican soda too." She chuckled. "A grown man and so much sugar."

"Do you own the store?" Addy asked.

"An old woman like me?" She waved a hand. "My son. He is owner."

"Is he here?"

She shook her head. "He does not come here often. Works from *la casa*."

"What's his name?"

Her expression went suddenly blank, and she picked up a rag and began wiping the glass countertop. "I must work now. You buy anything?"

Addy had crossed the line, and the woman was done talking. Mack could easily find out who owned the business, and he would because her response was suspicious.

Addy grabbed a few candy bars, a bag of chips, and two sodas, then paid for the items.

"Gracias," the woman said and turned her back to them.

Outside, in the warm dusty breeze, Mack unlocked the SUV with the remote and kept his head on a swivel until he had Addy safely inside the vehicle. He took a long look around and shot copious pictures with his phone until a husky man started his way.

Mack slipped into the vehicle and locked the door. He had to figure out their next move so he could maximize the time that was already slipping away today. "There are security cameras on the corner store. We need to get that video."

Addy looked at him. "What do you think the odds of that are?"

"Not good, but if we find an illegal immigrant working, we can probably convince them to talk in trade for not reporting them." He looked out the windows. "Once the bouncer takes a hike."

But the guy didn't leave. Instead, he stood staring at them from the sidewalk, then suddenly marched over to Addy's door.

"Show him your credentials," Mack said. "If he's here illegally, he'll be out of here in a flash."

She pulled out her ID. The large man with leathery skin took one look and bolted down the sidewalk.

"I hate scaring people like that." She shoved her creds in her pocket. "Sure, he shouldn't be in the country, but he could be a legit kind of guy just trying to eke out a living."

"Yeah," Mack said, wishing he could have such a rosy outlook, but his time in fugitive apprehension for the Marshals made him cautious. "Or he could be running guns or drugs or otherwise involved with a gang."

She met his gaze. "Are we like this? I'm the optimist, you're the realist?"

"Pretty much." His phone chimed. "It's a follow-up on the border crossings. A nearby cable is owned by the government."

"This really could be the place we're looking for."

Mack nodded but kept his enthusiasm in check since they didn't yet have the guns. "Let's go get that video."

He climbed out, and Addy met him at the hood. Together, they entered the tattoo shop. A long counter ran the full length of the store. The top was made of broken Mexican tiles. The irregular-shaped shards reminded him of how he'd literally smashed his life with Addy, walking out with little more than a one-hour conversation. A one-sided one at that. Before he'd talked to her, he'd already made up his mind so that nothing she said would have swayed him.

A guy who couldn't be more than sixteen stood behind the counter, a phone to his ear. He had inky-black hair buzzed short with equally dark fuzz above his lip. He also had a raging case of acne and a greasy forehead.

As Mack waited for the kid to finish his call, Mack looked at the neon-blue paint coating the door and window frames. And at the blazing orange sign in the window that announced *Little Baja Tattoos.*

Once the kid said good-bye and lowered his phone, Addy stepped right up to the counter. Mack joined her and noted the three-ring binders lying open, each one displaying tattoo pictures. She introduced herself and held out her ID.

The teen's brown eyes widened. He took a step back and looked like he wanted to flee.

"I'm not here on immigration matters." She gave him a smile that would make Mack do most anything. "If that's worrying you, forget about it. I just want to talk to someone about your security-camera footage."

"I—" He flashed a look at an open door on the far wall.

"Is there a manager here I can talk to?"

"Um . . . well."

"I meant it when I said I don't care about your immigration status or anyone else's."

He glanced at the door again and fled toward it. He moved at the speed of the many fleeing lizards Mack had seen since arriving here and closed the door behind him.

Mack was antsy and wanted to move things along. He faced Addy. "Want to go after him?"

"I do, but I think it's just going to spook them more." She sighed. "Let's give him a chance to send whoever's back there out to us."

Mack didn't want to wait, not at this point in the investigation. Yet he knew she was right. Despite the urge to act, he planted his feet. He glanced around the place and spotted three tattoo stations with black reclining chairs and tattoo paraphernalia littering some shelves. The spaces, divided by half walls, were organized and clean. Looked like a legit shop, but that didn't mean anything.

A woman who seemed old enough to be the boy's mother poked her head out of the door.

"Hi," Addy said and introduced herself, while Mack would've been firing questions at her by now. "I'm not here on immigration matters. I just want to ask about your security camera out front. Do you keep the footage?"

The woman stepped into the room but hung near the door. Mack noticed her neck tattoo, an outline of black flowers leading to a large rose below her chin. "It doesn't work, but my uncle leaves it up for security."

"How long has it been out of commission?" Addy asked.

"Years." A worried look crossed her face.

"Do you know a Dante Zamora?" Mack asked, moving them along.

"Um." She nibbled on a full bottom lip. "I know a Dante, but not his last name."

"May I show you a picture of him to see if he's the man you're talking about?" Addy asked.

The woman nodded and joined them, her long skirt that looked like it was made with handkerchiefs swishing as she walked.

Addy held out her phone, that comforting smile still on her face. It was a very good thing she was doing most of the questioning, as Mack feared his direct line of questioning would send this woman running back into hiding.

She cautiously inched closer, her sandals scraping on the tile floor. She looked at the phone and nodded, her long black hair falling over the shoulder of her denim shirt embroidered with bright flowers. "Yeah. That's him. That's the Dante who comes around here."

Addy slowly pocketed her phone, likely because she didn't want to startle the already skittish woman. "Do you know why he hangs out around here?"

"Yes, um, well . . ." She tossed her hair over her shoulder. "He gives guys a job."

"What kind of jobs?" Mack almost demanded.

Her eyes narrowed below thick eyebrows. "Driving cars. Not sure what's in them, but he sends them over the border to pick up cars and bring stuff back. He's not willing to cross the border himself, so I gotta think it can't be good stuff."

Okay, good. They were finally getting somewhere. "Do you know a man named Bruno Razo?"

She shook her head. "No Brunos."

Mack wouldn't let that answer slow him down. "Can you give me the name of anyone who has worked for Dante?"

She bit her lip and fidgeted with her hands.

"I'm assuming he only uses people who are U.S. citizens so they can legally cross," Mack said. "So even if you tell me their names, there won't be an immigration issue."

"Yes, but . . ." She shrugged.

"We aren't after these men. I won't arrest anyone." Mack firmed his tone.

She lifted her chin. "And if I don't tell you?"

"Then you don't tell us, and we move on." He tried to sound indifferent when he was anything but. "Just let me say that this involves the lives of many people, and anything you can share with us could help stop people from dying."

Mack paused and locked gazes with her. "Lives of innocent children and families. You could help stop a bloodbath."

"Fine." She fisted her hands on her hips and spouted several names. Addy quickly got out her notebook and pen and jotted them down. She repeated them back to the woman.

She nodded.

"Thank you," Mack said sincerely. "Do they live in the area?"

She nodded. "One of the guys is homeless. He hangs out across the street."

"And can I get your name?" Addy asked.

The woman bit her lip again but then shared her name.

Addy added it to her notes. "I promise we won't mention you when we talk to these men."

"Yeah, but everyone saw you come in here. It's all over the neighborhood by now." She looked like she wanted to cry.

"I'm sorry to put you in this position. I wish we didn't have to ask."

She clasped her hands together. "Will this man—this Dante—come after me and my family?"

"No," Addy said firmly. "He's in jail as we speak."

Mack wouldn't have given the same answer. He didn't think Dante being behind bars made a difference. If word got back to Dante about this woman, and he told Razo she'd snitched, Mack expected Razo would retaliate.

Mack handed the woman his business card. "If there's even a hint of a danger, you call me immediately. I'll make sure your family is protected."

Her big eyes widened. "You can do this?"

"I can and I will," he said with force. "You have my word."

"Mine too," Addy said. "Thank you for helping us."

She gave an uncertain nod.

Mack hurried Addy out of the building. He searched for the group of homeless men. They'd moved on, leaving the street corner empty.

Addy looked at Mack. "Displaying my creds made us pariahs for sure."

"Still, I think it helped this woman talk." He opened the SUV door for her. She settled inside, and he quickly closed it.

Once behind the wheel, he turned to her. "Let's head to

the office in San Diego and regroup. We'll look up addresses for the names she gave us and then bring the men in for questioning. We can get other agents to help us to move things along faster."

"I hate having to haul them in, but at least they're legal and we don't have that issue to deal with."

He searched her gaze. "Do you think we should pursue interviewing these men?"

"Don't you?"

"Yeah, but what if Razo really is bringing miniguns into our country and plans to use someone from here? If he hears that we're in town, he'll move the delivery to another location, and we'll miss catching him in the act."

She swiveled in her seat. "Good point. But then Zamora's in jail, and it's less likely he'll hear about us. So unless the locals have a way to get to Razo, we should be good. And with Zamora in jail, Razo might even postpone the delivery."

"Okay, we interview the men but still have the local agents stake out the places where Zamora got his drivers. And we get Cam on digging up background on these people."

Not wanting to waste even a moment of their precious time, Mack dialed Cam and rapidly detailed what they'd learned today. "I want all the information you can find on these businesses in San Ysidro, and I want it fast." Mack shared the bodega and tattoo shop names. "And get me info on the owner of the strip mall. Now that we're pretty certain on the crossing where Razo is moving the gun over the border, get me more info on the internet cables in the area."

"Can do."

"Good," Mack said. "And do it like yesterday. Lives are counting on you, and this is going down tomorrow whether we've figured everything out or not."

———

A long day of interviews ensued, and Addy felt the time slipping away as if it were being pulled out of her grasp. After closing the door behind the last man, she tapped a foot in the conference room, and glanced out the window at the sun sinking behind the horizon. They had to find a lead soon—they only had the rest of the day today and then tomorrow the guns would be moved. But where were they going to get a lead? The men they'd interviewed told stories very much like Pena's. Except they added that once a person drove for Zamora, they were never allowed to drive again. No matter how much they begged—and several of them had, especially the homeless man—Zamora was adamant. No more work.

Mack jumped up, grabbed a marker, and started scribbling the names of the men they'd interviewed on the board, his strokes fast and almost frantic. He'd been jittery all day. Obviously feeling the pressure of the deadline fast approaching, just like she was.

He noted the location where Zamora had hired each man. One outside the bodega and tattoo shop where this line of inquiry started, but also a man at a local taqueria, liquor store, vape-and-smoke shop, and pawnshop. Addy and Mack had also visited each store. Nothing new to go on, but they at least built a strong case against Zamora, *if* the men and women they talked to came through in the end and testified against the man.

Mack looked at her. "So if we can convince Pena and any of the people we interviewed today to testify against Zamora, we have him cold."

Addy could hardly believe his thoughts mimicked hers. Had they always been so in sync with each other? She suspected they had, and she liked the thought as much as it disturbed her.

She held his gaze. "I think very few of them will step forward when it comes time to take the stand. But what if we got the DA to offer Pena a plea deal in exchange for his testimony?"

Mack shook his head. "Pena will testify without a deal."

"Still, wouldn't it be nice if he could be home when the baby's born?"

He frowned. "Nice, yeah, but he broke the law, and he should have to pay for that."

"But he had extenuating circumstances." She lifted her chin. "Imagine having a son and not being able to support him. To put a roof over his head. What would you do?"

"I wouldn't break the law?"

"Are you sure?" She cast him a skeptical look. "Imagine us being together again. I'm nine months pregnant. We're going to get evicted. You have no legal means to stop that. Someone offers you money that you need. Cash. Right up front. Wouldn't you take it?"

He gave a guttural sound like a growl but deeper. "I don't know. Maybe. But I would never be in that position."

She arched a brow. "You know this for a fact?"

"No, no I don't but . . ." He paused and took a long breath. "We would first have to be together again, and unless you start remembering, that's not possible. And even then . . ." He shook his head.

"My appointment is tomorrow, if we're back in Portland by then. Maybe I'll recall something, and we can talk again."

"We can talk all we want. Talking about it doesn't change a thing." He locked eyes with her, his expression resolute. "I'm still toxic to you."

CHAPTER 22

IN THE LOBBY of their hotel, Mack read an email update from Eisenhower as he walked to the elevator with Addy. Eisenhower said Williams was holding out even longer than he thought would happen. Disappointed, Mack swallowed down his frustration over the girls needing him and the team and not being there for them. But there was nothing he could do about that, other than to wrap up the investigation and get back to the girls.

But how? It wasn't like he wasn't trying. They were all trying. Desperately. Cam included, as he'd sent an email with a thorough report on each business Mack and Addy had visited that day. He also mentioned that the strip mall was owned by a shell corp that he was still tracking down.

Mack sent a quick text to the team to say he would hold a video call in thirty minutes, and then he and Addy rode the elevator to the suite.

He'd made sure when making their accommodations yesterday that there were two bedrooms, but after the close proximity last night and waking up to find her sitting in the living area, he simply wanted to grab her up in a hug and forget about his nightmare. Being that close to her for another night wasn't going to be easy.

The tension between them was nearly unbearable on the ride up to their floor. What was it going to be like confined to a suite together?

Please, Father. Help us out here, he prayed as Addy stepped out and then got the door to the suite unlocked.

"I'm going to get cleaned up." She quickly charged toward her room.

"Conference call in thirty," he called to her fleeing back.

He'd never had a woman run away from him, and surely one had never moved so fast. He felt like a leper. He kind of was one, right? Except his condition was self-inflicted. He just had to man up even more and do more work.

Or maybe trust God. The thought came out of the blue.

Trust how?

Maybe believe once and for all that God was in control. In charge. And He worked everything out the right way. Even the PTSD. Even the potential of hurting Addy. After the incident with Addy, Mack had never asked God what He wanted. Mack had just ended his marriage. But maybe God wanted something else.

Do you? Did I act too hastily?

Addy returned in yoga pants and a T-shirt and was winding her hair up behind her head. She'd always changed out of her work clothes the minute she got home, kicking her shoes off wherever they landed, and he picked them up and put them away. He remembered relaxing with her on the couch so many nights after work. He could see taking her hand now and leading her to the couch. Snuggling in. Finding a movie. Making some popcorn. Or eating her favorite brand of kettle chips. A pipe dream. Not only because of their relationship issues but also the investigation. No time for TV watching. No time for anything else.

He made quick work of printing out the reports from Cam. They wouldn't have time to read them before the call, but they would be able to reference the pages if necessary. He connected his phone, and the portable printer whirred to life. While it spit out pages, Mack set up his laptop on the small dining table.

"We'll do the call here, if you want to get set up," he told Addy, then headed to the printer.

She pulled a chair next to the one behind his laptop, which would put her in the video frame of the call. And would put her in very close proximity. He took a long breath, snagged the pages, and sat next to her.

He set the reports on the table in front of her, hoping she would pick them up and turn those eyes that did all kinds of wonderful things to him onto the paper. "Cam's latest report."

She grabbed it like a lifeline.

Okay then. Mission accomplished.

He got the team connected, but Kiley wasn't looking at the screen. She had her nose buried in her laptop. Not unusual when she was on to something. She might physically be present in a room, but her mind was somewhere else completely.

Mack wouldn't say anything, as he knew it wouldn't do any good. "Great job getting the data together so fast, Cam."

"I aim to please." Cam preened. "You want me to let you read the entire report or cut to the chase and give you the interesting tidbits?"

"Interesting tidbits," Addy and Mack said at the same time.

"So, all these businesses are in strip malls, and the malls are all owned by a holding company, a Harp Holdings. In digging through the corporation's organizational records, it tracks back to owner Senator Jack Noble."

"Okay, so a senator owning these properties is interesting, but . . ." Mack shrugged.

"Can't be a coincidence that he owns all five of the malls where these businesses are located," Addy said.

"I don't think it is either," Cam said. "So I searched the senator's business holdings and discovered that he owns a sixth mall in the general area and doesn't publicly acknowledge this company."

"He doesn't want people to know he owns them." Addy

tapped her finger on the table, her thinking mode. "The properties aren't in the best condition and not in great neighborhoods. Maybe he thinks he'll be accused of being a slumlord."

"Could be," Cam said, though he didn't really sound like he believed it.

"What do we know about this senator besides that he owns these malls and comes from California?" Sean asked.

"Not a lot," Cam said. "I'm running background on him now, but it looks like he's pretty liberal."

"I've heard of him, but since he's from California, I never really paid much attention," Addy said.

"I don't know much about him either, but you all can't be thinking he's involved in gunrunning, can you?" Mack looked between his colleagues.

Sean shrugged.

Cam tilted his head. "Not the most farfetched thing I've ever heard."

"It's not like politicians these days keep their noses clean," Addy said.

Mack shot her a look. "But gunrunning? That's a far cry from some of the white-collar crimes we see politicians getting nailed for."

"Yeah, there is that," Addy said. "Yet we need to follow up on it."

"Shouldn't take me long to finish the background," Cam said.

"Can you get a phone number for him?" Addy sat up higher. "If he's in California right now, we should talk to him while we're here."

"I can get you that in a blink of an eye." Cam got a cocky smile on his face. "You want his home or cell number?"

"Those numbers must be private." She stared at him. "You can get them?"

"Cam can get almost anything," Sean said, his tone laced with sarcasm, even though his statement was true.

"I forgot. You're the Wonder Team." Addy shook her head. "Then both, I guess."

"You got it." Cam held up a finger and opened his laptop.

Mack was getting antsier by the minute and wouldn't waste a single minute by waiting for the numbers. "Kiley, are you still working on the dark web connection?"

"Uh-huh," she answered but didn't look up.

"She's closing in on something," Sean said. "That's the first time she's spoken in hours."

"Okay, here are the phone numbers." Cam shared them, and Addy jotted them down. "And before you ask, he's in town for fundraisers. Staying at his ranch."

"He's a rancher?" Mack asked.

"Alpacas," Cam said.

"That's not a *real* rancher." Mack rolled his eyes. "What about the business names I gave you? Any connection between them?"

"The taqueria and liquor store are owned by brothers, otherwise I haven't found another connection," Cam said. "I've got an algorithm running for that too, and it could still scope some additional data for us."

Addy set down her pen. "I assume that if you'd found any connection between the senator or these owners and Zamora or Razo, you would've already mentioned that?"

"That would've been the lead story." Cam chuckled, then immediately sobered. "On another note, Joshua Ross posted on the 8run site about a coming event that would prove the sovereign citizens' superiority over the Feds. No details. Just a hint that it would go down very soon."

"Sounds like he could be buying a minigun," Mack said, his gut clenching. "We gotta figure it will take time to get the gun from the border to Portland, so the event won't occur the same day as the arrival of the guns into the country. They might even need time to practice with the weapon. Keep watching for other comments and more specific dates."

"Already have an alert set," Cam said. "They say anything and I'll be notified."

"Let me know the second you get a post," Mack ordered.

Cam gave a sharp nod.

"Where do we go from here?" Sean asked.

"Let's run through our outstanding items." Mack got out his phone and opened a picture of the whiteboard from Oregon so he didn't forget a single item. "Let's start with the metadata."

"Nothing actionable there," Cam said. "Dead end."

Mack moved down the list. "What about personnel files for the cleaning crew?"

"I've narrowed it down to one name," Sean said. "A Sergio Smirnov."

"Seriously?" Mack asked. "Sounds like a bogus name."

"That's because it is." Sean met Mack's gaze. "The guy suddenly came to life when he went to work for the cleaning crew. Before that he didn't exist."

Interesting. "You have any leads on his real ID?"

Sean shook his head. "I ran the bogus driver's license picture through facial recognition and got nothing. We'll have to hope the fingerprints or DNA from the office are his and return a match."

"I'll text Harris to follow up." Addy grabbed her phone, her thumbs flying over the screen. She sat back and stared at the phone as if expecting an immediate reply, but her phone didn't make a sound.

Mack turned his attention back to the screen.

"No. Oh no." Kiley looked up, her eyes wide, and she took in a long breath. "This isn't good. This isn't good at all."

———

Addy's gut clenched, and she fixed her eyes on the screen. "What is it, Kiley? What did you find?"

"Razo," she said. "He's not only into gunrunning. He's also

a key player in human trafficking. Especially of young girls for prostitution."

Addy's stomach knotted. "That's sick and depraved."

Kiley's face paled, and she looked like she might throw up. She shared a look with her team members, and Addy checked them out. Anger darkened Sean's and Mack's eyes. Cam crossed his arms and slumped down.

Oh, right. They had to be thinking about the Montgomery girls who were missing. If they were still alive, they could easily have been trafficked, and everyone had to know that.

Kiley took a long breath and let it out slowly. "I'll dig deeper, but I'm going on record as saying I sure don't want to."

Sean turned to face his teammate. "I can take over for you."

Mack curled his hands into fists. "Or I will."

"Me too," Cam said.

Addy loved how these guys were so ready to support Kiley to keep her from having to face the ugliness of what a man could do to a young girl. They were all in law enforcement to protect the innocent, apparently Cam too, even though he was an analyst.

A tight smile found its way to Kiley's mouth. "I appreciate you all having my back, but I started this, and I *will* finish it. I'm going to nail this guy."

Mack pressed out his hands on his knees. "I know we're a long way away from Alabama and none of us wants to think the Montgomery teens are being trafficked, but keep your eyes open for any word on them, okay?"

Kiley nodded, her expression tight, that ill feeling returning to her face.

Addy hated that Kiley would have to keep working in such a tough area. Addy liked the internet. Used it all the time and could hardly remember life before it. But the criminal element had exploited it to such a degree that, like every avenue of life, it wasn't safe anymore, and she didn't like what it had become—

an instant gratification system for the sick people in the world and those who would cater to them.

She bowed her head for a moment and prayed they would be able to arrest Razo for murder and find and release any young girls he was holding.

Her phone rang, startling her. She quickly dug it out to see Harris requesting a video call.

"It's Harris. I have to take this." Addy smoothed her hair and answered.

"We'll stand by," Mack said.

"We have a match for the fingerprints on your keyboard and desk." Harris looked Addy in the eye. "They belong to Vadim Yahontov."

"Really?" Addy gaped at her boss. "It was Yahontov?"

Harris nodded. "I also compared the photo on Sergio Smirnov's employment record to Yahontov. They're one and the same. I'm heading over to the jail as soon as we finish up. This should be new ammunition to get Yahontov to talk."

Addy wanted to send the RED team instead, and she knew they would want to go. But the hacking had occurred at the ICE office, which made the crime personal to Harris. And she needed to seek her own payback, so Addy kept her mouth shut.

"What's going on in the investigation?" Harris asked.

Addy updated her boss on the recent findings, trying her best to be succinct and not blabber as Harris continued to stare at her.

"Senator?" Harris steepled her hands. "I don't like the sound of that. From what you said, there's very little to link him to our investigation. I'm not sure I want you questioning him."

Addy respected her boss and usually did as she instructed, but Addy would talk to the senator. She had to. They had no other leads. "I'll be diplomatic and not in any way let on that we think he could possibly be involved."

"I don't know." Harris pressed her lips together in an unusual moment of uncertainty.

Addy was going in for the kill. "I'll be as diplomatic as he'll be with me. I promise."

She would do her best to keep that promise, but if the senator sidestepped her questions, she would do what it took to get the answers they needed.

"Okay. Fine. Don't make me regret letting you do this." Harris scowled and disconnected the call.

Addy looked at the team. "We have a fingerprint match. Vadim Yahontov. *And* his photo is a match to Smirnov."

"You're kidding." Mack gaped at her.

"No," she said. "Harris will interview him again."

Mack narrowed his eyes. "Wish she'd consulted me first."

"She wants payback for breaching her territory," Addy said.

"I get that, but . . ." Mack shook his head, then looked at the screen and the teams' expectant gazes. "You able to get to this guy's computer files yet, Cam?"

"No. I hate to think he bested me, but I'm not giving up yet." He bent his head to his computer.

"I think it's best if you all catch a flight down here," Mack suggested. "If these guns are coming across the border tomorrow, you should be here and bring Bear. Sean, can you arrange a military hop? That way you won't waste time at an airport, and you can work on the flight. You'll also need a vehicle."

"Can do," Sean said.

"Let me know when you land. And let me know the minute you find anything." Mack closed the program with a tap of the touchpad.

"Calling the senator." Addy dialed his cellphone. His voicemail started playing right away, and she left him a concise and urgent message. Disappointed, she looked at Mack. "Voicemail. Hopefully he'll call back."

Mack started to speak when his phone rang, pulling his attention away. He glanced at the screen. "It's the ASAC from the local office."

"I want to hear." Addy slid closer.

"Deputy Jordan," Mack answered. "I'm with Agent Leigh, and you're on speaker."

"We had a report of a man fitting Razo's description outside the bodega," the ASAC said. "He's looking for a driver for tomorrow. We thought you'd want in on the bust."

"You thought right." Mack's frustration evaporated as excitement burst onto his face.

"Your hotel's right on the way. I'll pick you up."

"I'll be in the parking lot waiting." Mack ended the call but didn't look at Addy.

She assumed he planned to leave her at the hotel for her safety, yet she wasn't staying behind. She got up and grabbed her jacket.

Mack held up his hand. "I know you want in on this, but it could be a trap set by Razo. I'd rather you stay here."

She crossed her arms. "I want to go."

"I know you do, but would you please stay here?" He stood. "You should wait for the senator's call back anyway, right?"

She held up her phone and smiled at him. "I don't know if you've heard, but these things work anywhere."

Despite the tension in the air, he laughed. "I can't decide for you, but I would do my job better if I wasn't worried about you."

She wanted to be present for Razo's arrest, but she didn't want to distract Mack. To endanger his life. "All right. I'll stay."

He swept her into his arms with the force of a small cyclone. "Thank you," he whispered against her hair. "I know you're doing this for me, and I appreciate it."

He leaned back, his eyes filling with what felt like a familiar fondness for her. Sure, he'd been looking at her in a similar way for days, but this was different, and memories of such feelings were pressing in on her.

"I gotta go," he said, but looked like he wanted to stay.

The reality of the situation settled in. She was sending him off to potentially deal with a lethal killer, and she wouldn't let him go without a kiss. She slid her hands into his hair and drew his head down. His mouth formed a surprised O, but she kissed it away. He responded with gusto, tugging her closer. Kissing her with abandon. As if this were the very last time he could.

She forgot everything. Everything but the fact that she was married to him. And the new realization that she wanted this man's touch and love in her life again soon. Wanted it very much, and his response said he wanted the same thing.

He groaned and pulled back. "As much as I want to stay here, I have to leave." She relaxed her arms, and he stepped free. "I'll call as soon as I know anything."

"Be careful." She cupped the side of his face. "Razo wouldn't hesitate to turn a gun on any one of you."

CHAPTER 23

AS ADDY PULLED UP to the JH Ranch, she knew Mack wouldn't be happy with her decision to drive out to Senator Noble's ranch on her own, but she had no choice. The senator called and said he was hopping a plane in two hours and either meet with him now or don't come at all. So of course she had to go.

The tall wrought-iron gate stood open, and she rolled slowly down the winding drive. Since she really didn't believe Noble could be involved in gunrunning, she didn't think she was in danger, but she remained aware of her surroundings just in case. She drove past pastures with neatly painted fences, but dark shadows stopped her from seeing if alpacas grazed in the enclosure.

She approached a large two-story home that could be located in any affluent neighborhood in suburban America. Totally not the sprawling single-story house she'd expected to find on a ranch. She could easily imagine Mack's comments if he were here. He seemed to be a true cowboy through and through, and calling this place a ranch wouldn't sit well with him.

She parked and checked her sidearm, her bulky gloves in her jacket pocket making it hard to access the gun. She'd forgotten to take them out before leaving Oregon. She didn't need them here, so she tossed them onto the seat and peered in the mirrors.

Certain she was safe, she got out and hurried through a brisk wind to the double front door. A carriage-style light cast a warm glow over the sandstone pavers at her feet. She rang the doorbell and turned to look out over the property that seemed to go on forever. She'd researched the senator and read that the land had been in the Noble family for generations. It had at one time been a cattle ranch, and a forest fire had destroyed the original house.

The door opened, and she grabbed her ID as she spun to find the handsome senator standing tall, towering over her by a good six inches. Physically fit, he wore a crisp white shirt, black dress pants, and a politician's smile. His eyes were a deep blue, his hair silvery gray.

She held out her ID. "Special Agent Addison Leigh."

He shoved out a hand. "Jack Noble. Nice to meet you, Agent Leigh."

She often told people she interviewed to call her Addy to help them relax, but something about this man's demeanor told her to keep things formal.

"Thank you for seeing me on such short notice." She stowed her creds.

"I'm always glad to help in an investigation that makes the people I represent safer." Sincerity rang through his tone, and he stepped back. "Come in. I have fifteen minutes, then I'm afraid I'll have to ask you to leave."

"Fair enough," she said and vowed to squeeze every one of her questions into the time limit.

He closed the door and led her through a lobby with a sweeping staircase and sparkling chandelier, the air carrying the sweet, almost cloying scent of a woman's perfume. Addy wanted to comment on the smell and the lack of ranch feel, but she didn't want to lead them down a rabbit hole that would take time from her real questions.

He stepped into a dark study, the wall behind a large desk holding thick legal books. He'd been a DA before running for Senate so that made sense. He gestured at two leather barrel-shaped chairs that *did* look like they belonged on a ranch. "Can I get you a drink? Water? Coffee?"

"No, thank you." She forced a smile and sat. She didn't want to waste time with waiting for drinks.

He sat next to her and propped a leg on the other, then leaned back looking attentive. "Now, what's this about some of my properties?"

She hadn't talked to Mack about this but decided on the drive over that the best course of action was to be upfront with Noble. "We're investigating a gunrunner who is soliciting drivers to cross over the border and bring drugs and guns into our country. It turns out he's been hiring these men outside your malls."

He tipped his head and kept his focus on her. "I'm sorry to hear that someone is running drugs and guns. But I'm afraid you'll have to be more specific with me. I own a lot of commercial real estate."

"This would be properties listed under a holding company called Harp Holdings."

"Oh, that," he said, sounding casual, but a muscle twitched in his face.

When he didn't say anything else, she leaned forward. "Can you give me a list of all the properties for this company?"

"Of course, but I'm not sure how that will help you."

"First, let me say we don't believe you have anything to do with this gunrunner, but for some reason he's singling out your properties. It would help if we could confirm that our list is complete."

"Let me print one." He lurched to his feet and went to sit behind his desk.

She watched him maneuver his computer mouse and stare at his screen. If he was uncomfortable with this line of questioning, he didn't show it other than that muscle twinge, which could mean nothing.

The printer on a credenza whirred to life, and he came back to hand over the report. She ran down the page and noted several properties not on Cam's original list: "Does this include all the commercial properties you own?"

"No." He sat, informally crossing his ankles.

"So the other properties aren't part of Harp Holdings?"

"That's correct."

Okay, so he was cooperating, yet she was going to have to drag information out of him. "How do you decide which properties fall under this umbrella?"

He narrowed those sapphire-blue eyes. "I'm glad to answer, but I'm going to have to ask you to keep this confidential."

Interesting. "I'll only share it with the task force."

He gave a firm nod. "I wanted to do something to make a difference for the lower-income families in my constituency, yet I didn't want it to become public knowledge."

She met his gaze. "No offense, but as a politician I would think it would be seen as a good thing."

"It could also be seen as hypocritical." He gestured at the room. "One look at my home on my ranch, plus my other properties, and voters could see me as a slumlord making money from the hardworking store owners."

"Do you make money from these properties?"

"I do, but I put every penny back into updating and improving the malls, which benefits my tenants and their businesses."

"But also benefits you. The improvements increase the value of your properties."

"True. However, I charge a very low rent compared to many of the other landlords, and my tenants are happy with the deals I've offered them. They're always glad to renew their leases."

Did he really understand his tenants or was he wishing this was the truth? "How long have you owned these properties?"

He perched his arms on the chair. "I've accumulated them over the last three years."

She counted down the list. "Nine strip malls. That's a lot of property to buy in three years."

"It is." He gave her a tight smile. "But again, I want to give back in a way I know will help my constituents, and the timing was right for me."

Addy nodded, but something told her there was more to his story. "So why do you need to keep the properties under a shell corp?"

"As I mentioned, I don't want the leases linked to me. As a politician, my life is an open book. If I didn't somehow segregate them, word would get out."

She held out her paper. "Might I trouble you for an updated list that shows when you bought the properties?"

His gaze turned cold. "It's starting to feel like you're implying something untoward on my part here."

"I'm not." She gave him the best smile she could muster. "I'm just trying to be thorough. I know how busy you are, so I don't want to have to come back for additional information."

"I appreciate that." He stood and towered over her. "Let me get that information for you, and then I'm afraid our time is up."

"Thank you." She watched him cross the room with sure strides. "I'm assuming your tenants don't know you own these buildings?"

"That's correct," he said as he sat. "Word would get out if they did."

"You don't visit them, then, to see if they need any repairs."

"I have a management company who handles that for me." He looked up. "Did you visit the malls and find a problem?"

"No problems. Just another routine question." She smiled again and felt like her face was going to crack.

The printer started up, and she considered mentioning Razo's, Zamora's, or the three sovereign citizens' names just to see how he reacted. *No. Not a good idea.* The question would alert him to her investigation. He could have his people start digging, warning their suspects that she was hot on their tails.

That's the last thing she wanted to happen, so she stood and kept her mouth shut. She could always interview him again, though with his closed expression right now, she suspected he would dodge her calls, and she would have her work cut out for her if she wanted to pin him down again.

————

Mack charged out of his vehicle, along with ASAC Grant Ingersol and three of his agents. Wearing tactical vests and raising their rifles, they rushed down the street toward two men with caps pulled low over their eyes. Mack expected an air of intrigue to surround them. Instead, they looked like two guys just talking, and Mack's hope that they would find Razo waned.

The sun had long disappeared, and a cold wind whipped against Mack's body, pelting stinging sand into his face. Into his eyes too, but he kept them wide open as he approached.

"Police!" Ingersol yelled.

"Hands! Hands! Hands!" Mack shouted in case they decided to draw down on him. "Hands where I can see them."

They lifted their arms, and Mack got his first view of their faces. One of them looked a bit like Razo, and yet Mack couldn't be sure from this distance.

Three feet in front of the men, Mack took a stance. "Face-down on the ground. Now! Do it!"

They both dropped, and that was his second hint that he wasn't dealing with Razo. He would've balked. Maybe not outright, but he would've at least given Mack a look of disdain before he dropped to the ground.

"Cuff them," Ingersol ordered his men.

The local agents took charge of cuffing the worried men and started searching them.

"Names," Mack demanded.

"Santiago Gomez," the tallest man said.

The second man glanced up at Mack. "Alonzo Martinez."

"Verify their IDs," Ingersol instructed his agents.

A well-built agent dug into the first guy's jeans pocket to remove his wallet. "Driver's license confirms this one."

Mack snapped a picture of his ID with his phone and bent his head against the sharp wind still carrying the biting sand.

The other agent grabbed the wallet of the second man. "This one is who he says he is."

Mack took a picture of that ID too. "Get them to their feet."

They hauled them up, and Mack fixed his best intimidating look on the men. "What are you doing on this street corner at this time of night?"

"A guy paid me to find a driver for him," Gomez said, the resemblance to Razo uncanny.

"What guy?" Mack asked.

Gomez shrugged. "Came up to me and said he wanted to take a vacation in Mexico but needed a driver who knew the area and asked if I would do it. I'm born and raised here in California. Don't know much about Mexico. So I said no. He said he'd pay me a grand to find someone for him. So I started asking around. Was talking to Martinez here. Then you showed up."

"What did this man look like?" Mack asked.

Gomez tilted his head, looking like he was thinking. "Honestly, he looked a lot like me. Short. Shaved head."

Mack's adrenaline spiked. This guy was right. Razo did look like him, so maybe Razo was in town after all. "How's he going to pay you?"

"He said he would meet me at the laundromat down the street tomorrow at ten a.m. Said to bring the driver who should be prepared to travel right away."

Mack couldn't believe the things people decided to do. "And you trusted him?"

"Trusted him?" He rolled his eyes. "Nah. But I figured it was all done in a public place, so I should be safe enough to get my grand and go. Been out of work for a while. Need the money."

Mack had to admit to being disappointed in not finding Razo here. Maybe it was a waste of time. He didn't even know if these men were related to their investigation. Sure, Gomez described Razo, but the laundromat wasn't one of the businesses where Zamora had hired people in the past. It just didn't fit the pattern. But needing a driver for tomorrow? That fit the timeline all right.

Ingersol stepped to the side and nodded for Mack to join him. "You're calling the shots here. You want to bring these guys in for questioning?"

"Yes," Mack said. "Hold them until we can at least check out their backgrounds and until the laundromat meet tomorrow, which we'll stake out."

"You got it." Ingersol went back to his agents.

Mack's phone rang and he grabbed it from his pocket. "What's up, Cam?"

"The three sovereign-citizen guys have posted and are more connected than I first thought," Cam said. Mack heard the plane's engines in the background and knew they were on their way to San Diego. "Plus BloodyFox has started posting."

Mack's interest perked up. "Razo? What's he saying?"

"He's ranting about the federal government and taxes. Then goes off on a long tangent on law-enforcement oversight. He ends with a clear statement saying he's going to help ease that oversight. That the number of Feds harassing them will soon be less."

"That coupled with our other information is enough to put out a warrant for his arrest," Mack said, his mind racing after hearing this news. "Can you track the posts back to a location?"

"Not with the Tor browser that he's using."

Mack slammed his fist on the nearby car. They only had until tomorrow to find this guy and the guns, and he'd all but admitted what he planned to do. "Is it possible they're using some sort of code?"

"Doesn't look like it, but I could forward the messages to D.C. and get the cryptanalyst examiners working on it."

"Do that. I'll get in touch with Eisenhower to put pressure on them to work the messages right away."

"I've also narrowed down the targets, and I don't think it's the federal building."

"Then what?" Mack asked but dreaded hearing the answer.

"A regional meeting of several agencies starts tomorrow at the convention center in Portland. All the bigwigs will be there. A perfect target, as it has less security than the federal building. Plus they can attack the hotel where the attendees are staying." Cam shared the nearby hotel's information.

Mack's stomach filled with acid, and it burned up his throat. He had one priority and only one priority now. Stop hundreds, maybe thousands of government leaders in the region from sure death. But could he do it? The clock was nearing zero, and the guns would be arriving sometime tomorrow.

He swallowed down the acid and the pain burning in his gut and set his sights on being the agent he'd grown to be. A tough and get-it-done kind of agent. One who didn't let anything best him. "I'll tell Eisenhower when I call him. Let me know if any of the guys posts anything that could lead us to him."

Mack ended the call and got Eisenhower on the phone, first asking for him to put pressure on the cryptanalyst, then telling him about the convention center and hotel. He was met with silence at first. Not a good sign. Eisenhower was never at a loss for words.

"Then you should know," he finally said, "your guys are on the move. All three of them. Heading toward Portland."

Mack let the news register for a moment. "It's a day's drive from San Diego to Portland, so it's too soon for them to be picking up the guns. They could be meeting to plan."

"That's what I was thinking. We'll keep tailing them, and I'll let you know where they settle."

Mack felt like he was going to hurl. Time was running out, but the suspects were on the move, maybe planning to take control of the guns and put them into action. "Can you warn the convention center and hotel security?"

"We don't have any concrete evidence that they're the target. Once we get that, then yes. We'll be all over both buildings." Eisenhower fell silent. "Get me that proof, Jordan, and get it now."

He hung up, and Mack felt like a man alone on a deserted island, trying to get off but not finding the way. At least the team should arrive soon, and they could put their heads together to find that elusive lead before time ran out.

Mack's phone vibrated, reminding him of the earlier voice-mail. He tapped the icon and was surprised to see Addy had made the call. He played her message. *"Noble called back. Had to go talk to him now at his ranch or he would be out of pocket. Will meet you back at the hotel."*

Mack's gut tightened as he tapped her phone number to return the call. It went straight to voicemail. He didn't like her going out on her own. Didn't like it one bit. She could be in danger, and that was why she couldn't answer.

His heart started pounding, thumping wildly in his chest. He ran over to Ingersol. "Give me your keys. I need to leave now!"

Without question, Ingersol dug out his key ring, and Mack snatched it out of his hands. He ran for the SUV, praying as he went that Addy was simply interviewing the senator and her life wasn't in danger.

———

Questions Addy wished she could've asked the senator burned in her mind as she drove toward the hotel, but the light on her phone kept flashing so she pulled over to answer it. Mack's name appeared on the screen.

"What's so urgent?" she asked.

"Thank God, you're okay," he said, his voice shooting through the phone like a piercing bullet.

She blinked, trying to figure out why he was so concerned. "I'm fine, why?"

"You went off on your own, and I—" anguish deepened his tone—"was worried."

"Sorry. I had to go." She explained about the senator leaving town. "Did you arrest Razo?"

"No." He released a long breath of air. "It was some flunky who was looking for a driver for a tourist. At least that's what he claims. Ingersol has him and another guy in custody until we can confirm his statement."

Mack paused, and it sounded like he might be taking in big breaths but at the same time trying to hide it. "How did it go with the senator?"

"He was very cooperative." She shared the highlights of her interview.

"Do you think he's involved?"

Did she? "Honestly, I don't know. He was cooperative, but there was this undercurrent. He could just be playing me. He *is* a politician after all. He plays people for a living."

"What about his ranch? Did it seem like the kind of place drugs or weapons could be staged?"

"I couldn't really tell much in the dark, and he didn't offer me a tour."

Mack told her about Razo's online message. "We don't have any time to lose. We need to get a look around the ranch."

"It's not going to happen without a warrant." Addy thought about how she could make it happen, though it seemed to be a losing cause. "I doubt that Harris will approve such a thing when there's nothing solid pointing to the senator's involvement."

"Yeah, but it's our only real lead right now, so we have to

follow this up." He paused. "A drone. We could fly one overhead with a camera on it."

Really? He wants to pilot a drone? A big part of his PTSD revolved around having to fire from drones that killed innocent people. His suggestion showed how desperate he'd become with the investigation. She was thankful he would go the extra mile, willing to sacrifice his mental well-being like that. "We could do that if we had one," she said.

"We'll buy one."

She glanced at her watch. "It's almost eight o'clock."

"I'm sure I can find a store that's open. We don't need an expensive drone, and many retailers sell them these days." There was another pause. "I'm nearing the turnoff for the ranch. We'll meet up, and I'll lead the way to a store."

"If you're sure."

"I am," he said resolutely.

She ended the call and waited on the deserted road. She felt the heavy weight of the sovereign-citizen threat on her shoulders. Sure, she wanted to find Razo and put the guy away. Always had since her investigation started, but now it was more about saving lives. Lives of people she could now picture in her mind. Put faces to.

Flashing headlights cut into her thoughts, and she got her vehicle going to fall in line behind Mack. She trailed him down dusty roads to a nearby strip mall that was clean and well-maintained. Not the kind of mall Noble would own. The neighborhood was too upscale.

She parked next to Mack's SUV. He was out of it and at her door before she turned off the engine.

She pushed her door open, and he ran his gaze over her. "You really are okay?"

"I really am."

He shook his head. "I lost ten years of my life when I listened to your voicemail."

Her heart warmed over his concern for her, and yet she hated that he'd been so worried. "Sorry. I thought leaving a message was better than letting you show up to find a note at the hotel."

"No matter how I got the news, I would've lost it."

She looked at him. At this big, strong man with a tender heart basically telling her he loved her so much that he about fell apart just hearing she might have found herself in danger.

Would she react the same way for him? That was something she needed to search her heart to find out, although now wasn't the time.

He gestured at the small electronics store. "We need to get moving."

As they headed for the door, she looked at him, trying to find any sign of anxiety over the drone. "You sure you're good to do this?"

"You mean the drone?"

She nodded.

"It's only carrying a camera, so yeah, I should be fine." He sounded sure, but his expression darkened a little when he said it.

She squeezed his arm, and he placed his hand over hers for a brief moment, smiling at her. She felt his touch deep in her soul. Probably in the place where she knew she loved him. Because if anything had become clear to her regarding Mack, it was that if her memory returned, she would learn she was madly in love with him. And that thought sat just fine right now. She wouldn't think of all their problems. Of their separation. She would just enjoy getting to know him and falling for him again.

He removed his hand and opened the door to the store. The place was filled with shelves loaded with electronics, a full wall in the rear holding only drones. She hung back and watched Mack talk technical details with the skinny salesperson. The guy had a goatee and long hair bound in a ponytail at his neck. He fidgeted with the ponytail and kept reminding Mack that his name was Jeff. Addy figured the guy was on commission and wanted to be sure to get his cut of any sale. But he was the only salesperson in the store so maybe he didn't think Mack was ready to buy or Jeff was counting on repeat business. They finally settled on what Addy considered a pricey drone. Jeff beamed with happiness over the sale.

Mack paid for the drone and joined her.

She looked at him. "If you think that thing is inexpensive, then we have a far different definition of the word."

He chuckled all the way to the door. "This one's not cheap, but I decided it would be good to have greater range to provide more anonymity."

"Makes sense." She held the door open for him since he was carrying a big box. "Let's hope this will do the trick and we find where Razo is staging his guns."

His smile fell. "It's a long shot, but the only thing we've got right now."

They hurried toward the SUV, and Addy put her head down to manage the buffeting wind that threatened to push her back.

As they neared their rental vehicle, a man shot out from behind a wall. He hefted a tire iron.

She opened her mouth to warn Mack, but the guy slammed the tire iron down on Mack's head.

"No!" she screamed.

Mack and the drone dropped to the ground.

"Mack!" Addy called out, her hand shooting to her sidearm. Her fingers touched the grip.

A strong arm grabbed her from behind and pinned her against a solid wall of muscle. Not the guy who hit Mack, but a second man. He started dragging her backward.

She kicked and fought. Churning her legs. Lifting up on her arms to break free. The iron band held her in place.

"Help!" she screamed. "Help!"

The man clamped a hand over her mouth and tightened the

other one. She tried to open her mouth to bite him. His hand was pressed too firmly for her to move her lips. She dug in her heels.

He jerked harder. Her feet scraped along the pavement.

"Mack," she tried to get out, but couldn't as he lay deathly quiet on the ground. She watched him for movement. Looking for anything. A breath. A moan.

The man holding her shoved her back against an idling pickup truck. He secured zip ties around her wrists, cutting deep into her skin, then opened the truck door and jerked her gun from its holster. Then he pushed her into the cab next to the first man, who reeked of cigars.

"Nice piece," her abductor said, admiring her gun as he climbed in beside her and closed the door. He displayed it for the other guy.

"Really nice," the driver said. "Now put it out of her reach."

The truck roared off, racing past Mack. She took one final look at him. He didn't move.

Father, please let him be alive. Please. Please. Please.

CHAPTER 24

MACK WOKE WITH A SPLITTING HEAD and to sirens screaming so loud that he knew he had to be outside. He touched his throbbing head, and his hand came away bloody.

Blood. What in the world? What happened? Where was he?

He was too dizzy to stand so he slowly turned his head and looked around. He was lying on a sidewalk. Cars, streetlights casting shadows nearby. But where?

He pressed his hands against the rough concrete and tried to sit. Dizziness took him back down. He smelled a spicy scent in the wind that howled over him. Okay, a restaurant was nearby.

"You're in luck," a male said from above. "They didn't steal the drone."

"Drone? What drone?" Mack looked up at the skinny guy with a blond goatee and long hair pulled back in a ponytail.

"The one you just bought from me in the store." He jerked a thumb over his shoulder.

"I . . ." Mack glanced at the store, then blinked a few times, still trying to get his bearings. He'd never felt this out of it, other than coming out of anesthesia after surgery. Someone must have really clocked him hard over the head.

"Hey"—the guy pinned his gaze on Mack—"where's the chick?"

Chick. What chick? Addy. He meant Addy.

"Addy!" Mack pushed himself to sit up. The world spun. "Addy!"

He looked around. He could hardly remain sitting as everything swam around him. His stomach churned. He might hurl right on the spot. "Maybe she went for help."

"I called 911." The guy Mack now recognized as salesman Jeff narrowed his eyes. "Didn't have other calls as far as I know."

"Addy!" Mack grabbed the bumper behind him and hauled himself to his feet. He tried to take a step. Staggered. Rested on the vehicle hood and looked around as a police car came screaming into the parking lot. An officer got out and marched toward him.

He wore a khaki uniform, and his hair the color of coal was slicked back on his head.

Mack dug out his ID, the world swirling with each movement. He displayed his credentials. "There was a woman with me. Fellow agent, Addison Leigh. She's missing. I suspect she's been kidnapped. Put out an alert on her."

The officer's dark eyebrows went up, a heavy measure of skepticism in his expression. "You suspect kidnapping? Why's that?"

Addy didn't have time for Mack to get this guy on board, but he had no choice if he wanted the officer to take action. "I didn't actually see it happen, but she wouldn't leave me lying here unless someone forcibly took her."

The officer looked at Jeff. "And you? You see it?"

"Nah," Jeff said. "Just heard one of those big trucks with a loud muffler roar off. We've had some problems with theft in the area, so I went over to the window to see if I was in for trouble. Seen this guy on the ground. Drone was next to him. Called 911."

"Look," Mack said, "I don't have time to explain, but someone's been trying to kill Agent Leigh. Now she's disappeared."

"What if she went after them?"

Mack scanned the lot. "Both of our vehicles are still here. Put out that alert now!"

"Her description," the officer demanded.

Mack described her size, build, hair color, and cut his eyes to the salesman. "You get a look at the truck?"

He stroked his goatee. "Mighta been white or light silver. Big one."

"Pickup or bigger?" the officer asked.

"Just a full-sized pickup."

The officer leaned down to his radio and reported the information. Mack reached for his phone to call Addy, but his screen was shattered and the device wouldn't wake up.

He shoved out a hand to the officer. "Phone. Let me use your phone to call her."

The officer pulled it from the clip on his vest, and Mack snatched it up. Thankfully, Addy had the same phone number for years, and Mack had memorized it the same way he'd done for the RED team and Eisenhower for just such a situation.

The call went straight to voicemail. Addy had likely silenced her phone for her interview with the senator and forgotten to change it back. Or the person who took her had destroyed the phone. Yeah, that was more likely, and the thought sent a wave of nausea through his stomach.

He swallowed hard. Swallowed again, panic sitting on his shoulders and threatening to take him.

So now what? What did he do? Just what?

His brain felt like mush. Like a web of confusion. The pain sharp and all-consuming.

Think. Think. Forget the pain. Forget everything but Addy. She's depending on you.

He looked around for a lead. Searched the walls. The ground. Spotted a folded piece of paper near a car tire. He slowly bent to pick it up, his stomach clenching, his vision blurring. With his sleeve, he reached for it. Wouldn't do to contaminate evidence. If it even was evidence. He came up and rested on the SUV before his legs buckled. He opened it.

The words DEAD OR ALIVE were printed in shocking red at the top of the page, and a color picture of Addy leaving the bodega covered the bottom half of the paper.

Addy. A piercing pain cut through Mack's chest.

He displayed the flyer for the officer. "This is Agent Leigh. Obviously, I wasn't exaggerating. The threat to her life is real. Very real indeed."

———

Addy's wrists were already bloody and raw from trying to escape the tight plastic ties, but she wouldn't just sit between the two men and not do something. At least the goon sitting on her right had bound her hands in front, so she didn't have her arms jerked behind her back where she would be leaning on them and they would go numb. A mistake too. This way she had use of her hands. Given a chance, she could potentially break the ties.

The goon who'd restrained her leaned forward and rummaged through a pile of things on the dashboard. A piece of paper drifted to the floor. The yellow light from the dash highlighted it. She squinted but really didn't need to because the print was huge, and she couldn't miss the words DEAD OR ALIVE at the top. She moved down the page to the picture.

Me?

That was a picture of her on the paper. These men were hunting her. Her!

A gasp climbed up her throat. She quickly swallowed it away to keep from alerting them to her discovery.

Were they going to kill her? Or now that they had her alive, would they hand her over that way?

Goon One kept rummaging and found a pack of cigarettes. He cracked the window a fraction.

"No smoking in my truck, LeRoy," Goon Two said and glared at his partner.

"Big-man Holt," LeRoy snapped. "Always bossing me."

Holt's brown, nearly black eyes narrowed and focused, sending a chill over her. He was the dangerous one. The one she had to look out for.

LeRoy shook his head and tapped a cigarette out of the pack.

"I said *no*." Holt's icy tone held a warning Addy would never try to cross.

LeRoy tossed the pack back onto the dash.

Okay, so Holt was clearly in charge. And better dressed and groomed too. Clean jeans. Plaid shirt. Neatly cut black hair. Short on the sides. Longer on the top. His lips now pursed, and his focus back on the road.

"Where are you taking me?" she asked him.

"None of your business," LeRoy answered instead.

She turned her attention to him and memorized everything about his face. The narrow chin with a generous shadow of dark whiskers. A hook-shaped scar near his left ear. Small tufts of hair growing from the same ear. A pointed nose. Green eyes. Blond hair. Dirty and messy. And strong body odor.

"Are you working for Razo?" she asked.

She got a grunt in return.

"Might as well tell me. It's not like I'm going anywhere," she said, though she was keeping track of every turn to see if she knew where the driver was headed.

"Shut up," Holt said, his tone even sharper now.

She kept her focus on him and didn't give up. Not with so much at stake and so little time to go before the guns arrived. "I just want some information."

"Well, you ain't gettin' none." LeRoy glared at her. "Now shut up before I make you shut up."

"FYI," Holt said as he approached a stoplight and turned to lock gazes with her. "If you don't cooperate, neither of us is opposed to shutting you up. Permanently."

"For the Spirit God gave us does not make us timid, but gives us power, love and self-discipline." Mack repeated it again. _"For the Spirit God gave us does not make us timid, but gives us power, love and self-discipline."_

It didn't help for once. Nothing did as the next three hours passed in a blur. A nightmarish blur. One that Mack wished he was sharing with his teammates, who were winging their way closer. Thankfully it was only a short flight and they were due to touch down any moment. Mack was also thankful that they were bringing Bear. Hopefully the dog could help track Addy's scent.

But what about the guns? He couldn't forget they arrived tomorrow. Even if his head was splitting. He'd gone to the hospital, had been checked out, and was cleared. The doc said he might have a concussion but that was all. Mack had survived far worse in the past. Thankfully, because he had two priorities right now. First, he had to find Addy and then stop a mass killing. Addy had to come first, though, as she was in the most imminent danger. Yet he had to keep the sovereign citizens and their deadly plans in the forefront of his mind too.

His phone rang. He wished he had his real phone instead of this one he'd sent Jeff to buy for him, because then he'd know the caller's identity. He quickly answered, "Mack Jordan."

"Your suspects have met up," Eisenhower said.

"Where?" Mack held his breath.

"They checked into the same hotel booked for the convention."

Mack sucked in a breath.

"They're hunkered down in a room. We've got eyes on them now, but this is a big hotel and there are plenty of opportunities for one or more of them to ditch our guys. I hope it doesn't happen, but you should know it could."

Mack let out that breath and had to work to take another.

"Any word on Addy?" Eisenhower asked.

"Nothing."

"Call me the minute you know anything, and I'll keep you updated on the suspects."

Mack ended the call before he became emotional and Eisenhower pulled him from the investigation. Not like Mack would quit. Not without someone physically restraining him. No way he'd ignore Addy being held against her will, or the potential for his fellow Feds to lose their lives.

Mack paced the sidewalk, dodging forensic staff hunting for even a speck of evidence to find Addy. He held the phone and willed it to ring with the team calling to tell him they'd arrived.

Mack had requisitioned security feeds from each store in the mall and reviewed them until he found one that captured Addy being dragged to a white pickup truck. He'd scanned the video for plates, but the truck didn't have any. Likely removed for this kidnapping.

Kidnapping. Addy had been kidnapped. Right on Mack's watch. Unthinkable. Unfathomable. How had he let that happen? He'd let his guard down, that was how. Just for that moment. He knew better. How he knew better. Thought he'd learned his lesson. But no. He'd failed again. Not with just any person, but the most important person in his life.

He lifted his hand to slam it against his forehead and stopped. The pain cutting his head in two was already too intense. No way he'd make it worse and risk incapacitating himself.

He viewed the video over and over again but couldn't make out the features of the driver and the guy who was manhandling Addy. When Mack got his hands on that guy . . .

He growled and stared at the phone. "Come on, Cam. Call."

Mack had sent the video to Cam to improve the quality and run facial recognition. They had to get an ID. They just had to. They had nothing else to go on. Only other lead Mack had was a printout of malls in the senator's holding company that Mack had found in Addy's rental vehicle. Mack doubted it meant anything, yet he'd pocketed it for Cam to review the new properties listed to see if it gave them a lead.

The phone rang, and Mack nearly jumped out of his skin. "Please tell me you're on the ground."

"We are," Sean said, sounding far too calm for Mack's liking. "Just down the street."

A wave of relief washed over Mack. "Any ID on our guys?"

"Not yet. Cam couldn't enhance the video enough. He sent it off to D.C., and they're working on it."

Mack's heart fell. "So why the call?"

"Zamora finally talked. At least somewhat. He's still not giving up the name of his boss, but he mentioned an apartment he has down here. Said his boss—who we know is Razo—uses it sometimes."

Hope took purchase in Mack's heart. "Tell me Zamora gave up the address."

"He did, and we know you'll want to be in on that raid."

CHAPTER 25

MACK, SEAN, AND KILEY CREPT UP on the apartment located in a far nicer area of town than the seedy neighborhood where Zamora and Razo did their dirty work. Newer model cars filled the lot, and a cheery yellow color highlighted by the full moon covered the walls. Mack wouldn't hesitate to live in the upscale neighborhood, and it was going to shock the neighbors when they learned they shared walls with a drug lord and gunrunner, and even worse, a child trafficker.

Mack glanced back at the SUV, where Cam sat in the front seat, with Bear lying in the back. The dog had whined to join in, but Mack couldn't allow that. It would mess with their team's rhythm. Cam couldn't participate in the raid either, so he was babysitting Bear and reviewing the new mall information Addy had obtained from the senator.

Mack made eye contact with Sean and Kiley and questioned their readiness with a sharp look.

They each nodded.

Mack lifted the battering ram and slammed it into the door, fracturing the framing. The door swung in and clapped back at him. He dropped the ram and lifted his gun.

"Police!" he shouted before entering the dim room.

He swung the light on his gun over the living area holding leather furniture and piles of personal belongings. It adjoined a small kitchen. No sign of movement.

"Clear," Mack said.

The living room led to the left, and he followed it through a door and into the first of two bedrooms. The small room held an unmade double bed and tripod with camera. The closet was bare, the room unoccupied. Mack couldn't focus on what the camera equipment meant right now—he had to keep moving.

"Clear," he called as he backed out.

Kiley was stepping out of the hall bathroom. "Clear."

Sean marched to the second bedroom and shook his head. "No one here."

Mack wanted to curse. Shout. Punch. Do anything other than not find Addy. "We might have a storage space on the patio."

He crossed the room and whipped open the sliding door, disappointed when he didn't spot a door to a storage space.

"Let's get some lights on and see what we can find." Inside, Kiley flipped on an overhead light, revealing the tattered black furniture and personal possessions that turned out to be piles of young girls' clothing. Suggestive clothing and costumes too.

Kiley slung her rifle strap over her shoulder and glared at the piles. "He was filming girls here."

Mack's gut churned. "We'll need to get forensics out here so we can prosecute Zamora for trafficking girls, but first we search for a lead on Addy. Look for anything that might tell us Razo has been here and where he might've taken her. I'm gonna grab Bear and take the first bedroom. Sean, you have the second one. Kiley, you get the living area. Put gloves on and do a careful search so we leave the place like we found it for forensics."

They split up, and Mack rushed down the stairs to the SUV. He opened the back door and tapped his leg. "Come."

Bear eagerly bounded out of the vehicle and sat at Mack's side.

"I'm guessing you don't mean me," Cam's tone was rife with his usual sarcasm. "What'd you find?"

"Nothing other than proof that Zamora was filming girls in this apartment."

Cam shook his head. "Sick."

"You got anything?" Mack reached in to grab one of Addy's gloves that she'd left in the rental vehicle.

"Not yet." He looked back at his computer.

"We're heading back inside." He grabbed Bear's leash. "Come, boy."

They marched across the lot and up the stairs. He gave Bear a sniff of Addy's glove and released him. Nose down like a vacuum cleaner, Bear crossed the main area but didn't light on anything. Mack led him to the bedroom. Nothing. No sign of recognition, and he stopped to look up at Mack. He grabbed a treat from his pocket and gave it to Bear. The dog's wet tongue scooped it up and he devoured it one bite, then sat expectantly. He'd been trained to do his job in the police world for rewards. Usually not food but a toy that came out only after a search, but sometimes a snack was the easiest thing to have on hand.

"Sorry, boy." Mack ruffled the dog's fur. "That's it. Don't want you to get fat."

Mack's heart sinking, he ignored the pain of not finding Addy and looked at Sean. "No indication that Addy's been here. I'll get on searching that other bedroom."

As he left the room, Bear trotted behind him. If only Bear knew that Addy was missing, maybe he could lead them to something. The dog might be highly trained, but he couldn't know the person who loved him so much was in danger until he got close enough to her.

"Search," Mack commanded, and while the dog did his job, Mack went straight to the computer sitting on a scarred night-stand. He shouldn't touch the machine. Just waking it up would alter evidence, but finding Addy trumped evidential procedures. He could have one of the team image it first, except that would take hours, and if she was in the hands of a man who would traffic young girls, she was in very bad hands.

Mack put on latex gloves and woke up the device. Explicit pictures of a teenage girl who should be going to prom, football games, and movies filled the screen, and his heart tore. He'd seen bad things in his career, but trafficking of innocent girls was one of the hardest to take.

He minimized the photo to do a quick search, but only learned that the computer was used solely for capturing pictures and wouldn't help him at all. The only good news in all of this was that the quantity of photos on the machine would surely put Zamora and maybe Razo behind bars for a very, very long time.

Bear sat and looked expectantly at Mack. The dog had struck out too. Mack gave him a treat.

Before leaving the room, Mack checked under the bed with soiled bedding and found nothing. Disappointed, he joined Kiley and Sean in the living room and shared his findings or lack thereof.

"My bedroom held nothing of interest other than traces of illegal drug use," Sean said. "Toiletries in the bathroom suggested both male and female occupants."

"Zamora and the girls. Or maybe he had girlfriends here too." Kiley cringed. "The costumes he had them wear are all piled over there," she said, pointing. "Should be able to get good DNA from them, and maybe it will help bring home some missing girls."

Bear came to sit next to Mack. He handed over another treat and looked around the room. "How could neighbors not have seen this man bringing young girls here?"

"People mind their own business these days, even if it means others suffer." Kiley bent down and stroked Bear's head, likely needing some comfort.

Mack went to the kitchen and rummaged through cupboards and drawers. He found dishes and snack foods. The refrigerator held only beer, wine, and sodas.

He went back to his team. "Nothing in the kitchen to suggest someone actually lived here for very long at a time."

"And no hint of Razo," Sean said.

"We have to be missing something." Mack shoved a hand into his hair, his gloved fingers catching, and he jerked them out. He desperately looked around again. He spotted a folded piece of paper on the entryway floor, as if someone had slid it under the door. Likely a marketing flyer, but he went to pick it up anyway and unfolded it. He read the single line printed in large black letters.

This needs to end today.

"Odd." He held it out to the others.

"End the transport of a horrific weapon? Or the girls?" Kiley asked. "Or even something else?"

"I don't know," Mack snapped and resisted punching the wall. "I just don't know, and don't know how it impacts Addy. Or what to do? How do I find her? Just how?" His tone skated higher with each word as the pressure mounted.

Sean made strong eye contact and took a deep breath, letting it out slowly. Purposefully. "We need to calmly review the information we *do* have and formulate a plan."

"What do we have?" Mack gaped at him. "Nothing, that's what!"

"Not true," Sean said, that cool undercurrent to his tone not doing anything to calm Mack down. "We know Addy went to visit the senator before she disappeared. Let's start there. Retrace her route. Talk to the senator. Maybe find a lead that way."

"Let's go." Mack didn't wait for agreement but bolted out the door and down the stairs to the SUV. He opened the back door for Bear and found Cam leaning over the seat, connecting his portable scanner to his laptop in the cargo area, both sitting on the top of a storage bin.

Bear bounded in over his legs to curl up on the seat.

Cam looked over his shoulder at Mack. "Find anything?"

"Not much. Just this document lying on the floor in the entryway." Mack held up the paper.

As the others joined them, Cam took a long look at the page. "I'd like to scan it too."

"Because?" Mack gave Cam a glove, so he didn't put any prints or DNA on what might be evidence.

"I'd rather not say just yet." Cam put on the glove, took the page, and inserted it into the scanner. "I have a hunch, and I'll let you know if it pans out."

"Knock yourself out." Mack removed his gloves, ripped open the Velcro on his vest, and shrugged free to store it in a nearby bin.

He climbed in next to Bear and checked his phone, just in case there was information about Addy, but his blank screen stared up at him as if mocking him for failing to find the woman he loved. Not to mention also finding guns that could have taken her out in one burst of bullets. He was confident that he'd find the miniguns when he found Addy. He was struggling to find confidence in anything else.

God, please, he begged, *show me what to do here. Please. She needs me. The country needs me. Don't let me fail either of them.*

"For the Spirit God gave us does not make us timid, but gives us power, love and self-discipline." He tried to pay attention to his mantra and take some calming breaths, but the barely controlled panic joined the pain in his head and he could hardly think. Bear looked up at him, shifted, and rested his head on Mack's knee as if he knew Mack's pain. And he probably did know something was wrong. Mack stroked the dog's thick fur and continued to suck in air until he felt calm enough to think clearly.

Kiley took shotgun, pulling out her computer and setting it on her lap. "I'll get back to the human-trafficking angle while we drive."

"Thank you," Mack said, totally grateful that his teammates were able to work when he was a basket case.

Sean got behind the wheel and looked over the seat. "Where to?"

"Let's head back to the scene where Addy went missing, then try to trace her route back to the senator's ranch. We were planning on flying a drone over his place to see if he might be involved in this investigation, so that's a possibility." Mack ran a hand over his face. "Although I think it's a long shot at best." His head pounded.

Sean cranked the engine. "You don't think the senator's involved?"

Mack shook his head. "He's a family-values guy. Tough on crime as a DA. Revered by everyone. So clean, he squeaks. Not even a hint of impropriety in all his years in the Senate. Not exactly someone who would arrange a hit man and then kidnap a federal agent."

"You're probably right," Sean said. "I doubt he would get into bed with a guy like Zamora or Razo. Still, unless we find another lead at the crime scene, he's our best bet at the moment."

Mack nodded his agreement, the pain in his head intensifying, so he stopped. He didn't want to agree with Sean anyway. How could he when it meant that he had no real lead in finding Addy before her abductor did her harm?

———

Addy couldn't just sit between these two men and let them take her to her execution. They were headed into the country, but not on the same road she'd taken to the senator's ranch. They reached the foothills of the San Miguel Mountains, a range she remembered from studying the area map.

She had hoped momentarily that the senator *was* behind her abduction, as Mack would probably go forward with flying the drone over the ranch and might find her. But out here? He had no hope of locating her. Unless she found a way to tell him where their truck was headed.

They hadn't searched her or taken her phone, just her gun. Which was odd to her. Maybe they didn't usually do this kind of thing and didn't know what to do. The thought almost made her laugh. Hysterical kind of laughing. Not the let's-have-fun kind.

She swallowed it away. Steadied her mind. GPS was her best bet to be located, though she didn't routinely have it turned on for her phone, so they couldn't find her that way. She did have apps that were authorized to use GPS, if she could only open one of those.

What app could she use? Her brain blanked. Likely the stress. The pressure.

Think, Addy. Think.

She brought her phone screen to mind to mentally view the app icons. She ran through them row by row and landed on what3words.

Perfect.

She'd recently installed the app for emergencies. The app developers had assigned each three-meter square in the world a unique three-word address that would never change. After GPS triangulated your location, the app provided the three words you could more easily share with others instead of giving complicated GPS coordinates.

If she could get to her phone, place it on speaker and mute a call to Mack, then speak the words, he could find her. *If* he knew about the app. A big if, as many people didn't. But law enforcement used it, and so did emergency dispatchers. And he was a deputy, so she had a shot at him understanding.

The even bigger *if* was getting to her phone in her right pocket while sitting between these two men. She had to act quickly. Do it before they stopped. Before they searched her and took her phone. She faked scratching an itch on her left side and tugged her shirttail over her pocket, watching all the time to see if they reacted to her movements.

She looked at each one. Her heart thundered in her chest, and she held her breath.

Nothing. No interest in her movements at all.

She let out the breath slowly to keep from alerting them. Took another one. She was glad the phone was on LeRoy's side, as he wasn't the brightest of the two. She pretended to scratch again and slid her phone up, keeping the shirttail as coverage for her hands. Thankfully, the device was still silenced from her visit to the senator, and in nighttime mode so it wouldn't emit as much light.

She woke it up and got her thumb in position for the password, then tapped the app and waited for it to triangulate.

Please let me pull this off. Don't let the light from my phone alert them. Please.

———

Sean sat across the desk from the senator, but Mack couldn't sit. Not with Addy missing. He stood looking down on Noble, willing the man to confess to taking Addy and tell them where he was holding her. Yet Mack really didn't believe the guy had abducted her. They'd caught him in a lie when he'd told Addy he had to meet with her that night as he was leaving town, but that meant nothing. It could just be a white lie to get him out of talking to her for long. Or it could mean Noble was hiding something.

Time for Mack to home in on the guy and see what he really knew. "Have you heard of a man called Bruno Razo or a Dante Zamora?"

A sharp intake of air, barely noticeable but there, told Mack what he needed to know. The senator had heard of one or both of them.

"How do you know them?" Mack asked before Noble could answer.

Noble let his breath out slowly, almost imperceptibly. How many times had the senator done the same thing when trying to sidestep an issue in his political career? He would be a master at subterfuge, and Mack had to pay even more attention to each little nuance.

A tight smile crossed Noble's face. "What makes you think I *do* know them?"

"Come on, Senator." Sean sat forward. "Your reaction to the question was obvious. Just tell us about them."

Noble gritted his teeth. "Now that you mention it, I believe I've heard the names. I think they hire day laborers around town."

"Day laborers?" Mack asked. The senator's statement was so far from the truth that it was laughable.

"You know. Illegals who will work for pennies on the dollar." Noble pressed his hands flat on the arms of his chair but didn't grasp them. "Of course, if I ever witnessed such a thing, I would report it."

"Of course," Mack said, not trying to hide his sarcasm. "Now tell us how you really know these men."

Noble drew back and looked offended, but Mack thought he was putting up a front. Or maybe Mack wanted Noble to be hiding something because that meant Mack was questioning the right person and he would find Addy.

Fists pounded against the front door, and Mack spun, his hand going to his sidearm.

"Mack," Cam called out.

The door creaked open. "Mack. I need to see you right now."

"In here!" Praying Cam had a lead, Mack raced to the door.

The senator jumped to his feet. "What's the meaning of this break-in?"

"Sorry, Senator," Sean said. "That would be our teammate. He must have important information."

"But I didn't give him access to my home."

"He'll just be a minute." Sean kept placating the senator, but Mack didn't care if he was upset. Addy was missing and miniguns were ready to be shipped. Cam entering the house was a minor thing.

He was carrying his laptop, and his eyes were narrowed as he rushed through the big foyer and past décor that screamed of wealth.

"What do you have?" Mack asked.

"Not here." Cam grabbed Mack's arm and dragged him away from the door. "The letter you found at Zamora's place and the wanted flyer. They were printed on the same printer as the list of malls you found in Addy's car."

"The senator?" Mack gaped at Cam. "He printed the wanted flyer and the warning to stop? Are you sure?"

"Positive." Cam looked Mack directly in the eyes. "He has to be the secret boss Zamora refuses to turn on. The man who's in charge of smuggling the guns and who has Addy."

———

Addy held her breath and glanced between the two men, checking for any indication that they'd seen her wake up her phone.

LeRoy had his eyes closed. Holt was focusing on turning a corner.

Now was the time. She slid the phone up higher and opened the what3words app. The triangulation had completed. She memorized the words—*outpost, insertion, chocolates*—in case she was unable to do so when they reached their final destination.

She lowered her call volume down to mute and tapped Mack's icon.

Yes! She was succeeding. But her hands were trembling. She took another breath. Eased it out.

Holt slowed and turned to start climbing into the mountains. The truck bumped over deep ruts, the air rushing in from Holt's cracked window growing cooler.

"Where are we?" she asked loudly to make sure Mack could hear her.

"None of your beeswax." LeRoy leaned forward in anticipation.

Perfect. Neither of them was looking at her. She bowed her head.

"Mack, what3words," she said loudly and hoped the men didn't know about the app. Then she uttered the three words provided by the app even louder.

LeRoy looked at her. "Are you nuts or something?"

"Yeah," she said and shoved her phone deep into her pocket.

"Well, shut your yap. We're just about there. You're gonna soon find out your fate." He grinned at her, an evil smile that sent terror to her heart.

CHAPTER 26

MACK MARCHED ACROSS THE OFFICE to confront the senator. "It's you. You're the one behind it all. The gunrunning. The attempted murder. The kidnapping. Maybe even the upcoming massacre of federal employees with the miniguns."

Noble clasped a hand to his chest. "I beg your pardon."

"We have proof. This." Mack slammed their copy of the wanted *Dead or Alive* poster on the desk. "And this." He added the warning to Zamora. "Were printed on the same printer as the list you just gave Agent Leigh."

The senator paled. "You can't possibly prove something like that."

"We can actually." Cam stepped up to them. "Many printers add secret dots to pages as they print, and the dots form a pattern to tell us the make and serial number of the printer. All I have to do is match the number on these documents to your printer sitting there, and we have the proof we need."

Noble picked up the top page. "I don't see any dots."

"That's because they're microdots."

Noble eyed Cam. "Then how did you see them?"

"I scanned the documents into my computer, then used a photo-editing program to enlarge the files." Cam turned his laptop to face the senator. "Here's an enlarged image of the document you're holding. You can see the small yellow squares and the pattern they form. This pattern is unique to your printer and provides the information needed to identify you as the person behind the documents."

Noble dropped the paper and crossed his arms. "I've never heard of such a thing."

"Be that as it may," Mack said, "you're busted, Noble. Time to come clean. Where are the guns, and where are you holding Agent Leigh?"

Noble looked down his nose at Mack. "I don't know anything about guns, and I'm not *holding* anyone."

"Don't waste our time. Tell us what we need to know and we'll tell the DA you cooperated. Maybe he'll be lenient with you."

Noble scoffed. "I'm a former DA, remember? The current DA won't be offering me any deals. He'll milk this for all it's worth and use it to show how tough he is on crime."

"Either way, this is over." Mack crossed his arms. "No point in not disclosing her location."

He laughed. "You haven't a clue what you're dealing with. This isn't over. Maybe my tiny little part of it will end, but it will never be over. Not as long as Razo is breathing."

Mack shot around the desk and got in Noble's face. "I want to know where Agent Leigh is located. Since you put the wanted poster out on her, you're going to tell me, and you're going to tell me now."

———

Addy took in the scenery as Holt continued to climb a snow-covered road. Tree branches scraped along the vehicle's sides and snapped, the sound echoing into the quiet night as heavy snow plummeted from the branches. If she weren't a prisoner, likely heading to her own death, she might take the time to enjoy the picturesque scene in front of her.

They came to a clearing illuminated by three streetlights, the headlights shining bright on some brick buildings with tall antennas. The building directly in front of them held a sign for a local television station.

"Why are we here?" She continued to look around, truly baffled by their choice of locations, other than it was totally secluded.

"Meeting someone." Holt clicked off the headlights, casting the building in shadows. "Get her out," he said as he shifted into park.

LeRoy grabbed her arm and dragged her outside. She stumbled, and he jerked her upright.

"Not so rough," she said.

"You want rough?" He eyed her and pulled back his arm. "I can show you rough."

"Leave it alone." As Holt joined them, putting on his jacket, she caught sight of a gun at his hip. "He's not here yet. I saw a fallen log near that stand of trees when we scoped this place out." He gestured to the trees. "Let's go sit down and get comfortable."

LeRoy grabbed her arm again and headed toward the fallen log, pulling her along behind him through knee-high snow. She wanted to delay for as long as possible, so she tumbled over a snowbank to waste time.

LeRoy growled, dragged her to her feet, and shoved her onto the snowy log, a sharp branch stabbing into her thigh.

She bit down on her lip. She wouldn't cry out and give him the satisfaction of knowing he'd hurt her. She shifted to get as comfortable as she could in the cold without her gloves or scarf and peered through the snow falling all around them. The small clearing consisted of a large parking lot with several buildings, each with signs displaying the call letters for either a TV or radio station, their tall antennas reaching into the sky. The companies were obviously broadcasting from this location. Maybe she could get to one of the buildings. Make a call.

She estimated the distance. At least a football field away. No way she could get that far before the goons either tackled her or shot her in the back.

The wind whistled between the buildings, blasting snow into her face. She shivered. The temperature hovered in the fifties down on the flatlands, but it was likely in the low thirties up on the mountain. She was wishing now that she hadn't taken her gloves from her jacket pocket, but at least she was wearing a jacket and boots, although they weren't snow boots.

Holt grabbed a small stick and took out a pocketknife, then crossed his feet at the ankles and leaned back to start whittling on it. His cowboy boots reminded her of Mack, and tears wetted her eyes. Was he coming for her?

Did you hear my three words, Mack? Did you?

As much as she wanted him to roll up, guns blazing, she couldn't count on it and had to get more information on Holt's plan.

She looked at him. "What are you making?"

"Just passing time."

"Who are we waiting for?"

"I'm pretty sure we've told you to be quiet." He eyed her. "Don't make me gag you."

"Don't I at least deserve to know my upcoming fate?"

"No." He didn't even look at her, just kept slicing away at the wood.

LeRoy sat on a stump and poked a long stick into the snow, then pulled it out and started all over again. His eyes were glazed over as he stared at the snow.

She looked around again. Searching. Hunting. Seeking a solution. She could try to call Mack again. What did she have to lose? She couldn't very well just sit here and let them kill her.

She shifted on the log and cupped her hands to work the device up out of her pocket. She had to shift even more to get her thumb in the right place to unlock the phone.

Holt shot her a look.

She moved again to hide her phone from him. "I'm so cold," she said and pretended to shiver.

He went back to whittling.

She glanced down and found Mack's icon. She raised her finger.

"What're you doing?" Holt's deadly calm voice was scarier than if he'd shouted at her. He planted his boots in the snow, crossed over to her, his boots kicking up little puffs of snow swirling in the air. He grabbed her arms and jerked her up, then fished out her phone.

He cast a baleful look at LeRoy. "You didn't take her phone?"

"Um . . . well . . . no. We was in a hurry."

Holt lifted the phone. Slammed it onto a bare patch of ground and stomped it with the heel of his boot. The screen went dark. Black. Black as the night, and so did all of Addy's hopes for rescue.

———

"You want to go away for murder too?" Mack snapped at the senator, his face not more than a foot away. "Because that seems to be where this is headed, and you're complicit."

"I'm sorry." Noble clutched the arms of his chair, his face a mass of indecision. "I can't tell you. I just can't."

"Why?" Mack demanded.

"I can't tell you that either."

"I can." Kiley's voice came from the doorway.

Mack spun to see her standing there, laptop in hand, a look of utter disgust on her face. "The good senator here, the family-values man—Mr. All-America—is one of Razo's top clients."

Shocked, Mack stared at her for a moment before he got his thoughts going again. "He's buying drugs or guns?"

"No. He's buying time with Razo's girls. Girls the same age as the senator's daughter." She stepped into the room and showed Mack her laptop screen.

He caught sight of a video displaying the senator in bed with a young girl.

Mack jerked his gaze away, his stomach turning. He stared down at the senator, whose face had blanched.

"This is why you won't rat Razo out." Mack fairly spit the words into the senator's face. "You couldn't allow your secret life to come to light. Your career would not only end but you would go to prison. And you would likely do anything to stop that from happening. Even kidnapping Agent Leigh. Even paying blackmail demands to Razo. He's blackmailing you, isn't he?"

Noble nodded.

Mack's stomach roiled with revulsion. "What exactly did you do in return for his silence?"

"Made sure he had connections to tenants at my malls who would launder his money." His grip tightened on the chair, his knuckles turning white. "That's it. I didn't touch his money."

"Just his girls," Kiley snapped as she closed her laptop. "You're the lowest of the low."

Mack had to agree, but they could deal with the horrible things Noble had done later. They couldn't lose focus right now. "How long has this blackmailing been going on?"

"Two years, but I was getting tired of it. So I made a deal with Zamora. Get rid of Razo and he could have his job." Noble shook his head. "But then Agent Leigh got nosy. She would've exposed me. I couldn't let that happen."

Mack had to plant his feet to keep from stepping closer and pummeling Noble. "So you had Zamora try to kill her?"

Noble shook his head. "I just wanted him to scare her off. Not kill her. Zamora was a little zealous, so I told him to back down."

Mack gaped at him. "Kidnapping her is backing down?"

"I didn't authorize that. Zamora must've decided to go out on his own."

"Zamora couldn't have taken her. He's in jail."

"Jail? But I . . . no wonder he isn't taking my calls." The senator sighed. "This has gotten out of control."

"You think?"

"If Zamora isn't behind this, then it's Razo. He must've taken Agent Leigh." Noble's eyes flashed with fear. "And if he has her, God help her. Razo is one of the most brutal men I know."

———

Bile rose up in Addy's throat as she had to endure the rough search by LeRoy. He tried to grope her. She shoved her shoulder into his stomach, sending him flying. He landed with a thump on the concrete, snow puffing into the air around him. She smirked at him and relished the moment.

He was growling and scrambling to his feet when Holt grabbed his arm and held him back. "Enough! We don't want to look like amateurs when he arrives, do we?"

"He?" she asked.

Neither of them answered.

The sound of a vehicle coming up the mountain drew everyone's attention toward the road.

"It's showtime." LeRoy cracked his knuckles and grinned. "Now you'll get what's coming to you."

Panic assailed her, and she wanted to flee into the wooded area behind them.

Give me courage to face whatever's coming.

She pulled her shoulders back and stood her ground. The car stopped behind the pickup. A single car door opened and then slammed. Footfalls crunched over the snow. A stocky figure emerged from the dark. The short guy wore black gothic track pants, a black hooded puffer coat, and a black beanie. But it was his square and yet chubby face that captured her attention.

Razo. The man she'd been hunting for months.

"Imagine running into you out here, Agent Leigh," he said, a snide smile on his face.

She didn't respond. There was nothing to say.

"What's the matter? Cat got your tongue?"

Holt nudged her. "Go on. You been wanting to talk."

She remained quiet, as she wasn't about to give him what he wanted.

"Okay." Razo glared at her. "You want to get right down to business? Fine. I hear you've been having some problems. A visitor to your house. An accident. A shooting."

She pressed her lips together. Why speak? He knew all about these incidents as he was the perpetrator, so why say anything and stroke his ego?

"I was sorry to hear about it. I believe one of my men was to blame." Razo smiled. "I had so hoped to deal with him at the same time as you, but then you arrested him and that was no longer possible."

"You're saying Zamora was acting on his own," she clarified.

"She speaks." He chuckled. "Yes. My number two decided he wanted to be number one. I went along with this fumbling effort to take over, but I was growing tired of it, so I planned to intervene. Now I'll have to settle for you. And the good senator, of course. He can't team up with Zamora to plan my demise without paying for it."

"Ah, yes, Noble," she said and worked hard not to let her surprise and intense interest fill her words or Razo might figure out she didn't know how the senator was involved and not explain Noble's role. "He poked his nose where it shouldn't be."

"He did indeed. Trying to squirm out from under my control." He sniffed as if he found something distasteful. "But when the pictures of him and underage girls I send to the news hit the airwaves, he'll wish he hadn't."

The senator and young girls? Addy felt like she might hurl. Instead, she stood silently, swallowing her disgust with this man for providing young girls for the senator, which she had to believe he'd done. Disgust with the senator for taking advantage of the girls. Both men were the lowest of the low and should be locked up and never released.

"At first I thought to take him out," Razo continued. "But this will be far more humiliating and painful. Imagine a life in prison after his pedophile conviction." He smiled again, clearly proud of himself.

She didn't want to stand here and listen to Razo brag about his cunning, yet she also didn't want to push him into action. She had to hope that someone was coming to save her and buy as much time as possible. Because just looking at that cocky smile, the dark glint in his eyes, the gun holstered at his hip . . . she would not be escaping from his clutches on her own. Of that she was certain.

———

"Where?" Mack demanded of the senator. "You have to know where Razo stages his guns or drugs in this area."

"I don't. I really don't."

Mack pressed closer. He didn't know if he was going hit the senator or strangle him. He couldn't predict how his burning rage was going to manifest itself.

Noble lifted his hands. "I really don't know. Honest. I had nothing to do with the actual guns. You have to believe me."

Problem was, Mack did believe him, and that left him understanding what was going down and why, but without any leads on the *where*.

Cam returned carrying a cellphone. He handed it to Mack. "All restored to your latest backup and set up with your original phone number so you're back in business. By the way, there's a voicemail."

Hoping it related to finding Addy, Mack grabbed the phone. "It's from Addy!"

He tapped the speaker so everyone could hear. "Mack, what three words? Outpost. Insertion. Chocolates."

The call went dead. He looked at his team. "What in the world?"

"She's telling you where she is," Cam said.

"She's using the what3words app." Kiley dug out her phone. "I'll enter the words in the app, and it'll show us her location."

Mack charged over to Kiley. "I'm not going to waste time asking how that works. Just give me a location."

Kiley held out her phone, and a map displayed the words and location. "She's on the top of San Miguel Mountain."

Mack spun on the senator. "And how far away is that?"

"About forty minutes if there's no traffic," the senator said.

"That's too long. We need a helicopter." Mack grabbed his phone and dialed Eisenhower. The minute he answered, Mack explained his need.

"I can have a military chopper to you ASAP if one can land on the ranch," Eisenhower answered, not at all shocked at the request.

Mack looked at the senator. "Is there a spot where a helo can land?"

He nodded. "I have a heliport on the property."

"Does it have lights?"

He nodded.

Mack looked at Sean. "Go with him to light it up."

Sean grabbed the senator's arm, and they headed out.

Mack turned back to his phone. "I'll text my GPS coordinates. There'll be a lighted heliport for the helo."

"Perfect," Eisenhower said. "I'll text when it's finalized."

He ended the call, and Mack checked his GPS before texting the information to Eisenhower. Mack finally understood how the what3words app would have been easier to let him know via words where she was located instead of a bunch of numbers that would be easy to make a mistake with.

Mack shoved his phone into his pocket and tried to formulate a plan to rescue Addy, but he didn't know enough about where Razo had taken her to begin to do so. He looked at Kiley. "Can you get me a ground-level view of the location?"

"Already done." She held out her phone. "There's only one way in and out."

The map on her screen showed a narrow drive that wound up the mountain. At the top, the drive circled around several buildings, then ran back down to connect with the same road.

Mack looked up. "The single driveway makes our rescue far more difficult and dangerous for Addy."

"We sure can't land a helo up there," Kiley said. "I mean, there's plenty of room, but it wouldn't be a secret, and we would likely put Addy in a hostage scenario."

"Exactly." Mack studied the map again. "We'll land in the foothills. Drive up. Use our drone to get eyes on them."

"Might work," she said, looking like she was trying to play the scenario out in her mind. "The drone can fly high enough not to be detected. And you can even load it with a weapon if needed."

Mack nodded, but his stomach clenched. He was going to come face-to-face with his worst fear. Use a tool he hated to save the most important person in the world to him.

Was he up to taking someone out with a drone again, or would he fail the love of his life?

CHAPTER 27

DESPITE THE COLD TEMPERATURE, Addy was sweating nervous bullets. Her back was soaked, and yet she shivered in the cold wind and the snow and ice under her body. Razo was going to kill her up here on this mountain. Likely shoot her in the head. Or maybe in the back like a coward would do.

She'd been shot once before, but she hadn't had time to sit around and wait, not knowing it was coming then. No time to think about dying. No time to think about never seeing Mack again. No time to think about not seeing her friends on the RED team again. Because they were her friends, and Mack was her husband. She knew that now. Not that she remembered, but that feeling that kept coming to her, screaming at her to pay attention, was stronger than ever. She might never remember, but she could start over. Begin again with all of them. If they would let her.

"We do it my way," Razo shouted and stabbed a finger into Holt's chest. "You've messed things up enough as it is."

Holt firmed his stance, surprising Addy with his fortitude in front of Razo. "We didn't mess up. It was LeRoy."

"And yet you let him live." Razo turned and curled his finger at LeRoy. "Come here, man."

Eyes wary, LeRoy got up from the log. He crossed to the men, his feet dragging. "You want something?"

"Yeah," Razo said and drew his gun. "This."

He pointed the barrel at LeRoy's head and fired.

Addy screamed, but nothing came out of her mouth. Blood and brain matter spurted over the white snow—over Addy.

LeRoy dropped to the ground near her feet.

Addy clamped a hand over her mouth and stared. She'd known Razo was a cold-blooded killer, but to see it in person?

Her stomach convulsed, and she thought she might be sick. She swallowed hard and watched the two men. Holt gaped at Razo but remained standing next to him. His eyes darted around, likely looking for an escape before he met the same fate as LeRoy.

"You'll take over for Zamora." Razo frowned, his already sharp features looking more pointed. "I want those cables cut at San Ysidro for tomorrow's shipment. We got five minis ready to roll, and three buyers on the hook. One possible in the wings. If I miss my deadline for delivering these bad boys to those sovereign-citizen nuts, heads will roll."

Holt's face blanched. "But I don't know how Dante was cutting those cables with Yahontov."

"Then you better find out real quick or you'll be joining LeRoy here."

So they *were* working with Yahontov, and they planned to cut cables. She'd been right all along. And they were also right about the sovereign-citizen guys. She couldn't let this shipment make its way into the U.S., with the guns finding their way into the hands of these fanatics. Somehow she had to get away and stop them.

Razo turned his attention to her. "I want to kill the woman right now, but we'll be better off if she serves as a warning. Anyone who might think about messing with me will think again before acting. I can't get to Zamora just yet, so she'll have to stand in for him. Carry my message that betrayal never pays."

Addy cringed. She could only imagine what he had planned for her. She'd seen terrible, horrible videos where people were mutilated and paraded through villages in Mexico to show others what happened when you crossed the cartels, and Razo was as brutal as the cartel leaders.

"You're the boss," Holt said.

Razo jabbed his finger in the man's chest harder. "Remember that." Then he spun and marched over to her, his boots thudding in the quiet night.

She looked up at him. "We know you sold the guns to Ross, Woods, and Turner with the sovereign citizens. You'll never get away with delivering the guns. We'll see to that."

"We?" He scoffed. "You won't be part of anything for long. And so what if you know? I'm a whole lot smarter than any of you."

"So you admit these guys are your buyers," she clarified.

He responded with a deep growl and rolled a large stump into the clearing. He looked at Holt. "Get the lights and camera from my trunk. I'll get the ax."

Ax? Addy's heart clutched, and she had to swallow not to be sick on the spot.

Razo took off into the dark and came back carrying a large ax, the blade glinting in the streetlight. "We usually reserve this punishment for people who steal from us, but the severing of your hands will still be effective in warning off any other agents who would try to come after me."

He laughed, and the brittle sound carried behind him like a sick melody meant to haunt. Maybe to scare. And it did. Clear to Addy's bones.

He didn't want to kill her, so now was her chance to run, and she had to hope he didn't shoot.

She jumped up and bolted. Plunging through the deep snow that threatened to take her down.

"After her!" Razo shouted.

She plowed through the snow, stiffening her back for the potential gunshot.

She heard footsteps behind. Coming closer. Closing in.

She kicked up her speed. Her feet got caught in an icy ball of snow, and she tumbled face-first into the snow. Air rushed from her mouth. Winded, she lay for a second.

No. Get up. Go!

She clawed her way to her feet. Started to move.

Holt flew through the air and dragged her back down. She landed face-first again, the icy cold cooling her body, heated from the run.

He grabbed her by the hair, hauled her to her feet, and jerked her back against his body. "He's gonna make you pay for that," he whispered.

"Probably you too," she snapped back.

"Shut up." He grasped her wrist, punishing her already raw skin with a bruising force. He dragged her forward, and she had to run to keep up with his long strides.

Razo glared at her and pointed at the stump. "Drop her there."

Holt shoved her to the ground. She knelt in the wet snow, her legs freezing, her body starting to shiver. From cold or fear, she didn't know, but soon it wouldn't matter.

Razo made a big production of setting up his camera on a nearby tripod. She lifted her face to the sky. To the fluffy white flakes falling. Gorgeous. Just as God planned.

I know you're here, God. I can see you. Feel your presence.

Razo eyed her from behind the camera. "Place your hands on the stump, and if you pull back, I'll put a bullet in your head."

She rested her zip-tied hands on the cold stump, breathed in the chilling air, and closed her eyes to ease her fear. She couldn't possibly watch while Razo maimed her with his sharp ax. As he hefted it overhead and swung down, she could simply pull back. She wouldn't. No matter how much her brain would scream for her to do so. He'd told her he would put a bullet in her head if she did. Better alive with no hands than dead.

She oddly felt at peace. Her only regrets were not being able to say good-bye to her mother and not telling Mack she loved him in case she bled out and died up here.

"You will think twice about coming up against me, no?" Razo asked.

She didn't answer. Why would she when it would just stroke his ego? Better to let him do this without her flinching or reacting. That way he wouldn't get as much enjoyment from it.

She took a long breath and held it. God was with her so everything would be okay. She just had to keep repeating that to herself, and all would work out for her good.

Snow continued to fall, peppering her body with cold needles. She heard Razo's footfalls moving across the clearing toward her. The greatest terror she'd never known usurped her good thoughts, and she lifted her face in prayer.

———

The blades of the helicopter thumped overhead at Noble's ranch, each spin urging Mack to act and raising his heartbeat. The aircraft hovered and slowly settled down right on schedule. Mack made a mental note that when this was all over, he'd thank his boss for coming through as usual.

The sand and dirt whipped into a frenzy, biting into Mack's face, and he bent his head to join his team and grab equipment from the back of their SUV and load it into the helo. Thankfully, local deputies had arrived in time to take the senator into custody, and Mack would take care of pressing charges after rescuing Addy.

Mack set the bin with their drone near the seat he would occupy. "Thanks for the speedy response," he said to the pilot.

"Welcome." The young Navy lieutenant looked over his shoulder. "Captain has a vehicle ready and waiting for you at your destination."

Mack wasn't going to ask how he arranged that. He was

just going to get in that vehicle and plow through the snow up the mountain to Addy.

He went back to the team, who were grabbing assault rifles and slinging them over their shoulders. They'd finished loading equipment and had donned tactical vests and their comms units. Mack moved to the back seat, disconnected Bear's leash from the headrest, and dressed him in his body armor. Mack didn't know if he would need Bear to free Addy, but if so, he wanted to be sure the dog was protected. Mack led him into the helo. He had no idea if the dog had ever flown in a helicopter before, but his calm acceptance of jumping in said he probably had.

Mack looked back at the team. "Let's move."

Sean and Kiley climbed into the helo and buckled up. The aircraft lifted from the ground.

Thump. Thump. Thump. The rotors beat through the air.

Just minutes now before they landed. Before Mack had to perform.

He looked at his teammates and signaled a moment of prayer. They all bowed their heads as they rose up through the clouds into what felt like oblivion.

Mack searched for the right words to say. This was too important to get it wrong. He started his plea. Then stopped. Started again.

God, you know my request. Addy needs you. Help me—us—rescue her. And to find the guns before they reach our country.

Bear's head came to rest on Mack's knee. Mack's heart soared for a moment at the close contact with the animal who knew Mack needed support, and he flashed his eyes open. "Good boy, Bear. Let's go bring Addy home."

Bear barked his agreement, and Mack smiled despite the heaviness of the mission weighing him down.

"Flying time five minutes," the lieutenant announced.

Mack slid over to the drone container. He opened the bin, his pulse pounding hard. Just the sight of a drone could be enough to send him into a flashback. The worst thing that could happen. Fear of failing Addy climbed up his throat, threatened to choke him. He swallowed it down, his gaze shooting around the helo.

Kiley squeezed his arm and focused in on him. "You got this. I know you do."

He gave a sharp nod, but his hands trembled, and that didn't bode well for a steady hand on the drone's controller.

Kiley took Bear's leash and drew him over to her. Bear sat next to her, but she didn't pet him. This wasn't playtime. They were heading into a mission.

Mack peered inside the bin and took a long breath, letting it out in a shuddering wave.

You can do this. You have to do this.

Their drone wasn't an off-the-shelf retail system like he'd purchased at the mall, but a custom instrument made for their team. Weighing fifty pounds, it had a range of just over six miles and could reach an altitude of over nine thousand feet. It was equipped with a day/night camera that transmitted real-time video. In this instance, it would also carry a rifle that Mack could use to take out whoever was holding Addy if necessary.

He inspected the gun's ammo and mounted the gun on the drone. He checked the drone batteries, his stomach churning as fast as the rotor blades overhead, and he thought he might hurl. He swallowed. Breathed. He wouldn't fail Addy.

The helo thumped away in rhythm, bringing them closer to the time he would have to use the drone. His worst fear could very well play out in slow motion. Using a drone again to take a life and potentially injuring or killing an innocent. In this case, the love of his life.

"We good?" Sean asked, his two words loaded with such meaning that Mack wanted to scream, *No, we're not good! We're never good. Haunted at times. Still.*

Instead, he nodded and closed the bin. The helo began to descend. Mack's heart started racing faster. Faster. Adrenaline coursed through him.

Once they hit the ground, he was as jittery as if he'd pounded a dozen Red Bulls. They landed in a small field, where a man wearing khakis and a leather jacket stood by a silver SUV, keys dangling from his hand.

Mack hopped out, and the man handed over the keys. "Would be great if you could bring it back to this location."

"We'll do our best," Mack said. "If not, we'll let the captain know where to find it."

"Roger that," the man replied, making Mack think former military or law enforcement. "FYI, there's a report of snow falling up top. So take it easy."

That's all Mack needed. Snowfall to interfere with the drone, maybe cause his shot to go wide. Yet he couldn't think about that now.

He carefully set the bin in the back seat of the SUV. Kiley led Bear to the same seat and settled him inside the vehicle. They made quick work of loading their equipment.

"I'll be standing by," the pilot said, "in case you need a lift home."

Mack thanked him, and back at the SUV, he looked at his teammates. "Kiley, you find a place near the target where we can observe them, and Sean, you get us there. I'll do the rest." Mack climbed into the vehicle next to Bear. Sean took a seat behind the wheel, and Kiley rode shotgun.

Sean pointed them to the narrow drive, and they started to climb. Snow flurries soon danced around their vehicle, an earlier snowfall having covered the unplowed road. Tires left deep ruts, and Sean kept the SUV in those ruts.

"I have just the spot," Kiley said over the seat. "I'll give you directions."

"Great." Mack prayed that it really was a perfect spot, because they had no margin for error when it came to saving Addy's life.

They continued to climb the narrow road, moving closer to Addy. Closer. Mack's phone rang, startling him. He quickly answered the call from Cam.

"We got them." Cam's excited voice shot through the phone. "The suspects. I infiltrated a private message board where they laid out their plans, and I was right. It's the convention center and hotel. Plus they were going to use the third gun on the federal building."

"Is it enough to get an arrest warrant for them?"

"At a minimum we have them threatening via online messages."

"Let Eisenhower know. He can decide if we roll on them now or wait until they have the guns so we can get them for more serious charges."

"Will do."

"We're about to approach the location where they're holding Addy. I'm silencing my phone. I'll call you as soon as we have her safely in hand."

"Praying for a successful op."

Mack disconnected, his nerves pressing him to move. He shook his leg. Tapped his foot. And the moment Sean parked in a small bump out in the road, Mack jumped out. For once, he didn't care about ruining his boots but plunged into calf-high snow and raced to the back of the vehicle. He opened the tailgate and set the bin down to remove the aircraft. He dropped onto the tailgate and balanced the controller on his lap. His hands were trembling—hard—and he could barely maneuver the drone's joystick as he launched the aircraft.

How sad was that? The most important flight of his life and he might botch it. Should he give the controls over to Sean or Kiley? They were both trained to fly the drone. Sure, they didn't have Mack's skills, but they might be able to do the job regardless.

"You sure you got this?" Sean asked.

Mack thought for one more second. Decided. Better him with a bit of tremble than novices flying the drone.

"Yeah. Got it." Mack looked at the video screen on his lap with the controller on the side and maneuvered the drone through the air. He had to keep the aircraft high enough so Razo didn't hear the propellers and motor and yet make sure the camera was getting good coverage so they could see what was happening on the ground.

Sean and Kiley sat on either side of him, their focus pinned on his screen.

He ignored them and winged the drone over the treetops, through snow falling heavy now, and reached a clearing lit with streetlights. Thankfully that gave him a perfect view of the scene, and he wouldn't need to turn on the infrared camera. He hovered the drone above and focused his camera below. The first live video of Addy's location opened on his screen.

Kiley gasped and grabbed his knee.

"No!" Mack shouted. "No."

Razo had Addy kneeling by a large stump. Her hands rested on the wood, and he had an ax sitting on his shoulder.

"He's going to cut off her hands." Just saying the words terrified Mack, and the blood drained from his head.

"He's using her to send a message," Sean said. "Like the drug cartels are known to do."

"You have to stop him. Now!" Kiley cried out.

Mack didn't hesitate but brought the drone down into firing range.

He aimed the gun. Hovered his finger over the button. Held his breath.

Memories flashed before his eyes, flickering like irritating bugs swarming at him, yet he couldn't just swat them away. They were woven into who he was. The fabric of his life. His very existence.

Razo moved closer. Lifted the ax high above his head.

Mack ignored the memories. Ignored the strong pull that wanted to take him back in time to his military past. He tried to press the button. His finger wouldn't constrict. But he had to shoot the gun. Addy was counting on him.

God, help me! I can't fail her. I just can't.

CHAPTER 28

ADDY NEEDED to look. She also needed to keep her eyes closed. Seeing won out. She flashed her eyes open and glanced up. Heavy snow peppered her face, cold and biting, her eyelashes icy. She ignored the snow and focused on Razo.

He brought the ax over his shoulder.

No. No. She couldn't watch after all.

She closed her eyes tight. Waited, her body trembling.

A rifle cracked in the distance.

What in the world?

A loud thump sounded next to her. Not the ax. Farther away. She opened her eyes. Razo lay on the ground, a bullet hole in his forehead.

She shot a look around, searching for Holt. He ran toward his truck. A bullet pierced a tire. Quiet save for the rustling of grass, and then another tire went. Holt was scrambling to hide.

Was this friendly fire? Mack's or Razo's rival? Was she safe?

She wouldn't sit there and wait to find out.

She shot up. Grabbed Razo's gun and fled as fast as her frozen feet allowed through the deep snow and into the copse of trees. She took a stance behind a large tree and watched as bullets took out the remaining truck tires. She looked around, trying to figure out where the shots were coming from. At a distance and up high, that was for sure. Trees maybe. Or a drone? Could you even fire a rifle from a drone?

Mack had talked about dropping missiles, but not firing guns. If it could be done, Mack would know how to do so. But would his past allow him to pull the trigger? She hoped he hadn't been put in that position again. It would hurt him so terribly, and she didn't want him to be hurt. But a rival would more likely shoot Holt than the tires. Had to be Mack.

A dog came bounding into the opening. *Bear!*

He charged at Holt. He raised his gun, aiming for Bear.

Addy couldn't let Holt shoot Bear. No way. She bolted from the trees, Razo's gun in her hand. "Stop or I'll shoot!"

Holt glanced at her. Shifted his gun to aim at her.

"No!" Mack shouted from the other side of the clearing.

Holt shifted again, and Bear lunged for Holt's arm. He clamped on and took the man down. They flew through the air and sank into the deep snow.

Mack, Sean, and Kiley came running. Mack stood over Holt, gun in hand, but he didn't try to pull Bear free. He growled and tussled with Holt's arm. Holt cried out in pain.

"Get him off me!" Holt yelled, anguish in his voice.

Sean and Kiley subdued a moaning Holt. Addy let out a breath. Took another, the muscles in her legs refusing to hold her. She dropped into the icy snow and rested Razo's weapon on her knee. She wanted to call out to Bear and Mack, but they had to finish apprehending Holt. She watched them for a moment, then looked down at her hands. She'd almost lost them to an ax, but Mack had found her. Had intervened.

"Come, Bear." Mack grabbed their dog's leash.

Bear released Holt, and Mack pulled him back. "Sit."

Bear sat, and Mack dug out a treat from his pocket to give to the dog. Bear gulped it down.

"Stay," Mack said and spun. His gaze locked with hers. He charged in her direction. "Are you hurt?"

"My legs gave out. I—" She tried to get up.

He dropped down next to her and leaned against a soaring

tree. He scooped her up into his arms and settled her on his lap. Wrapping those powerful arms around her, he buried his head in her neck. "Thank God, I got to you in time. I saw Razo. The ax."

He shuddered, breaking her heart that he had to go through such a traumatic experience. "You flew the drone. Shot Razo."

"I did."

"Any problems?"

"You mean flashbacks?"

"Yes," she whispered.

"Not a one." He leaned back and tipped her face up. "God was there with me. With us. He brought us through. Together. Where we're supposed to be. I thought I was going to lose you," he whispered against her neck. "You were only minutes away from harm. I'm so sorry. So, so sorry I let that happen. I will never let you out of my sight again."

The terror of the night. The thought of the ax. All of it fell away, and she let herself be held and let the warmth of his strong body seep into her. She inhaled the unique scent of his strong mints and woodsy aftershave and thought about what he'd just said.

She held his gaze. "Not letting me out of your sight might be kind of difficult since we live on opposite coasts."

"I don't care," he said adamantly. "I want us back together."

"What about your PTSD issues?" She hated to ask, but she had to spell it out. She didn't want to admit her love for him and find out his issues would still keep them apart. "Are you comfortable with that now?"

"Comfortable, no. But I know we can figure it out. I've had this mantra since I started counseling. A Bible verse. 'The Spirit God gave us does not make us timid, but gives us power, love and self-discipline.' It's helped me make progress, and I've learned in the last few days to take strength and hope from those words. To know that God doesn't want me to be worried or be timid about wanting to be back with you. He'll take care of us as He always promises."

Her heart overflowing with love for this man, she smiled at him.

"And that goes for your memory too," he continued. "I know you hoped to have it fully back by now, but God will see you through that struggle."

She cupped the side of his strong jaw. "I don't need it to know I love you."

"What?" His mouth fell open.

She held his hand over her heart. "I can feel it here. That's all that matters."

He gently brushed snow from her cheek. "Then, Addison Leigh, will you be my wife again?"

"Yes. Without a doubt."

He whooped and bent his head to kiss her. She forgot about everything. About the horror. About the cold. She returned his kiss with every emotion coursing through her body. What had been simmering between them for days exploded into fireworks of joy. She really was home. Was where she belonged and would never let this man go again without a knockdown fight.

Something tugged on her sleeve. She tried to shake it off, but the pulling grew more insistent. She leaned back and drew in a deep breath, relishing the smitten expression on Mack's face before looking at her problem. Bear released her shirt, sat down, his focus fastened on them.

"You want in on this, huh, fella," Mack said.

Bear barked.

Addy leaned back farther, and the eighty-pound ball of fur burrowed in between them.

Mack looked at Addy over the dog's head, a fond smile on his face. "Looks like we have one more obstacle to overcome before we can be together. At least alone together."

———

Mack picked up his binoculars as Sean turned in to the defunct manufacturing plant in northeast Portland and pulled behind the dilapidated building. He left the SUV's powerful engine idling.

Mack glassed the lot. "No sign of suspects yet."

Sean nodded, his hands at the ready on the wheel.

Mack continued to look into the drizzling darkness at the empty lot, wishing he was with Addy instead. He'd hoped for time alone with her, but it turned out that Bear wasn't the only one keeping Mack from realizing his hope. Eisenhower had ended that thought with one phone call.

He wanted the sovereign citizens for more serious charges than threatening messages, which meant delivering the guns to them, then arresting them on the spot. Cam had found the three men's contact information on Razo's phone and arranged a meet via text. So Harris went back to question Zamora, and upon learning Razo was dead, Zamora hoped to lessen his sentence by giving up the location of the guns and plans to smuggle them. Eisenhower contacted Mexican officials, and the RED team was soon in possession of five miniguns and had flown back to Portland with Addy to meet up with the sovereign citizens.

Addy had to sit out the op, though. She still hadn't been medically cleared for duty, so Eisenhower wouldn't let her join in. Mack didn't mind her staying home, because then he didn't have to worry about her safety during the op.

Headlights cut through the lot, and Mack forgot about everything but bringing this sting to a successful close.

"Suspects are in sight," Kiley said from an unmarked van.

The sovereign citizens were expecting Razo, but the RED team convinced them to let his girlfriend make the drop. Kiley was wired and would be posing as the girlfriend, while Sean and Mack, along with an FBI SWAT team, waited in the wings with one of their snipers on overwatch.

Mack followed the rented U-Haul truck's progress through his binoculars and watched them stop at the designated area. Kiley drove up to them and slid out of the van. Her eyes were tight, her posture assured.

A tall, heavyset guy with a bald head who Mack recognized as Ross got out of the truck.

"It's Ross," Mack said into his comms mic so that both his team and the SWAT team could hear.

"Roger that," the SWAT commander replied.

Kiley didn't respond because Ross was within earshot and would hear her.

"Macy Wallace," Kiley said, using Razo's last girlfriend's name.

"I'd like to see some ID."

"Sure thing." She slowly reached for her pocket and pulled out the driver's license they'd quickly made for her. She held it out. "Same for you. Let's see your license."

He dug out his wallet from the back pocket of worn jeans and held it out. "Now that we both know who we are, let's make the exchange."

"Money first," Kiley said and drew back her jacket to reveal her holstered gun. "Just in case you think you can play me because I'm a helpless female."

Mack waited for the guy to get mad or even draw down on her.

Instead, he grinned and curled his finger at the truck. "Shoulda figured Razo would have a strong chick by his side."

Mack could imagine Kiley cringing inside, but as a very capable agent, she would never show her emotions to this creep.

Sean ran the wipers to clear away the drizzle on the windshield, the scrape across the window sounding almost like an explosion in the quiet to Mack, and he feared the others could

hear it. But they were too far away, and he was just being paranoid.

Another man slid down from the truck, a large bag in his
hand. His mousy-brown beard ran to the middle of his chest,
and his hair was pulled back in a ponytail. No doubt it was
Turner. "Guy approaching is Turner."

He dropped the bag on the ground in front of Kiley.

"Pick it up and open it." She eyed Turner. Mack knew she
wasn't about to put herself at a disadvantage and get down on
the ground to check the bag.

He stood, stroking his long beard and looking at her with
contempt.

"Quit wasting time and do it," Ross said.

Turner glared at Ross, then grabbed the bag and tugged the
zipper open. He held out the handles, displaying a bag filled
with cash.

Kiley inspected the money without losing her focus on the
two men.

"And just what is it you think you're buying?" she asked to
clarify for the investigation.

Ross fired her a testy look. "You're not trying to pull something, are you?"

"Just confirming. We deal in a lot of weapons."

Ross shrugged, seeming to accept her response. "Three miniguns plus power supplies and ammo."

"Then bring the money with you." She gestured to the back
of her van and stood waiting.

They started moving in the right direction, glancing back
at her along the way. She circled around them, giving them
a wide berth, unlocked the van, and opened the door. "Your
merchandise."

"Check it out," Ross said to Turner.

Turner dropped the cash bag and hopped into the truck. He
opened the first box. "Sweet. Just what we ordered."

"Have your other guy bring the truck around," Kiley said, moving back a bit and in a ready position to make a safe exit if needed.

Ross stepped around the van and waved on the other guy, who Mack believed to be Woods. The truck set into motion, the engine growl breaking through the quiet. On a normal sting, they might move in, but Eisenhower wanted the sovereign citizens to actually take possession of the guns so there was no chance of their getting off.

"Stand by," Mack said into his mic.

Kiley gave a subtle nod of her head.

The U-Haul backed up to the van, and the last guy climbed down to open the back. Mack got a good look at his black slicked-back hair and knew it was indeed Eric Woods, the youngest of the three men.

"Woods makes all three," Mack said and noticed Kiley grin.

Ross stood watch as the other two loaded the weapons weighing over eighty-five pounds apiece minus the ammo or power supply into the truck.

After the second weapon was loaded, Sean shifted into gear.

Mack waited for the men to transfer the final box into the vehicle. "Move! Move! Move!"

Kiley drew her weapon. Sean roared their vehicle forward, as did the driver of the SWAT truck. Sean pinned the men in from one side, SWAT the other.

Ross squirted, but Kiley charged after and tackled him to the ground. A SWAT guy had Woods by the collar. Mack flew out of the truck and grabbed Turner, taking him to the ground and cuffing him before looking up.

Kiley was hauling Ross by the cuffs toward them. Woods was on the ground, cuffs in place.

"Good job, everyone," Mack said as he lifted Turner to his feet, then looked at Sean. "Take control of this guy while I arrange for transport."

Sean moved in, and Mack stepped away to call the Portland Police Bureau to send units to take these guys in. He hung up and phoned Eisenhower to give him the good news.

"Excellent work, Jordan."

Mack took a moment to enjoy the compliment, as they were few and far between from Eisenhower.

"Too bad things aren't going as well here." Eisenhower's tone was filled with disappointment. "We hit a dead end again on the Montgomery Three Investigation."

The girls. They were still out there. Waiting for rescue.

Mack's joy in capturing these men disappeared, and his months-long desperation to find the girls came flooding back.

"Maybe it's time to take Zamora up on his offer," Eisenhower said.

Mack cringed but held his tongue.

When Harris interviewed Zamora, he claimed he could reach out on the dark web to Razo's contacts to help find the girls. If they were being trafficked, he said he had a good chance of finding them.

Mack thought about the creep drugging Addy, almost killing her. About the girls Zamora had trafficked. Mack's heart rebelled at working with him. But the girls' faces came to mind, and Mack knew he would swallow down his disgust and do what needed doing. "I'd rather not work with the scum of the earth, but yeah, let's see if he's full of it or if he can help us finally bring these girls home where they belong."

CHAPTER 29

A WEEK LATER, Addy leaned against the counter in the Portland safe house. She was starting to regret volunteering to be the local agent assigned to Zamora's babysitting detail. They'd made sure word got out on the street that Razo had died and Zamora had taken over his business. To make things appear real, they had to release Zamora from jail. They were keeping him at the safe house under guard, and he issued orders from there to Razo's posse, claiming he was hiding out, as he feared whoever had killed Razo was after him.

She looked at him where he sat at the round table, computer in front of him. Kiley sat next to him, keeping an eye on his computer habits. Sean and Cam were sitting on the sofa, wrapping up paperwork from the Razo investigation and waiting for any lead Zamora might produce.

Mack, who had been gone on an urgent errand, came jogging down the stairs, a huge smile on his face as he crossed over to her. He took her hand. "I need you to come with me."

"Where to?"

"It's a surprise." Mack tugged on her hand.

She crossed the room, glancing at the others, and their sly expressions told her they were in on the surprise. She had no idea what he could have waiting for her, but her pulse tripped faster. Bear whimpered from his bed. She left him behind, as she had no idea what to expect.

Mack held the door open, and she stepped out. There in

the driveway sat her cherry-red Mustang completely repaired, polished, and shiny.

"My dad's car. They said it was totaled . . ." Tears flooded her eyes. "But you had it fixed."

"I know how important it is to you." He led her down the steps.

She ran a hand over the fresh paint. "She's even prettier."

"I have to admit, there are parts we had to cannibalize from another vehicle. Everything you see, though, is just as your dad left it."

She turned and threw her arms around Mack's neck. "Thank you. This is the nicest thing anyone has ever done for me."

He smiled. "Just the first of many, I hope."

"You're going to spoil me."

"That's my plan." His smile disappeared. "I love you, Addy."

"Right backatcha," she said with gusto.

His eyes darkened and he kissed her, his lips warm and insistent. He held her so tightly, she couldn't imagine a thread fitting between them. She could go on and on kissing him, but she had a job to do, and she took it very seriously.

She pushed back. "As much as I would like to take the car for a spin, we need to get back to Zamora."

"See. Someone coming between us again." He chuckled and held her hand as they returned to the basement.

She received smiles from the others, minus Zamora, whose face was glued to the computer screen.

"Is it pretty?" Kiley asked.

Addy nodded. "We can go for a ride later."

"Hey, what about the rest of us?" Cam faked a pout.

"We all can go when this guy is back behind bars." She went to the counter to brew a cup of tea. Mack followed her. Except for when he'd gone to get the car, he'd been like a magnet for the last week, just like Bear who traipsed after him.

She poured water from the electric kettle into a mug and

leaned against the counter to dunk her tea bag, the peppermint scent rising up to greet her.

She looked at Mack over her mug. "I still can't believe we agreed to offer Zamora a deal."

"Not much of one," Mack said.

Addy thought using Zamora's connections was a long shot, and she really didn't want to work with a creep like him. Just being in the same room with the person who'd tried to kill her—and worse yet, someone who trafficked young girls—was hard to take. Much less working with him for seven days. She *did* want to find the missing girls, though, so she was on board with the operation.

Zamora grabbed a slice of pepperoni pizza from the nearly empty box, chomped off a bite, and followed it with a swig of cola. Then he belched and laughed about it. This was the guy they'd been pinning their hopes on for a week now. Seemed ludicrous.

She shook her head. "Prepare yourself for not succeeding. He could just be blowing smoke."

"But why?" Mack asked. "His deal is only good if we find the girls."

"Yeah, but this plan gives him a few days of freedom, plus the food he wants, and for that, he might lie to us."

Mack frowned. "You could be right."

Zamora suddenly shot forward and squinted at the screen. "Different colored hair and skinnier, but I think this is one of your girls."

Mack, Sean, Kiley, and Cam ran to the computer, but Addy hung back to let them get a look at the screen first. Addy set down her mug and stepped over to the group. She caught sight of the image on the screen and was fairly certain it was Becky Vaughn looking at them with lifeless eyes ringed with heavy makeup.

"It's Becky." Mack looked over his shoulder at his team. "Right? It's really her."

"Yes." Kiley gulped in a breath. "She's alive."

"Was, anyway," Zamora said without any emotion, as if they were talking about a possession and not a person. "My guy seen her two weeks ago."

"Where?" Mack demanded.

Zamora raised a bushy eyebrow. "Now, getting that information is gonna cost us. He wants ten grand before he coughs up the location."

"Done," Sean said, his usually even tone deep with angst. "Tell me how to get it to him, and he'll have it within the hour."

"Well, shoot. You guys know how to roll." Zamora started typing in a private browser window, where he and his source exchanged comments.

"Bitcoin." Zamora tapped his screen. "Here're the directions."

Sean leaned forward. "What about the other girls?"

Zamora shrugged, looking indifferent. Not surprising for a man who willingly trafficked girls. "He didn't know nothin' about them, but for this kind of coin you better believe he'll do his best to find 'em."

"Tell him we'll double the amount for each girl," Sean said.

Addy almost gasped at the easy exchange of large sums of money, but then this team had been looking for the girls for some time, and she would probably do the same thing if she had budgetary freedom like they had. Or if she didn't, she might even pay the money herself.

Zamora typed in the information about the added incentive. A message filled with emojis and exclamation marks came back. The guy would do his best to find the other girls.

"Move." Kiley jabbed Zamora. She was even less thrilled that this guy was out of jail than Addy was. "Let me get the bitcoin transaction going so we can rescue Becky ASAP and put you back where you belong."

Zamora glared at her. "You might want to be nicer if you want to actually see these girls."

She gritted her teeth. "Please get up."

"That's more like it." He sneered at her and stood.

Addy wanted to wipe that look off his face, but she shoved her hands into her jean pockets instead.

Kiley slid into place. Cam went back to the sofa, setting his laptop on his legs. Addy grabbed her tea and returned to her club chair. Mack settled in the chair nearby, with Bear dropping to the floor between them, his ears perked, eyes closed.

Sean sat on the sofa and looked at Cam. "I've never known you to take paperwork so seriously."

Cam looked up. "You guys should all know. I finally did it. I put my application in for agent a few months ago, and the process is moving along. It's looking good."

"That's great news," Addy declared.

"Yeah, for you maybe," Mack grumbled. "But the team is never gonna be the same."

"Congrats, man." Kiley grinned at Cam. "I'm gonna miss you, but it's what you've wanted for so long that I can say I'm happy."

Cam lowered his computer screen. "Maybe I can stay on the team."

"We can try to make that happen," Sean said, looking as disappointed as Mack. "But it's doubtful they'll give you such a prestigious assignment for your rookie year."

"Yeah, I didn't think they would, but . . ." He shrugged.

"But it's your dream and that's what's important," Mack said, looking at Addy. "Follow your dream."

She nodded. "Look at me. I'm coming back to the RED team and Mack. What could be better?"

"Nothing." Mack smiled, and the warmth of his gaze curled her toes.

She thought about her mom. Addy would have to arrange for her mom's relocation to D.C. Normally that might be a tough transition, yet her mother was at the point of needing to go into a dementia care home with special safety protocols. Her life would soon be majorly disrupted anyway, and it didn't matter if that happened in D.C. or Portland.

"Okay, bitcoin's on the way." Kiley stood, and Zamora sat back down. Kiley remained at the table. She'd taken him on as her own personal project and kept her eye on him every minute he was near a computer. Which was a good thing, as they couldn't give him free rein.

"Okay," he said. "My guy got his money, and he's giving me the address. It's in Atlanta."

"Atlanta." Sean turned to Mack. "It'll take us at least six hours to get there. Way too long. Her kidnappers could get wind of us on their tail and move her. We'll need local agents to make the bust now. I'll get the Atlanta office SWAT team out there right away."

"I always thought we'd be there to rescue the girls, but that's not gonna happen." Mack ran a hand over his hair, and Addy knew he was upset. He stood and looked at Zamora. "Still, all that matters right now is that someone raids that house and frees the girls from creeps like you."

———

Mack wished he could do something to calm his team, but he was just as jittery as they were. All of them were standing in front of the TV. Too tense to sit. Watching. Waiting for the Atlanta FBI SWAT commander's video feed to go live on the TV.

Eisenhower had hopped a quick flight to Atlanta and convinced the office's Special Agent in Charge to let Agent Newkirk wear a camera and microphone to broadcast the home invasion for the team in Oregon, and for Eisenhower, who was waiting in the Atlanta office.

Sean started pacing. "What's taking them so long?"

"You know it takes time to prep for an op like this," Kiley

said, but her foot was tapping, and she was madly fluffing a pillow.

Mack was about to say something when the video on the TV went live.

"Go time." Newkirk's deep voice boomed over the speaker.

Everyone crowded closer to the screen, and Zamora sat in a club chair where they could keep an eye on him.

Newkirk moved up a sidewalk toward a ranch house located in an older area on the east side of Atlanta. An officer pushed past him and slammed a battering ram into the door.

"Go! Go! Go!" the commander shouted and charged forward.

His camera caught two men sitting on a sofa, going for their guns. The SWAT team fired before the men could take them out and moved deeper into the house. The commander headed down a dark hallway, the light from his assault rifle sweeping side to side. He ducked into a bedroom holding only a double bed with covers tossed into a heap. He checked the closet, then backed out and charged into another room holding a similar bed. The rooms were empty. He shouted "Clear!" and continued down the hall to check one last bedroom and a bathroom with bright aqua tile.

"Where are the girls?" Sean slammed a fist into his palm. "Where?"

Mack spun toward Zamora. "Looks like your friend lied to us."

"He didn't say they'd be there today." Zamora clamped his lips like he was holding back a smirk.

Mack watched and waited, hoping he'd go ahead and smirk. Then Mack would wipe the sneer off the guy's face, because he was itching for a fight to release his pent-up tension.

"Let's check for ID on the men in the living room," Newkirk said and marched back to the room.

His camera captured one of the agents removing wallets

from the deceased's pockets. He opened the first one. "This guy's Bobby Gaines."

"Bobby Gaines," Sean said. "Not a name we ever came across."

"Second guy is Reggie Downs," the agent said. "Both are from here."

Mack looked at Sean. "He was never on our radar either."

"So maybe this isn't the right house after all," Kiley said, looking so disappointed, Mack wanted to give her a hug.

"We got a basement," someone yelled from the TV.

"Yes!" Kiley pumped her fist, and her eyes lit up.

Mack tried not to get his hopes up, but they soared—way up—and he didn't know if his heart could take another disappointment. He felt so out of control. So frantic. Desperate. Nearly as bad as when Addy was missing.

She slipped her hand into his, the warmth a comfort for his nerves. He turned to smile at her. He still couldn't believe she'd agreed to resume their marriage. He couldn't believe he'd agreed to let her. Not only agreed but encouraged it. He still feared he might hurt her, but he wouldn't let that fear dictate his life any longer. He would live the life God wanted him to have, and Mack knew without a doubt that Addy was included in that life.

He heard boots pounding on the TV speaker and turned back to see Newkirk's camera catching the stairwell as he marched down the steps. He looked around the unfinished space with gray cinder block walls and concrete floors. He swiveled and paused, his camera facing a door with a hasp lock.

"Cover me," he called out. He broke the lock and drew open the door, which groaned on its hinges. "Going in."

Mack listened for any sound of terrified girls, but silence greeted them. "If they're in there, they aren't saying a word."

Newkirk swept his lighted rifle over the room. He landed on a pair of eyes staring from the shadows. He moved on.

Another set of eyes. Another and another. Yet one more. Five girls cowering in the darkness.

"They're there!" Kiley exclaimed. "We did it. We found them."

"Slow down, Kiley," Sean warned. "We don't know who these girls are yet."

"We're with the FBI," Newkirk said. "No need to be afraid."

He moved to the first girl and shone the light over her head to protect her eyes, giving them a clear view of her face. "What's your name, sweetheart?"

"Izzie," she said, her voice barely audible. "Izzie Dilman."

Addy squeezed Mack's hand, and his heart took flight.

"It's official. We *did* find one of them." Tears flowed down Kiley's cheeks.

"Well, Izzie, would you like to go home?" Newkirk asked.

"P-p-lease."

"My agent will help you."

An agent assisted her as she slowly came to her feet. Newkirk's light shone on her, and she looked healthy but dirty. He moved to the next girl. Before he asked the name, Mack recognized her as Becky Vaughn.

"It's Becky," Mack said. "It really is her."

"Two of the three," Sean said, his voice barely there. He'd been lead on this investigation and had blamed himself for a long time for not bringing the girls home, and Mack couldn't begin to know what he was feeling.

Newkirk helped her to her feet.

"Did you get him?" she said, her voice barely a whisper.

"Who?" Newkirk asked.

"Bobby Gaines. The guy who took us."

Newkirk nodded. "He won't ever hurt you again."

She shuddered. "It was all my fault. He came on to me one night when we were out. I started a secret relationship with him. I should have known a city guy wouldn't be interested in me and he was gonna do something bad."

"This is not your fault," Newkirk said. "It's all on Gaines. Don't ever forget that."

Becky started crying, the pain in her sobs cutting Mack to the quick.

Newkirk patted her shoulder, then had one of his team take her out of the room.

"If only we'd known," Mack said. "And found this guy . . ."

"She hid him from everyone," Addy said. "There's no way you could have."

Mack heard her words but didn't believe them. At least not yet. Maybe after time passed, but not now.

Newkirk continued down the line. The next two girls were unknown to the team. Mack held his breath as Newkirk moved to the last girl. Her eyes were narrowed, and she didn't have red hair like Felicia, but her kidnapper had likely insisted they dye the girls' hair.

"And your name?" Newkirk asked, his voice cracking under the stress of such a tough discovery.

"Felicia Wallings."

"Yes!" Mack shot his hand up and turned to high-five his teammates.

Then he swept Addy into his arms and twirled her around. When he set her down, her expression wasn't jubilant but sad.

"Why so sad?" he asked. "It's a good day."

"I'm glad the girls were found, but I was just thinking about the road they have ahead of them. It's going to be tough."

He hadn't thought that far, but she was right. The girls were safe now and heading home, and yet it would take months, maybe years for them to recover from the terror of their captivity.

Sean's phone rang.

"It's Eisenhower," he announced. "I'll put him on speaker."

"Congratulations." Eisenhower sounded more jubilant than Mack had ever heard their supervisor sound. "I just saw each of the girls on the video. They appear to be healthy but are on the way to the hospital to be checked out. FYI, Bobby Gaines is one of the friends Williams named, but we couldn't find him."

"Well, we have him now," Sean said, disgust in his tone.

"We do indeed," Eisenhower agreed. "We'll need to notify the girls' parents."

"I'd like to call them," Sean said.

Eisenhower didn't answer at first. Mack suspected he'd wanted to go out to their homes himself or send an agent out to notify them in person. "That sounds fine. Tell them I have an agent on the way to take them to the hospital to reunite with their girls."

"Will do, sir." Sean disconnected and tapped his screen. He looked at the team. "First call goes to Vivian Vaughn."

The call rang over Sean's speaker.

"Sean." Despite all that she'd suffered, hope lingered in her voice. "Do you have a lead?"

"No." Sean smiled. "We have the girls. We finally have the girls."

EPILOGUE

AN EXCITED HUM OF CONVERSATION buzzed around the FBI Academy auditorium that was quickly filling up with guests. Addy couldn't be happier to be here right now with the RED team and their significant others. Zamora was back in prison and so were the sovereign citizens. All of them charged and awaiting trial. And, she hoped, awaiting many years behind bars.

Mack slid an arm around the back of her seat, and she leaned into him. Sean's fiancée, Taylor, a special woman with a big heart for her protectees in the WITSEC program, sat next to her on the other side. Though Taylor couldn't really talk about the details of her job, her love for her position shone through what she could say. And then there was Evan, a guy who was almost as protective as Mack. She believed that Evan's and Kiley's hands were permanently locked together. They sat together now just down the aisle.

Addy strained in her seat, looking for Cam. "There's Cam. Third person, second row."

Mack leaned forward. "I see him."

"Me too." Kiley's voice rose with excitement. "I'm so happy for him. He's wanted this for so long."

The FBI director came onto the stage, and the room quieted down. He addressed the agents in training and had them stand. As he swore them in, Addy's heart swelled for Cam. She remembered her own graduation day with ICE and was sure that Mack and her friends next to her were doing the same thing.

It was the moment the candidate went from being someone who wanted to serve, protect, and defend others to someone who had the obligation and privilege to do so. To someone who would do so every day for the rest of their career. The day changed everyone's life, including family members in the room.

The trainees filed out of the room to go stand in a hallway offstage. One by one they would cross the stage and receive their credentials and badge. They entered in alphabetical order, so it didn't take long for Cam Linn to appear.

Dressed in a dark suit, white shirt, and dress shoes like the rest of his class, he strode proudly across the stage and clasped the director's hand. They turned toward the audience, pausing for a quick photo, and Cam's beaming smile told them everything they needed to know. He was honored and excited to be an FBI agent.

Addy squeezed Mack's hand and smiled at him. He looked so proud of Cam, much like a dad or mentor. Addy and Mack remained hand in hand until they stepped out to greet Cam. Soon he burst through the crowd and joined them.

"Congrats, man." Mack clapped Cam on the back. "You made it."

Cam grinned as he stared at his shiny new badge. "Almost. Gotta stop by the weapons vault to pick up my FBI-issued pistol and ammunition."

"Right." Sean pumped Cam's hand. "Then you'll be ready to head off to your first assignment in Chicago."

"Isn't it cool that I got such a major field office to start?" Cam asked.

"Lots of analysts there to boss around." Kiley chuckled and gave Cam a hug. "Just know we'll miss you and hope you'll someday be able to come back home to us."

"That's my goal, but you know, I got a lot of living to do before that." Cam's cute smile widened.

"And maybe find someone to share your life with," Taylor suggested.

Cam waved a hand. "I've got lots of time for that once I get my agent feet under me."

"Hey, man." Another new agent bumped shoulders with Cam. "Let's get checked out and pick up our pistols."

"Gotta run," Cam said.

"Keep in touch," Kiley told him.

He nodded and bolted with the other guy, not at all looking sad about the parting.

"This must be what a proud parent feels like when their kid flies the nest." Kiley wiped a tear from her eye. "Proud and sad at the same time."

"Aw, honey, don't cry." Evan took her hand. "Remember today is all about happiness."

"Yeah, it is." Mack smiled at Addy, a promise in his eyes.

At the mere thought of their wedding vow renewal set for that afternoon, butterflies took flight in her stomach.

"Speaking of which." Kiley looked at Addy. "Time for the girls to get going so we can take care of a few last-minute things. That is, if I can pull you away from Mack."

Addy chuckled and kissed Mack on the cheek. "Have to go."

"You call that a good-bye kiss?" Mack swept her into his arms and looked at the others. "If a real kiss makes you squeamish, go now, because I am about to engage in a very public display of affection."

Addy laughed, but it was broken off by Mack's mouth pressing against hers. He kissed her until she could barely breathe and had to come up for air.

"I love you." He gave her a wide smile.

She returned it. "I love you."

Kiley grabbed Addy's arm. "C'mon. You have a whole afternoon dedicated to kissing."

Addy waved good-bye to Mack and let Kiley lead her and Taylor out of the parking lot. Addy had hoped by now that she would've remembered Mack and the others, yet she had only gotten bits and pieces back. Just little flashes really. She'd kept up her hypnosis, and her doctor was encouraged, thinking it was just a matter of time.

She honestly didn't care today as she was getting a chance that she doubted few women got. She was going to have her wedding all over again. Since she couldn't remember the first one, the same emotions and joy saturated her heart, as did the man who held it. She couldn't wait to begin the first day of married life with him again.

———

Mack stood near the altar in the tiny church in the country and tugged on his tie. The pastor stood behind him, tapping his toe. The little traditional church had ornate woodwork and rich burgundy carpet running down the aisle. Solid wood pews were lined up like soldiers and were empty save for his family on the right side of the aisle and the RED team on the left. Mack did everything in his power to get Addy's mom here today, but she was having a tough day and it would've been too taxing on her. He did convince the nurse to stream the event live for Addy's mother in case she was lucid for a few moments.

Kiley and Taylor had hung white bows at the ends of the pews and placed a pretty arrangement of purple-and-white flowers on the altar.

The organ started playing, and Mack came to attention, pinning his focus at the end of the aisle. He and Addy didn't have a huge wedding the first time around, and today was even less so, but she didn't remember her first walk down the aisle and was going to wear her wedding dress.

He felt incredibly blessed that she not only came to love him once, but twice, telling him that God clearly wanted them together, and Mack would trust that he wouldn't do anything to hurt her ever again.

She stepped out from the shadows. Her dress was simple, floor-length with bare shoulders. Mack had no idea the name for the fancy things sewn on it, but they were lacy and sparkly. He really didn't have eyes for the dress anyway. He only had eyes for her. Her shiny red hair was piled up in a fancy do, and her bare shoulders were creamy and inviting.

She glided toward him, a small purple-and-white bouquet in her hand, a smile of sincere joy on her face. But it was those sparkling blue eyes fixed on him as she reached the altar that got his heart beating harder.

She gave her flowers to Kiley and took his hand. They faced the pastor, who began reading through the liturgy, making it clear that this was a renewal of vows, not an official marriage ceremony.

He asked them to face each other, and Mack took Addy's hands, his gaze pinned to hers. Her eyes were glistening with tears, and he sure hoped they were happy tears.

"Go ahead, Mack, and share what you've written," the pastor said.

Mack looked deeply into Addy's eyes. "On our wedding day, I made a choice. It was the most important choice of my life. I didn't take it lightly. I chose you to be my wife. I thought then that such a decision was final, but life threw us a curveball, and now I have the chance to choose you all over again."

He took a long breath but held her gaze. "No other person has moved me to the feelings I have for you. And I have never wanted to marry anyone else. I will honor, cherish, and protect you for the rest of my life."

"That was beautiful, Mack." Tears ran down Addy's cheeks, and she dabbed them with a tissue she'd tucked in her waistband.

"I don't remember our wedding day. Not for lack of trying, but I have come to accept that God has a reason for it. Whatever it is, He gave me the chance to fall in love with you a second time. You're an amazing man. Caring, kind, and strong. Compassionate, thoughtful. And I continue to take you as my loving husband to have and to hold, for better or for worse, until death do us part."

"Perfect segue," the pastor said and looked at Mack. "What are you waiting for? Kiss your wife."

Mack crushed her to him and kissed her with everything he was made of. Her mouth was soft and warm and inviting him to linger for eternity. He was vaguely aware of his team and family applauding, but none of that mattered right now.

He pulled back. "I love you, Mrs. Jordan."

"And I love you too, Mr. Jordan."

He kissed her again, then whispered in her ear, "I'm the luckiest man in the world."

"Me too." She leaned back and smiled at him.

"Oh, honey," he said, running his hands over her back. "Trust me. You're not a man. Not a man at all."

ACKNOWLEDGMENTS

THANKS TO:

Ron Norris, who continues to give of his time and knowledge in police and military procedures, weaponry details, and information technology. As a retired police officer with the La Verne Police Department, and a Certified Information Systems Security Professional, the experience and knowledge you share are priceless. You answer all my questions so very patiently, and I couldn't get the law enforcement or weapons info right without you. The depth of your knowledge astounds me.

My wonderful agent, Steve Laube. You are there whenever I need a question answered, and you reply so quickly and make me feel like your only client when I know you represent many superstar authors. I thank God for the day we met.

My editors, Dave Long and Luke Hinrichs. Thank you for helping me bring the RED team to life so that readers could get to know and enjoy them as much as I have enjoyed writing about them.

As always, to my super talented friend and romantic suspense author, Elizabeth Goddard. You know the friend you can go to and can tell just about anything and they understand and make you feel better, that they're there for you whenever you need them? That's you, Beth, and thank you from the bottom of my heart for being such a loyal friend as we navigate the crazy waters of being an author.

And most importantly, thank you to God. You have blessed

me in so many ways, and my writing career is one of them. Thank you for inspiring me with stories that share your amazing Word and for giving me the outlets to bring them to readers. I could never in my wildest dreams have imagined what you are doing in my life right now! Thank you for the wonderful ride.

Susan Sleeman is the bestselling author of *Minutes to Die* and *Seconds to Live* plus more than forty romantic suspense novels with sales exceeding one million copies. She's won several awards, including the ACFW Carol Award for Suspense for *Fatal Mistake*, and the *Romantic Times* Reviewers' Choice Award for *Thread of Suspicion*. In addition to writing, Susan hosts the popular Suspense Zone website, www.thesuspense zone.com. She's lived in nine states but now calls Portland, Oregon, her home. For a complete list of the author's books, visit www.susansleeman.com.

You May Also Like . . .

When authorities contact the FBI about bodies found on freight trains—all killed the same way—Alex Donavan is forced to confront her troubled past when she recognizes the graffiti messages the killer is leaving behind. In a race against time, Alex must decide how far she will go—and what she is willing to risk—to put a stop to the Train Man.

Night Fall by Nancy Mehl
THE QUANTICO FILES #1
nancymehl.com

After one of her team members is murdered and the CIA opens an internal investigation on her, Layla Karam reluctantly turns to her ex-boyfriend and private investigator Hunter McCoy to help clear her name and uncover the real killer. With threats on all sides, Layla must put her trust in the man who broke her heart and hope they both come out alive.

Backlash by Rachel Dylan
CAPITAL INTRIGUE #2
racheldylan.com

In 1928, Bonaventure Circus outcast Pippa Ripley must decide if uncovering her roots is worth putting herself directly in the path of a killer preying on the troupe. Decades later, while determining if an old circus train depot will be torn down or preserved, Chandler Faulk is pulled into a story far darker and more haunting than she imagined.

The Haunting at Bonaventure Circus by Jaime Jo Wright
jaimewrightbooks.com

BETHANYHOUSE

More from Bethany House

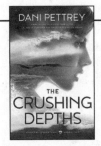

When an accident claims the life of an oil-rig worker off the North Carolina coast, Coast Guard investigators Rissi Dawson and Mason Rogers are sent to take the case. But mounting evidence shows the death may not have been an accident at all, and they find themselves racing to discover the killer's identity before he eliminates the threat they pose.

The Crushing Depths by Dani Pettrey
Coastal Guardians #2
danipettrey.com

When multiple corpses are found, their remains point to a serial killer with a familiar MO but who's been in prison for over twenty years—Special Agent Kaely Quinn's father. In order to prevent more deaths, she must come face-to-face with the man she's hated for years. In a race against time, will this case cost Kaely her identity and perhaps even her life?

Dead End by Nancy Mehl
Kaely Quinn Profiler #3
nancymehl.com

On a mission to recover the Book of the Wars, Leif and his team are diverted by a foretelling of formidable warriors who will decimate the enemies of the ArC, while Iskra uses her connections to hunt down the book. As they try to stop the warriors, failure becomes familiar, and the threats creep closer to home, with implications that could tear them apart.

Kings Falling by Ronie Kendig
The Book of the Wars #2
roniekendig.com

BethanyHouse